THE SPHINX PRINCIPLE

RISE OF MAGIC
BOOK 5

STEFON MEARS

Also by Stefon Mears

The Rise of Magic Series
Magician's Choice
Sleight of Mind
Lunar Alchemy
Three Fae Monte
The Sphinx Principle
Double Backed Magic
Mercury Fold (forthcoming)

Cavan Oltblood Series
Half a Wizard
The Ice Dagger
Spells of Undeath

Power City Tales
Not Quite Bulletproof
No Money in Heroism

Standalones
The Hireling
The Captain's Cat
Save Whiskers!
The Ogre of Threepeaks
Between the Cracks
Sects and the City
Prince of a Thousand Worlds
Devil's Night
Portal-Land, Oregon
Stealing from Pirates
Fade to Gold
With a Broken Sword
Twice Against the Dragon
The House on Cedar Street
Sudden Death
On the Edge of Faerie

Short Story Collections
Spell Slingers
Twisted Timelines
Longhairs and Short Tales: A Collection of Cat Stories
Dangerous Space
Confronting Legends (Spells & Swords Vol. 1)
The Patreon Collection, Vol. 1-8 (Vol. 9, coming soon)

Nonfiction
The 30-Day Novel and Beyond!

Spells for Hire Series
Devil's Shoestring
Zombie Powder
Spirit Trap
Dragon's Blood

The Telepath Trilogy
Surviving Telepathy
Immoral Telepathy
Targeting Telepathy

Edge of Humanity Series
Caught Between Monsters
Hunting Monsters

Jumpstart Duchy Series
Into the Torn Kingdoms
The Dragon's Gold
The Gift Castle
The Deadly Feast
The King's Test
Triumph in the Torn Kingdoms

Published by Thousand Faces Publishing, Portland, Oregon

http://1kfaces.com

Copyright © 2023 by Stefon Mears

Starfield image © Ashestosky | Dreamstime.com (File ID: 11418999)

Fae Portal illustration © dgstudio | Dreamstime.com (File ID: 227406846)

ISBN: 978-1-948490-06-1

AUTHOR'S NOTE

All of the novels in the *Rise of Magic* series that star Donal Cuthbert have titles derived from stage magic and card tricks. This is the first such title that I felt should probably be explained.

Thus, do I quote the Glossary of Magic page from Wikipedia:

The Sphinx Principle:

"The concept that two mirrors at 90 degrees and with their apex facing the audience can be used to reflect the side curtains or walls, which are the same pattern as those at the back, enabling an object to be hidden behind the mirrors[. F]irst used in the Sphinx illusion."

The year is 2027
Six decades after the Rise of Magic

1

"I told you you were doomed," Fionn said, in tones pitched so that only Donal could understand them.

Donal Cuthbert didn't bother to hush his *cú sidhe* familiar. That the great, emerald green deerhound was right was nothing new. And anyway, Donal didn't have the attention to spare.

No, right now, Donal faced just over a meter-and-a-half of angry Irish steel.

His mother.

This should have been a triumphant homecoming. By all rights, Donal should have returned to Santa Cruz like a hero, striding once more among the redwoods and beaches of his childhood. Through the halls of the U.C. Santa Clara campus, where Donal had done his undergraduate studies.

Perhaps the cold December rain had been an omen.

Still, since Donal had last been home, he'd completed three semesters of graduate work at Cal Thaum San Luis Obispo toward his Doctorate of Thaumaturgy. A rare enough accomplishment, on its own, and one that could lead to him becoming the first Hierophant in his family.

An education at one of the finest thaumaturgic universities in the world, paid for by no less than the interplanetary business magnate whose life — *and very mind* — Donal had saved.

Donal was even tied for the head of his cohort with his new girlfriend, Esmeralda Villaseñor.

Heck, most mothers would have been thrilled that Donal's new girlfriend *wasn't* a megalomaniac trying to establish an interplanetary shadow government with herself in charge.

Like Donal's last girlfriend.

But that wasn't all.

This past summer, Donal'd flown to *Ganymede* and helped *save a newly discovered, sapient species of life* — actual nonhuman, self-incarnating spirits — from falling prey to the uses and abuses of corporations, the military, and politicians alike.

Donal's actions had influenced political developments here on Earth, as well as on Luna, Mars, and — if Hierophant Nicholas Mason was to be believed — even among the newly developing settlements on Venus.

Donal had even returned not with a load of laundry, like most graduate students home on break, but wearing good airsilk clothes — a pale blue shirt with grey slacks — and fine doeskin loafers.

But none of that seemed to matter.

Donal's mother wanted to focus only on one little detail in all of this. The detail he'd managed to avoid discussing in his occasional links home over the last semester. The detail he knew she'd hone in on like a striking falcon.

Donal's new relationship with the fae.

"You serve the good neighbors? Of *both Courts*?"

That was the sixth time his mother had said just those words.

No. The seventh. Hard to keep track, with all the yelling in between repetitions.

And this seventh time, those words seemed to echo. Quite a trick, since there wasn't much room for an echo to develop.

Both Donal and his mother were seated at the round, oak table in his parents' small kitchen.

In truth, Donal had forgotten just how small was the house he grew up in. His parents had never had much money. His grandfather had built this house himself, out of local redwoods, not long after the Rise of Magic.

It was all built of lovely, warm woods. Very welcoming. Easily heated by the stove and two fireplaces. Three little bedrooms, a combination living room-dining room, and two efficiency bathrooms.

And the whole thing would fit inside the apartment Donal kept down in San Luis Obispo. With some room to spare.

Donal had hoped to surprise his parents with an offer to buy them a new, larger home. He'd come into more than enough money to do it.

But so far, he hadn't gotten a word in edgewise.

Donal had come home, dropped his valise, garment bag and messenger bag. He'd been lured into the kitchen with the promise of his mother's licorice root tea and hand-ground peanut butter sandwiches on fresh wheat bread, with clover honey drawn from his father's hives.

Donal hadn't even gotten to taste his sandwich before his mother started in. And now his tea was even getting cold.

Donal's mother had the fine-boned features and light brown hair that Donal had always imagined in the princesses of the stories she'd told him, when he was a child. And when she was happy, it was as though the sun shone brighter and even the air tasted fresher.

Donal had her eyes, but his father's black hair and, Donal liked to think, his father's more rugged features.

Still, his mother's smile could raise the spirits of everyone in a five hundred meter radius. Even if they couldn't see her.

And her anger lashed like a bullwhip, whose crack gave ghostly aches to all who heard it.

But Donal's years of magical training had not been for nothing. He was skilled enough at meditation that he could listen to her, hear every word she said, and still let the raw power of her emotions wash over him without harm.

"May I defend myself?" Donal said at last.

"Can't imagine you have any excuse for this that I'll want to hear." His mother shook her head. "Not as though I hadn't warned you about getting involved with the good neighbors. Not as though both your grans didn't warn you. No, you still had to go and commit yourself to their aid all the same."

"Mother—"

"Honestly, Donal, did you ever pay heed to any of the warnings we gave you? Some of them might just be old superstitions, I know. But as my mother says. Since magic has come back into the world full-force, there's no way to be truly sure what's just superstition, now is there?"

"Mother, the crying of an owl does not portend death as surely as the cry of the *bean sidhe*."

His mother leaned forward. Both the elbows of her fine white cotton blouse on the table now. Her brow lowered, her cheeks crimson, and her blue eyes furious.

And her own tea likely getting cold.

"Oh, and I suppose you know all there is to know about the *bean sidhe*, is that right? Bran's told me how your fancy schools don't teach even the most basic facts about the good neighbors that your own people have known for hundreds of years. Your father's Scottish kin as well as my own Irish forebears."

Bran. Donal's older brother, and his personal cross to bear. Donal still felt inferior enough to the great Bran Cuthbert that hearing his mother invoke his brother's name almost broke Donal's focus.

One more breath before he spoke.

"I don't know everything there is to know, mother. About the *bean sidhe* or anything else."

"Well, thank Brigid for that. It might just be that you haven't grown too big for your britches just yet."

"May I defend myself?"

"Oh, go on then. Give us a laugh, while I heat up our tea."

"Allow me," Donal said. Then with a moment's focus and a few mumbled words, he channeled a small amount of elemental power. Water-aspected fire of water.

Perhaps a dozen breaths later, the tea steamed as hot as it had been when fresh-poured.

"Well," his mother said, one eyebrow arched high. "Can't say I understood that. Have you abandoned Gaelic then?"

Trick question. Donal's mother knew that Gaelic was the official international language of thaumaturgy.

"Of course not, Mother. We speak more Gaelic in class than English. But the spell was Enochian, as was the language. Enochian is the focus of my graduate studies."

"Well," she grumbled after acknowledging with a nod that Donal had heated her tea just right. "Good to know you haven't abandoned the tongue of your people, even if you don't 'focus' on our magic. But no more distracting me. What's your excuse for the severe lapse of judgment that led to you serving the good neighbors?"

"I'll show you."

"This ought to be good," Donal's mother said, while Donal stood. In five strides he retrieved his valise from the living room and returned to his seat.

Donal pulled out his zephyrpad. Called up the right document. Held onto the zephyrpad when his mother reached for it.

"Not yet," Donal said with a smile.

He waited for her to settle back in her chair before he continued.

"You remember me telling you about Donatello Mancuso?"

"Of course," Donal's mother said, with the first smile he'd seen since his hug of greeting. "He's that rich businessman who set us up for retirement after you saved his life ... what was it, twice?"

"I say twice. He says three times."

"If he says it's three, it's three. Certainly that 'retirement fund' is more than your father and I could ever spend."

"Point is," — Donal smiled again — "he's been very gracious with his time as well as his money. And one of the things he taught me is: negotiate like hell yourself, but bring in the lawyers before you sign anything."

"Lawyers?" One of her fine brown eyebrows arched with actual interest.

"That's right," Donal said. And now he pushed the zephyrpad across the table so that she could read the document he called up. "You always taught me the lesson of Great Uncle Rory's ill-fated duel. Get every agreement in writing. So when I told Donatello that I had to negotiate a position with the Fae Courts, he was only too happy to lend me his personal team of contracts attorneys to help with the paperwork."

Donal tapped the table beside the zephyrpad. "Every detail of the agreement between me and the Courts is expressed in this document. My responsibilities, my compensation, and most importantly that there can be *no debts* accrued by either side without a rider added to the contract that has been signed by both parties."

"No debts?" She sounded skeptical, but for good reason. "You realize they'll hit you with a never ending stream of riders when the time pressure will keep you from getting to your safety net of lawyers. You'll agree to the wrong thing, then you'll be stuck."

"I don't think so," Donal said with a smile. "Look at section seven."

Donal's mother frowned, but started skimming down while Donal explained.

"It's term-limited. It lasts exactly one year and one day, and no provisions, including riders, may survive the contract. It may be extended only by the free and untrammeled agreement of both parties."

"Untrammeled? How do they prove that?"

"It's a legal term these days. It means that court certified specialists must prove that I am acting of my own free will if and when I agree to an extension. And that certification must be registered before the extension could go into effect."

Donal smiled wider. "There's also an escape clause. There's a big ... event coming up. If I want out when it's over, I only need to give them the warning of 'a single sunset.'"

"You've missed something," she said, pushing the zephyrpad back toward Donal, but now she sounded more worried than angry. "I guarantee it. They've been making bargains longer than we've been out of caves. Even their ancient enemies the *Fomhóraigh* and the *Fir Bolg* could never best them in a bargain. They'll find a loophole."

"They might," Donal said. "But they might not use it. They need me right now. On their side and doing my best for them."

"Why? What's this special event?"

"I can't tell you," Donal said, shaking his head. "But it's the reason they need me badly enough to let me bring in lawyers in the first place."

Donal sighed. "It's also the reason I'm only here for two days."

"What?" She sounded scandalized. "Well, then eat your sandwich. I've got to feed you while I can. And in between bites you better tell me all about this Esmeralda of yours, and when I'll get to meet her."

Donal couldn't help smiling around his first bite of that wonderful sandwich. And not just because the wheat bread was fresh, and the peanut butter and honey amazing.

No, if his mother was fussing over him again, then he'd survived her wrath.

For now, at least.

Tucked away in a forgotten neighborhood on the outskirts of Santa Monica, California, sat the single finest Mexican restaurant that John Jacobs had ever tasted.

And he included the restaurants in Mexico in his estimations. Their food might have been more "authentic," but he always considered it a little over-spiced. Not that it was too hot. Jacobs had grown up in Atlanta, where the fumes of good barbecue were hot enough to peel paint. It was just that ... in his mind most Mexican restaurants tried too hard to be flavorful.

Certainly the case, when compared to Casita Rosana, which got it just right.

It was a family-owned establishment, with a history stretching back a good hundred years. Which meant that Rosana Gutierrez had opened her doors some four decades before technology fell.

The building looked like it was made by Spanish missionaries, and the artwork painted right on the walls continued the theme.

The restaurant was always full, which just went to show that at least some people these days still had good taste. Only maybe fifteen little tables total in the front part — with another room in the back for parties — and at least a ten minute wait for a table anytime he stopped in.

Still, whenever Jacobs was in this part of the world, Casita Rosana was worth his time.

The tacos here had a combination of spices that Jacobs had never tasted anywhere else. They managed a ratio of ninety percent savory to ten percent sweet, that lingered on the tongue in just the right way. Especially when followed up with their own brew of iced tea. It would leave his mouth tasting good for hours.

No thaumaturgy or alchemy involved. Not in the flavoring, anyway. This was one of the few restaurants that Jacobs could name that had changed very little when technology fell and magic rose. Oh, the sources of their heat changed, and they had closed for about two years, but when they reopened — or at least, as of the first time Jacobs had gotten back here, which was about five years after magic rose — their food tasted just as wonderful as he remembered.

A little taste of the old life, for a man nearing his ninetieth birthday.

Eighty-eight years old and dating again. He hoped his dear, departed Rhonda would forgive him.

She had to though, didn't she? She and their son Carl had died during the early days of the Rise. More than sixty years ago now.

Yes, Rhonda would probably approve of the woman sitting across the candlelit table from Jacobs. Slim and proper Elinore Bellefleur, with her pale Creole skin, and the traces she'd kept of her New Orleans accent, though she'd lived in California for decades.

She was younger than he by about a decade, but she was old enough to remember little things like electricity, and cars that ran on gasoline, and movies that got projected onto flat, white screens.

And she had actually sailed on one of the old steel ships. Only a ferry, but to an old Navy man like Jacobs, it was something at least. If Jacobs waxed nostalgic about the way those huge engines sent vibrations all through the ship that dug right down into the bones, she actually knew what he was talking about.

And that was every bit as delightful as her soft brown eyes and sweet smile.

She'd dressed for their date in a magnolia print dress and a little yellow hat with a magnolia blossom tucked into the brim.

Jacobs still dressed like a spacer. Couldn't help it. Too ingrained a habit. Navy blue pants with more pockets than he needed, and a stiff white shirt under his matching jacket.

At least he wasn't wearing the hat. And he'd let his tight, close-cropped curls go gray. The only obvious concessions to his retirement.

"I don't know," she said, going over the menu. "Usually I favor enchiladas, but they can vary so much from place to place. Maybe I'd better play it safe and try the tamales?"

"You can have anything here," Jacobs said with a smile, "and it will be perfect."

"Oh, you're no help," she replied, but in a teasing tone.

"He wouldn't know anyway," said little Marcella, stepping up to check on their order. Not so little anymore, perhaps. Into her twenties, surely. Still, in Jacobs' eyes the waitress was that little girl with pigtails who used to run around making sure every table had fresh chips, as though it were the most sober and serious task ever undertaken in the history of the human race.

A task performed these days by little Andre.

"He only ever orders the tacos," Marcella continued. "Hasn't ordered anything else in my lifetime."

"Not much of a sample set," Jacobs said, but they went on without him, discussing the different dishes until Elinore settled on the chicken enchilada, with extra guacamole.

Jacobs had just raised his glass of iced tea to propose a toast when Elinore said, "Who's that man? He looks like he's coming this way."

Jacobs didn't really want to look over his shoulder, but he did. And he saw just about the last person on this or any other world that he would want to run into.

A man in a dark blue suit that probably cost more than this restaurant had earned in its whole history. Hell, his shoes, belt, and pale blue tie alone probably cost as much as Casita Rosana made in a year.

"That's Donatello Mancuso," Jacobs said with a sigh as he turned back around.

"*The* Donatello Mancuso?" Elinore said, eyes blinking as though she couldn't have heard that right.

"I don't want to believe it either," Jacobs grumbled.

Donatello Mancuso, the chief executive of 4M, the most powerful collection of businesses around, with offices scattered around the Earth, Luna, Mars, Venus, and probably Hell itself.

Still whip lean as the last time Jacobs had seen him, his curls just as black as though he hadn't aged a day, and still carrying himself as though he were the most important person in the heliosphere.

Mancuso left his twin executive assistants back at the door. The two blondes. One male, one female. One his business secretary and the other his social secretary. Jacobs could remember which was which if he cared to, but he didn't.

That Mancuso approached without them meant something, and Jacobs was pretty sure he didn't want to know what.

"Captain Jacobs," Mancuso said, a touch slower than his usual whirlwind of speech. "Good to see you. You're a hard man to track down."

"Just Mister Jacobs now," Jacobs said, his voice as full of caution as his expression. "I'm retired."

And he may have hit that last word a little hard.

"Don't I know it," Mancuso said, his smile not budging a centimeter as he turned his attention to Elinore. "I'm the one who bought him out of Starchaser Spacelines with a more generous package than you'd believe. But I don't believe we've met. I'm Donatello Mancuso, and I'm very pleased to make your acquaintance, miss..."

"Elinore Bellefleur," she said, her glance darting to Jacobs' and back, "and I prefer mizz, but otherwise I'm pleased to meet you."

"Of the New Orleans Bellefleurs?" Mancuso asked, and Jacobs didn't like the idea of Elinore getting on this man's scanners.

"Why, yes," Elinore said, pleased.

"I thought I saw a family resemblance."

"What do you want, Mancuso?" Jacobs said firmly.

"Well, first to tell this lovely woman that I had lunch with a son or nephew of hers just last week, so we could discuss developments at the New Orleans port. They're trying to put in a space dock."

"My grandson," Elinore said, smiling as though despite herself. "But thank you for the compliment."

"Let me guess," Jacobs said. "Mazatlán is fighting them and you plan to sweep in to the rescue for a percentage?"

"What do you care?" Mancuso said with a shrug. "You're retired. Although, speaking of your retirement, there was another matter I wanted to talk to you about."

"How did you even find me?" Jacobs shook his head at Marcella, who looked as though she wanted to come help. "I left clear instructions at the port—"

"That you didn't want to be found," Mancuso finished for him. "And believe me, you're well-respected enough that no one would rat you out. However, there are only a handful of restaurants in the greater Los Angeles area that use no magic or alchemy..."

He didn't need to finish the sentence. Jacobs already realized that his own proclivities had made him easy to find for a man like Mancuso.

"I'm surprised you came to talk to me yourself," Jacobs grumbled.

Mancuso cocked an eyebrow exactly one millimeter. "Would you have listened to an underling?"

Jacobs snorted. They both knew the answer to that.

"Why don't you have a seat?" Elinore said, and gave Jacobs a don't-be-rude look.

Jacobs sighed, and wondered if dating again at his age really was a good idea.

"Thank you," Mancuso said, taking that seat. "I won't stay for dinner though. Davis back there has already ordered food to-go for us. I just want to ask *Mister* Jacobs here about something."

"Out with it then," Jacobs said, drawing another disapproving look from Elinore, who clearly didn't know what this man could be like.

"On your last official flight as a commercial captain," Mancuso said, "you got chased out of a no-fly zone near Venus."

"Chased is putting it mildly," Jacobs said. "The Terran Navy fired on us."

"They *didn't*," Elinore said.

"Not even a hint of exaggeration there," Mancuso said. "Even if I weren't inclined to take Jacobs here at his word — which, of course, I do — I've seen the logs."

Jacobs knew that Elinore wasn't questioning his veracity. He knew her just well enough now to know that shocked tone. She might not have wanted to believe it, but she certainly did.

"What about it?" Jacobs said. "Suing them on behalf of Starchaser Spacelines? Need my testimony?"

"No, nothing like that," Mancuso said, sounding offended. "Honestly, if you think I need to go to the courts for recompense when something like that happens, you haven't really been paying attention."

"What then?" Jacobs said, drawing another frown from Elinore by making a get-it-moving gesture with his hand.

"Simple," Mancuso said, leaning forward. "How'd you like to pop into that no-fly zone and see just what the Navy's hiding?"

"I'm too old to get shot at doing stupid things anymore."

"No shooting," Mancuso said, and Jacobs could feel the trap springing. "You'll even have a gunboat escort."

Damn if Jacobs wasn't still every bit as curious as he'd been his whole life. It was curiosity that had kept him flying as long as it did. The need to see just one more port. Set foot on just one more planet. Log one more accomplishment on his already historic list.

And now, the chance to see what the Terran Navy had been ready to *kill* to hide?

"What's the catch?" Jacobs said. "I have to fly *you* there?"

"Me?" Mancuso smiled, and Jacobs reflected that the devil must have just such a smile as the man kept talking. "I wish. Even my best friends in politics won't let me near this one. No, I volunteered to foot the bill as a gesture of goodwill to the Fae Courts. Part of the reason I want the best captain alive flying it. No, the man you'd be carrying is—"

"No," Jacobs said, suddenly realizing the only person Mancuso could possibly mean. The only person they had in common that Mancuso would go out of his way for. "You've got to be kidding."

"—Donal Cuthbert."

"He's a Jonah," Jacobs said. "That kid draws trouble like morning draws the dawn."

"Not saying he doesn't," Mancuso said. "He's pretty good at getting out of it too. But this time it's all above board in every way. He's got the approval of every party involved. He's not trying to stop any conspiracies. And so far as I know, no one's trying to kill him."

"So far as you *know*," Jacobs said, raising a finger to make his point. "Not very reassuring."

"Donal Cuthbert..." Elinore said. "Any relation to *Bran* Cuthbert?"

"His brother," Mancuso said. "Brilliantly gifted magician. Maybe better than Bran. Couldn't say for sure. I do know Donal has more courage than ten firefighters. Too much, probably. Tends to bite off a little more than he could eat in a day, let alone chew in a bite."

Jacobs nodded agreement.

"He's also," Mancuso continued, "the ambassador of both Fae Courts. Which means no one in their right mind is going to try to kill him."

"No one in his right mind would try to kill you either. Or Hassan al Rashid. But he's dead, and you're only alive—"

"Because of Cuthbert." Mancuso smiled. "Look. Judging what people want is a critical part of what I do. I'm the best at it. And I *know* you want a peek into that no-fly zone. Not only is this the only way you're ever going to get to do it, but you'll be flying with a military escort, a crew and ship of your own choosing, and a passenger list of exactly two. What do you say?"

Jacobs frowned.

There was no way he could turn this down.

AFTER TWO DAYS AT HOME, DONAL FELT ALMOST MOTION SICK FROM THE emotional roller coaster.

One moment, he's up. His father, praising Donal for his work on Ganymede. Work done for the famous Hierophant *Nicholas Mason* yet.

The next, he's down. His father, going on at even *more* length about the agreement Bran had forged just last week between the settlers of Ganymede and the Terran Navy. They'd be working together now, instead of sniping at each other nonstop, and the news everywhere was hailing the possibilities.

After all, in terms of natural resources, there had been no big developments since the discovery of carterite on Mars. And that was years ago now. Everyone believed that the next great find would be on Ganymede.

And Bran would likely get credit for that too.

Then, Donal was up again. His mother, praising him for his grades, and for being tied at the top of his cohort despite all the "running around" he'd been doing.

The next, Donal was down again. Both his parents flatly refused to let Donal buy them a new house. Been offended by the mere idea.

The yelling had gone on for quite a while, at the prospect of the family 'abandoning' the home built by his grandfather's own two hands...

To make matters worse, Bran himself had arrived home in the middle of that one. And Bran had had a few choice words of his own for the prospect of their mother and father moving. As though their father were some great Scottish Laird, being asked to leave the castle where generations of their family could live together in harmony and move into a shack in the swamp.

Wasn't even as though Donal wanted to get rid of the house. He just thought it would work better as a vacation home, now that they had the resources to do better for themselves than Cuthberts had done since before the fall of technology.

But no one wanted to hear it. Not Mom, not Dad, and not even Bran.

Bran, who had an estate down in Mazatlán that made the old homestead look like housing for his servants' servants.

That was why Donal had finally taken his leave to go for a walk. Oh, that the sun had finally started shining had been the excuse. In December in Santa Cruz, it was important to enjoy sunshine on the rare occasions it made an appearance.

One more walk under the blue sky of Earth before going back to space, and all that.

But really, Donal just needed a break from getting yelled at.

He wandered down close to the peanut butter colored sands of the beach. The spot where he used to go to think when he was a kid.

Down, maybe a hundred meters from the small drop that led down to the beach, was a huge gray rock. Like the nose of some sleeping titan.

When Donal had been maybe five years old, scaling that rock had been the biggest accomplishment of his life. He'd stood proud and tall — perhaps drawn up to his full one-meter height at the time —

atop its jutting edge and looked out over the beach below as though it were his own kingdom.

Later, in his teen years, Donal had returned here to practice meditating. Or just to think. About life. About magic. About girls. Whatever nagged at Donal's mind, this rock was the perfect place to contemplate it.

His feet now followed the familiar, narrow trail between redwoods. His soft, doeskin loafers hushing among the redwood needles. The dirt dry here, under the canopy of redwoods, despite all the recent rain.

As he walked he called Fionn forth out of the silver faun pendant that served as the fae hound's housing.

The great, slightly transparent deerhound fell into step beside Donal without a word. Those emerald eyes glancing up from time to time, full of questions that remained unspoken for now.

When Donal reached his rock, he scaled it easily. So easily compared to the triumph it had been almost twenty years ago.

Fionn merely leaped to the top, with barely a whisper to his landing. But then, Fionn could have flown up, had he chosen.

"A lot of change, your parents have had to deal with," Fionn said, as Donal assumed his usual cross-legged pose. Worked equally well for meditation, or just for sitting.

Donal said nothing. Just gazed out across the sands at the dark blue of the waves. Their frothy tops crested high, and a good dozen surfers fought to tame those waves.

Donal didn't want to see surfers right now. Any more than he wanted to see the people frolicking and playing on the beach. Scores of people, with their towels and picnic baskets and guitars and dumbeks and other instruments.

He wanted the simple sea of the horizon. And even that was denied him now.

"Two sons," Fionn said, looking not at Donal, but out at the sea. His accent wasn't quite Irish, and it wasn't quite Scottish, but it was unmistakably Celtic. "Neither following into the woodworking business. Both talented wizards."

"Magicians," Donal said without thinking.

Fionn's ears flicked, and his tongue drooped in a quick smile. A trap. Fionn knew that the word 'wizard' was out of fashion. He just wanted to see if Donal was listening.

"And both those sons covering themselves in fame and glory ... while facing down dangers that likely keep their parents awake at night."

Donal blinked at that.

"You downplay the dangers when you talk to them. I have heard you do it. And from what your brother's familiar tells me, your brother does the same."

"You have chats with Res?"

Res. The raven familiar that — rumor said — the Morrigan herself gifted to Bran.

Fionn, of course, ignored the question.

"But you both must know that your parents are not fools. One son a Magister who completed the licensing certification without completing the formal training first? One does not develop such skills without facing weighty risks along the way. Risks such as those that might make one wealthy enough to afford a grand estate in Mazatlán."

"You expect me to believe that *anything* could challenge the great Bran Cuthbert?"

"His brother could."

Bran's voice? Here? A glance showed Donal he was right. Bran stood down at the base of the rock, looking up. The "after" image, to Donal's "before."

Bran stood five centimeters taller, his eyes a brighter shade of blue, his chin stronger and cleft. He even wore clothes better. His simple pale blue shirt and soft gray slacks — both airsilk — fit him like they'd been tailored by elementals. Of course, they probably had.

But Donal didn't sense his approach. Even though Donal could usually sense Bran's aura of power at a good hundred meters. And Fionn should have sensed it farther away than that...

"Please, Magister Bran Cuthbert," Fionn said, not sounding at all surprised. "Allow me to finish my point."

"Of course."

"You blocked me from sensing his approach," Donal said to Fionn, tone accusatory and one eyebrow high.

Fionn ignored the accusation.

"The other son has not yet completed his education. And yet, he is showered with gifts and opportunities, and now, financial resources well beyond anything a certified Journeyman should ever expect to see. Accomplished men and women have lauded that son's achievements privately and publicly. And your parents are expected to believe this is all done out of the goodness of those people's hearts?"

Fionn shook his head, making his ears flop. "They have guessed more about the risks you've faced than you would imagine."

Donal wanted to say something to that, but instead he nodded for Fionn to continue.

"When you offered them a more expensive home, what they heard was that you were undertaking all these risks for *them*."

Donal blinked at that.

"Do you think so?"

"*May I now intrude, wise one?*" Bran asked in Gaelic.

"*Of course, Magister Bran Cuthbert. I believe I have made my point,*" Fionn replied in the same language. The emerald deerhound then turned around three times and lay down, as though he were any other kind of dog than he was.

From Fionn, it was merely a gesture of finality.

Donal raised an eyebrow at Bran as he scaled the rock and sat facing Donal. Same pose. But then, it was the basic pose of meditation taught to students of magic as far back as high school.

It was like looking into a mirror, if that mirror were enchanted to make one look better and more capable.

Donal felt the old frown start before he could stop it.

"Oh, knock it off," Bran said with a laugh. "We're not kids anymore, Donal. And the only one putting you on the wrong side of a comparison with me is you."

Donal drew breath for a rejoinder, but Bran wasn't done.

"If that's the reason you're doing this crazy thing with the Fae Courts, get out of it. Want me to say you're a better magician than I am? I'll say it. *You're a better magician than I am.* Now can you call this madness off?"

Donal felt a brief moment of irritation, that he'd come out to this rock to get away from the emotional roller coaster of this visit, and so far he'd only gotten more of an emotional wild ride.

From dejection to curiosity to understanding to guilt, a hint of betrayal, then back to curiosity, and now, just good old fashioned anger. Brewing in Donal's guts, and tightening half the muscles in his body.

Well, anger and something else. But the anger was the important thing.

"Is that what you think?" Donal asked, in a voice he didn't recognize as his own. This voice was quiet, and harsh.

Fionn's head snapped around to look at Donal, ears perked attentive and eyes worried.

"Well," Bran started, but it was Donal's turn to interrupt.

"Look," Donal all but hissed. "Growing up in your shadow, that was rough. I'll grant you. Hearing about your greatness at every single port of call when I was a courier? Not easy either. Neither was getting asked daily if I was any relation. But let me tell you something."

Donal rolled his tongue around in his mouth, tasting his words and seeing if Bran would be foolish enough to interrupt. But Bran stared back at Donal with almost meditative focus.

"I don't run risks trying to outshine the great Bran Cuthbert. I just live my life. When I see something wrong, I try to fix it. And when I see a problem I can help with, I try to help that too."

"Sure," Bran started, but stopped when Donal raised a hand.

Donal felt power crackle around that hand. But that was just the intensity of his emotion. Wouldn't do anything. Not without intention added in.

But the thought of his calling up that much power without trying was the surest sign of Donal's anger. That kind of loss of control, even for a moment...

Donal drew a calming breath and finished in a more normal voice.

"So if you think my working with the Fae Courts has anything to do with you, you better get your ego in check. It's the sort of thing that can bring a magician down."

"So is working with the fae, Donal."

"Then I guess you'll get your chance to say 'I told you so.'"

Donal stood. Fionn, clearly knowing an exit line when he heard one, leapt to his own feet.

"Wait," Bran said, brow furrowed in frustration. "Don't go. I wanted—"

"Right now, Bran, what you want is the last thing I'm worried about."

Scrabbling down the side of that boulder, while Bran tried again to get Donal to stay, was not the exit he had in mind.

In fact, nothing at all about this day was going right.

San Francisco was one of the few cities on the west coast of the UNAS that not only had both a seaport and a spaceport, but kept them separate. The spaceport wasn't even in San Francisco proper, but down just past its southern edge, where there used to be a whole separate city, if Jacobs remembered right.

A city with an obvious name, like South San Francisco.

The seaport, of course, was down at the bottom of the hills, at the bay. Where the docks looked out at Alcatraz — newly brought back into use as a prison for magical crime — and at the Golden Gate. Still standing tall and red after all these years. Jacobs could never return to San Francisco without wondering what spells or alchemy preserved what mechanics had built.

Were there places that magic crossed over with science and technology? Or was the bridge now no different than a great boulder, to be worn away over time by the bay, unless alchemy preserved it?

He would never ask though. Not any of these questions, or the others they brought to mind. They were only idle curiosity he worried at the way he might worry with his tongue at a sore spot in his mouth.

Jacobs liked setting down at the seaport instead of the spaceport. It felt more natural, somehow. More human.

Plus, it helped keep the line separate in his head between retirement and his old profession, running an interplanetary cruise line and captaining its primary ship.

And since his custom combination helioship and houseboat looked for all the world like a big old, technological flat-bottom boat — and could sail almost like one — Jacobs could set down anywhere he damn well pleased. So long as he filed his paperwork, and made sure to get a competent magician to check it over every so many flights.

Paperwork. Even in retirement, it seemed that Jacobs spent almost as much time doing paperwork as he did reading. Especially in San Francisco, where the paperwork was as bad as anywhere this side of Mars.

San Francisco in December. Socked in with the kind of fog that soaked down into the bones. Made his knees and knuckles ache. Seeped into his joints as one more unwelcome reminder that he was no longer a young man. And rain would hit before nightfall. Jacobs was sure.

But San Francisco was where Jacobs needed to be right now. Not someplace warmer and drier. Even if being here now meant saying goodbye to Elinore sooner than he intended. She understood, though. Or at least, she pretended to. With women, Jacobs was never quite sure. He knew that Rhonda, bless her soul, could pretend to be perfectly fine with whatever unexpected development Jacobs dropped in her lap.

Perfectly fine. Right up until the eruption.

On the other hand, one advantage of leaving southern California was that he wouldn't be there, if Elinore had a Rhonda-like eruption.

At least, Jacobs *thought* that was an advantage. Oddly enough, he wasn't sure. Too long alone, perhaps.

And yet, here he was, strolling down the smooth crushed stone walkway. Heading for Steve's Joint, like he were a younger man in town on shore leave.

Steve's Joint. Only been open a decade, maybe a decade and a half. Big hit with those who still sailed the waves though. Even if most people who did so these days did it for entertainment or to answer the call of the sea.

The hobbyists outnumbered the working fishermen and deep sea explorers by a good ten or twenty to one. And there weren't many other professional options left for those who felt that ancient call.

But when in San Francisco, it seemed they all came into Steve's Joint, and this night was no exception. Sun only down an hour, and already the sea shanties blared loud enough to be heard on the street. But then, there wasn't much crowd to compete with. Not here on Pier Six. Just about the only people walking the pier were heading to or from Steve's Joint, and most of the crowd was already there.

Four windows in the weathered wooden front of Steve's Joint. From the outside, the walls looked on the brink of collapse, and the roof looked as though it should have leaked in dozens of places.

All for appearances, of course. Just like the small iron anchor on the thick front door.

Jacobs hadn't been inside Steve's Joint yet, but he'd seen it a number of times over the years. And tonight this bar was the specific request of the man he needed to talk to.

Jacobs tried the handle. Locked?

He pounded on the door.

It opened a crack. Jacobs saw a pair of brown eyes set in a cragged man's face that probably looked twenty years older than it was.

A bad imitation of a shadow play pirate accent said, "What be the password?"

"Password?" Jacobs asked. No one said anything about a password.

"Arr," the doorman said. "Give us the password or ye'll walk the plank."

Jacobs fixed those eyes with a glare that had wilted naval officers at ten paces.

"Open the damn door."

"Jeez," the doorman said in a perfectly normal voice, opening the door with impressive speed, considering the door's weight. "Lighten up, man. I'd've taken 'Arr, matey,' or 'Fifteen men on a dead man's chest.' Any of the classics really.'"

The doorman was dressed as a pirate, complete with fake peg leg and three gold earrings.

"Boy," Jacobs said, shaking his head, "I've been sailing long enough to know that pirates aren't a joke, and bars shouldn't insult their patrons with passwords."

The doorman straightened up, surprised maybe, but Jacobs stepped right past him and into the sea of noise. The tides of conversation and laughter crested high over the blare of sea shanties from hidden speakers.

The whole place was built to look as though it had been fashioned from cast off bits of wrecked wooden ships. Ropes hung about the rafters like ship's rigging. The stools were old wooden barrels. The tables were all old ship's wheels, right down to the handles, with their gaps filled in with what looked like old flyers or pennants. Solid enough, though, for people to slam down their big glass tankards of beer.

Plenty of those tables, all full. A bar at the end that looked to have been made from three different figureheads, all mermaids.

The bar half-full with drinkers. The barman wore a pirate captain's hat, and an eyepatch. The waitresses were all dressed like pirates too. At least, in that they all wore red bandanas to tie back their hair. Jacobs doubted, however, that pirates ever wore their skirts short and their blouses unbuttoned that far. And the heels on those calf-high boots wouldn't fare well in a storm.

At least the patrons, men and women alike, were dressed like proper modern sailors, even if they carried on like pirates out of a shadow play. Jumpsuits, or shirts and pants, all with plenty of pockets and all with good work boots that could handle the weather.

Of the ones that wore swords, some did affect cutlasses. The rest wore rapiers or sabers.

Jacobs made his way between the raucous tables to the bar. Sat on a barrel.

The bartender came over with impressive speed.

"What'll ye have, matey?"

Jacobs had to draw in a breath through his nose to avoid saying something impatient. Not a good sign. First Mancuso brought out Jacobs' old temper, now this bar.

Jacobs knew he was too old to meet every problem with a fist. So why did every problem have to have such a punchable face?

"He'll have your best honeyed Irish whiskey," a familiar voice said, from behind Jacobs. "Fifteen years old, at least. Brigid's Own, if you have it."

Kristoff Tunold heaved himself onto the barrel seat beside Jacobs. A skinny blonde man with a lantern jaw — and not more than half Jacobs' age — but Tunold still managed to carry himself like a grizzly bear.

Jacobs turned to his old ex oh with a smile and a greeting on his lips, but both died when the bartender spoke.

"We don't have any single malt Irish. Only blended."

"Sacrilege," Jacobs said, turning to Tunold to finish, "just what kind of place is this?"

"We've got plenty of good scotches," the bartender hurried on, abandoning his faked accent, which was a help. "Try some MacAvoy. Eighteen years old, and smooth as a windless sea. If you don't like it, it's on me."

Jacobs raised a disbelieving eyebrow while the bartender poured Jacobs a drink with one hand, and filled Tunold's order for some sort of swill bourbon with the other.

Jacobs brought the glass to his lips while the bartender watched with more amusement than Jacobs liked.

Then Jacobs found out why.

He slipped maybe a third of the glass past his lips to test it on his tongue. The honey was subtle, under the complex flavors of the whiskey. Smokey, and it made Jacobs think of a storm at sea, when he had a good crew and ship to meet it.

He smiled and nodded appreciation to the bartender before he was finished enough with that swig to let it ease down his throat.

Tunold, as usual, had already slammed down one glass and gotten a refill.

Jacobs shook his head. "Two years a captain now, and you still don't know how to drink."

Tunold opened his mouth for a rejoinder, but Jacobs gave his old friend a smile that killed those words unspoken.

They exchanged greetings, finally, including even a one-armed hug. And Jacobs did not hug many.

"I don't usually do my drinking in an amusement park," Jacobs said, while the bartender hurried off to deal with other customers.

"Couldn't resist," Tunold said. "Speaking of, what was so urgent you had to see me in person? I mean, it's always good to see you, John, but nothing's ever urgent with you these days. Not since…"

Realization spread across Tunold's face like the dawn rising in the east.

"You're kidding," he said.

Jacobs explained the offer. Most of it, anyway.

Tunold tossed down another bourbon, while Jacobs finished his own scotch and got a refill.

"All right," Tunold said. Then shook his head and tossed down another bourbon while Jacobs let the mere suggestion of his scotch past his lips to stretch out on his tongue.

Tunold shook his head again.

"All right," he said. Then slapped an open hand down on the bar. "No. It's not all right. What the hell are you thinking, John?"

"Wrong question," Jacobs said, fighting down a smile.

"No," Tunold said firmly. "You don't get to play that game now. You're not my captain anymore, and you're not my boss."

True words. Still. Anyone else spitting that kind of attitude in Jacobs' face would probably have gotten a fierce response. But Tunold had earned the right to speak to Jacobs like that. And Jacobs knew that Tunold would get past the attitude on his own.

"And this idea," Tunold said, while the bartender refilled his glass. "It's crazy. Pulling the *Horizon Cusp* off its routes is mad enough, but running it all the way to Venus for *two passengers*? That's..." — Tunold's head bobbed as he ran numbers — "maybe zero-point-five-six percent of capacity? Madness."

Tunold started waving his hands around as he continued, just like a bear raising up on its hind legs as it roared.

"*Plus*, Venus still isn't all that wild about commercial traffic. They won't welcome us, and they won't want to ship any people or cargo back with us. This is a *terrible* idea. If you want to do it at all — which you shouldn't — at least take a smaller ship."

"We won't quite be going *to* Venus," Jacobs said, staring into his glass. A small smile playing on his lips. He turned to face Tunold to finish. "We'll be going into that no-fly zone *near* Venus. With a military escort."

Fifteen different expressions warred their way across Tunold's face with all the grace of a drunk scrabbling for the toilet. Tunold finally slammed his fist down on the bar to get hold of himself again.

Jacobs sipped more scotch while he waited. It really was fine scotch.

"Okay," Tunold said, at last, running his hands across his face and through his short blonde hair. "Okay, I get why you want to do it. And I admit, that idea tempts me too. I'd love to see what they're hiding. But how far can you trust this? I mean, if Mancuso's involved..."

"Mancuso will be fine," Jacobs said, surprised to hear himself defending the man, but unwilling to deny the truth. "I don't like the man. It's true. But ever since he's been freed of Tai Shi's mind control, he's been past eager to make up for the trouble he caused. Even if he still manages to do it while running his corporations like a virtuoso."

Jacobs shook his head. "The military, though, is another matter."

Tunold started chuckling, and Jacobs knew he had him.

"You don't just want the ship," Tunold said, and the realization had forced a grin onto the man's face. "You want the crew you've led into and out of scrapes. And you want Mash's wards between you and any possible naval betrayal."

Jacobs raised a toast. Enjoyed a sip.

Mash. Magister Ronaldo Machado. Finest ship's mage in the business, and more than willing to push the limits of what civilian wards were allowed to do.

"That's most of it," Jacobs admitted as he lowered his glass.

"All right," Tunold said, then spun on his barrel to face Jacob. The booze was already turning the younger man's face red.

Jacobs set down his half-full glass, only his second to Tunold's … fifth?

Tunold raised one steady hand, index finger extended and rigid.

"One stipulation."

"I'm not giving up the conn," Jacobs said simply. "I'm doing this as captain."

"Knew you'd say that, you stubborn old shark," Tunold said with a grimace. "No. This is the stipulation. Ramirez checks you over daily. If, in his medical opinion, you need to step down. Or even take a break. *You take it.* He gets the *final* say about your fitness."

Jacobs opened his mouth to object, but Tunold got even louder.

"I mean it, John." Tunold shook his head, and his next words came out softer. Only just loud enough to be heard over the dull roar of the other patrons. "I'm not letting this trip kill you."

Damn if that didn't suck all the wind out of Jacobs' righteous sails.

"Fine," Jacobs grumbled. "I agree."

He had to repeat those words louder, for Tunold to hear them. Or maybe Tunold just wanted to make Jacobs say them one more time.

Either way, the rest was just working out details.

ONE OF THE GREAT JOYS OF BEING A MAGICIAN, SO FAR AS DONAL WAS concerned, was meditation.

Yes, it focused the mind. Yes, it calmed the body. Yes, it eased spirit contact, facilitated the ability to sense and interact with magical energies, and provided a host of other benefits critical to his calling.

But meditation had a social benefit, and it was one that Donal spent hours exploiting, after his little confrontation at the rock.

No one wanted to interrupt a meditating magician.

It was like interrupting a priest during prayer. Simply not done.

Hours, Donal spent deep in meditation after his argument with Bran.

Meditating that long was a skill in itself. Most students new to the practice could scarcely keep their minds clear for seconds at a time. Initiates could usually handle ten minutes or so, if they kept up the practice as often as they ought.

Journeymen were expected to be able to maintain a clear mind for at least half an hour at a stretch. And Journeymen usually had familiars, to keep them honest.

Most Magisters could handle an hour or three. The licensing requirements varied a bit from place to place, but most adhered to the one-hour standard for meditation when it came to Magisters. Some could handle more. Perhaps because they enjoyed it, or it aided their chosen focus, or they hoped to move up to Hierophant one day.

Hierophants, representing the pinnacle of thaumaturgic certification, were expected to be able to maintain a clear mind for no less than twenty-four hours consecutively. Only part of the reason so many who hoped to join their ranks had to settle for lesser titles.

And the truest masters — such as Nicholas Mason or the great Aiofe Durnin — were said to live in a state of perfect clarity.

Donal was nowhere near that good. Yet.

But dedicated practice had gotten him to the point that he could meditate for hours at a time.

And so, when Donal finally felt the gentle nudge from Fionn's mind, telling him it was time to return to the world, dusk had already fallen.

The last of the sun's warmth was absent on Donal's skin. Only the rough, cool ocean breeze, carrying its smells of salt and decay.

Donal blinked his eyes open to adjust to the light, but there wasn't much to adjust to.

He was yet seated where he last sat — always the first thing he checked, after the pranks undergraduates played on one another — on a dusted rock at the base of a small cliff, facing the beach and the ocean beyond.

He faced west, but the sun was already gone. Sunk below the distant horizon. The only light came from the twinkling stars in the moonless sky and from a small bonfire down on the beach, where a good dozen or more men and women Donal's age frolicked. Their swimwear covered by baggy cotton garments, and their voices raised in laughter and joy.

They would have welcomed Donal, if he went down to join them. Not because he was Donal Cuthbert, but only because they looked to be the sort to welcome strangers with a smile, a beer, and a hot dog.

"You would miss dinner," Fionn said, following Donal's gaze. "But your father would approve. Your mother would as well, I think. They would smile to see you do something they consider normal, such as join a bonfire party."

"You say that," Donal said, standing and moving his limbs to get blood flowing through them. They didn't fall asleep while he meditated, not anymore, but still Donal felt the need to wriggle and shake them all the same. "But you've never skipped one of my mother's dinners. Especially since we're leaving tomorrow."

"True," Fionn said. "But if you will not, then we should return. I received word from Res only ninety seconds ago that your mother was pulling dinner out of the oven."

Donal turned and started walking back through the woods towards his parents' house. He could scarcely see where he was going between the redwood trees, but his feet knew this area so well, he didn't need to see.

How many times had teenage Donal snuck back from the beach late at night, with nothing more than faint starlight to light his way?

Perhaps not as many times as Bran, but plenty.

Fionn immediately fell into step with Donal, eyes scanning the ground for any problems that Donal's own eyes couldn't pick out.

After all, knowing the path was good. But old memories wouldn't include new fallen branches, or any recent divots. Especially if they were covered over by redwood needles.

"Master," Fionn said in his thick Celtic accent as he guided Donal's feet around a fist-sized hole where something had been dug out, "Are you angry with me for concealing Bran Cuthbert's approach earlier?"

"I'm not thrilled that you did it, but it's not as though I can pretend he had any bad intentions. And you'd never have gotten to speak your piece if I'd known Bran was approaching. So no, I'm not angry."

Fionn said nothing more on the walk, but unless Donal was mistaken, the *cú sidhe's* steps were lighter.

THE CUTHBERT FAMILY DINNER TABLE.

It was too big for their house, and none of them pretended otherwise. It didn't even live in the house, most of the time.

No, most meals eaten by the Cuthbert family — when relatives weren't visiting — were eaten at the little kitchen table. Small, but big enough for four, especially when the entrée and side dishes could sit on the counters until needed.

But for visits by relatives, and for special occasions, they brought the big beast in from the woodworking shop out back, and set it up in the living room. The upholstered couch and chairs had to be relegated to the edges and corners to make space. And the coffee table had to hide underneath its giant cousin, as did the two end tables that usually sat by those big, comfortable chairs.

The family dinner table had been hewn from a single huge log of redwood, by Donal's grandfather. The slab was a good meter and a half across, and two and a half meters long. Easily over a dozen centimeters thick.

A mighty tree had yielded all that wood. A tree that, the legend said, had been felled by twin simultaneous strikes of lighting. When Donal's grandfather had heard the roaring crack of that falling tree, he had rushed out into the rain, carrying blankets and buckets.

Fire often followed lightning into the heart of a tree.

But when Donal's grandfather reached the fallen titan, it smoldered, but did not burn.

The twin strikes had left their charring, but this tree had been too mighty to burn.

Well, that was what the neighbors said. Donal's grandfather told the story a little differently. The Cuthbert family patriarch declared that this tree was a gift from Taranis himself. That ancient Celtic god of thunder.

And so he had spent weeks smoothing and leveling the wood of the tree, while maintaining all of its character. The pattern of its rings. The twin marks left by the lightning (which designated the head of the table). The wood itself was a gloriously warm, yellow-red color.

The table's six legs came from the same tree, narrowed to a meager fortyish centimeters across and rounded, with Celtic knotwork designs in rings that matched the trim work decorating the table itself.

The great beast of a table must have weighed as much as the rest of the house. Only horses and patience had allowed Donal's grandparents to fetch the fallen titan as far as their woodworking shop. And even after all of Donal's grandfather's work, the table had not been able to come into the house at all for many, many years. It split most of its existence between the woodworking shop and the Cuthbert family backyard.

It was Bran who first made moving the table ... practical. Bran was still a freshman studying Thaumaturgy at the University of California at Berkeley when he summoned two earth elementals and bound them into the table as part of an independent study project.

Karom and Oggain were a tremendous help, when it came to lugging that table around.

Donal and his family were seated around that table right now. Donal's father, at the head. A slender man made strong by years of hard work, Robert Cuthbert had the kind of callouses and roughness to his skin that Donal and Bran would probably never have. But otherwise, he looked like a vision of the future, save that his eyes were green instead of the blue that Donal and Bran shared with their mother. But his hair was just as black as theirs, and his chin just as determined.

Donal's mother sat at the foot of the table, while Donal and Bran faced one another in the middle of the long sides. Res perched casually on Bran's shoulder, although a quarter-meter of slightly transparent raven did look a little big for Bran's shoulder. At least from where Donal sat.

Fionn, of course, sat on the floor beside Donal.

Scattered all across that large surface were the handiwork of Donal's mother's cooking.

The entrée for tonight was a shepherd's pie, with rich, savory beef as a base, supported by a series of root vegetables and topped with his mother's own recipe for garlic mashed potatoes. Buttery soda bread, of course, to go with it, as well as dishes of peas and beans, mixed with bacon and some variety of spices.

And to wash it all down, bottles of Uncle Rory's dark beer. Uncle Rory had been brewing for decades now, and had two or three beers that were good enough he'd begun selling them and doing quite well with them. His IPAs were the most popular, followed by his Hefeweisen, but it was his dark beer that the family all agreed was best.

Rory didn't do anything stupid with his dark, like try to add flavors to it. It was a simple beer, and all the better for it.

The dark beer was the perfect complement to the night's meal. And for Donal, so was the conversation.

For what felt like the first time in days — well, really it *felt* like the first time in years — the conversation wasn't focused on Donal and things he was doing wrong.

They discussed Bran's plans to work with sea spirits around Mazatlán to help encourage fishing while controlling the risks of overfishing. This could be seminal work, if he pulled it off, and Bran's excitement was infectious.

Right now, the recent developments in thaumaturgic fishing had increased the number of fish drawn from the seas and rivers, without adequate attention paid to the effect this would have on fish populations.

Fodder for a good half of the meal right there. And beyond that, Donal's parents had plans for a cruise out to Luna, their first trip farther than San Francisco.

Here, Donal was even able to help. He'd been to Earth's moon many times by now, and knew the hotels to recommend, the sights they had to see, and even the touring company to use.

It felt good. It felt ... it felt as though Donal was in high school again, with Bran home from college on break. Excitement going different directions, and all of them met with enthusiasm.

The conversation was only just coming back to Donal and Esmeralda when, in the same moment, Donal felt two *plings*. The sounds of two somethings tickling at the wards.

Bran's eyes went wide. He'd felt them as well, of course. The wards on the Cuthbert property were one of the few joint spells Donal and Bran had worked together.

And their parents knew that look well enough to stop talking.

"One east, one south," Bran said.

"I know the feeling of the one to the south," Donal said, confirming his suspicions with a glance at Fionn, who nodded. "Admit her, Fionn, and escort her here."

"You're sure?" Bran said, and Donal just raised his eyebrows.

"Fine," Bran said. "I'll take east then."

Without a word from his master, Res took wing and flew straight through the wall before Bran could stand up.

Fionn, similarly, leapt into the air and plunged through the south wall as Donal stood.

Donal's mother pushed her plate back, unwilling to continue eating until her boys returned to the table. His father picked up another forkful, but lowered it at the sight of his wife's raised eyebrow.

Bran stepped out the front door.

Fionn returned through the wall, followed by a jaguar. A slightly transparent jaguar that stood about a meter tall at the shoulder, to be precise.

Tsindu. Esmeralda's familiar.

"Greetings, Journeyman Donal Cuthbert," Tsindu said, in an accent that wasn't quite Mexican. Tsindu turned to Donal's parents. "My greetings as well to you, Colleen Cuthbert and Robert Cuthbert, on behalf of my mistress, Esmeralda Villaseñor."

"I'm supposed to link Esme in a couple of hours," Donal said. "Is something wrong?"

"Not wrong," Tsindu said, "though my mistress sends her regrets. She will be unable to speak with anyone on a link for at least the coming week. Possibly not before the second turn of the moon."

"She got the internship!" Donal said, happiness in his voice and spreading all over his face. "Tsindu, do *please* remind her who pushed her to try for it in the first place."

"I already have, but I shall again." Tsindu bowed from the shoulders. "Do you have a brief message I'll be permitted to convey?"

"Only my congratulations," Donal said with a smile, "and, of course, my lack of surprise."

"Of course. On her behalf, I thank you."

The jaguar exchanged a brief word with Fionn in that language that only familiars seemed to speak, then turned and flew straight through the wall.

"Will you be telling us what that was about?" Donal's father asked.

"Or why you didn't send your girl something a little *warmer* than 'congratulations' as your last message for so long?"

Donal and Fionn looked at one another. Donal's mother cleared her throat.

"As to the second," Donal said, still smiling, "that's pretty much all I'm allowed to say. Any message beyond congratulations might get redacted or investigated. She might not even get the reminder about who pushed her to apply. That internship she just got was with Hierophant Cesar N'Kembe, First Magician of the United North American States. The first intern he's taken since his appointment."

"N'Kembe," Donal's father said, snapping his fingers. "I've been meaning to ask. Is this the same Cesar N'Kembe who was your old professor?"

"One of my favorites," Donal said. "In fact—"

Donal didn't get to finish that thought, because Bran came back in through the front door. Alone. And he didn't look happy.

THE LOOK ON BRAN'S FACE WAS ENOUGH TO DRIVE ALL THE JOY OUT OF Donal's mind.

The marvelous shepherd's pie meal that Donal's mother had prepared. The pleasure of eating at the great dinner table, a table Donal hadn't even seen in more than a year and a half. The fantastic news about Esmeralda's internship.

All wonderful things.

And all of them flew straight out of Donal's mind, at the sight of his older brother, standing framed in the front doorway of the house they'd grown up in.

Bran's face was ashen. His brow troubled. His shoulders slumped, and his posture less than perfect.

Donal hadn't seen *any* of these signs in his brother since before Bran had gone away to college. But to see them all at the same time?

Unprecedented.

And Donal's parents knew it too. Their chairs scraped the hardwood floor in unison as they stood to run to their son.

"Stop," Donal said, his voice not nearly loud enough. It was supposed to have been a firm command, to ensure he got their attention. Instead, it came out little more than a whisper.

Both parents got two steps closer before Donal could repeat his command loudly enough to get their attention.

And hearing Donal address them that way was too shocking for his parents to ignore.

"Bran," Donal said, trying to affect a lecturing tone, the way his professors did, "report."

He must have gotten the tone right, because it had the same effect on Bran it would have on Donal.

Bran shook his head. Then again, followed by his shoulders, and that shake worked its way down his body. By the time it reached his feet, Bran's posture was back to the perfection trained into it by years of proper meditation technique.

Bran blinked at Donal, then frowned, but started talking.

"That one's for you too, Donal," he said, his voice as unsure as it used to be when Bran was a teenager, talking about girls. "But don't rush out there. Might be better to let Res take a message. He can't do it without your permission, though. So just say—"

"Who is it?" Donal asked.

"The question isn't who, but what," Bran said. He shook his head again. "One of the good neighbors is here for you."

Both parents hissed in a breath.

Donal started forward, Fionn falling into step beside him.

"Donal, listen to me" Bran said, trying to stop Donal with a hand on the shoulder.

Donal frowned, but hesitated long enough to hear at least another sentence.

"You don't get it. This isn't a human messenger. *This is one of the good neighbors.* Standing out there in the flesh. Or as close as they come to it. Let Res take a message."

"You haven't heard anything I've been telling you since I got here, have you, Bran?" Donal said, shaking his head. "I'm working with them. And I'm not afraid to talk to them."

"Donal," his mother said, but Donal was done being delayed. And he was even more done keeping his fae guest waiting. He started forward.

"Donal Tormey Cuthbert!"

The magic of names was hotly debated in certain circles of thaumaturgic enquiry. But the magic of Donal's own name, thundered in just that tone by his mother, certainly had a magic all its own. It froze Donal's feet in mid-motion and made him turn to face her, fighting the urge to hang his head as though he'd done something wrong.

"I can't stop you from working with them," she said, her voice as arch as that lethal right eyebrow of hers. "But if you intend to walk out to meet one from the house that has been in your family for generations, you will certainly not do it empty-handed."

"I told you," Donal said, as patient as he could be while his mother strode past him into the kitchen, "I cannot incur debt from them, or accrue debt to them, while the contract is in effect."

"For yourself," Donal's father said. "But I'm willing to bet your contract said nothing about debt for others."

Donal's mouth slapped closed with a pop that he hoped was only audible to himself.

"And that is why they likely sent someone to you now," his father continued, patient as his mother was not. "You're a member of this household, but you're not its head."

"He does raise a point," Fionn said, in words pitched so that only Donal could understand them. "His interpretation is questionable, but not impossible. I cannot guarantee that he is wrong, so you should take their precautions."

Donal's mother thrust two ceramic bowls into his hands. One of milk, and a smaller one of clover honey.

"I *trust*," she said, tone still speaking volumes about her opinion here, "you haven't forgotten the right way to handle these?"

"I remember, Mother."

"Go then," she said. "Be about your fool's errand."

Donal pushed through the doorway and out into the cold evening air. Too cold, really. He should have had a jacket. Couldn't stop himself from shivering despite the warmth of his own anger. Each redwood-scented breath came in with another chill of its own, until Donal had to shift awareness and use pure technique to let him ignore the cold.

The front walkway was a dry dirt trail, or as dry as it ever got here during the wintertime. Which meant that small bits of mud would have to be cleaned from the soles of...

Deep breaths, Donal. Focus. And don't spill.

The wards ringed the border of the property, which meant that the fae visitor would be waiting at the end of the walkway. A hundred meters down the path.

Most of the time Donal took that walk, that hundred meters felt like a kilometer. More than enough time for Donal to think. Sometimes time for him to think too much, and manage to tie his mind up in knots it didn't need.

But not tonight. Tonight, those hundred meters passed in mere moments. Or so it felt, at least.

Donal was perhaps a dozen steps from the edge of the property when Res intercepted him.

"Don't do this, Donal Cuthbert," Res said. "They are amending your bargain already. They—"

"*Fuist,*" Donal said, angry enough to revert to Gaelic to hush his brother's familiar. Those were his brother's words anyway.

Donal didn't consider it likely that a fae raven — especially not one rumored to have been granted as a familiar by the Morrigan herself — would be against humans working with the fae.

Besides. Neither Res nor Bran knew the particulars of Donal's agreement.

Donal reached the edge of the property at last. The edge of the Cuthbert property abutted a road. Crushed stone, pressed smooth by elementals and left sparkling clean by regular maintenance. The entirety of the road was under the open sky. The redwoods surrounding the road had been trimmed back to ensure it.

Bright moonlight lit the road under skies yet clear.

Donal picked a spot near a tree at the edge of his parents' property and set down his bowls. Only then did he look to see about this fae visitor.

But no guest stood on that road.

DONAL FROWNED AND LOOKED AROUND. THE ROAD WAS EMPTY ALL THE way to its bend in either direction. The chill air itself was empty, so the fae visitor was not some air sprite.

Fionn waited by Donal's side, staring into the trees opposite Donal along the road.

Among the trees, he saw only patches of moonlight. At first.

But then, between two slender young redwoods, Donal realized that one pool of light was not moonlight.

It was the silvery glow coming off of a woman.

A slender woman. Perhaps two full meters tall, with long silver blonde hair that fell to her ankles in glorious waves. She seemed to be clothed in moonlight itself, a gossamer gown that flowed around her slender frame.

The very sight of her seemed to draw Donal in. Made him focus on every detail of her ethereal beauty. Her eyes like the setting sun. Her lips the color of fresh raspberries, smiling as though she knew secrets she shared only with a chosen few.

Those eyes took in the sight of the offering with pleasure, and those lips smiled at Donal as though he were alone in the whole, vast universe.

"Donal Cuthbert," she said, her voice tinkled like chimes, sending shivers of pleasure through Donal with every word. "Thank you for meeting me yourself."

Before Donal could reply, she spoke next to Fionn, and her words sounded for all the world like the language familiars used among themselves.

That language always reminded Donal of Gaelic, but he had reason to believe that it was not even related. Esmeralda had told him that the speech of familiars to each other sounded to her as though its etymology owed its roots to an older form of Spanish, combined with the ancient language of the Aztecs.

But though she spoke both Spanish and what had been restored of the Aztec language, she couldn't begin to understand familiars when they spoke to each other. Any more than Donal could understand what the fae woman and Fionn were saying now.

"Thank you for coming," Donal said, resisting the urge to bow. "What pleasure brings you here on this fine evening?"

"The pleasure of bringing you news," she said, her smile broadening. The playful tones of her words seemed to creep down Donal's back. Filled him with the urge to step forward to meet her. The shape and movement of her lips even seemed to invite kissing...

Donal drew a deep breath through his nose, and shifted his awareness along the magical trajectories.

No change...

Donal pushed deeper.

Still no change...

Donal shifted his awareness deeper still. Deeper than he could have gone, even over the past summer break.

But now, he saw changes in his visitor.

The fae woman remained surpassingly beautiful, but she no longer seemed to emanate that silvery glow. And the urge to go to her, Donal could still feel that, but he recognized it now for the glamour it was.

His heart lurched to double-time. Despite the cold, sweat broke out on his brow and down his back.

Donal snatched up a handful of dirt and redwood needles. He flared power through the handful and flung it into the air at the fae creature while hacking out the right words in Gaelic, faster than he'd ever spoken them before.

The glamour shattered. The sound of a dozen crystal bells, ringing discordant notes as their structures cracked apart and fell to the ground in a cacophony.

The creature hissed. Fangs visible now. Its skin almost translucent. Its hair now a silvery cloud behind its head.

She remained still oddly beautiful, in her way. The pure natural beauty of an apex predator.

But Donal wasn't finished.

He slipped his tuning fork out of his sleeve while Fionn took up the proper position between Donal and the creature, the *cú sidhe's* head lowered, fangs bared and growling, feet apart.

Power rose across the road, where the fae creature — Donal felt at least ninety percent certain it was a *leannan sidhe* — brought its hands together.

Donal rang the tuning fork, channeling outward pure power of the fifth element. Not earth nor air nor fire nor water but the fifth, considered by some to be spirit, proven by others to work as space, and summarized by many simply in a catch-all term like azoth or mana.

Fionn howled the right counterpoint, twisting the power that Donal pressed forward, and their combined effort slammed into the growing power of the fae creature and blasted it apart.

She fell to her knees. Dazed. Head shaking. Body trembling.

"Mercy," she mewled. "Mercy, great wizard."

Fionn approached, head low and growling. He sniffed at her, testing her nature more truly than Donal could ever have himself.

"*Leannan sidhe*," he confirmed. "And young. She's seen no more than perhaps two centuries."

"I long only to aid you in your travels," she pleaded. "I could love you as no mortal woman could, and inspire you to great magics you cannot yet imagine."

"And he would flare so bright he would burn to ashes, which you would then devour," Fionn said.

"No," she cried in a long wailing note.

"You are beaten," Donal said. "Acknowledge."

"I do acknowledge," she wailed. "And now I must serve as your slave."

Fionn's ears flicked in that way that Donal interpreted as a frown. "That *is* tradition. And her nature."

"I do not wish your servitude."

"And yet you have it," she said in closer to her normal voice. Her words still tinkled like chimes, but no longer did they shiver pleasure down Donal's back. "You may find the idea less disagreeable, when you discover the pleasures and wonders I can show you."

"Who sent you to me?" Donal asked. "Who broke the compact?"

"His Grace, the Duke of Shadows bid me come to you."

"Unseelie," Fionn clarified, choosing tones that only Donal could understand, before continuing in more normal tones. "This did not break the compact. It was not meant as an attack."

"I can aid you, great one," the *leannan sidhe* begged from her knees. "You will never bed a better lover, and I truly can inspire you to works beyond anything you ken."

"Both statements are likely true," Fionn said, ears still back in that frowning posture. "But a partnership with a *leannan sidhe* would not end well for you, master."

"How is sending her to me *not* an attack?"

"His Grace likely only wanted to ensure your magic reached its fullest while in service to the Courts. Her gifts would see to that. And you would certainly survive a year with her, and so nothing bad would likely happen within the term of the arrangement. Once the arrangement was over..."

"Can I release her from my service?" Donal asked. "Safely?"

"Do not destroy me, great one," the *leannan sidhe* begged. "At least let me prove my worth before you decide."

"Dismissing her isn't an option," Fionn said. "She could not trap you, and so she must serve you."

"*I don't want a slave,*" Donal said.

"No longer an option, I'm afraid," Fionn said. "It is her very nature. If she is not your mistress, she must be your slave. Only the death of one of you will end that."

"Please, master," the *leannan sidhe* implored. "Please do not kill me."

"This is..." Donal drew a deep breath to avoid calling the situation ridiculous. He knew all too well that the nature of spirits did not always include free will.

But that didn't mean he liked it.

"Very well," Donal said, his face a grimace of distaste. "You acknowledge that you are defeated and pledge yourself to my service?"

"I swear, great one," she said, vibrating with sincerity. "I am yours. I will serve you in every way you wish, and every way you will allow."

Donal wasn't sure about that last part. He made a mental note to ask Fionn about it later.

"Very well," Donal said. "I accept and acknowledge your service and declare Fionn my representative in all matters that pertain to you. You will obey his orders as you would my own. Give me a name to call you."

"I would have you call me Morna, master."

"Very well, Morna it is. Morna, I wish you to be my eyes and ears at the Courts. Report to Fionn nightly about activities there. Especially anything that might pertain to me or my duties for the Courts. Do you understand?"

"I am uncertain, master." She fluttered her beautiful eyes. Tilted her chin so that her hair, a spill of silver, formed a cloak behind her. "You do not wish me by your side?"

"This task is of great importance to me," Donal said, meeting her eyes with complete sincerity of his own. "You will be doing me great service this way."

"Then it shall be as you say, master. May this lowly one beg a kiss before she leaves your presence?"

Fionn caught Donal's eye and nodded firmly.

Donal fought against a sigh.

"On the condition that you never again refer to yourself by such a debased term as 'lowly one.' You are a noble creature, and should never forget it."

Morna blinked at Donal, her brow furrowed and lips pulled in uncertainly. But she nodded. Fionn said something Donal couldn't understand. Morna nodded again, more certainly.

"As you say, master," she said.

Donal leaned down. Morna spread her arms and lips to welcome him, but Donal crossed those lips with a finger. She blinked at him again, puzzled, and Donal kissed her on the forehead. Morna pressed her forehead back against his lips, and caressed his shoulders with her hands as though this were the deep kiss she expected.

"Now go," Donal said as he pulled back, and she faded away like moonlight behind a cloud.

"You handled that well," Fionn said.

"And I'm about to handle it even better," Donal said, smiling at Fionn.

"How is that?"

"I'm going to let *you* explain this to my mother."

2

With every ragged breath, Carl Jones tasted blood and licorice.

The blood was his. That last bastard had gotten in a lucky blow. Split Carl's lip, before Carl had finished him with a tight cut across the throat.

The licorice, well, that was just the taste of the air everywhere in Kennedy. Even in a narrow back alley between a green-bricked pizza joint and the off-white of one of those boxy prefab buildings that rented office space short term.

The air smelled like pizza dough ground from soybeans instead of grains, and whatever the place used for marinara had never encountered a tomato.

But still, that licorice scent was stronger.

First human settlement off Earth, and they never did get the air or water right. It'd be the great embarrassment of Luna, if they admitted it was a mistake.

Carl leaned heavily against the green brick. Not ducking behind the matching ceramic waste bins. That might have drawn attention.

No, Carl leaned there and fixed his face in a slightly dopey expression, as though he were drunk, or playing with pixie dust. His hands held low, where neither stiletto nor rapier would be seen by passersby, much less the blood dripping from them.

More of Carl's own blood had ruined his muted red shirt with its darker brown stain.

Wouldn't matter though. Not if he got back to Edik and Anna with what he'd learned. Not if he evaded or ended the rest of the killers between him and them.

Four more blocks to the spaceport itself. Maybe two klicks to Edik's office.

If Carl were fresh, he could have sprinted the whole way and still have enough wind to explain everything he'd learned.

But Carl had already fought his way past a dozen killers and three klicks of bad streets and back alleys. He was tired. His muscles had started to ache from the neck on down. And one of those killers had been good enough to wedge a knife between two of Carl's ribs, under his left arm.

He'd have to get that seen to. And sooner, rather than later.

But the mission came first. It was true when Carl was still on the job, fixing problems for the government. It was true when he free-lanced now and again, to keep in shape between gigs as a licensed champion.

Most of all, it was true right now when the lives of his friends were on the line.

Another few breaths. And with them the deeper calm of his off-the-books magical training. Even now that Carl was off the job, he could never seek certification as a Journeyman, or even as an Initiate. Could never charge money to cast spells, or register any magical discoveries. That was part of the exit agreement he'd had to sign.

Licensed practitioners of thaumaturgy had to certify where and how they'd gotten their training, for tracking and verification purposes.

But certification wasn't needed to gain the benefits of meditation. Nor to learn the spells of his trade. Which included the servitors watching the ends of the alleys for him. Tiny little artificial spirits that looked like dragonflies.

The servitor at the far end of the ally buzzed a warning, fractions of a second before the one at the near end did the same.

Carl came off the bricks. Rolled his shoulders.

"No point in hiding," he said, hoping he could still cover weariness in his voice as well as he used to.

"Not for you either, Jones." Far end speaker. Common formation. The speaker would have at least two backing him on that end. Probably four at Carl's other side, closing the trap.

But they'd talk first.

"Still haven't said what this is about," Carl said, casually nudging one of the ceramic garbage cans a few centimeters. "Don't you looneys like to admit why you're trying to kill someone?"

Looneys. Pathetic attempt at insulting slang for the locals here on Luna, but Carl was surprised just how agitated it got people.

Worked this time too. Carl could already hear the speaker's voice heat.

"Insults aren't your best play here, Jones."

Russian. Carl was sure of it now. Oh, this guy tried to cover the accent, but there was a dip to the right vowels that Carl could pick out no matter what the man was saying.

"Well, do you want to tell me what this is about?" Carl rolled his shoulders again and shook his wrists to keep them loose. "Or will I have to hope you'll tell me with your dying breath?"

"What does anyone want?"

The man stepped into the light now. The streetlights here in Kennedy were bright, even in this part of town. They shone with a pale white light that Carl always thought looked more like moonlight than sunlight.

One of life's little ironies.

This man wore the same as the last speaker. The same kind of clothes all the killers tonight had worn. Brown jumpsuits. Like they were trying for cheap spacer chic. But they'd obviously cut patches off the sleeves and chest. Which meant that they weren't afraid of admitting they were here at the behest of one of Luna's great families. They just didn't want to admit which one.

Problem was, it could have been either of the two big ones — Romanov or Lukyanov — which meant that they might as well have been from any of the twelve contenders, so far as solid information went.

"Information, Jones. You have it, and I need it," the man said. This one was a little taller than the last one. Almost as tall as Carl. And maybe as well-muscled. The pair at his back were shorter. And they carried slingers.

Slingers...

That was enough to make Carl smile.

Slingers were a little like handheld crossbows, except that what they flung weren't arrows. They were tiny balls of alchemical concoctions. Sometimes pure alchemy, such as one of the acids, and other times an alchemical base holding a spell.

But slingers were still notoriously unreliable, when it came to crunch time. Illegal for civilians to carry, not that such a worry would stop one of the great families. Not on Luna, where the great families were practically a law unto themselves.

But slingers had little vulnerabilities. The kind that Carl was a past master of spotting and exploiting, even if he hadn't been specifically trained to defeat slingers.

One of the little facts of his training that could never become common knowledge.

The other killers tonight, they had only carried blades. That this pack carried slingers meant something. Carl suspected he knew what.

"Your orders have changed, haven't they?" Carl smiled a vicious smile.

The dragonfly servitor behind him trilled a different note that only he could hear. Oh, if they had a decent magician, that magician might have sensed the magic of the warning, but nothing short of a Hierophant could have picked up what the flare was, or what it meant.

And it meant that the four behind Carl had fanned out at the mouth of the alley, and taken two steps inside.

Good.

"You're supposed to bring me in now, aren't you?" Carl nudged that ceramic trash can a few more centimeters, then took two steps closer to the speaker. "You're not supposed to kill me."

"Kill or capture," the speaker said with a shrug Carl wasn't sure he believed. "My choice, to be honest. And I'd prefer to capture. I'd prefer not to even torture you."

The man drew a deep breath through his nose, and Carl used it as an excuse to slide forward another half-step.

"Given my choice in the matter," the speaker continued, "I'd just as soon pay you off, get the information, and *then* kill you."

"Why pay me off then?"

"Because good information should be paid for." The man smiled, a pale smile in the streetlight. The contrast with his slicked back black hair made it dramatic. "But payment is never a guarantee that one lives to spend one's money."

"See," Carl said, loosening his arms again. His breathing now cool and steady. His heart rate down to its usual slow rhythm. "That's the problem with you lunar thugs. You just don't understand the proprieties of these things. You pay a man for information, you need to let him live so you can buy from him again."

"Not someone who's already killed a dozen of my men."

Ah. The real leader then. Of tonight's pack of killers, anyway.

Better and better.

"*Your* men?" Carl said with a broader smile. One he was sure the two behind the leader could see. "Well, then you must feel wronged. Aggrieved, even. How about the two of us fight a duel over it? I win, your dogs back off and I go my way in peace. You win, I'll tell you whatever you want to know."

The men behind the leader glanced at each other. It was a good offer. Better than he deserved. There was certainly no legal basis for a duel, not even here on Luna where the strictures were not as ... ironclad as they were back in Europe or the United North American States.

"I don't duel with a man carrying a DeGarmo blade."

Carl smiled a different smile then. His old working smile. Predatory. Some might even call it evil. He raised the blade and tilted it so the light glinted off the capital *D* and the tiny *e* in its upper right-hand corner, down by the steel crossbar.

Alonzo DeGarmo only made swords for masters he considered worthy. And only when those swords were petitioned for, and paid for, by people other than those masters.

"Last war—" The leader never got to finish his lie.

As he lied, his men raised their slingers to fire.

Before they could, Carl did two things at the same time.

One, he dove forward, tucking his body into a roll while flinging his stiletto into the throat of the leader.

Two, he sent out just the right pulse of magic to cause those slingers to misfire.

Six triggers were pulled.

Six balls of alchemical ammunition misfired.

Six men died screaming in eruptions of green alchemical fire that burned hot enough to slag a ship hull.

The seventh man, the leader, was consumed by the flames as well. But he was already dead.

Those idiots! Talk about overkill.

The whole block was in danger now.

Both buildings surrounding Carl were already on fire. Burning with that evil green flame. Hot enough that getting past them without getting fried would be almost impossible.

And the fire was spreading. Alarms were sounding. The dragonfly servitors pinged constant alerts to danger Carl could feel on his skin. Even his blood-and-licorice flavored breaths were uncomfortably hot.

No time.

Carl grabbed one of those ceramic garbage cans. Dumped it. Charged the far end of the alley where the fires were smaller, caused by only two slingers, instead of four like the fire behind him.

As he neared, Carl dove into the can, tucked himself small, and rolled, clutching his precious rapier to keep it from either stabbing him or breaking.

Carl screamed as he rolled through the flames. The garbage can melted to slag that clung, burning Carl's body as he straightened out and started running.

The dragonfly servitors flashed an all-clear. So Carl wasn't actually on fire. That was something at least.

Pain blazed across every millimeter of his anatomy. And that on top of the stab wound. But Carl could not afford to stop.

He ran his mind through the meditations to ignore pain, and forced effort from his exhausted body.

He could only hope it would be enough.

THERE WERE TIMES THAT EDIK BARSHAI REGRETTED HIS PARTNERSHIP with Roger North.

Well, to be honest, there were times *every day* when Edik regretted that partnership. Even if the two of them together were making more money running their tourist routes and charter flights than they could have made when they were still competing, the fact was that their partnership meant that Edik had to deal with North every ... single ... day.

One of them was likely to end up dead. Both of them knew it. The only questions were who and when.

The way North was carrying on right now, it would be him, and it would be tonight.

Most of Kennedy Spaceport was shut down by this time of night. It should have been peaceful. The glow of the lights around here was pale enough to make even the blue-white stone of the spaceport walls and floor easy on the eye.

The black night sky above, almost the sky of Earth, with only a hint of the day's greenish hue visible now.

None of the other landing bays in this area were busy. Edik had hoped to stretch out on the top of the *Third Son*, his firebird-shaped helioship, enjoy some late-night borscht and watch the stars while chatting with Dola, his familiar.

But the night's peace had been shattered by the shouting of North.

North looked as he always did. Which was to say, like a pirate masquerading as a Navy man.

First, he was short. As though someone took a proper human being — say, one about Edik's height — and squished him a good quarter-meter shorter while packing on another ten kilos of pure barrel-chest.

Then there was the short, scruffy black hair that sprouted not only all over the top of his head, but also above his bloodshot eyes, and finally out of his chin in a ragged, disorganized attempt at a beard. Not nearly as sophisticated as Edik's own blonde Van Dyke and clean-cut hair.

Where Edik wore proper spacer clothes — a fine black jacket with multi-pocketed black pants and a pale red shirt — North affected a faux-Navy uniform, complete with fake insignia.

And while Edik wore a proper saber, as any good man of Russian descent would wear to defend himself, North had to have that big cutlass.

He was also carrying a duffel bag, and that made no sense at all.

"...now get down here, you bastard!" North finally finished. "You've got a lot to answer for."

Edik looked longingly at his bowl of borscht. It was spiced just right, and the beef had just the right texture. The texture it only got when the pot was three days old. Old enough for those spices to settle into every grain of the beef...

"You can heat it again," Dola said. Edik would have sworn that the ripple going down the meter-tall, shaggy gray cat's fur was one of displeasure. "Better to deal with this sooner than later. You know what he's like when he's had all night to stew about something."

"You don't like this partnership any better than I do," Edik muttered.

"I don't like that the two of you don't get along," Dola corrected him. "Ivan Tsarevich knows you have enough reason to set aside your differences."

Now that wasn't playing fair. Using Edik's favorite Russian folk hero against him.

"*Now*, Barshai!" North roared.

Was it Edik's imagination, or did North's hand stray toward his cutlass?

"Fine," Edik said, "but not because I take orders from you. Your yelling is hurting Dola's ears."

Edik whistled to Magom, the earth elemental Edik had bound into the *Third Son*, and Magom helped ease Edik down smoothly across the hull and finally down the firebird's legs to set his shiny black, knee-high boots on the blue-white stone of the landing bay.

Dola, of course, merely jumped down, then paused to bathe himself.

Or perhaps he was excluding himself from the immediate discussion. If so, he was a smart cat.

But then, Edik already knew that.

"What's your problem this time, North?" Edik asked. "Don't like the way I track my expenses? Don't like that my ship costs more to maintain than yours does? Only drawback to having a proper helioship over your little airship, after all. Or is it that you don't like—"

"Why don't you let him tell you, Edik?" Dola asked, in tones pitched so that only Edik could understand them.

Edik frowned at Dola, but stopped talking. Looked at North expectantly.

North grabbed his heavy black belt with both hands, and adjusted it. More as a show of size than out of any need to do so.

"What's this I hear about you and a voyage away from Luna? Again?"

"Don't see what's puzzling about that," Edik said. "Anna needs a lift to someplace near Venus. Not like your *Sparrow* could handle the jaunt. Payment's all arranged."

"That's not what I mean," North growled, "and I'm betting you know it. You left my name off the crew manifest."

"No mistake there either," Edik said with a one-shoulder shrug.

"Don't need your help flying my ship. Figured you might as well be here making money—"

"I'm not letting you fly Anna into danger without me."

That made Edik blink.

In all the time Edik had known North, the man had shown exactly two emotions: greed and lust. Anna was a dead end for North's lust, thank God, and Edik couldn't see how greed applied here.

"I'm sorry," Edik said. "I couldn't have heard that right."

"Edik," Dola admonished, sticking to tones only Edik could understand.

"You heard me," North said, stepping closer, his jaw and chest jutting forward.

"Fine," Edik said, raising one hand in an attempt to look soothing instead of flabbergasted. "I heard you. But come on. She's going to have *Carl* along, and that Hierophant. Mason. Think about that. A Hierophant almost as legendary as Lloyd Bird himself, and Carl? I don't know exactly what the hell he is, but I know I'd rather face that Hierophant than Carl. Just what the hell could you do to protect her that *they* couldn't?"

"You saying you've never seen a fight, one more sword couldn't make the difference?"

"There's not supposed to *be* any fighting," Edik said, trying to keep to those soothing tones, though from the look Dola was giving him, Edik doubted he was doing a good job.

"And if there is?"

"Look," Edik started, but then he heard the echo of steady, swift boots coming this way.

He didn't need to say a word. One glance at Dola and the cat became invisible to non-magicians and took off, investigating.

Dola hadn't gone three steps before Edik had his saber drawn, just in case.

North, perhaps aware enough of his surroundings to realize that all was not well, drew his own cutlass. He even had the good sense not to threaten Edik with it.

Dola hadn't made it out of the landing bay before Carl came tumbling in.

Carl was drenched in sweat and blood. His ebon skin looked ashen. And something green clung to him all over.

"Don't say it," Edik said to North, then rushed to his fallen friend's side.

MOST PEOPLE SUFFERING AS MUCH PAIN AND EXHAUSTION AS CARL would, very sensibly, pass out.

Even most magicians. And Carl knew for certain that magicians of Journeyman grade and higher knew how to shunt away pain and exhaustion, even if they knew it was a bad idea to do so.

Such efforts could keep one conscious and active, yes, but at a price...

Unfortunately for Carl, even if he wanted to be sensible right now, his training had long since tamped down the inclination to avoid that awful price.

And to make matters worse, the *way* he'd been trained to shunt aside pain and exhaustion allowed him to assess his condition with an almost clinical detachment.

His pain level exceeded safe limits. He knew that even before he began to enumerate the causes, from the outside in.

He'd been scalded over most of his body, and even now chunks of ceramic garbage can clung to his flesh. Legs, arms, shoulders, hips, back, chest — all seared, and all restricted by reshaped ceramics.

He'd suffered a number of bumps and bruises from earlier fighting. Difficult to assess the extent of trouble there, past the fiery pain of the molten garbage can. Best estimate, three contusions on his chest — one front, two back — another on his left cheek, and one more on his hip.

Stab wound, left side of ribcage. No lung damage. No organ damage at all. Just pain, and lacerations to muscles and tissue. Also, small issue with blood loss, but that had been ameliorated by the ceramics, some of which had cauterized the wound.

All muscles suffering from fatigue past the point of exhaustion. Even without any combat damage, the exhaustion would require a dozen hours of good sleep, and two good meals before anything like real improvement.

This level of fatigue, however, was sufficient to impair healing. Combined with the combat damage, Carl could not feel certain that he would live to see the dawn.

That had to be at least part of the reason he was still awake, when every fiber of his being demanded unconsciousness.

Carl believed he had made it to the right landing bay, at least. His face was currently planted on blue-white stone — which could have meant he was anywhere in Kennedy Spaceport, but he could smell the licorice flavoring of the air. That meant he was in a landing bay, which was open to the sky, and not inside the port somewhere, where air elementals filtered the too-familiar scent away.

More importantly, Carl could smell borscht. That meant he had to be in the right landing bay. Only Edik's landing bay ever smelled like borscht.

Boots. Rapid steps. Vague tick against Carl's awareness said a familiar stood nearby as well.

A 'caster. If Carl was wrong about where he'd fallen, he could be in enemy hands right now.

With a herculean effort, Carl raised up to his knees. Couldn't see much. His sight had narrowed down to a tunnel of blackness and blur.

He hefted his rapier to something close to a defensive pose. Just in case. He kept listing to the left. He'd have to ... try to counter that...

"Careful, North. Even like that he could probably still stick you."

Edik's voice.

Safety.

Carl sagged. His wrist reflexively bent so his bloody blade did not smack the stone, only the steel of the hilt.

"Easy, Carl." Edik's voice right beside him. Likely Edik's hands checking wounds. "Easy. What the hell happened?"

Not the official words demanding a report, but close enough. Words came pouring out of Carl without any conscious effort on his part. Though they did slur here and there.

"Went to sh-sh-check Anna's worry. Figured new recruits ... would get pulled ... from the Russian and Romanian bars-sh ... on south side, near the Temple."

Deep breath. Too lightheaded. Not sure if he could continue. But the words flowed all the same.

"Great family recruiting. They made me. Pursued. Wanted intel. Tried to cap-sure. Failed. Tried to kill. M-M-Maybe s-s-s-ucceeded..."

There was more Carl needed to say. But his lips refused to move.

Blackness enveloped him.

Edik caught Carl before the poor, half-dead man collapsed.

Dola, knowing his role, had already returned from the ship with Edik's medical kit — a small, red canvas bag filled with bags and bottles of alchemical solutions, along with a brief refresher book — and was even now zooming away to fetch the port doctor on call.

"Get his boots off," Edik said to North.

North hesitated. Edik looked up from rummaging through the medical kit and arranging supplies.

"Shouldn't die like that," North murmured, in as close to a respectful tone as Edik had ever heard from the man. "Should die with his boots on."

"He's not going to die, Roger," Edik insisted. "Now help me. Get those boots off of him. Socks too."

Just where the hell was that Hierophant when it mattered, anyway? Off doing something glorious, no doubt. Far too political to do something as important as save the life of a good man.

And Edik had long since decided Carl was a good man, even if Carl didn't seem to believe it himself.

North was finally moving, at least. Might have been the overhead avian swoop of a blue jay-shaped airship that jarred him back to awareness. He pulled Carl's boots and socks off, while Edik arranged his meager supplies and tried to remember the first aid training he'd learned while studying for his Initiate's license.

Fortunately, the alchemists who assembled this medical kit seemed to know that most magicians wouldn't necessarily have those first aid lessons foremost in their mind, in an emergency. Or have time to rummage through the brief first aid booklet they included.

Edik looked Carl over. Tried to determine priorities.

The burns were the most obvious. But burn creams would have to wait until the green gunk had been stripped from Carl's skin.

Carl's skin was ashen, and tacky with foul sweat. His muscles shivered, and some of that might have even been convulsions. But Edik didn't know how to judge that.

No. He needed to go simple and straightforward, bringing the big guns into play immediately and pray for the best. He could only really try to stabilize Carl and hope a real doctor got here soon.

Edik started with a fingerfull of pain cream, slathered just below Carl's nose where he would inhale it with every breath, and a little more at each temple, completing the triangle and speeding the effects through Carl's system. Edik smeared the little bit of excess across the middle of Carl's forehead.

It might have been Edik's imagination, but already Carl seemed to ease a little where he lay.

The man wasn't even moaning. Much pain as he'd been in, shouldn't he have been trying to moan? Just one more thing Edik didn't know.

He shook his head. Returned his attention to the kit.

Next came a handful of powdered mixture that smelled like a forest after a rain. As directed, Edik rubbed that into Carl's hair and scalp from the forehead to the soft spot in the skull, while easing just a little power into the mix and muttering the written incantation in his own poor pronunciation of Gaelic.

Why did the official language of magic have to be Gaelic? Tribute to Lloyd Bird or something? Why couldn't it have been English? Or better still, Russian?

Hell, *French* would have been better than Gaelic.

Focus, Edik.

After the head mixture came the foot mixture. A different powder. This one had to be made tacky with spittle from the "healer." Edik added the spit — ignoring the snide comment from North — and smeared that mixture on the soles of Carl's feet.

That would complete one essential connection. It would begin shifting outside energies through the channels of Carl's body.

How many channels were there? Six? Seven? Edik couldn't remember. He hoped it wasn't important.

The white candle came next. Edik whispered just a little power into it, then lit it and set it on the blue-white stone on Carl's right side. Then he did the same with a black candle on the left side.

Incense next. A stick. Edik lit it and waved it seven times above Carl's body, then set it into its holder up by Carl's head. If he'd done it right...

Yes! The smoke from the incense was trailing down Carl's body before it began to waft up with its smells of camphor, ambergris, and a few other things Edik couldn't place.

Now there was a blessing to chant. A six-word thing, but full of those harsh Gaelic syllables. Edik couldn't begin to translate this one. It was some older form of Gaelic than he knew. Or maybe it wasn't in Irish Gaelic — which was all he'd had lessons in back at that community college — but one of the other forms. Like Scots-Gaelic.

Doesn't matter, Edik. Just shut up and chant.

Power flowed. Edik could feel it flowing through him and into Carl.

Still, Edik's chanting efforts were weak. His mind kept flitting back to the medical kit. Maybe there was something else he should have done first. Maybe there were more herbs to apply. Or a concoction to pour into Carl's mouth.

I should check...

No. Keep chanting.

So many harsh syllables. How could these even be words? They just sounded like Dola pretending to cough up a hairball. And the power Edik felt moving. Was it enough? Was there a way he could make it more? Maybe if he...

Edik shook himself. Tried to focus. But those other thoughts, they just kept intruding.

The way Carl trembled. Didn't Edik see something in the medical booklet about shakes? Maybe Edik should check...

No. He needed to chant. Focus on the ... syllables. If they could be called syllables.

Sounds. Whatever. Edik kept making them all the same. Repeating them over and over. In his own mind, it sounded like "Rach, nechech, swee-lach-natrech, moash, krich, toe-roash."

Not even close to any words he recognized.

Fever! Didn't Edik see something specifically against fever? Fever would explain the sweating and shaking. Yes. Edik should check. Surely he could keep chanting while he checked. These were just noises anyway. Probably only there to give a helpless Initiate something to keep his mind busy while waiting for a real magician to save the day.

Edik gave up trying to hold his thoughts together. But he made himself stay on his knees there by Carl's side, repeating those nonsense syllables over and over. Letting the power those sounds called up move through him and into Carl.

Suddenly Dola was there.

"The doctor is moments behind me," Dola said.

A snake appeared in front of Edik. A huge red-green adder, maybe three or four meters long, and a good twenty centimeters across.

"No!" Edik cried, reaching for it. He had to stop it from biting Carl.

Edik's hands passed through the snake...

...familiar. There. Edik could see the slight translucence to it now. It was moving over and through Carl. And now Edik could hear rapid, approaching footsteps too, echoing in the hall outside the bay.

"It's all right, Edik," Dola said, in tones only Edik could understand. "Let the doctor's familiar help Carl."

Edik fell back on his butt on the cold blue-white stone. He was sweating. When had he started sweating? And his heartbeat was beating so fast it was like it was trying to beat for Carl as well as Edik.

And why did Edik feel so lightheaded?

"Breathe, Edik," Dola said. "That chant is ancient, and it can take a lot out of you."

"What?" Edik managed. The landing bay ... was it spinning? He lay on his back, and the great opening into the night sky above seemed to try to spin, but got no more than about a quarter rotation before clicking back into place.

"You need to meditate more, Edik," Dola said, sounding a little worried. "The chant would have taken less out of you if you only had more focus."

"Easy there," North said ... to Edik? Sure enough, North had stripped off his faux-navy jacket and was tucking it under Edik's head.

"He'll live," North said, sounding strangely subdued. "You kept him alive until the doc got here. More than I could have done."

"I..." Edik frowned. He wasn't sure what to say to that.

"Take it easy now," North said again. "Or the doc will have to work on you next."

Edik lay back and tried to rest.

<hr>

Six times, while still on the job, Carl passed out from pain and exhaustion after giving as complete a report as possible.

Each time, Carl had not expected to wake up.

Each time, he did indeed wake up. Most often in the infirmary, and always with the understanding that he would be sent out to endure the same sort of treatment, if necessary, in service to his country.

This time, at least, there were no superiors to send Carl back out onto the field against his own desires.

No, this time, if he went back, it would be for friendship. A far greater cause than even loyalty to the nation that birthed him.

These were the sort of thoughts that flitted through Carl's head and let him know that he was awake.

Typical, really. Like so many things in Carl's life, it came back to his training. The first thoughts on awakening had to do with recollection of where he was and why, so that he would be better prepared for whatever met his eyes when he finally opened them.

In those first moments, though, it wasn't likely anyone could tell that he'd regained consciousness. Without even trying, his lungs maintained the same rate of breathing. His heart the same pulse. His limbs would not even move, not unless they had been twitching in his sleep.

And so, as soon as Carl realized he was awake, he had a moment to assess what he could of his situation before taking any action that would alert potential enemies.

After all. For all Carl knew, some of those killers from earlier had survived the fire, and might even now be in pursuit.

He could hear voices talking softly in the background. That could mean anything though. He'd get to them. He needed more information first.

He lay on something cold and hard. Last he'd seen, or what little his eyes had been able to determine, he'd been certain he'd arrived in Edik's landing bay.

That would mean he lay on the blue-white stone of Kennedy Spaceport. Likely, but not enough for certainty.

Carl could smell the licorice scent of the air, and under it the aromas of ambergris and camphor. Healing incense? Likely. No guarantee of friend or foe there. Ambergris and camphor incense was usually a field medicine concoction. Anyone might have it...

There. Faintly. Only just still something his nose could detect.

Borscht.

That eased his next breath, while Carl turned his attention to those voices...

No good. The sound of Carl's own blood rushing past his ears was still too loud. And they rang, as though he'd endured loud sounds as well.

Sirens? Perhaps. No way to be certain right now.

"He wakens," said the voice of a familiar Carl didn't recognize. He was certain it was a familiar though. Perhaps because he was now aware enough he could sense magical entities nearby. Or perhaps simple the way the voice seemed to almost hiss those esses. As though the words it actually spoke were "He wakensssss."

A quick tightening of all of Carl's muscles told him he still had two daggers hidden on his person.

Also, that much of his clothing was gone, including his boots and socks. And that he lay under a soft, wool blanket.

How did he not notice that first?

Just how messed up was Carl?

He let his eyes flutter open slowly, adjusting to the light as quickly as he could.

The light stabbed pain into Carl's eyes. Too bright in these damned landing bays...

No. That was sunlight. And the sky overhead was the pale green of just after dawn. Almost more white than green.

Footsteps. A tilt of his neck, and Carl saw a sight that eased him even more.

Edik. That was good. Dola was with him. Even better. And neither looked harried. Better and better.

North, right behind them. That was ... well, the man wasn't an enemy, anyway.

Entering Carl's vision from the right, a doctor. Middle-aged woman. Skin almost as dark as Carl's, and her hair in a bush of short curls around the back of her head. She wore a dark purple dress — an African cut, consistent with local trends — with the universal medical symbol of the red caduceus over her heart.

Edik and North moved back behind her, giving her room to work.

Now that Carl could see her, he could feel her magic all around him. And that the giant adder familiar was hers. Carl began to sit up...

"Ah," the doctor said in a sharp voice. "You stand up right now and I'll confiscate your pretty sword and turn it in to port authority."

"You wouldn't," Carl said, ignoring the dizziness the fogged his head and the pains radiating all through his body and sitting up anyway. "I'm a licensed—"

"You're a licensed fool is what you are," she said, shifting her awareness. Likely so that she could check Carl's healing along several lines. "You were caught in that fire, weren't you? Fighting, if I had to guess. And rather than stay there like a good boy and get medical treatment immediately, you tried to run from the law."

She shook her head. Took Carl's wrists in her hands. Checked the pulse points first, then the energetic channels flowing down there from the central channel that followed the spine.

She arched an eyebrow. "Blood on your sword, and I'm betting it's not yours, Carl Jones. If that *is* your real name."

"Might as well be," Carl said. "No one knows me by any other name these days."

"Uh huh," she said, then whistled to her familiar. "Hush now."

And the woman made passes with her hands over Carl's physical body, extending into his etheric body, and even into his astral body, while her familiar assisted in ways Carl wasn't quite sure he understood. He knew a little of the magic of emergency field medicine, but not much more than that.

It could have been that the doctor's familiar was describing a limit that gave her senses scope they could follow. Or perhaps it was sensing in a different direction. Down, as it were, to her up.

Whatever it was she did, she finished it faster than Carl would have expected.

"You'll live," she pronounced, as though she weren't sure it was a good thing. The way she arched that judgmental eyebrow reminded Carl of the women Carl's mother knew through church. They had all looked at Carl that way, back before anyone ever called him Carl Jones.

"Thank you Doctor..." Carl said. The landing bay started to spin, but a deep breath held it still. Reduced the dizziness to a discomfort in his head, hardly noticeable under his pains.

"Johnson," she said. "Doctor Monique Johnson. And before you ask, I'm a Journeyman with specializations in several forms of medicine, including" — she looked pointedly as some old scars on Carl's chest — "field medicine."

"Thank you, Doctor Johnson," Carl said with as much dignity as he could muster. He still felt shaky.

"Save your thanks until I'm sure you're not one of the bad guys. Port security will—"

Carl spoke over her. "If you have a specialty in field medicine and not just experience, then you likely got your training in the Terran Navy. If I'm right, check my etheric body in the third official location."

That got a frown on the good doctor's face. A frown that seemed to extend from the neck up.

She arched that judgy eyebrow again and peered to the spot behind Carl's left ear.

She hissed in a breath through pursed lips.

"I've never seen that symbol before," she said, leaning closer.

"It's need-to-know," Carl said, exhaustion creeping into his voice. Lying down sounded like a really good idea. "And you don't. But that's the reason why I was fighting, and the reason port security won't bother me, when they get here."

Doctor Johnson frowned again, but nodded. She turned to Edik. "He still needs a hospital, no matter what he tells you after I leave. Even with magic, bodies just don't heal fast enough for him to pretend he's up and about."

"I'll get him there myself," Edik said, and Carl heard the lie in his friend's voice. Though Edik covered it pretty well, all things considered.

Carl lay back down, and let out a small moan for good measure. Might help convince her that he really would go to the hospital.

And Carl lay there until he no longer sensed her familiar.

EDIK WATCHED THE DOCTOR AND HER SNAKE FAMILIAR LEAVE HIS landing bay. He listened until he could hear her steps echo out there to blend in with the rest of the early morning noise of the port.

No flights were schedule to leave for another hour, which meant that at many of the landing bays, crews were rushing to get ready. Some of them may even have been boarding passengers.

Though this part of the port was reserved for smaller traffic. None of the big space liners or anything. Made it all more convivial, as well as less noisy.

Nothing in a spaceport could compete with the sound of those great commercial cargo movers lugging boxes around. They looked like hollowed out giant gorilla bodies — if gorillas had been lizards instead of mammals — and every step those things took seemed to shake the ground nearby.

But none of those near here. From the rest of the port Edik could only hear distant voices and the general bustle of activity. And from the pale green morning sky overhead, only the occasional flap of airship travel.

Edik stared harder at the arch that led out of the bay and into the rest of the port. As though she might turn around, and come back in leading a pack of port security guards.

Dola sighed at Edik. Zoomed to the edge of the bay. Turned back and made a show of nodding at Edik before returning.

Edik nodded at North.

Edik and North turned together to look at Carl, who still lay under a single woolen blanket on the cold, hard blue-white stone.

"She's gone," Edik said.

Carl didn't immediately sit up. Stupid that Edik should have expected him to, especially the way he practically fell back down from a sitting position only a moment ago. It's just that actually being hurt this way seemed so much more ... human.

Edik hadn't been sure *anything* could hurt Carl like this.

And if he was honest with himself, he found the whole situation disquieting.

Carl might not have sat up, but he did shift about like he was considering it.

"Oh, you stay there," North said. "Don't be stupid. Leave port security to Barshai and me."

"Port security isn't coming," Edik said, frowning at North. "A great family's involved."

"They'll come," Carl said, and his voice sounded shivery, even if he seemed to lay still enough.

"Do you need more incense?" Edik asked, desperate to have something to do to help.

Carl just shook his head.

"You heard him earlier," Edik said, whispering to North now. Though his voice, despite himself, got louder as he continued. "A great family caused that fire. And it was outside of the port proper. No way they're going to let port security investigate Carl. They'll just throw money at the problem until it goes away."

"Maybe," North said, tugging at his patchy black beard. "Wouldn't trust it though."

"You're both wrong," Anna said, striding into the landing bay and followed by Hierophant Nicholas Mason.

They looked like they'd walked out of a picture book together. Anna, the tsarina. So blonde and beautiful it might have hurt to look at her, if Edik had not already relegated her to the role of younger sister in his head. So instead of finding the sight of her attractive, he wondered instead what important meetings required her to wear a high-necked turquoise business suit and have her hair bound back in those complicated braids today.

And Mason, he looked the part of a hero in ways Edik never would. Mason was a good two centimeters taller than either Edik or Carl, which made him quite tall. He wasn't muscled like Carl, but he was slender as a whip. He dressed in dark blue and brown airsilks today, that seemed to set off his blue eyes and long brown hair as though he'd been arranged by a shadow director, looking for just the right image to sell his new work.

And the rapier at Mason's side. A DeGarmo, for crying out loud.

Through most of Edik's life, DeGarmo blades had been a rumor. Just this side of a folk tale. Something people talked about, but no one had ever seen. The highest praise a rumor would attribute to some local fencer would be that DeGarmo was *considering* designing a sword for him or her.

Now Edik not only saw a DeGarmo sword on a regular basis, he knew not one, but *two* men who carried blades made by that master of swordsmiths. And both of them were commonly in Edik's presence these days.

Whether that was a good thing or a bad thing, Edik wasn't sure.

But it was Anna's words, not the troubled brow of the Hierophant — or his sword — that had Edik's attention right then.

"How can we both be wrong?" Edik asked. "Either port security are coming or they aren't. There's no third option."

"When the great families are involved," Anna said slowly, shaking her head as though she couldn't believe Edik didn't understand this yet, "there are *only* third options."

Mason was already kneeling beside Carl, and muttering spells that he probably should have cast hours ago. Except that he hadn't been here when Carl needed him.

He was casting them now, at least, and Edik could feel immense amounts of power flow from the Hierophant and into Jones.

"How do you see this playing out?" North asked Anna with more deference than Edik would have believed possible. Just how did he view her, anyway?

"Have you warded?" Anna asked Edik.

"Not recently. I mean, they're in place, but not active."

While Edik tried to stammer an explanation as though he'd already been caught in the wrong, Dola moved to the wards and activated them.

"Connect them to the port wards while you're at it," Edik said. "If trouble's coming, at least an official report should help us."

"You're not listening, Edik," Anna said, patiently. "That fire last night, that could only have been the work of misfiring slingers that should not have been carrying the kind of payload they obviously were."

Edik almost — *almost* — asked how she could be sure. But then he recalled that, though Anna herself was not a magician, she had a real flare for alchemy.

"Every great family will realize that. And the great family who *caused* that fire is not going to be satisfied with last night's results. Which means now that word of Carl's survival has gone out…"

"We're not just looking at one great family coming," Edik said, a drop of sweat forming on his brow. "Others will investigate this too."

"And none of it will be above-board," North added in a growl.

"He can be moved," Mason said. Addressing Anna.

"Good," she said. She knelt beside Carl and stroked his cheek in a way that made Edik wonder if she held feelings for Carl that she hadn't admitted to. "I'm sorry, Carl. This should never have happened to you. And if we had time, I'd take you to my family's home and have you restored to health. But we don't have time."

"They've passed the first marker," Mason said, standing.

"Then we are out of time," Anna said, voice crisp. "We must leave now."

For a moment, Carl could only lie on that blue-white stone and blink, while the others discussed his fate.

Discussed. Argued. He wasn't sure which.

Not at the moment, anyway. Not with so much of Carl's attention inside himself.

Carl still had all his pains. He could count them, in order of descending sharpness and magnitude.

Oh, it was true that some of the alchemical mixtures had worked right with his system to dull the worst of his suffering. But not nearly to the extent that Carl had experienced from medical treatment in the past.

Just more evidence that good Doctor Johnson might have considered Carl one of the bad guys.

It was a fair concern. In her shoes, he would have made the same assumption. Hell, even where he lay, Carl was never quite certain himself where he fell on the good-bad spectrum. Especially now that he was an independent operator.

But for all the aches from his skin, and his stab wound — the bruises, at least, he couldn't feel under the alchemy and the competing worse injuries — there was something more going on.

Some of that was the doctor's healing magic. That was plain enough, even if it would be just as Doctor Johnson had said — altogether insufficient to get Carl back on his feet and active anytime soon.

In fact, were it not for Carl's own training and experience, the good doctor would likely have been right that he would have died without medical attention.

But Carl had been hurt worse than this and survived. Unpleasant though it most certainly was.

Still. There was something else going on inside Carl. Something along magical lines. Something not quite what the good doctor had done.

Just what, exactly, had that Hierophant done to him?

Carl had felt the spellwork, of course, as well as the movement of energies. Felt them surge into him. Some of those energies had even done what he expected — attempted to augment the healing done by the doctor.

But that was only a small portion of what Mason had done.

And though Carl's focus was foggy, he found his attention seeking inside himself. Seeking traces of the Hierophant's signature and attempting to track them. To determine just what those spells were doing.

But it was no good.

Maybe Carl was just too hurt. Or maybe the Hierophant was just too subtle. All Carl knew for sure was that Mason's spells had moved into the energy centers of Carl's physical and etheric bodies, and carried on deeper into him in a way he didn't understand and couldn't follow.

Into the astral component of his self, certainly, but there was more to it than that, and Carl couldn't tell what. Or how. Or why. Or what it was doing.

All Carl knew for certain was that, despite the depths of his injuries and exhaustion, Carl could sit up.

It hurt. And he couldn't do it without rocking side to side, but he could do it.

The woolen blanket fell to his waist, exposing his naked chest and the various solutions covering his burns and stab wound.

His sitting up also threw the discussion into silence.

They were all looking at Carl now. Mason, Anna, Edik and Dola, even North.

"You're not helping my cause here," Edik said, and just like that the whole of the argument fell together.

Edik, arguing that Carl needed proper medical attention. That taking him off-world without a doctor was murdering him.

Anna, arguing that Mason could keep Carl alive until they reached ... wherever they were going, where Anna sounded certain that help could be had.

Mason, agreeing with Anna and speculating that the Rhian people might be able to help as well.

North, arguing that Anna was right and we should do what she said.

Edik, reminding everyone whose ship the *Third Son* was.

But now Carl was sitting up, and they were all looking at him.

"Let's ... go," he said, and tried to stand.

The bay spun. His limbs scarcely seemed to follow his orders. And the blanket felt like it weighed a ton. But he was moving.

"This is stupid," Edik boomed.

North hustled over, even ahead of Mason, and started to scoop Carl up like a baby.

Perhaps the least dignified thing to happen to Carl in years, but he couldn't bring himself to protest.

Movement in the green sky above.

A port security airship. An *armed* port security airship.

Looked like an old Earth submarine, maybe ten meters long. A channel on each side for rock throwers. Old siege equipment style. Nothing as powerful or complicated (or alchemical) as a naval helioship might carry, but it could do a lot of damage to the *Third Son*.

Especially while the firebird helioship remained on the ground.

To make matters worse, port security guards were hustling into the landing bay right now. At least a dozen of them.

Carl didn't have his sword. Why didn't he have his sword? Where...

Oh. Yes. There it was. No more than two meters from his hand. The small, faceted sapphire in the hilt glinted in the morning sunlight.

Too far. But one of the knives Carl had hidden was in his hand before he even thought about it. It would have to do.

He tried to get up. Failed.

Roaring sound in his ears. Louder even than the alarm he could hear coming from above.

Too loud. And the light too bright.

Carl gritted his teeth. Pushed to stand up.

Collapsed back down to the deck. Unconscious.

OF ALL THE THINGS THAT ANNA LUKYANOVA HAD LEARNED ABOUT MEN in her nineteen years, the most common element was also the most irritating.

Violence. Nearly all men seemed to believe that violence, both the ability to inflict it and the willingness to use it — whether personally or through others — represented some essential ingredient in masculinity.

And thus, in conflicts between men, violence always breathed about the air. One wrong word or deed away from exploding into action and removing all opportunities for reasonable resolution.

An exaggeration? A slight one, perhaps. But all too slight.

And at the moment, it seemed not an exaggeration at all.

Anna stood in a landing bay in Kennedy Spaceport. The landing bay leased by Firebird Travel, which was to say by Captain Edik Barshai. Although, technically, it was now leased through Edik's partnership with Skipper Roger North of Northbound Tours.

Despite this partnership, neither man was willing to surrender or modify the name of the business he had built. So they appeared to remain in competition, even though their businesses had merged.

Appropriate, perhaps. Cooperation was hardly the hallmark of their relationship. Both men had been ready and willing to come to blows multiple times a week for all the months she'd known them now.

Violence. Men. Not quite synonymous, but all too close.

Both men stood behind her now. Edik with a saber in his hand, and Roger with a cutlass in his. Edik's familiar, Dola, had his shaggy gray head lowered, was letting out a low, yowling sound of warning.

Hierophant Nicholas Mason — a man with a *Doctorate* in Thaumaturgy — stood with a hand on the hilt of his sheathed rapier. More violence implicit in his ready stance.

Even poor, dear Carl. Half dead, at the least, and still trying to stand, with a knife in his hand. Amazing that he could even hold that knife, under the circumstances.

And all of them trying to stare down the interlopers. The men who wore the pale blue uniforms of Kennedy Port Security right down to the silver crescent moon badges. Those white clubs at in their hands, Pacifiers that could render a person unconscious with even a near miss.

A score of these men — and they were all men, and all under the age of thirty, if Anna was any guess — and they all stood ready and willing to offer violence.

They all looked to be of Russian or Romanian descent as well. And when one considered the high percentage of the local populace that could trace its roots to western and central Africa, seeing so many white faces among a port security team could simply not happen by accident.

And in the air above them, their support. An airship ostensibly belonging to Kennedy Port Security. Ugly thing. No grace at all. Like a gray sausage, with holes ready to rain down rocks on all who "fail to comply" with orders.

Whoever was behind this lacked a proper touch of subtlety. Why the composition of the team alone told Anna that they were not sent by Natalia Romanova or by Anna's father, Alexei Lukyanov.

And the airship flying support? Already hovering overhead and menacing with its weapons? Right over the center of the spaceport, where *all of Kennedy* could see?

They might as well be carrying the Pajari crest.

Rasputin Pajari possessed sufficient wealth and connections to rally his family from perhaps the least of Luna's great families when Anna was born, to a current position of somewhere between third strongest and fifth, depending on a number of shifting factors.

But Pajari was a thug. His family would never ascend higher than third while he held the reins.

And today Anna would remind him why.

The man droning on for the "port security" team stood a little short. Scarcely a dozen centimeters taller than Anna herself. But his black hair came to a widow's peak. His eyes were a clear shade, but brown. Likely he had some blood from one of the old noble families of Earth, but too far back to do him any good, and the wrong surname here on Luna.

He had been going on for some time with the usual sort of spiel. Surrender this, throw down your weapons that, consequences, consequences, and all of it teeming with the threat of violence.

Anna had listened to just about enough of this. Carl needed rest. And Anna had to get her people into space before either her father got involved, or worse, Natalia Romanova.

And the scent of Edik's borscht had set her stomach to rumbling and reminded her she had not yet broken her fast for the day.

"That will be quite enough," Anna said in the proper tone of command.

The captain of this would-be guard found himself shutting up so fast he frowned in confusion.

As though Anna had needed any further proof that this man had worked for a great family for some time...

"It is plain enough to anyone with eyes to see it that you are not here at the behest of any superiors you might have in Kennedy Port Security — and I have no doubt that your superiors in this life are so many as to be without number — but at the command of Rasputin Pajari."

And the mention of the name, this guard captain's eyes rounded wide enough that she half expected the man's eyeballs to fall out and bounce along the cold floor.

"As I thought," she said. She held up her right wrist and slid down her sleeve to reveal a simple gold bracelet, only a subtle hint of scroll-work around the edge. "This bracelet is a gift from my father. Alexei Lukyanov. I have only to twist it and he will be notified of my precise location and that I am under threat. And if I speak the name of Pajari as I do, which I can assure you I most certainly will, then my father will hear that as well."

Anna gave the poor man a condescending smile.

"Yes, you outnumber us and yes, you have Pacifiers. But you are not so foolish that you could not recognize a famous Hierophant such as Nicholas Mason. Which means you must know that neither you nor your ship are likely to emerge victorious from this conflict."

Anna shook her head with slow surety while the guard captain seemed to count his resources a second time.

"But let us say, purely for the sake of argument, that you *could*. Let us be generous enough to even suggest the possibility that you *would*. What then would happen?"

Anna tapped her chin, while pretending to think.

"Well, you would no doubt please your master. That *is* a point to recommend it, I suppose. But what of *your* consequences?"

Anna dropped her pretense and showed a smile that held only malice.

"First, you would make an enemy of my father. And do you think that Pajari would raise a hand to protect you? From the *Lukyanov* family? You, who do not even bear his crest? Oh, no. Pajari would *fling* you at my father's feet as part of a claim that you were acting on your own, to get into that family's good graces. But that is not all."

Anna shook her head again.

"Even if we do not consider the Hierophant, and his many friends and allies who would look into each of your lives. Even if we do not consider the many friends that Edik and Roger here have developed among the agents of *actual* Kennedy Port Security."

Anna had no idea if Edik had any such friends, and she was quite certain that Roger did not, but the lie sounded plausible enough, tucked in among the rest of what she had to say.

"Let us leave all of these things aside for a moment," Anna said, taking a single step forward. "You would make an enemy of *me*."

One of them had the temerity to laugh. But the leader could no doubt see the storm clouds that laugh brought into Anna's eyes.

"I am Anna Lukyanova. I have been the voice of the Rhian people since their discovery. I have been in the courts, in the news, and in private meetings with more politicians and military leaders than you could name."

Anna drew herself straighter. Allowed her voice to become coldly menacing, in her best impression of Natalia Romanova, the single most frightening woman Anna could think of.

"I have built up resources beyond anything you can *imagine*. If you touch any one of us, it will mean the end of you, your families, and quite possibly your friends. You will have no work. You will have no money. You will have no homes. You will likely be arrested on charges far worse than any crimes you have ever actually committed, and the remainder of your lives will be spent in such abject misery that even a slow, painful death shall seem the most pleasant dream left to you."

Anna let those words hang *just* long enough for them to sink in.

Restlessness and uncertainty rustled through the "port security" team's ranks like a quick breeze through thin branches.

But the leader actually tried to bargain.

"We only need Jones. We weren't expecting you or Hierophant Mason. We rescind all threats against either of you, expressed or implied. Just give Jones to us and—"

"We are leaving now. Impede us at your peril," Anna said, turning away. "And I suggest you clear that ugly thing you call an airship from our sky."

3

The *Horizon Cusp*. Jacobs had called it home for more than a decade.

He'd been worried about how he would feel, returning to the great helioship after having a couple of years to himself, flying nothing larger nor more complicated than his personal ship, the *Sweet Dream*.

The *Horizon Cusp* measured more than two hundred fifty meters long. Its *shuttle* was larger than the *Sweet Dream*.

And the *Horizon Cusp* was built when the trend in helioships was to make them look like creatures out of myth and legend. And so its outer shell had the shape of a gigantic golden gryphon. Even its shuttle looked like a hippogriff, with its landing bay painted to look like a nest.

The *Sweet Dream* had only a handful of cabins. Tight quarters, like the ships Jacobs knew in his youth. There was comfort to that. For Jacobs, at least. Elinore had called it "cramped" and "tight as a dog kennel."

The *Horizon Cusp* berthed three hundred fifty passengers or so, depending on current configuration. It had a dozen restaurants.

Shadow play theaters. Massage parlors. Bowling and other entertainments.

Practically a small tourist town unto itself.

Yet returning to it felt as natural as swallows must have felt, returning each year to Capistrano.

And sitting once more in the captain's chair on the bridge, Jacobs' life of retirement almost seemed the sweet dream he'd named his vessel. As though he'd wakened from a nap, and almost nothing had changed.

Almost nothing *had* changed.

The bridge of the *Horizon Cusp* still sat on the gryphon's back, right between the wings. Its top and sides were spaceworthy ceramics shaped like a dome and enchanted for safety and transparency. As though the bridge itself were open to the sky. A full, unrestrained view to the sides and above.

Right now, a view of the light gray ceramic walls that bordered the landing bay here at San Francisco Spaceport, and above a dark gray, cloudy sky filled with organized traffic. Dozens of airships and helio-ships about their daily journeys.

Only the door down into the ship gave lie to the illusion of an open-air bridge, and even the door was sloped downward.

The phantasmal workstations of the bridge were arranged in a ring inside the rail of the dome's outer walkway: helm, communications, scanners, damage control, and the executive officer's station.

The conn itself, smack dab in the center. Raised on a dais at the end of a short spiral staircase.

Jacobs sat in that chair now. His phantasmal workstation remained the same as he remembered. The scanners pad, currently inactive with the ship in port. One wave of Jacobs' hand and he could call up a view of the port and the skies above (as though he couldn't just look up right now), fed by the air elementals who handled everything for the ship while it was within a planet's jurisdiction.

Jurisdiction. Once Jacobs would have called it an "atmosphere." Now, questions of space and distance worried about "jurisdictions."

The air elementals handled everything until they got far enough from a planet that space elementals, lacunas, took over.

Once that happened, the scanner display would be an amazing, manipulable three-dimensional view of space around the ship. Expandable to include all information in the latest charts. Perfect for viewing, plotting and replotting routes.

There was also the holographic log, which apparently Tunold had made extensive use of. That thought made Jacobs sigh and shake his head. He'd avoided looking at one of these since retirement.

He slashed his hand through it to close it, and slapped down his preferred method of keeping his log. An actual paper-bound book of blank pages, and a pen that used ink. That would be the only captain's log for this voyage, and if anyone in Starchaser Spacelines — Mancuso, just to pick a name — had any trouble with it, they could find another captain.

Then, of course, the red slap-pad for communications. On Jacobs' own ship, he'd had to handle his own communications. The slap pad sat beneath a snarl of pale blue, glowing lines, representing all the links the ship could reach. On the *Sweet Dream*, Jacobs had to select and manipulate them himself.

Here on the *Horizon Cusp*, the communications officer handled a snarl far larger and more complex than the one aboard the *Sweet Dream*. All Jacobs had to do was order a link, and use the slap pad when it was ready.

Or, for shipboard links, he could work with his favorite part of this phantasmal workstation. An element far more complex and powerful than the version aboard his *Sweet Dream*.

The miniature representation of the ship itself.

One touch to a section could bring up the current reports that affected that station, from security and damage control to the state of maintenance and repairs.

Oh, how Jacobs' first captain, Captain Nemeth, would have turned green with envy over such a thing.

Modern magic did have a few advantages over the old way of doing things.

Yes, Jacobs' station, basically the same as he had left it. The bridge layout, exactly the same.

Jacobs turned and looked down at the only way the ship had changed since Jacobs last sat in this chair. His bridge crew. Only just different enough to cause a little dissonance in him.

Mr. Burke, still a steady hand at the helm. Perhaps a little heavier than Jacobs remembered. Marriage must have agreed with him. Burke smiled a little easier now, and his brown eyes smiled too.

Mr. Grabowski, still on scanners. Still jittery, thin and pale, though Tunold assured Jacobs that Grabowski had gotten a better handle on running the scanners in tight situations.

Jacobs hoped so. He didn't relish the thought of rushing down there to grab the scanners where there was trouble. Not again.

Ms. Jefferson, the communications officer who had served with Jacobs for so long, was absent. For good reasons, at least. When Jacobs had turned captaincy of the *Horizon Cusp* over to Tunold, his old ex oh had followed Jacobs' recommendation and promoted Jefferson to new ex oh. She'd done well enough that apparently she was on a trial run as skipper of the small San Francisco (Earth) to King (Luna) run.

Good for her. Well deserved.

In her place at the snarl was a Mr. Hernandez. A boy who didn't look old enough to shave, despite that little excuse for a black mustache.

And handling damage control, another face Jacobs didn't know. Ms. Chiba, by name, and she had the kind of fierce demeanor, twice-broken nose and lean muscles that implied she interesting ideas about "damage control."

She looked as though she had transferred from Goldberg's ship security team. Tunold swore she hadn't though, and Goldberg claimed that Chiba had never worked security. At least, not according to her background check. And hard experience had made Goldberg one of the best when it came to background checks.

This Chiba was someone to keep an eye on during shore leaves then...

Jacobs snorted a laugh. There would be no shore leave on this voyage for the crew. And it wasn't as though he intended to return to work full time.

So long as Chiba could handle damage control, Jacobs had no reason to worry about her.

And if Jacobs had any luck, he wouldn't need any damage control reports on this voyage.

Jacobs snorted for a different reason this time.

He reached a finger to the right spot in the gryphon's belly with the smooth precision of old habits. Twisted his finger.

The rough and tumble face of Saul Goldberg appeared quickly, his head floating above the gryphon.

"Aye, Captain?" he said.

Jacobs caught himself grinning and straightened his face. Goldberg was still Goldberg. No taunts about how long it had been since Jacobs sat in the chair. No jokes about Jacobs' age.

No, in person, Goldberg would likely have been a little more casual until Jacobs established official protocol. But over a link, Goldberg always answered as though he might be getting the call to battle.

"Did Tunold ever institute my recommended Cuthbert Protocols?"

"Well..." Goldberg cracked his neck as though he was expecting trouble. "They're on the books, but the truth is that we haven't carried any Cuthberts since you retired. And since there are only two passengers on this voyage, it seemed ... excessive."

"Pity," Jacobs said. He liked the idea of Cuthbert being isolated off at one end of the ship, away from everyone else. Perhaps even with restrictions about which restaurants he could use, or when he could visit the Main Deck, where most of the passenger amenities were.

Jacobs sighed. "I suppose it's a fair point. Can't worry about him causing trouble that threatens the VIPs—"

"*Technically*, Captain," Goldberg said, wincing, "Cuthbert only *started* trouble the one time. And Mash read him the riot act, magician style."

"He brought a pair of zuglodons down on us, Saul. I just want to make sure we don't get a repeat performance." Jacobs shook his head. "Anyway, since there are only the two passengers, they're both VIPs."

"From what I hear, they know each other, too," Goldberg said. "Keeping them apart ... would cause problems."

"Fine, but I want Mash to—"

"He's already on it, Captain."

Jacobs raised one eyebrow.

"Honest," Goldberg said, holding up three fingers as though he'd been a Boy Scout. "Mash is over there right now."

DONAL STOOD IN THE DOORWAY OF HIS CABIN AND GAWKED.

"Well," Fionn said. "I'd say this is a trifle fancier than you've stayed in before. On this ship, at least."

The last time Donal had stayed aboard the *Horizon Cusp*, he had berthed in one of their good cabins. Fine appointments and all that. Indeed, it had seemed very good to him at the time.

Of course, he had also seen the suite that Mr. Mancuso stayed in on the same flight, which was orders of magnitude fancier than Donal's own. But that was to be expected.

This, however. This was ... beyond...

First of all, it didn't look as though it were part of the ship at all. It looked like a palace. No simple ceramics for the hull or interior bulkheads. No Starchaser Spacelines logo on the wall. Oh, there were small landscape depictions of Earth, Mars, Luna and Venus, as well as a full-length mirror near the closet. But those walls. Everything, from the ceiling to the deck under Donal's shoes seemed to be made of *marble*.

And not just any marble. It looked to have been done in three shades of white, with veins of gold running through. And every so often, tiny gemstones.

Gemstones that might represent stars...

"Night," Donal said, guessing the code word.

Sure enough, the whites of the marble darkened to hues of black and deep blue. The gems now twinkled softly like starlight.

"Day," Donal said, and the change reversed itself.

And that didn't count the furniture.

There was a living room setup, with an opulent throw rug beneath a coffee table that looked like hand-carved and engraved teak. And Donal knew a thing or two about carved woods. Impossible not to, growing up in his family.

The couches had the smallish look and elegant design that often went with old French furniture from hundreds of years ago. But Donal would have given good odds that they were enchanted with earth magics to make them even more comfortable than the deepest, plushest couches could manage on their own.

A wet bar stood in one corner of the room, beside a doorway. The door looked to have been carved from teak as well, as did the bar. All of the engraving had a Celtic pattern to it. Knotwork, and similar designs.

Along the other wall, a desk that matched the style, with six drawers. Not that Donal could imagine why a traveler would need six drawers in a desk.

And on the floor beside the desk, a magic circle.

The circle was inlaid in the floor. Black marble in the white, which meant it likely swapped to white in the black at "night."

Simple design. Nondenominational, and large enough that if Donal stood inside it with his arms stretched out, he would still have several centimeters of play before he reached the edges of the circle.

So, room to add any chosen names or words of power. Thoughtful.

"That must be what's in the drawers," Donal said suddenly. "Reagents."

"Do you find it likely that Magister Ronaldo Machado would give you reagents?" Fionn asked, one ear bent in skeptical askance.

Finally, there was the far wall. It looked stable enough, and seemed to lack even a small porthole. But Donal doubted that.

"View," Donal said, again guessing.

And again, guessing correctly. Chances were, it responded to any of a number of keywords that were backed by attention from the speaker.

No portal appeared though.

Instead, the entire outer hull vanished.

Donal could see straight into the spaceport, and the edges of the sky up above the gray ceramic walls of the landing bay.

"I imagine it's more impressive at space," Fionn said.

Donal agreed. The view would be. But the magics involved were certainly impressive enough even in port. Donal didn't need to shift awareness to know he was standing inside a complex webwork of enchantments.

Donal nodded, and stepped into the room. His soft leather shoes even sounded as though they were walking on marble.

"The illusion is thorough," Donal said. "I'll have to study it later."

"You're sure it's illusion?" Fionn asked, and Donal knew that tone. Fionn liked to give him little tests every so often. "Could be that they simply paid for a thin layer of marble on the ceramics. Enough for the appearance without interfering with the hull's spells."

"Illusion," Donal said firmly. "The cost versus benefit wouldn't pay. Besides, by using illusion, they can configure it dozens of different ways without the greater expense of redoing the room."

"What about maintenance?"

"What do you think the maintenance would be to replace chipped marble floors and walls on a helioship?"

"Fair enough," Fionn said with a nod. "What about the furniture?"

"Real," Donal said. "Who would argue with teak?"

Fionn blinked at Donal. Nodded.

Donal shifted awareness and allowed himself to scan the room's magics.

Many. Almost without number in so small a space. Building upon the enchantments that kept the ship running of course, as well as air flowing (in and out through the veins of the marble) and such.

Donal needed a moment longer to stretch his attention along the right lines to find the illusions. But only a moment. Illusion and conjuration were his two thaumaturgic specialties.

"Hah," Donal said, finding the elements that gave the walls, ceiling and floor the multi-sensory appearance of marble.

But apparently "hah" was a keyword of its own, or close enough, because an air elemental manifested at shoulder height in front of Donal.

This one was male, with skin the color of an overripe lemon, and the kind of slender build that, in a person, suggested not eating enough. His hair was long and thick, though, falling about his shoulders and moving constantly. And his eyes were bright orange.

"Yes, Mr. Cuthbert?" the air elemental said in a voice that Donal could only think of as breezy. "What do you require?"

Donal looked at Fionn and back at the elemental.

"I apologize," Donal said with a slight bow that made those orange eyes wider for a moment. "I had not intended to call you forth."

"It is no trouble, I assure you."

"Not the point, but thank you." Donal nodded. "As you already know, I am Donal Cuthbert, but please call me Donal. And this is Fionn. What name should I call you?"

The elemental smiled. His teeth sparkled like yellow diamonds. "My name is Veriss."

"Then it is my pleasure to meet you, Veriss. With what tasks are you charged?"

"The pleasure is mine, Donal. And I am charged with seeing to your needs. If you need anything delivered to your room, I shall call for it. If you need any aspect of the room adjusted, you need only ask. I am at your service in all ways you require, in order to make your stay as pleasant as possible."

"Definitely a nicer room," Donal said. "Thank you, Veriss. What is the proper way to call you?"

"My name will suffice, Donal. Or, if you prefer, you need only say, 'help.'"

"Thank you, Veriss. I require nothing but information."

"We are due to lift off within the hour, as soon as permission comes from the San Francisco Port Authority," Veriss said, apparently anticipating Donal's questions. "Rains are due this morning, but will not affect our liftoff. The journey is expected to take three days to reach the no-fly zone, where our escort will meet us. From that point, our travel time is considered classified."

"Who would I tell?" Donal said.

"You could have a memory circle, with a second point of access," Fionn pointed out.

Veriss bowed to Fionn's answer.

"That will be all for now, Veriss," Donal said. "Thank you."

The small air elemental vanished in a puff of yellow mist.

Donal finally entered the sitting room of his suite. Odd, not to be carrying his own luggage, but he had no doubt that his bags were already in the bedroom.

The door closed itself behind Donal, and scarcely had the door closed before someone knocked.

A rapid knock. One might even call it a *troubled* knock.

***

DONAL KNEW HE WASN'T GOING TO HAVE THIS TRIP TO HIMSELF. HE'D heard there was another passenger. He hadn't been told who the other passenger would be, but he had his suspicions.

Still, the last thing he expected, the moment he stepped into his room, was to have someone start pounding on his door.

Well, perhaps *pounding* was too strong a word. But it was definitely an insistent knock.

Still, in a room so fancy that it seemed to be made entirely of marble and teak (granted, the marble was illusory), Donal half expected the air elemental butler to answer the door for him.

But that didn't seem to be happening.

Donal looked down at Fionn.

"Who is it?"

Fionn's ears flattened down low. "I can't tell."

"You can't—"

"The moment the door closed, so did a circuit of spells. While within, it seems we are contained within."

Donal ripped open the door.

Two knocks on his chest before the knocker stood back and regarded him.

Donal knew this man. This Magister. He would never forget the heavy Brazilian, who had been angry with Donal and grateful to him at various times.

The look on Magister Ronaldo Machado's face right now was not gratitude.

And the first words he muttered weren't English. Some Latin-based language though. Portuguese, Donal thought.

"About time," Magister Machado said when he switched to English. "Planning to keep me in the corridor all day, Journeyman?"

"No, Magister," Donal said, stepping back and sweeping one arm to invite his ... guest? ... inside.

Machado didn't enter.

"Right," Magister Machado said. "By now you've had time to notice a few things." He pointed to the magic circle. "Yes, that's available to you. There are reagents and a reasonably good portable alchemy lab in the desk."

"But—"

"Second," Magister Machado said, sharply enough to cut off the rest of Donal's question. "You've no doubt noticed the wards on the room. You can come and go as you please. Physically or astrally. No complaints there."

Magister Machado stepped closer to Donal and raised a finger.

"However. This trip is of an especially sensitive nature. You will not cast any spells that stretch past my ship's wards. Do you understand me?"

"I was thinking of using a memory circle."

"If you want one, let me know. I'll set up an unused cabin, and you can hold your memories there and collect them when we get you back to Earth."

"What if I don't make it back to Earth?"

"Then any memories from this trip are gone too." Magister Machado raised both hands now, to cut off Donal's objections. "This is a political matter. Official word from the United Terran Government. This trip is classified for the time being, and that means no civilians leaking information. Not even to a memory circle."

"I never agreed to that."

"Tough," Magister Machado said. But then his tone softened as he looked at Donal. He even smiled a little. "I know. I don't like it either. You're a good kid. But right now you have two problems."

Magister Machado held up one finger. "First, you're a diplomat for a nation that no one knows what to do with. The Fae Courts." He shook his head so quickly his jowls gave a quiver. "No, don't tell me. I don't even want to know."

"But why does—"

"Think, Journeyman," Magister Machado said, sounding for all the world like one of Donal's professors. "You're acting as an agent of a foreign intelligence, and you'll be escorted into classified territory. Believe me when I tell you that they don't want you seeing or knowing anything they can't control."

Donal frowned. "Let me guess. Even the vanishing wall will be mysteriously unable to vanish in certain areas. And at such times, the viewing areas on the Main Deck and the entire Observation Deck will be mysteriously closed."

"Mysteriously," Magister Machado agreed. "And I suggest you don't try to interfere with that. You're gifted. I've always said so. And I have no doubt that you're at or near the top of your cohort at Cal Thaum S.L.O. But if you think you can take me—"

"I wouldn't even try, Magister," Donal said firmly.

"Good." Machado tried to see through Donal for a moment, then nodded. "Good. Now, your second problem. You overstretch yourself. Can't count how many times you've done it, and I haven't spent all that much time around you. Can't risk you doing it again on this flight. You have to be intact when we get where we're going."

"I wasn't planning on any experiments."

That got Donal the hairy eyeball.

"Well, anything involving space or anything outside the ship."

Magister Machado nodded. "Now *that* I might believe. *Might*. But the wards on this room will insure you keep your word."

Magister Machado stepped inside now. Allowed the door to close behind him. He lowered his voice when he spoke again.

"Look," Magister Machado said, sounding more like a confidant now than a lecturer, "I like you. Despite yourself. You want to try something big while you're on the ship, come talk to me. If I approve, I'll let you use one of my circles. Hell, I may even help."

Magister Machado narrowed his eyes. "But if you try to work around me, *Oxalá* will not save you."

"Yes, Magister," Donal said, splaying his hands in the universal not-casting gesture.

Magister Machado stared a little harder at Donal. Turned to Fionn.

"As lord of this demesne," Magister Machado said, "I command truth from you about your master. Is he being sincere?"

A dirty trick that. Magicians, in their own demesne, had abilities that visiting magicians did not. Donal could only challenge Magister Machado's right to question Donal's familiar by challenging the Magister to the *Comórtas Draíocht*, the magician's duel.

And Donal would likely get trounced. Quickly.

"He is," Fionn said. "Further, I can assure you, Magister Ronaldo Machado, that Donal understands the gravity of his mission and plans no flights of fancy that might endanger himself, nor the mission, nor the ship, nor the crew."

Magister Machado nodded.

"All right, Cuthbert," the Magister said, nodding. "I think maybe you *have* learned a thing or two since I last saw you. Behave yourself and I won't give you any problems."

The Magister took his leave then. And once the door was closed behind him, Donal said, "You'd think I was the scourge of space or something."

Fionn cocked his head sideways. "Not space. Possibly this *ship*, but not space."

Donal sighed and turned to explore the bedroom and bathrooms.

EVERYTHING ABOUT THIS MISSION WAS A BAD IDEA. KRISTOFF TUNOLD was as sure about that as he'd ever been sure about anything. Flying into a no-fly zone was bad enough. Doing it with a so-called "military escort" was worse.

At least, if they'd flown into a no-fly zone on their own, they'd have time before any gunboat managed to train weapons on them. A chance to flee.

Flying with an "escort" just guaranteed they'd have a clear shot, if the time came to start shooting.

And Tunold felt all too confident that there'd be shooting. If only because every naval officer Tunold had gotten a hold of had promised him that there'd be no shooting on this voyage.

Well, that wasn't entirely true. Pulling every string Tunold still had in the Terran Navy, linking everyone he possibly could, he got more non-answers than answers.

Very few people even knew this mission was happening.

But Tunold's old naval captain, Pike, was Admiral Pike now. And Admiral Pike knew all about this little mission. Knew enough to offer plenty of reassurances. Even put Tunold in touch with a few others in the navy, and two in the UNAS government, who doubled-down on those assurances.

It was all just a little too much protesting, for Tunold to trust it. He'd seen his share of clusterfucks in the navy, and this had the distinct odor of insipient unwanted group sex.

Worst of all, there were only two passengers on this flight.

Now that was just stupid. Even beyond the waste of resources. No way that only two humans were coming from Earth to take part in this big fancy meeting. Odds were that the Terran Government would have more people there, but they were flying separately.

Hell, for all Tunold knew, Luna, Mars, Venus, and maybe even Ganymede were going to have delegations at this shindig.

The *Horizon Cusp* berthed three-hundred-sixty-five in its current configuration. No reason to take multiple ships.

Not if all those ships are supposed to come back.

And then, there was the passengers themselves to consider.

Donal "Jonah" Cuthbert. All right, maybe Jonah wasn't actually the kid's middle name, but it might as well have been. That kid was a menace to space travel.

Yes, he'd saved this ship multiple times. But Tunold couldn't help but notice that this ship only really *needed* saving when Cuthbert was a passenger.

And from what Tunold had heard, Cuthbert'd even shown up for a shuttle flight from Kennedy, on Luna, back to San Francisco at a *dead run*. Chased by a Romanov goon squad, yet. Had to have his bacon saved by a *Hierophant*.

The man was just pure bad luck.

Still, Cuthbert, at least he was a known quantity. So long as the *Horizon Cusp* had a top-notch ship's mage like Mash along, he could handle Cuthbert.

But this other passenger? MacPherson? He'd never heard of her. Not that he could recall. There was something familiar about her name though. Something he couldn't quite place...

That was just enough to get his stomach acids trying to give him an ulcer again. And if he complained to Ramirez about stomach pain one more time, the doctor was likely to ground him for a month.

Not quite a death sentence, but nearer than Tunold ever wanted to come.

He might feel at ease if he could meet this woman.

Assuming she ever arrived.

Right now, Tunold stood down on the gangplank. Well, that was Jacobs' old nickname for what was officially the reception hall, but he'd been using it so long that the whole crew had picked it up. No one called it anything else these days.

The large room was designed to look and feel like a mountain cavern, complete with a blue sky view along the aft wall where the shuttle would enter.

Right now Tunold was standing between rows of comfortable chairs and benches decorated in a gryphon's nest theme with gold and silver chasing. Each breath tasted like clear mountain air, like the time Tunold had gone mountain climbing in Switzerland during a shore leave contest with his ship's navigator.

Tunold stared at that empty blue sky view, waiting to see the hippogriff shuttle coming in to land among the illusory great eggs and cave walls of its "nest."

Tunold was just about to link the bridge — again — to see if there was any word from the port, when, at last, he heard the shuttle approach.

The shuttle didn't actually flap its wings. Not that Tunold ever saw. And yet every time it took off from or approached the landing bay, Tunold would swear he heard the flap of wings and the rustle of feathers.

The shuttle landed now, its clawed legs catching the deck in just the right spot, and settling down.

What felt like an hour later, the starboard wing rose, and the hatch beneath it opened. And, finally, out stepped the *Horizon Cusp's* only other passenger for this voyage: Rowan MacPherson.

And Tunold knew he was looking at Trouble with a capital T.

This woman wasn't just beautiful. No. She was *beautiful*. Or maybe BEAUTIFUL.

Yeah, that sounded right. She was beautiful with all caps. Amazing that she hadn't been scooped up by shadow play producers or modeling agencies and turned into some huge star. She had that kind of *look*.

Everything about her. From her curves to her glory of long red locks and immaculate skin, all of it seemed to have been designed by some magician to appear perfect.

Her eyes weren't just green. They were a vivid emerald green, with flecks of gold. And her hair wasn't just red either. It was crimson, also with flakes of gold.

Illusion? Machado and Goldberg had both sworn that this Rowan MacPherson had no history of magical training, but it was possible that she carried some item of enchantment to make her look more beautiful than was humanly possible.

If she was, legally, it should have been inactive during boarding so as not to interfere with proper identification procedures. Then again, her ID was cleared in the port, so maybe she had some leeway to activate any vanity magic on the shuttle.

And real or illusion, the effect was the same.

Tunold's jaw might have dropped when he saw her. If he'd been another man. Instead, it clenched. Tight. Because Tunold's unfortunate experiences with women over the years had left him with one singular, distinct impression.

Beautiful women were trouble. The more beautiful the woman, the bigger the trouble.

Oh, he knew others disputed him on this. Machado in particular had spent hours railing at Tunold about what he called "a ridiculous prejudice." From different angles, too. Sometimes defending beauties on their own merits, other times simply arguing that first impressions — especially those based on appearances — had no true merit.

But Tunold knew what he knew. Beautiful women were trouble.

And this woman had to be a goddamn volcanic eruption, earthquake, and tsunami all in one. Clad in the kind of soft white dress that looked simple, but probably cost more than a year of Tunold's salary.

And worst of all, she looked vaguely familiar. And there was that nagging familiarity about her name...

If only he'd had time to run her name past his contacts. Maybe he could have learned something. Tunold did feel certain he'd never actually *met* her before. If he had, he'd never have forgotten. Not a woman like her.

Alas, he hadn't had the time. The identity of their second passenger had only been made known to him twenty minutes before she was due to arrive. And Jacobs swore he'd passed it along as soon as he'd had it himself. Goldberg and Machado had both taken the name and run their own checks at top speed. But they'd learned nothing about her.

Troubling in itself.

Rowan MacPherson's heels clicked on the ceramics of the deck as she approached.

"Impressive," she said. "I'm a little surprised though. Given the general elegance reputation attributes this ship, having the shuttle land in something like an *actual* nest seems an odd choice."

"Ma'am," Tunold said snapping to attention. "I am given to understand that it cements the idea for passengers that they are entering a wonderland where their everyday thoughts and cares can be left behind."

Rowan MacPherson looked him up and down. Frowned, and even that looked good on her. "Now that *must* be the official marketing version."

"Yes, Ma'am," Tunold said, but he smiled. "I'm Executive Officer Kristoff Tunold. Here to welcome you aboard the *Horizon Cusp*, Ms. MacPherson."

"Thank you, Mr. Tunold."

She held out her hand to shake. Had a good grip, too. Tunold had half-expected her to tilt her hand as though he should kiss it, but no, she gave a proper business handshake.

"Has Donal Cuthbert checked in yet?" She asked. "I was hoping to speak with him before liftoff."

Of *course* she knew Cuthbert. More proof that this woman was trouble.

"There won't be time, I'm afraid," Tunold said, escorting her toward the bubble tube beneath the Starchaser Spacelines logo, a star trailed by a stylized arrow. "We only have a few minutes, and you have to be in your cabin for liftoff."

Was that a troubled expression in her eyes? If so, it flitted away as quickly as it showed up. She covered almost immediately with a small smile.

"That's fine," she said. "I'm sure it won't matter."

Tunold frowned as he pulled the lever to call water elementals who controlled the bubble to bring down the transport cage.

He knew a lie when he heard one.

* * *

TENSION SANG THROUGH EDIK'S SHOULDERS AND BACK AS HE SAT AT THE controls of the *Third Son.*

Everything looked normal. Safe even.

Edik didn't trust it for a second. Not after what happened in the landing bay. Sure, Anna's social flexing might have gotten Edik room to lift off — and immediate permission from the port, which was something unto itself — but that offered no guarantees beyond this very moment.

Edik surveyed his situation. Again.

The green sky around his ship: empty but for normal traffic. That threatening port security airship: long gone.

The holographic display of the space above the port itself — fed from the port's lacunas to ships still in air-elemental range like Edik's: normal traffic, all flowing along the expected channels.

Edik's route: clear. Apparently.

He could have grabbed the golden, phantasmal handles under the scanner display and honed his view in any direction. If he suspected there was something to see.

Edik was tempted, but knew better. If his air elementals told him the skies looked clear, they looked clear. And if the information from the port was flawed, his sylphs wouldn't be able to tell.

He glanced left across the curved, smooth ceramics of his helm/captains' station. All the ship's functions routed through here, including the ones Edik had re-routed himself.

The miniature image of the firebird helioship: five by five.

The red communications slap-pad: dull and unlit. No emergency incoming links.

The blue tangle of communications links: all shedding only their diminished, standby glow. Nothing actively linking at all.

Out the front viewport, the green sky ahead of Edik looked empty.

Well, a few smears of grayish clouds, but even those weren't in Edik's path.

Still his muscles buzzed with tension.

His right hand gripped the red phantasmal lever that controlled the helioship's main engines, itching to jam forward from all-stop to full-ahead. Even though it would have no effect until Xincapph, the *Third Son's* lacuna, could feel proper space around himself.

A smaller lever beside it, for airborne acceleration, was ahead three-quarters. It would vanish once the *Third Son* was far enough from Luna for Xincapph to take over the flying, but right now it controlled their speed.

In fact, half the reason Edik kept his hand on the main engine accelerator was to keep himself from pushing the airborne lever to full-ahead.

Breaking the local speed laws wouldn't do Edik any good though. Just get the *real* port authority sending ships after him.

Edik's left hand danced over the phantasmal dials for pitch, yaw and roll. Not adjusting anything. But ready.

"What's that off ten points to starboard?"

North's voice. North wasn't supposed to be on the bridge. He was supposed to be back in the main cabin. Yet those words came from no more than a meter behind Edik.

The fact of North's presence was almost as irritating as the question, and not just because Edik already knew the answer.

"That's just part of the usual port patrol, North," Edik said. "A *proper* captain would know that."

Edik allowed himself a tight grin at the sound of North's grinding teeth. He hated being reminded that he wasn't a helioship captain. That he'd only ever commanded an airship, and that made him a skipper. At best.

Still, North had asked for it.

He didn't leave though. Instead North dropped audibly into the bridge's only other chair. Aft and starboard of Edik, the chair sat at what was once the ship's communications station, before Edik's modifications. Now, only a small ceramic counter.

"What are you doing here, North?" Edik demanded, voice tight as his shoulders.

"Wondering why we're pushing the port's speed limits when we've no cause to do it."

"We're within mandated limits."

"Yeah," North said, drawing the word out, "but even a skipper knows they prefer us doing half that. Just can't get the official change approved."

"Shut the door," Edik said.

Took longer than it should have, for North to close that door and resume the seat he hadn't been invited to take. Maybe Edik'd managed to shock North? Unlikely, but possible.

"Any news on Carl?" Edik asked.

North growled. "If there had been, I'd've told you right out, now wouldn't I?"

Edik spared North a droll glance over his shoulder, then snapped his eyes right back to watching the skies and scanners.

North chuckled. "Well, *maybe* I'd've made you wait."

Then Edik realized that bastard was filling a pipe.

Edik whispered a few quick words in Russian to Sparakat, the *Third Son's* chief salamander.

North's lighter refused to spark.

North growled when he sensed the interference of a fire elemental.

"No smoking on the bridge," Edik said, voice still tight. "You interfere with the lovely smell of my morning coffee, and I'll throw you out the hatch."

North harrumphed, but Edik could hear the rustle of cloth.

"He put it away, Edik," Dola said, pitched so only Edik could hear the words. Dola was curled up under the workstation, on a small pad that Dola insisted he didn't need. But Edik would be damned before he failed to provide comfort for his familiar.

"Thank you," Edik said.

"Can I smoke in the main cabin, at least?"

"I always allow smoking in the main cabin only. And announce it first, so the sylphs have a chance to control the smoke and the odor."

"I closed the door so you could tell me that?"

"No, you closed the door because I need to know what you've heard about this voyage."

Silence. And silence from North was a rare thing.

"Look," Edik said. "We've got at least three great families involved in this thing, if I understand it right. Lukyanov is involved, because Anna's involved, and no way her father intends to get cut out. Romanov is involved, because nothing happens on Luna without Natalia Romanova knowing about it. And once she knows about something big, we'd have better luck keeping Baba Yaga away."

Edik shook his head through a tight breath. "And if Anna is right — and I'm sure she is — Pajari is involved too. But I've heard exactly fuck all about it."

Edik shot North a quick look over his shoulder. "So what do you know?"

"I hear Volya's making a move. At least, that's what I heard a couple of days ago in King. I was drinking at the Green Cheese, and overheard some Volya pilots talking in hushed tones about the number of soldiers they've been ferrying up from Earth. Mercenaries."

"I thought all the Earth mercs were out on Mars, fighting in that independence thing."

"Me too. Guess not."

"Hear anything more in there?" Edik tilted his head back to indicate the main cabin.

"Anna seems certain that Romanova's going to be at the big to-do. Mason doesn't believe it though."

Edik almost lost those words, because he could see something now that lifted his heart.

Space.

Glorious, wonderful space.

Let the great families fight things out while he was gone. In a few seconds, Edik would have space around him, and the fastest ship in the heliosphere.

"What's that?" North asked, but this time there was no humor in his voice. "Twelve degrees off to port, maybe a thousand klicks out."

Edik spared a glance. Three bogeys, flying in formation.

Flying an intercept course.

"Nixia," Edik said, "how long until Xincapph can take over the engines?"

"Perhaps a minute, Edik," his chief air elemental said. She didn't manifest though. Likely too busy coordinating the *Third Son's* crew of air elementals.

"Can we go any faster?"

"Not without violating port protocols."

"Minute's a long time," North said. "Rate they're closing."

It was true. They had to already be just far enough away from Luna that their lacunas were engaged.

"Dola, port authority, please."

Dola sprang out from under the helm and activated the correct link.

The ghostly image of a young Chinese woman's head appeared in the air above the blue strands, while one strand glowed bright.

"This is port authority, Xu speaking."

"Ms. Xu," Edik said, "this is Captain Edik Barshai of the *Third Son*. I have three ships on my scanners, flying intercept. Twelve degrees off to port from my nose, approximate distance nine hundred kilometers. Please advise."

The few seconds between Edik's question and her answer seemed to take a year.

"Our scanners show nothing near those coordinates."

"Dola," Edik said, and Dola transmitted the scanner information.

"I'm sorry, Captain Barshai, but our scanners show that section of sky as clear. Perhaps your scanners need—"

"*My scanners are in perfect order,*" Edik snapped. He knew it for a fact. He kept all the systems on his ship five-by-five as much as he could. And with a flight like this one coming up, he and Dola had triple checked every system.

"Captain Barshai, there is no need for that tone."

"She's either lying or in on it," North said, and apparently he said it too loud.

"I resent that accusation," Ms. Xu said, "and it is being logged in your records. And I assure you, *that section of sky is clear.*"

She cut the connection.

Those bogeys were close enough now that Edik could see their shapes on the scanners. They looked like two-headed eagles. Maybe twice the size of the *Third Son.*

"I don't know the design," North said.

"Me either," Edik said. "But I don't intend to wait to find out. Nixia, the moment Xincapph can take over, tell him full-ahead on the route we worked out."

"Of course, Edik," Nixia's breathy voice assured him.

"And tell everyone in the main cabin to strap in."

Edik banked hard to starboard.

"Damn it!" North swore as he fell on his tail.

"Better strap in," Edik said, allowing himself a small grin as he thrust the airspeed lever to full-ahead. "I never let the gnomes stabilize the bridge too much. I like to feel the action when I fly."

North muttered something about a "cockpit, not a bridge," but Edik didn't grace it with a response.

Well, he did add a little extra nose-up to his flight path, and smiled when North swore again.

The slap pad glowed red at the same instance one strand of the communications tangle flared bright blue. Likely port authority sending a priority link.

No reason to bother with it. It would connect in a few moments anyway. So Edik focused on trying to put sky between himself and those double-headed eagles.

Dola said something in that language familiars spoke among themselves. Edik pushed for more speed.

"Captain Barshai!"

Xu again. Edik ignored her.

"Captain Barshai, you will return to port mandated speeds and your approved course at once."

"Sorry, Ms. Xu," Edik said. "Lunar Space Law affords me leeway when my ship is under threat."

"Those port boys are swinging back around," North said. Probably the quietest words ever spoken by the loudmouth.

North was right though. The two port security ships were turning back and angling for an intercept course.

And those three double-headed eagle ships were no more than five hundred klicks and closing.

"Your ship is not under threat!"

The floating head of Ms. Xu was screaming at Edik from above the glowing red slap pad.

She was wrong though. Coming from the port side, three double-headed eagle ships. Definitely on an intercept course with the *Third Son*. And they were helioships, which meant fast enough that Edik couldn't lose them easily.

Then there were the two port security ships. Airships, so Edik could leave them behind soon enough. But they'd be fast enough until Edik reached space. Worse, they had a legal right to weapons. And Edik had the feeling that Ms. Xu was clearing them to shoot even now.

"Sorry, Ms. Xu," Edik said. "I need to clear the links."

Dola, knowing a cue, cut the link. Edik twisted and rolled his ship, trying to find an angle that put the maximum distance between himself and all five pursuing ships.

The slap pad glowed red again immediately, while three separate strands of the communications tangle flared bright blue.

Immediately another head appeared in the air above the slap pad. Another woman, from the sound of her voice, but Edik couldn't spare the attention to look at her.

"Captain Barshai, this is Skipper Jamison of the *Port Three*. You will return to Kennedy and land immediately."

"No can do, Skipper," Edik said. "Have important interplanetary business meeting to get to. Check my registered flight plan."

"Captain Barshai!"

"Cut," Edik said, and Dola cut the link.

No more than three hundred klicks to those double-headed eagles now. Edik was pulling out all his tricks, but the trick he needed most was speed. And he couldn't have that so long as…

So long as he headed straight for space…

A warning shot came across his bow. A chunk of greenish rock that probably weighed half of what the *Third Son* did. Would cripple the ship, if it connected.

Point made, Edik thought as he swallowed.

He flipped dials and spun his ship back toward the surface of Luna, angled for maximum distance from those port security ships.

"They're holding course, Edik," Dola said, keeping an eye on the scanners while Edik focused on not slamming into the lunar mountain ahead of him.

Dola was talking about the helioships, of course. They were the ones Edik was worried about.

Closer…

The mountain loomed larger and larger in the forward viewport.

Closer…

Edik could practically count the striations on the largest boulder when he spun the dials and banked away.

The belly of the *Third Son* missed scraping the stone by no more than a dozen meters.

"Watch it, you damned fool!" North yelled. "That was close!"

Close enough that the second "warning" shot slammed into that mountain and kicked up one hell of a lot of dust. His forward viewport was nothing but a greenish white cloud.

Which meant none of the other ships could see *him* right now either.

Trusting his scanners, Edik dove back down, but danced close to the surface of Luna, hoping to draw the port ships down there with him.

They didn't follow.

Worse, they started coordinating fire...

... and missed? Badly?

Skipper Jamison's voice again. Must have been her head above the slap pad.

"No more tricks, Barshai! You cut your speed and fly right back to Kennedy."

"Not kidding," Edik said. "Can't do it. And don't you see those helioships tailing us?"

They were. After a fashion. Clearly Edik was out of scanner range, down close to the lunar surface. They were staying up out of air elemental range of Luna, but they were definitely moving the right direction.

So Edik reversed course a hundred and eighty degrees.

"Those helioships have nothing to do with you." But Jamison didn't sound confident of that.

"Can't risk it. VIPs on board and all that."

No shots now. In fact, a good dozen seconds had passed since the last shot.

Edik spared a glance at the scanners. The port security ships. They weren't following.

"Cut," Edik said, and Dola cut the link.

"Hierophant Mason," Dola said. "He must be intervening."

"Well see if he can do anything about those helioships."

Edik nosed up and started straight for space.

"He has to give priority to the port security," Dola said. "It is important that official pursuit be—"

"Fine," Edik said, trying to figure out how he could leave three helioships behind when they could stay between himself and space.

"Gonna answer those links?" North asked.

And sure enough, two of the links in the communications tangled remained bright blue.

"Dola," Edik said, and now a male voice came over the link. With a Russian accent, which made Edik glance. Out of the corner of his eye, Edik saw pale skin and tight-cut black hair.

"Captain Barshai." Man that accent was thick. Thick as Dola's. "I am Maximillian Pajari. I require ... some of your time before you leave Luna."

"Sorry," Edik said. "I really am pressed right now. Leave a message at the office. We'll do lunch when I get back."

Edik nodded at Dola, who cut the link.

"Bad move," North said. "He might have only wanted to talk. Now he's going to get pissy."

"He's linking again, Edik," Dola said, "and there's another."

"Nixia, how long until Xincapph can take over?"

"Ninety seconds, Edik. And you aren't far enough from those helioships. They'll pick you up before you reach space."

"Damn it," Edik said, diving back down toward the surface.

"Don't take the link," North said. "Might be he could track it."

"Dola, open the other link then."

"Well, Captain Edik Barshai," said a voice that Edik knew all too well. It was a voice that sent shivers down his spine, and reached Edik in the place inside him that was still a small boy who feared that monsters were real and that trolls lived under bridges.

The voice of Baba Yaga. Known here on Luna as Natalia Romanova.

"It seems to me," Romanova continued, "that you're having some trouble with Pajari. Shall I intervene on your behalf?"

"No need, really. We're part of the same book club, and he's worried that I won't get the reading list before I'm off Luna. Hell of a guy to run it out here for me, wouldn't you say?"

"Come now," Romanova said. "Surely you will not allow your foolish fears of me to place our dear Anya at risk."

So she was calling Anna "Anya" again. Apparently Anna was somehow back in her good graces. It had been nothing but "Anka" for the last several weeks, so far as Edik knew.

"Where is she?" Edik asked Dola, in words only his familiar could understand.

"Can't tell," he said. "Her ship's not on the scanners."

Edik blinked. Nodded at Dola. Dola flattened his ears, but cut the link.

"Are you nuts?" North said, and Edik thought he heard admiration in his voice. "You just cut on *Natalia Romanova*."

"Links," Edik said, hanging close to the lunar surface. "If you think Pajari can track us, you can be sure *she* can."

"You'll still pay for it."

"Nixia," Edik said.

This time the elemental manifested herself, only just within Edik's line of sight. Like a tiny ballerina she was, all in yellow from her hair to her skin to her dress, but her orange eyes carried mirth.

"Yes, Edik?" she asked in soft tones.

"Find me an angle to space that should put us outside Pajari's scanners, and head for it full speed."

"Of course, Edik. And I'll make sure Xincapph takes over as soon as he can."

"Thank you," Edik said.

Edik turned and saw North staring as wide-eyed as Edik had ever seen him.

"You're trusting our safety to an *elemental's* choices?"

"I'd trust Nixia at the helm before I'd trust you," Edik said, standing. "Now come on."

And Edik herded North off of his bridge.

———

Pure relaxation.

One of the best things about flying on the *Horizon Cusp* was that their masseuses had to have been trained by the gods themselves. That was why it was third on Donal's to-do list for the first day of the voyage, after showering and eating.

The masseuse Donal had today — Inga was her name — had managed to slowly and steadily work out every single knot from Donal's neck to his arches.

He had no idea how long he'd been in there. He'd started meditating during the massage, and returned to his body to find himself more relaxed than he'd been in weeks.

He was dressed again now. Back in a pale blue airsilk shirt that brought out his eyes, and black airsilk pants that worked well with his black leather belt and loafers.

Between the clothes and the massage, Donal felt like royalty. So very different from his first flight on this ship. Back then, he hadn't known how to dress, much less how to present himself with authority or any kind of mystery.

The mystery part he might not have had down — truth was, he had no way to judge it — but he was getting pretty good at authority.

So it was with his head held high and the smell of lavender and rose hips in his nose that Donal strode out of the massage parlor to seek other entertainments on the Main Deck.

Under the lavender and rose hips, Donal could just make out the scents of the Main Deck itself. Clean sea smells, and a hint of dust. Subtle touches of illusion to air scrubbed clean by sylphs on a steady basis.

Illusory details that laid the foundation for the design of this deck. Suggested to passengers that they were not on a helioship flying through space, but in a simple port village in ancient Greece.

Details.

One key thing that Donal had learned as his studies of thaumaturgy progressed. Details were everything. In his observations, as well as his spell designs.

And so the buildings of the Main Deck didn't just look like ancient Greek construction to Donal anymore, with their faux marble style of fitted blocks without mortar, polished to a shine.

Donal could tell now that the designer had taken as influence the shadow plays of the early 2000s. *Plato's Rebellion*, the speculative tale of one of the early attempts to shift the world from magic to science, and likely *Caesar's Portents*, about Julius Caesar and the omens that presaged him throughout his life, both in triumph and defeat, even unto death.

The ceiling here was distant. Probably only twenty meters up, but with the illusions that made it resemble the sky above Greece, it could have been kilometers away.

The illusion was of a rich blue sky, with small, fluffy clouds meandering slowly past to the rhythm set by the air elementals as they freshened the air of the deck.

The deck itself appeared to be smooth, hard-packed dirt under a glistening layer of shine. Worth a chuckle unto itself. Donal knew from past shifts of awareness that the deck was actually ceramic, just like every other deck of the ship. But dirt completed the image of an ancient village, and the shine must have reassured passengers that their fancy shoes wouldn't get dirty.

Fionn, trotting next to Donal as they walked, took it all in without a word.

"What do you think?" Donal asked Fionn. "A sandwich? Breakfast was hours ago, and there's a deli two rows down that has marvelous honey roasted turkey, as I recall, with a spiced mustard I still haven't found on Earth."

"I think your snack will be delayed," Fionn replied, nodding down the street to Donal's left.

Rowan MacPherson. Not a woman Donal could mistake. And not just because she was some magnificently beautiful redhead. He'd known that from their first meeting — just like he'd known there was more to her than there seemed to be.

Now he knew she was a changeling. Though whether that meant she was of fae blood or a *Daoine Sidhe* left to be raised by human parents, he did not know.

She claimed the latter. And truth to tell, her beauty *did* seem to have a commanding presence beyond mere physical appearance. But Donal could not imagine that the good neighbors would be willing to abandon one of their own just to steal a human baby. Interbreeding seemed so much more likely.

Either way, she approached now, in a Kelly green gown that was cut for modesty. Which meant the dress did all it could, but the woman would have been eye catching in a snow storm.

Donal paused at the corner and waited for her.

"Donal," Rowan said when she was close enough for conversation. "Lovely to see you again."

She moved in as though she intended a hug, and perhaps a kiss.

Donal forestalled her with a handshake, which got him a droll expression.

"Really?" she said. "Are we no closer than you and Donatello Mancuso?"

Donal sighed. "I don't want to give you the wrong impression."

"Donal," Rowan said, holding up a hand before he could explain further. "Trust me when I say you've done an admirable job of rejecting me. More thorough and complete a job than anyone before you. So is a friendly hug too much to ask?"

Fionn gave Donal an encouraging nod.

Donal held his breath, but gave Rowan a hug...

...and had to try very hard not to think about just how good she felt pressed against him. Or about how, at this range, she smelled like heather and fresh spring air.

But she didn't try to make the hug linger, and she didn't come in for a kiss.

Still, Donal, to his chagrin, found his pulse racing and a trace of sweat on his brow from the contact. He wanted to shift awareness as far as he had around the *leannan sidhe*, to see if there was some element of magic to it all.

But he also suspected that Rowan would probably be able to tell he'd shifted awareness. Which meant there was no reason not to ask.

"So, is part of your ... heritage ... irresistibility?"

"Hardly," she said, but her emerald eyes were laughing. "*You've* managed to resist me so far."

An evasion. Of course.

"There was something you wanted to talk about?"

"How did you know?" Rowan's smile dazzled. Made the imitation sun above pale by comparison.

"Turn it down a notch," Donal said, shaking his head.

"I'm sorry?" Rowan gave at least the good imitation of a puzzled look.

"Look," Donal said, and sighed. "We both know you aren't entirely human, if you're human at all. And we both know that the fae have otherworldly beauty. But you make it hard to have a conversation with you sometimes."

Rowan arched one crimson eyebrow. Then gave Donal a conspiratory smile.

"Has it occurred to you," she asked slowly, "that you never had so much trouble before?"

"Yes," Donal said, "which is why I know you need to turn it down."

Fionn cleared his throat. Muttered words only Donal could understand. "She's not glamouring you."

Mirth danced in Rowan's eyes.

Donal looked away, a flush creeping up his neck. "So, business?"

"Here?" Rowan scoffed, "in the middle of the street where anyone can hear?"

"There's no one to eavesdrop," Donal said. "We're the only two passengers."

"Oh, very well," Rowan said with a small frown. "But may we at least adjourn to a park and *pretend* to be civilized?"

Rowan pointed to a small bit of green halfway down the block. Illusory grass and maple trees, shading a marble bench.

Not quite as much space as Donal would *like* to put between himself and Rowan MacPherson, but it would have to do.

The marble of the bench was real enough, and cool to the touch, but more comfortable than Donal expected. Good craftsmanship, though, rather than thaumaturgy.

Rowan sat properly enough at her end of the bench. In fact, her beauty seemed to have a little less ... intensity again. No longer that verge of otherworldly beauty she'd seemed to have only a moment ago. She looked more like the woman he'd first met than...

"You *were* glamouring me, weren't you?" Donal turned to Fionn. "How could she slip it past you?"

"She couldn't," Fionn said at the same time Rowan denied the accusation.

But Donal started to stand up all the same.

Rowan stopped him with a hand on his shoulder.

"I promise," she said. "I'll explain everything."

Donal resumed his spot on the bench, crossed his legs and his arms, and shot Rowan a disbelieving look.

"No glamour," she said. "I've never directed glamour at you. It's just that my nature ... provides me with certain benefits when it comes to body language. Most can accomplish only the most basic of statements through poses and movement." She shrugged one shoulder. "I am capable of intricate, extended speech through gesture and posture alone. Speech that you will understand on a deep level, though you might not be able to interpret it in words."

"Did you know she could do that?" Donal asked Fionn.

"I know of a few of the *Daoine sidhe* who have this gift. I did not know she possessed it."

"I'm very careful with it. But I had to use it this time."

Donal relaxed his shoulders a bit, which just made him realize he'd tensed up again. And so soon after his massage...

"I needed to know if you were having sex with the *leannan sidhe*. If you were, she would ... dominate that side of you. You would not have responded to me."

"I don't respond to you anyway," Donal said.

"You blushed," Fionn murmured, so only Donal could understand him.

From the look in Rowan's eyes, she didn't need to hear the *cú sidhe's* words.

"You could have asked."

"And if you were her creature, you would have lied," Rowan said. Then frowned. "It's true that you sent her to the Courts then. Some are taking that as an insult."

"I need *someone* warning me about attempts to circumvent my contract."

Rowan must not have liked the look on Donal's face.

"Donal," she said, sitting straighter, eyes wide. "I knew nothing about this. Not until after she appeared at the Courts as your representative."

"Of course not," Donal said, giving Rowan a smile that didn't extend to his eyes. "Why would the Duke of Shadows tell you? Unless…"

"No," Rowan said wearily. "I'm not working against you. We *are* on the same team here."

Donal glanced at Fionn, who nodded. Fionn was convinced, at least.

"All right, teammate," Donal said. "Do I have to worry about angry *sidhe* nobles coming after me because I want some heads-up about what's happening at the Courts?"

"No," Rowan said. "Even the ones who chose to take it as insult agree that it was clever. If you let your contract expire though, you should pull her from the Courts."

"She's right," Fionn said. "The *leannan sidhe* would become a liability at the Courts, without the contract protecting you."

"You do have their attention though," Rowan said with a slight frown. "Which means they may send you more help."

"Great," Donal said through a sigh.

"And someone in the Summer Court may decide to balance the Duke of Shadow's efforts."

"The Duchess of Mirrors?" Fionn said, sounding as concerned as Donal had ever heard him.

"She's the one I'd worry about." Rowan turned to Donal. "You might want to cover any reflective surfaces in your quarters for, well, the duration."

"That will only do so much," Fionn said.

"It's better than nothing."

"Wait," Donal said. "I don't know anything about this duchess."

"You might say she is the duke's opposite number," Rowan said. "And she will see the duke as having scored a point in their ongoing match, through the *leannan sidhe*."

"I can't even trust her service?" Donal said to Fionn.

"You can," Fionn said. "She is entirely yours. But if she aids you and you succeed, then the duke will receive credit for assisting you anyway."

"And the duchess will not want him to get ahead of her," Rowan added.

"Lovely," Donal said, thinking quickly. "How does this affect the big meeting? Any thoughts on how we can plan for it?"

"We can't," Rowan said with a frustrated shake of her head that set her hair dancing like fire. "The Courts are mercurial and the humans untrustworthy. Present company excepted, of course."

"Of course," Donal said, his mind rushing ahead of his words as usual.

"All we *can* do," Rowan said, "is figure out how we can work *together* so that you and I, at least — and Fionn here, of course — come out of this experience intact."

"You think it'll come to that?" Fionn said.

"I'm worried that it might. The Courts are worked up about the Rhian, and especially about the Du Mak, in a way I've never seen before. It's been so long since they've encountered anything new. There's no telling what they'll do."

"Then I believe I have an idea," Donal said with a slow smile.

Rowan and Fionn looked at one another. It was Rowan who asked, hesitantly, "A plan involving the Courts?"

"No," Donal said, his smile still in place. "A plan in case it all goes wrong at this big meeting..."

THERE WAS NO JUSTICE IN THIS UNIVERSE.

Edik went back and forth about whether or not he believed that, but walking back into the main cabin of the *Third Son* right then, he felt *sure* of the universe's sense of unfairness.

Half of Edik's body was still so clenched he was likely spaceworthy. He'd been sweating and struggling to find a way to avoid getting himself and his passengers killed while just trying to leave Luna. Not to mention avoiding port security ships, and not one but *two* great families. Probably pissing off both in the process.

But here in the main cabin, it looked like business as usual.

Yes, technically, that was how it was supposed to be. Most flights. Most flights, Edik would have been ferrying around eight wide-eyed tourists, wanting them to be as comfortable as possible in their big leather recliners. Each with its own meter-long porthole to gawk out of.

Tourists never needed to know what maneuvers Edik was flying to get them their views. In fact, the drinks and snacks they kept on their personal shelves — and all eight seats had personal shelves, as well as the ability to rotate three-hundred sixty degrees and to recline flat, if desired — should never move so much as a millimeter during Edik's fanciest moves.

And yet.

And yet it just meant that his passengers had no reason to realize Edik had done anything out of the ordinary. Certainly nothing worthy of notice or thanks.

Mason looked just like Cuthbert so often did during that long trip to Ganymede and back. Eyes closed and deep in meditation. Although, if Dola was right, odds were that the Hierophant was doing something to help the ship get away.

Carl, of course, was unconscious on the seat beside Mason. Carl's seat reclined all the way back. Edik could smell the blend of herbal odors of his alchemical treatment from where he stood.

Anna sat opposite Mason, on the other side of the plush, red carpet that ran the length of the main cabin and divided the gold-painted bulkheads below, the way the cabin-length depiction of a red firebird tailfeather did along the ceiling.

Anna was only looking up from a book now, as Edik entered the main cabin. Hers was even an old, printed book, not one of the modern refillables.

She marked her place with her finger.

"Edik?" she said, as North stepped past her and took the seat beside her. "All is well?"

"Not sure." Edik turned to Mason. "Can you hear me, Hierophant?"

"I can hear you, Edik," Mason said, his voice as casual as though he had only been reading himself. But he kept his eyes closed. "I believe I have drawn the port security ships sufficiently far away that you should be out of their scanner range."

He opened his eyes. Gave a mischievous smile.

"Thank you," Edik said. "But now we've got Pajari and Romanova to deal with."

"Which Pajari?" Anna said.

Edik would have asked about Romanova first, but then, Anna was the one who had known the woman all her life.

"Maximillian."

"An errand boy." Anna snorted. "Of course Rasputin feared to come himself."

"Isn't Maximillian Pajari's eldest?" Mason asked, in a tone that said he already knew the answer.

"Yes," Anna said through a sigh, "but he'll never be allowed to take over the family business. He isn't fit for it."

"He's got three helioships, and they've been following us," Edik said. "I think I've lost them, but I can't be sure."

"He does have a small gift for hunting," Anna allowed, then frowned. "What's this about Natalia Romanova? I wouldn't think she'd … oh. You refused her, of course."

"He cut the bloody link on her," North said.

That got a smile out of Anna. "I'll deal with her then."

She stood to walk toward the bridge.

Edik held up a hand to stop her.

"North here thinks they can track us through an open link."

"It doesn't matter if the link is open," Mason said through a sigh. "If they have a Magister or a Journeyman with enough experience and enough of the right kind of space certifications, they could track you whether the link was open or not. The links work because no ship can join the communications web without making a portion of its ceramics available."

Edik slapped himself in the forehead. "That's why they're called *links*. They're literally using a ship's thaumaturgic link to contact it."

"Exactly," Mason said. "So open or closed won't matter."

"Maximillian Pajari is a Journeyman," Anna said, and Edik thought he heard a trace of jealousy in her voice. He knew her father had denied her the chance to study alchemy. Had she developed aspirations of thaumaturgy as well?

"And he has certainly been spending time at space," Anna continued. "It might be that he could track us."

"And if he opens fire?" Edik said. "I mean, I know civilian ships aren't supposed to carry weapons, but—"

"They will be armed," Anna said, as casually as though she were dismissing thoughts of rain on a clear day. "But they will not shoot on us. Pajari's place in lunar society is too tenuous to risk killing the daughter of Alexei Lukyanov. More likely he would offer escort, or simple try to follow us and intrude on the coming meeting."

"So what do we do about them?" Edik said.

"For now? Nothing," Anna said. "I was going to contact Aunt Natka, but let her stew. If she links again, I will speak with her myself. Otherwise, she will have to wait until we return to Luna to speak."

Edik sucked in his lips to avoid responding to that one.

North had no such control.

"And you think she's going to let you be Luna's only representative at this big to-do?"

"I *think*," Anna said, "that I am not representing Luna, but the Rhian people. Further, if Luna is to have a representative that Earth will acknowledge, it will have to be an elected official. Earth does not officially acknowledge Luna's great families nor the influence we wield. She has no reason to attend."

Edik didn't believe that for a moment. He wasn't sure Anna believed it either, from the slight frown she wore now.

No, officially this meeting was to determine the status of the Fae Courts as well as the Rhian people and the Du Mak people, who may just be a type of fae no one had ever seen before.

There was no way a powermonger like Natalia Romanova would miss it.

4

THIS TIME, CARL JONES RETURNED TO CONSCIOUSNESS KNOWING exactly where he was.

Even before he opened his eyes, or gave any sign that he might have awakened, he knew.

He knew because for three days he had drifted in and out of consciousness while healing. And while none of those moments had been truly *conscious*, strictly speaking, he had been aware enough of his surroundings to take in all the details such as location, people surrounding him, and the passage of time.

So Carl knew for certain that it had been almost exactly three days since he was carried aboard the *Third Son*. He knew he was still fully reclined in one of those big, brown leather chairs in the main cabin.

He knew that the passenger and crew complement — excluding spirits — included only Edik, North, Anna and Hierophant Mason. Apart from himself, of course.

Knowing those details within reasonably safe limits — it was always possible they had landed and picked up or lost passengers while he was fully unconscious, though Carl doubted it — made him comfortable enough to flutter his eyes open as he properly assessed himself.

Thus he saw the expected white light shining into the main cabin from the red tailfeather motif painted on the gold ceiling. Through his peripheral vision he saw North, pacing at the aft end of the cabin, and Anna and Hierophant Mason seated nearby, both reading.

Thus more confident of his situation, Carl began his assessment.

He hurt.

He hurt a lot.

Not nearly as much as he had three days ago, which was good, but altogether he hurt entirely too much.

Too much for comfort, at least. Not necessarily too much for action. He wouldn't know that until he started to move.

Those burns all over his body were no longer fiery pain dominating his thoughts. They ached though, and he suspected he would feel them with every movement.

Bad, but he could shunt that pain away if necessary.

The stab wound in his chest, that was worse. The muscles on the left side of his torso were still insulted. Deep breaths would likely provide sharp discomfort for the next few days, at least.

That was ... less good. Tolerable, but it would inhibit the depths of his meditation. And meditation would help.

Worse was that his left arm would be ... maybe twenty-five percent less useful in a fight.

The rest of his bumps and bruises — what Carl thought of as the cost of doing business — had quieted down. Not even the dull roar he'd expected.

Clearly Mason knew a thing or two about healing magic. But then, Carl figured that Hierophants knew a thing or two about pretty much every kind of magic.

Carl's mouth was dry, but not the cotton field he'd been expecting. He only needed to smack his lips once before he could rasp out, "Water?"

Anna was there in a flash with a glass of water for him. An actual glass, too, complete with the firebird logo of Edik's company.

Figured.

And then, of course, Anna asked the stupid question that people always asked at times like this.

"How are you?"

Carl chuckled, which was a mistake. It sent off a litany of complaints all through his torso, and tugged at every millimeter of skin on his body.

"Watch that," Hierophant Mason said, not looking up from his book. "The old saying might be that laughter is good medicine, but right now it's just a pain."

"How much longer?" Carl tried to sit up, but realized that the full restraint harness was in place. As though the ship were expecting combat.

He also noticed that Mason wasn't wearing the harness, and the Anna hadn't had to remove one.

"Well," Mason said, looking over now. "If you were anyone else, I'd expect you to be out of commission for at least a month. Two or three before you could fight. But your etheric body has been modified for healing. Shunts and refines energy in interesting ways. Never seen anything like that before. Subtle work too. That doctor back on Luna might not have been able to tell."

Carl nodded, noncommittal. Sipped a little more water, that felt as welcome on his tongue as rain in the desert.

"Given what I could tell without probing deeply, I expected you not to return to consciousness for another three days." Mason shrugged. "So for all I know you're going to get up and demonstrate obscure forms of lunar folk dancing."

"I'd expect that to be Anna's department," North growled, stomping over to peer at Carl as though Carl's eyes held the secrets to his recovery.

"What's ... your problem?" Carl asked, feeling the desire to sleep further pull at him.

North just started swearing.

Carl looked at Anna, who sighed and shook her head.

"Edik won't let him on the bridge. Won't let him take a shift at the helm. Won't even leave the door open at this point, when he's in there."

"As though I'm not pilot enough to handle his precious ship," North spat, then went back to stomping and swearing.

Carl looked over at Mason.

"How long has this—"

"Practically since we hit space," Mason said, one eyebrow raised. "I admit there have been times I've envied you on this flight."

"Me too," Anna said softly.

"Fine," Carl said with a grimace.

He brought his chair to a sitting pose.

"Whoa now," Mason said, sitting forward quickly and extending a restraining hand. "Don't do anything stupid, man, you're still healing."

Carl unclicked the restrained harness.

"Hey!" North barked, and stomped over, putting his big ugly mug in Carl's face. "What the hell you think yer doing? We didn't bring you out here to die!"

Carl looked right into North's brown eyes. Deep.

"Sit the hell down," Carl said.

North sat down. Apparently without thinking about it, because rage started into his features.

Carl held up a hand. That didn't look like it would be enough, so Carl spoke as loudly as he could.

"You're giving Edik what he wants."

That stilled the storm before it started dumping rain and thunder.

"What do you mean?" North asked, so much suspicion on his face, it might have been that Carl had said the North could double his profits by ferrying daisies to the great families.

"I mean Edik loves tormenting you as much as you love tormenting him. You think his elementals aren't telling him just exactly how you're stomping and swearing?"

Carl shook his head. "You're giving Edik in-flight entertainment more satisfying than any shadow play."

"Bastard won't even let me into the galley," North grumbled.

"Of course not," Anna said, picking up the thread. "You would eat all of Edik's favorite snacks, wouldn't you?"

North tried to look outraged, but nodded his head in reluctant admission.

"And you'd do it even if you didn't like them," Carl said. "Just so Edik wouldn't have them."

"You're like children, the both of you," Anna said.

"Which means you're both distracting Anna, when she has to prepare," Carl said.

"Prepare?" Anna asked, as though she had no idea what Carl meant.

"Aren't you representing the Rhian people?" Carl asked the question, but from the looks on their faces, either North or Mason could have asked it just as readily.

"Yes and no," Anna said. "I'm their liaison, that is true. And I'm sure they'll have many questions for me during the proceedings. But they'll be *representing* themselves."

She pulled a small green rock from a hidden pocket. Held it up. "Once we arrive, I just have to let them know."

Carl blinked. That rock. It carried enchantment of some kind, and yet it didn't. Not by any form of magic Carl had encountered.

He hadn't even known she was carrying it.

"May I see that?" Mason asked, hand extended.

"You may investigate it from where you sit," Anna said, evidently enjoying the surprise of her revelation. "But only I am permitted to touch it."

Mason shifted awareness so far and fast that Carl felt his head spin. And he was surprised he could tell at all. Usually Mason could shift awareness around Carl seemingly at will without Carl noticing. No small point of irritation there.

But this time. This time Carl spotted it, and it scared him more than anything he'd seen from a Hierophant before.

Just how good *was* Mason?

"It both is and is not fae magic," Mason said, wonder through his voice. "I've never seen anything like it. Not even around the Rhian themselves. The way they take form leaves a different kind of resonance."

"Yes," Anna said, "well, it seems that they are more flexible than they were ready to let on."

"Well that's disturbing news," North said.

Carl was inclined to agree with him.

A small, throat-clearing sound, and everyone turned toward the front of the ship.

The door to the bridge stood open. Dola sat at the edge of the red, runner carpet, looking quite pleased with himself.

"Edik invites you all to join him on the bridge."

<hr>

THREE DAYS BACK ON THE *HORIZON CUSP*, AND IT WAS AS THOUGH Benny Sugg never left. The grizzled white tomcat lay sprawled across the large oak desk in Jacobs' office, getting his belly scritched in just the way he liked best. Three passes against the grain, then one pass to smooth it.

"What do you think, Benny?" Jacobs asked. "You like it here better than our little boat?"

Jacobs looked around as he petted his cat. The walls were disturbingly bare. It was Tunold's office now, not Jacobs', so Jacobs had expected the new captain to have his share of images on the walls, tchotchkes, and the like on the shelves behind the desk.

Instead, those shelves held the same set of spacetime law books and manuals that Jacobs had left behind. Only the current, modern ones, of course. The others, Jacobs had taken with him, along with his refillables.

But the walls were bare. And that just disturbed Jacobs.

Even the big red couch under the porthole on the starboard side looked little used. True, he didn't expect that Tunold was sleeping on it or anything, but Jacobs was starting to suspect that Tunold rarely even used his own office to meet with his officers on any kind of casual basis.

Benny Sugg gave an irritated mew.

"Sorry," Jacobs said through a chuckle, realizing he'd stopped petting. He resumed Benny Sugg's belly scritch. "You didn't answer my question, though, Benny. Would you be happier living out your remaining years here on this ship? Or on the *Sweet Dream*?"

The look Benny Sugg gave Jacobs was inscrutable, alas. Unless it meant *keep petting and no one gets hurt*, which was likely.

A brief rapid knock on Jacobs' office door.

Kelly. Smart move on Tunold's part, keeping Kelly on as his yeoman. Hard to find a better one.

"Come," Jacobs called.

The door opened approximately thirty degrees. Kelly leaned in at precisely a forty-five degree angle. Even his crisp haircut was exacting down to the millimeter.

Jacobs still thought that Kelly's parents had to have been mathematical aids. A compass and a protractor, perhaps.

"Your officers are here, Captain," Kelly said, his words as precise as his movements.

"Send them in," Jacobs said, and at those words Benny Sugg rolled over, jumped down off the desk, and resettled himself on the back of the red couch, under the porthole. As though he might see a bird flit past.

In filed the officers Jacobs'd sent for. Tunold first, taking the chair furthest to Jacobs' right of the five arrayed on the other side of the captain's desk. Machado followed, taking the furthest left. Goldberg sat next to Tunold, and Ramirez next to Machado.

Ramirez. Even now Jacobs could feel those big, dark owl eyes of his boring into Jacobs. Trying to discern what ways the captain was lying to him about his health.

That was the damnable hell of it all. Even when Jacobs told Ramirez *exactly* how he felt, in words even Kelly would have admired for their accuracy, Ramirez *still* thought Jacobs was hiding something.

Turned out that years of doing just that were coming back to haunt Jacobs.

The final seat, dead in the middle, went to Jang, the chief engineer. So small it seemed she could barely see over the desk, but vibrating with the need to do ... some damned project that Jacobs would consider a bad idea.

A chief engineer, in Jacobs' mind, needed a more level head when it came to experimenting on the ship. But then, all the modern engineers were mages, and Jacobs would swear that *all of them* lived to tinker.

Speaking of which...

"All right," Jacobs said. "Been uneventful so far, but the wind is likely to pick up."

Fortunately all these officers had served with Jacobs long enough that he didn't have to explain his shorthand for "possible trouble incoming."

"We're going to be at the rendezvous spot in about an hour," Jacobs continued. "And I want to go over any last things we need to. Starting with Cuthbert. Mash? Chief? What's he been up to?"

Machado and Goldberg looked at each other. Goldberg nodded for Machado to go first.

Interesting. Were those two getting along better these days?

"He's experimented a bit," Mash admitted with reluctant slowness, "but he's followed every restriction I've given him to the letter. Even offered him a better magic circle, one of my own, if he'd tell me what he was up to." Mash shook his head. "No dice. Hasn't even tried to use the permanent circles I set up on the Observation Deck."

"I don't like the sound of that," Tunold said.

Jacobs didn't either, but he let the ex oh take lead here.

"Maybe you could put a moratorium on all his spellwork for the duration?"

"In my *professional opinion*," Mash said, "that isn't necessary. And I'll be damned before I'll hamper the thaumaturgic research of a promising young mind, when he's already following my edicts."

"Nevertheless," Tunold started, but now Jacobs intervened with a raised hand.

"Ex Oh, let him talk. Continue, Ship's Mage."

"Honestly," Mash continued, "I don't think he's doing anything space-related. I must have set two dozen different kinds of alerts around his room, and I have him watched when he's anywhere else. When he touches a thread of power anywhere on this ship, I know about it. But whatever he's doing, it just seems like the normal experimentation we might expect from a grad student fitting in extra homework when he has a chance."

"He's a graduate student," Jacobs said. "I'm not sure I trust his homework. Keep tabs."

"Already done," Mash said, making notes on a zephyrpad that Jacobs hadn't realized he was holding.

"Chief?" Jacobs asked.

"Well," Goldberg said slowly, "it seems to me that what he's up to isn't magic. Or at least, it isn't thaumaturgy."

"Explain," Jacobs said.

"He's spent at least half of every day with our other passenger. Rowan MacPherson. In fact, I keep getting surprised that the two of them split up at night instead of just sharing one bunk."

"They know they're being watched," Jang said.

"Even so," Goldberg said with a one-shoulder shrug. "They don't spend all their time on the Main Deck or Observation Deck. They go back to one of their cabins at least a couple of times a day. If they're hooking up, they're—"

Jacobs slapped a hand down on his desk hard enough that Jang and Goldberg both jumped.

"This is not a sewing circle. This is not a locker room. If you want to play at gossip, do it on your own time, and don't waste ship's resources on it." Jacobs shook his head. "Chief, is your official report that Cuthbert and MacPherson are staying entirely to passenger-permitted zones of the ship?"

"Aye, sir," Goldberg said quickly, while his cheeks gained a touch of color. "Main Deck and Observation Deck or personal quarters."

"They've shown no signs of interest in anyplace or anything off-limits?"

"No, sir."

"They've taken no actions that risk bringing them afoul of your security teams?"

"No, sir."

"They haven't asked for a formal meeting or dinner with myself or any other ship's officers?"

"No, sir."

"Then your report is complete, unless you have anything else *security related* to add?"

"No, sir. Sorry, sir."

"Ms. Jang," Jacobs said. "How's the Deception Drive handling?"

"Smooth as a greased bobsled run, sir," Jang said with a smile. "In fact, I was thinking of—"

"Denied."

Jang blinked at him. "But, sir, this is the perfect opportunity to—"

"Denied, Ms. Jang." Jacobs met her eyes with an unyielding gaze. "In just over an hour, we'll be escorted into what is *literally* uncharted space for any of us. I'll not have you taking unnecessary risks."

"Aye, sir," she said glumly.

"Dr. Ramirez," Jacobs said, then paused when those owl eyes blinked slowly. "Find anything in their medical records we need to be worried about? If there's a history of heart attacks in one of their families, we need to know."

"Nothing like that, sir," Ramirez said, but he frowned. "In fact, by all accounts Rowan MacPherson's health is absolutely impeccable."

"I'll believe that," Mash mumbled, but Jacobs pressed. "Think her records are faked?"

"If so, not all of them." Dr. Ramirez took off his glasses and wiped them on a cloth from his pocket. "I'm personally acquainted with two of the doctors in her records. Both straight as Mr. Kelly's posture."

"But it troubles you," Jacobs said. "Why?"

"John," Dr. Ramirez said in a gentle voice, "you told me once that no ship at space is perfect."

Jacobs nodded. It was derived from an old saying from Jacobs' first captain, Captain Nemeth aboard the *Decatur*, back when ships were made of steel and powered by huge machines.

No ship at sea is perfect, Captain Nemeth used to say. *When all the reports are five-by-five, you've missed something.*

"Humans are the same way," Ramirez said. "Take Cuthbert for example. He's in a top-tier grad school for Thaumaturgy. Spends more time meditating and flushing clear energy through his winds, channels and energy centers than even Mash does. Plus, he's on some kind of exercise regimen."

"Latest thing," Mash added, face contorted in an expression of distaste. "All the top grad schools are requiring it of their doctoral candidates these days."

"So this Donal Cuthbert," Ramirez continued, putting his glasses back on. "He's in solid health in every way. But even *he* shows signs of stress, signs of a diet not quite as regimented as his exercise, that kind of thing. The ebb and flow of health that comes from actually living."

"And you don't see this in MacPherson?" Jacobs asked.

"*All* her reports are five-by-five," Dr. Ramirez finished. "Hierophants don't have bodies as perfectly tuned as hers, and she's not even a magician." He shook his head. "I've never *heard* of anyone like this before, John. If it weren't for the agreements we signed before taking this voyage, I'd be talking to her about a deeper study of her family tree."

"Right," Jacobs said. "Well, if its honest, God bless her. If it isn't, we're not responsible for knowing what she doesn't tell us. Anything else?"

"All other reports are coming in within safe parameters, sir," Tunold said.

Jacobs stood. "All right, folks. Back to your stations. I think our lives are about to get more interesting."

SEVEN SHIPS?

Edik counted the bogeys on his scanners one more time. This would be the fourth time. He knew the number wasn't going to change. But he counted again anyway.

Yep. Seven ships.

Nothing was ever as simple as it was supposed to be. Why was that?

Not leaving the port back in Kennedy. Not the flight from Kennedy to the rendezvous point...

Well, that was true and it wasn't.

As far as Edik was willing to let anyone else on the ship know — apart from Dola, of course, but Edik told Dola everything — the flight from Kennedy to the rendezvous point had been perfect. Open space. No signs of anything ... untoward.

Or at least, nothing had been shooting at the *Third Son*, or sending threatening links. So as far as Edik had been concerned, there was nothing to worry his passengers about.

The truth, of course, was that Edik had spotted ships at the edge of scanner range that were probably following them.

Still, the sightings weren't constant, and the ships showed no signs of gaining.

Plus, the *Third Son* was a civilian vessel. It carried no weapons. And as often as it got "randomly" searched since news broke about the Rhian people, Edik couldn't risk trying to hide anything even close to non-spec on his ship.

Hell, even his wards these days were just exactly down the center of the official specifications mandated by Earth and forced on Luna.

Not that Earth or Luna would have put it that way.

The point was, Edik flew a legal ship, on a legal — if classified — mission. If someone or someones (there might have been as many as three ships back there) chose to follow Edik, he couldn't control that. All he could do was get his own ship to the rendezvous point at speeds that would get him there within the allotted window.

He could have been here as much as a day ahead of schedule, but that would have raised questions about how he did it. And Edik had taught the Terran Navy all he intended to about lacunas. If they didn't understand the spirits that made space travel possible, it wasn't his responsibility to teach them.

Hell, he was only an Initiate. By all rights, he shouldn't have been teaching them anything. But every time Edik had made that observation to Dola, Dola got very interested in cleaning his paws. Sometimes even including droll expressions, as though Edik should have known was Dola was trying not to say.

Besides, if Edik had told his passengers about those possibly tailing ships, he knew exactly how they would have handled it.

Anna would have gotten on the link, figuratively breathing fire at their presumption, and devoting the full force of her charisma to getting them to go away.

Whatever would have come of that, she didn't need the distraction.

Hierophant Mason would probably have thrown spells in their way. Illusions, maybe, or other impediments that forced those ships to turn back.

Edik wanted Mason to save his efforts for the upcoming meetings. Edik had the feeling Mason might need every spell in his arsenal before this was all over.

And North. North would have stomped around, trying to tell Edik how to fly. Trying to commandeer the helm himself. Some damn thing along those lines.

Edik wouldn't have it. Not on his ship.

So Edik had enjoyed the excuse to keep everyone — especially North — off his bridge.

But now he'd reached the rendezvous site. Where he was supposed to be meeting two ships total. Some passenger liner from Earth, the *Horizon Cusp*, and an escort gunship.

Instead, there were seven ships here. Not including the *Third Son*.

One of them *was* the *Horizon Cusp*, at least, according to scanners. Gigantic thing, compared to the *Third Son*. A gryphon big enough to snatch Edik's firebird in one talon and fly back to its den.

Instead of one gunboat, there were two. The *Kansas* and the *Lexington*. And a cruiser. The *MacArthur*. Three big, ugly ships — especially the cruiser — that looked like shadow play depictions of seafaring ships from the second World War. Back a couple of decades before magic rose, and gave the world a whole new set of problems to deal with.

Why anyone would want to memorialize those old ships, much less recreate them for space travel, was beyond Edik.

The gunboats were big enough to dwarf the *Third Son*, and the cruiser was big enough to dwarf the gunboats.

Then there were the other ships.

One was another gryphon. Smaller than the *Horizon Cusp*, but still at least twice as big as the *Third Son*. Scanners read it as the *Spear's Tip*, which was not what Edik considered an encouraging name.

The next was a black bear, just about the size of the smaller gryphon. This scanners read as the *Tsar Nikolai*.

Finally, approaching from behind, a double-headed eagle a little larger than the *Spear's Tip* and the *Tsar Nikolai*, but still much smaller than those gunboats.

The double-headed eagle scanned as the *Boyar*.

Seven ships.

Edik sighed.

"Dola," Edik said, "would you please invite our passengers onto the bridge?"

"Including North?" Dola asked, one ear back in that suspicious expression Edik knew so well.

"Hell, Carl can join us if he's up to it."

The sound of his cat familiar snickering never ceased to bring a smile to Edik's face, even if it was lopsided and quick to fade, as it was in this case.

Anna stormed through the door first.

"What is it?" she asked, then spouted some Russian so fast that Edik almost couldn't parse it. Just not enough time speaking it these days. Well, also, Anna's upper-crust accent didn't help. Edik's father had raised him on what even he called "peasant Russian."

Still, Edik had gotten the gist: *how have things gone wrong?*

Mason didn't ask any questions, just came through the door,

moved to one side, and let his scary-good thaumaturgic senses tell him everything he needed to know.

North stomped in and stopped short of grabbing the handles under the scanners by maybe ten centimeters.

"Back," Edik said, slapping North's wrist.

North growled. Made a fist.

"*Stop it, both of you,*" Anna said. "We don't have time for this. Why are there so many ships?"

"That's the question of the hour," Edik said. "Who do we link first?"

"The cruiser," Anna said, in the same instant that Mason said, "The *Horizon Cusp.*"

Anna and Mason looked at each other.

"Obviously you believe there's a reason not to go right to the authority here?" Anna asked, one eyebrow high.

"I've never met any of these captains," Mason said, "but I know Captain Jacobs of the *Horizon Cusp* by reputation. And I *have* met his ship's mage, Magister Ronaldo Machado. They're trustworthy. And from the size of their ship, if there's a problem, we could dock aboard it."

"Not a bad idea," North said at the same time Edik said, "Not happening. I'll trust my elementals ahead of anyone's, regardless of ship size."

Three strands in the tangle of communication links flared bright blue.

North started to reach for one, but checked his hand.

"May I?" Anna asked, but Edik shook his head.

"Chances are, one of those is the military power in charge. Which means if I don't answer, he's likely to use military privilege to force my civilian vessel to accept the link."

Edik only just got the words out when his slap pad bonged and glowed bright red.

"See?" Edik said, and slapped it.

The head of a young man appeared above the communications station. He looked to be Japanese, if Edik was any judge.

"This is Communications Officer Riku Nakagawa, of the *MacArthur*, and I addressing Captain Edik Barshai?"

"You are," Edik said, "and my VIPs are on the bridge and part of this conversation too."

"One moment for Captain Yamato."

The head morphed into the head of a much older Japanese man. Gray haired, with a wispy waggle of beard.

"Good afternoon. I am Captain Haru Yamato, commander of the official Terran Naval escort. I understand I am addressing not only Captain Edik Barshai, but also Anna Lukyanova and Hierophant Nicholas Mason?"

"Me too," North said. "Captain Roger North."

Edik had to bite his tongue not to correct North's title. Anna was right though, this wasn't the time for games.

"You are not on my list, Captain North," Captain Yamato said.

"He is here at my direction, Captain Yamato," Anna said smoothly, stepping in close enough to be seen. Which also meant that Edik could smell the honey of whatever scent she was wearing. Made his empty stomach growl at the memory of his mother's honey cakes.

"Captain North," Anna continued, "is part of my two-man security team."

"Nothing in my orders permits you a security team."

"I didn't ask," she said, and Edik had to *fight* not to raise his eyebrows at her. But Captain Yamato couldn't have missed it if he did. "Luna attempted to impede my leaving Kennedy, and Luna specifically ignored third-party vessels intent on shooting us out of the sky. Thus, extra security."

Edik chose not to observe that the "extra security" would had to have already been aboard the ship, or she couldn't have brought them along. Which meant she'd made the decision before there was a need.

"I'll have to run it past my superiors," Captain Yamato said.

"Certainly," Anna said graciously. "And while you do, perhaps you can find an explanation as to why the rendezvous has changed without proper notice?"

"The escort—" Captain Yamato started, but Anna cut in right over him.

"The escort was to be one ship, but I count three. We were supposed to meet one civilian vessel, but I count four. The Rhian people object to Earth changing the rules without following due process."

"Noted and logged," Captain Yamato said. "For now I can tell you that the size of the escort changed in accordance with the number of ships appearing at the rendezvous without invitations. Believe me, Earth is as interested in why this is as you are. Captain Barshai, for the time being, you will not deviate from your current location until instructed by my ship. Understood?"

"Understood," Edik said, but Anna wasn't finished.

"We understand," she said, "but the Rhian reserve the right to take such steps as are deemed appropriate by their liaison. If that means moving this ship, then this ship will be moved. Understood?"

"I am being as patient with you as I can, Ms. Lukyanova, but I do not appreciate power plays," Captain Yamato said. "I am giving you instructions necessary to keep your ship safe. Ignore them at your peril. *MacArthur* out."

The link cut.

"*Bravo*," North said.

"You mean *brava*," Mason corrected, but he frowned as though he were thinking along the same lines that Edik was: pissing off the Terran Navy was not a good idea.

———

Jacobs stood at the conn and leaned over the railing as he addressed his bridge crew, arrayed in a ring about his station.

"Ladies and gentlemen, either the navy is lying to us, or they are not in full control of the situation here. Communications, get me the *Third*

Son. Helm, I've just sent you three escape routes. Be ready to move along escape route alpha on my mark. Scanners, I want to know the *second* any weapons chutes heat up. Ex Oh, please advise our passengers that we recommend they stay in their quarters. And tell Chief Goldberg to have a team ready to secure said passengers, if they make it necessary."

Jacobs resumed his chair to a chorus of ayes. He hoped this didn't turn into a clusterfuck. The universe would be doing him a huge favor if it let things go smoothly just this once.

Truth was he hadn't been sleeping as well as he should have these last couple of nights. Even admitted it to Ramirez, though he refused the sleeping draughts Ramirez offered.

Wasn't any real insomnia. Just ... command again. After taking a break from it the way he had, coming back just wasn't as easy as he'd expected it to be.

Benny Sugg might not notice the differences in returning to command, but Jacobs was feeling the strain. More than he wanted to admit. More than his nightly boxing sessions with the heavy bag could take care of.

Even with only two passengers, there were more than two hundred human lives aboard the *Horizon Cusp*. All of them depending on Jacobs' skills as a captain.

And he did not need this many civilian ships where they shouldn't be. Plus, that the Terran Navy had tripled its escort without a word of warning wasn't good either. Implied that they weren't expecting so many ships to show up themselves.

This many unexpected factors? For a mission as diplomatically sensitive as Jacobs expected this one was?

Just the thought of it set his teeth on edge.

"Captain," Mr. Hernandez said from the communications station. "I have the *Third Son* for you."

"Link them through," Jacobs said.

And immediately had to fight a grimace.

When did they start giving command to children? The head that appeared above Jacobs' slap pad... This boy may have managed a blonde Van Dyke, but he couldn't have been thirty. And he was a captain?

"Captain Barshai," Jacobs said, wedging a smile onto his face if not quite into his voice. "I'm Captain Jacobs. You have any warning about the party invitations?"

The phrasing — Jacobs attempt at levity — seemed to take the kid a moment to parse, but then he gave a grim smile of his own.

"No, I did not," he said. "Looks like we have crashers. What do you think?"

"Ever been in a real firefight before? With naval ships and proper fireballs?"

"Run from a couple. We don't carry any weapons, so we don't go picking fights."

"Smart man," Jacobs said. "Listen. We have the best ship's mage within a good hundred decans of this site. He makes sure our wards are the best available. Maybe even better than the navy's if you take my meaning."

That got a whistle of appreciation from Barshai, while someone spoke in the background. Male voice.

"You're welcome to dock with us," Jacobs said. "We're going to the same place, and you'd be safer in our wards than your own. No offense intended."

"None taken," Barshai said, looking as though he'd taken offense. "But I respectfully decline. Wards are nice, but speed is better, and I have the fastest ship in the heliosphere."

"You don't," Jacobs said, letting his tone get flat now. "Your ship's not big enough for a Deception Drive, and no other drive can get that kind of performance out of a lacuna. Not to mention that your ship is too small for anything but a *young* lacuna, which means it simply can't move as fast at crunch time."

"Trust me, Captain," Barshai said. "I know how to get more out of my lacuna than even your vaunted ship's mage can."

"Fine," Jacobs said through a sigh. If the kid wanted to get his people killed for his ego's sake, Jacobs couldn't stop him. "Let me do at least this much for you. I've been in this section of space before. Let me send you the escape routes we have planned. If this whole thing goes south, we can take the same route out. If your ship is so fast, then you'll still have my wards between you and the fireballs. Fair enough?"

Barshai turned and spoke to some people Jacobs couldn't see. He also thought he heard Barshai asking what "goes south" meant, which just said poor things about today's educational systems, far as Jacobs was concerned.

But just then a blonde woman thrust her head in front of Barshai. And not quite in alignment. The communications system did its best to resolve this, but it left a very pretty girl's face in front of a head that was slightly misshapen and shifting, with two different shades of blonde hair.

Very disquieting.

"Captain Jacobs," the young woman said with the precise syllables and the slight accent of one of Luna's great families. "My name is Anna Lukyanova."

Yep, a lunar great family. Lovely, Jacobs thought as she continued.

"May I ask, do you have Donal Cuthbert aboard?"

"I'm not at liberty to discuss my passenger manifest, Ms. Lukyanova."

"Of course I understand," she said as smoothly as though Jacobs had actually given her an answer. "However, if he *is* aboard your ship, please send him my greetings. And tell him as well that the Rhian people say they look forward to meeting him."

Jacobs frowned at that, but before he could say anything else—

"Captain!" Grabowski yelled from scanners. "Gunboat chutes are heating up."

"Take care of yourselves," Jacobs said to ... whoever was listening on the other end of the link. "*Horizon Cusp* out."

He cut the link and slapped the beak on the miniature version of the gryphon at his station.

Jacobs' voice came over the internal comm system, issuing the call to general quarters and confining all passengers to their cabins.

"Details, Mr. Grabowski," Jacobs called as he craned his head to see what he could through the transparent dome around him.

"The gunboats are shifting positions, moving out from the cruiser. The cruiser is moving between us and the *Third Son*, course set to interpose itself between our ships and that double-headed eagle and the black bear. Looks to me like they're objecting to the presence of the *Boyar* and the *Tsar Nikolai*."

"What about the *Spear's Tip*?"

"On our side of the picket."

"Captain," Mr. Hernandez said, "from what I can pick up, the *MacArthur* is in contact with the *Spear's Tip* right now."

"Lovely," Jacobs muttered. "Just what we need. Another gryphon in this flight." Louder, he said, "Get me the *Spear's Tip* as soon as their link is open."

Jacobs tapped a spot in the gryphon's midsection and twisted his finger, opening up communications with the ship's mage's lab.

The dark face and close-cropped hair of the assistant ship's mage, Cromartie, appeared.

"Aye, Captain?" Cromartie said in his deep voice.

"Tell Mash I said to be ready."

"He has me ready to pull the keys right now, Captain, and he's standing by for the emergency ward upgrade."

"Good men, bridge out."

Jacobs cut the link. He should have known Mash would have things ready.

Every civilian vessel was required, by law, to have certain thaumaturgic keys built into their wards. Keys that could be exploited by police and military vessels.

In much the same way, civilian wards had ... limitations that military and police wards did not have. Jacobs couldn't begin to understand exactly what those differences were, but he understood the salient points: civilian wards were downright porous, compared to military wards. Mash had used the analogy of trying to stay dry in a storm by standing under a colander.

So, a couple of years back, Jacobs had approved Mash ... taking precautions. Building sockets for those ward keys, that could be pulled and remove those blatant vulnerabilities.

Further, Mash, bless the man's focus and dedication, had spent the better part of a year not-upgrading the wards. By which he and Jacobs meant that Mash had been building spell structures within the network of spells that held the *Horizon Cusp* together and flying through space. Structures that were certainly not wards, and could never be detected as wards by any inspectors.

However.

Those spell structures needed only a series of adjustments that Mash could make on the fly to *turn* them into ward modifications. More than tripled the strength of the *Horizon Cusp's* wards.

And Jacobs had seen how effective those wards were against naval alchemical fire. And maybe even against attacks from those great beasts, the zuglodons.

Not that Jacobs wanted to see them tested against zuglodons, if he could avoid it. Truth was, there was a huge zuglodon feeding ground no more than ten thousand klicks from this rendezvous spot...

"Mr. Grabowski?" Jacobs said, letting his tone fill with impatience.

"No shooting yet, sir," Grabowski said. "The *MacArthur's* heating up its chutes though. Only on the away side."

"Well thank God for that much," Jacobs grumbled.

"Sir, I have the *Spear's Tip*," said Mr. Hernandez, looking up at his captain.

Jacobs nodded, and above his slap pad appeared a head without anything like a military haircut.

True, even Barshai's haircut hadn't been properly military, but it was still reasonably short.

This woman, though. She had paler blonde hair that fell past her shoulders. Strong features, but eyes like arctic ice. And from the way she held herself, she was used to command.

She looked familiar, too, but Jacobs couldn't quite place her.

"I'm Captain John Jacobs of the *Horizon Cusp*," Jacobs said, trying to add a smile he didn't feel.

That got him a raised eyebrow. "I've dined at your table, Captain Jacobs."

The voice brought it home. Natalia Romanova. From that trip to Venus.

Two lunar great families involved in this mess. Terrific.

"Please forgive an old man a lapse in memory," Jacobs said. "That Venus flight ... had a number of pressing matters that took precedence in my mind."

"Very well," Romanova said, and the damned woman sounded as though she were pardoning his life against her better judgment.

Jacobs hated the self-styled aristocrats of Luna. But he let her continue.

"Tell me, Captain Jacobs," Romanova continued, "is your ship armed?"

"Certainly not. We're a passenger liner."

"Then I suggest you follow Captain Yamato's instructions and sit still. Who are your passengers?"

"That is classified information."

"This is a classified situation," she said, as though her answer were the most obvious thing in the world. "My presence here is classified as well. But I must know whom you transport."

"Take it up with Captain Yamato," Jacobs said. "I was only trying to—"

"I'm not interested in what you were trying to do," Romanova said. "I know you're carrying Donal Cuthbert. There's no reason they should have classified that. The news has been telling us all for months that he represents the Fae Courts. But I know you have a *second* passenger. Who?"

"Ms. Romanova," Captain Jacobs said, his nerves fraying, "I do not answer to you."

Jacobs cut the link. "Get me the *MacArthur*!"

"Shots fired!" Grabowski yelled. "Shots fired!"

Jacobs fell back in his chair, fast as he looked up.

Sure enough, in the distance he could see twin balls of green flame soaring through space.

WHEN THOSE FIREBALLS APPEARED ON THE SCANNERS, EVERYONE ON Edik's bridge froze. Even North.

It was the gunboats that fired. And they were shooting at that double-headed eagle. The *Boyar*.

And the *Boyar* started shooting back at them.

Meanwhile, that cruiser, the *MacArthur*, was closing the gap between itself and that black bear ship, the *Tsar Nikolai*.

"No!" Anna cried. "Get them on the link, Edik! Now!"

Edik hesitated, unsure which ship she meant, but Anna didn't wait anyway. She grabbed a link.

While she did that, North leaned in. Spoke in what, for him, had to be hushed tones. But for anyone else it would have been normal conversational volume in a busy restaurant.

Worse, North's breath smelled like ham sandwiches.

"This is getting ugly, Barshai. Maybe you oughtta think about—"

"No," Edik said, cutting off the docking discussion with the one word, before turning to his left.

Anna was deep in conversation with a pale man with a widow's peak in his black hair.

Well, "conversation" was a gentle term for what she was doing. A more accurate term would be "browbeating."

Edik couldn't quite follow her Russian, but Anna was giving the poor fool on the other end of the link a very hard time.

Then Edik picked out one word, from sheer repetition: "*Otet.*"
Father.

So the *Tsar Nikolai* was a Lukyanov ship. That was just perfect.

Anna cut the link, then grabbed another.

"Edik."

Dola's voice, from under the console. Edik looked down, but Dola pointed with his nose.

Hierophant Mason had dropped into a meditative sitting position. His legs were crossed, his eyes were closed, and Edik knew there was no way he could look so perfectly at ease sitting like that. Especially with his back so straight without any wall behind him.

"Meditating?" Edik asked.

"No," Dola said. "He's not in there. And he sent his familiar out too. Do you want me to—"

Edik lost the rest of that under Anna's tirade.

"—*public section of space, rendezvous or not.* You have no right to open fire on civilian vessels that are not posing a current threat. And the *Tsar Nikolai* has already surrendered itself to me as a representative of the Rhian people."

Now, Edik might not have been able to follow most of what Anna had been yelling at that poor pale man a few moments ago. But he knew for certain he'd never heard her mention the Rhian people, and neither had he.

Right now she was yelling at someone in a uniform. The young Japanese man from earlier. So that had to be the *MacArthur*.

So now she was yelling at the Terran Navy and trying to boss them around?

Yeah, Edik could see no way this could go badly.

"Nixia," Edik whispered, continuing in his own poor Gaelic, to try to keep Anna from understanding him. Just in case she could yell and listen at the same time. *"Tell Xincapph to get ready. We may need to flee."*

"Of course, Edik," Nixia whispered from next to Edik's ear.

"Get 'im!" North roared, thrusting one fist in the air.

The *Boyar* had taken at least three direct hits. The double-headed eagle ship looked battered and barely able to keep flying. It certainly couldn't fire back anymore.

Still.

"Celebrating?" Edik didn't hide the disgust in his voice, made stronger still by the sudden silence on the bridge.

Anna had cut the link?

Yes. Either she had, or the *MacArthur* had. She was staring at the scanners now. Watching the *Boyar*. Watching as it began to break apart.

The *Kansas* and the *Lexington* kept firing.

Anna began muttering an old Russian prayer for the dead.

Edik began praying with her.

DONAL PACED BACK AND FORTH IN THE LOUNGE OF HIS SUITE. FIONN paced right beside him, but more as a show of solidarity than out of any need of his own.

Rowan, seated on Donal's couch and drinking blackberry tea as though nothing in the world could be wrong, had asked Donal four times to join her.

At each invitation, Fionn had looked up at Donal, ears perked.

By the fourth, Donal had stopped even refusing.

The fifth invitation came anyway.

Donal whirled on her. He pointed at the Starchaser Spacelines logo on the wall, still flashing red, though Captain Jacobs' voice no longer boomed about passengers returning to their cabins.

"We have to do something."

"We are," she said, eyebrows raised. "We are waiting. That's what diplomats do when the military must resolve something, Donal. We wait until they finish their work, so that we may continue ours."

Donal huffed out a breath.

He gazed again at the wards in frustration. Magister Machado had done quite a job of shutting him down in here. Donal's signature specifically, clamped down. It was almost as bad as what was done in anti-magician cells, but not quite. Donal could still work magic in here, he just couldn't send any spells out *there* where they were needed.

And the *Horizon Cusp's* security team had specified that Donal had to return to his own cabin. Even if Rowan was permitted to accompany him.

Rowan, of course, was not bound by wards keyed against Donal. She could have worked her own form of fae magic all she wanted.

Not that she had any intentions of doing so.

So Donal had to remain here, with no idea what was going on, much less any visible way he could help.

Even the porthole-wall was locked in wall mode, so that Donal couldn't even look outside to see what was happening.

This was intolerable. He had to...

Wait. What had Magister Machado said? Donal was allowed to send forth his astral form...

"Fionn, tether," Donal said and dropped into a meditative pose right there in the middle of the faux marble floor (currently white, for "daytime").

"Donal," Rowan said, but whatever she said to finish that sentence was lost as Donal shifted his mind deeply into a meditative state.

He felt Fionn take hold of a portion of his essence. Ready to snap him back, just in case Donal found himself ... unfit to get himself back to his body on his own.

And then Donal projected his sense of self right out of his body, outside of the room, past the wards, and into space.

Out here, it looked worse than Donal had feared.

A shooting match had begun. Two Terran Navy gunboats, shooting great balls of green alchemical fire at a double-headed eagle ship. And that ship looked ready to shoot right back.

Closer to where Donal's essence floated, he could see a Terran Navy cruiser, moving in on a helioship that looked like a black bear.

Black bear...

Why did that sound familiar?

Donal shook off that thought, and finished assessing.

He could see the *Third Son*, over by another ship that looked like a miniature version of the *Horizon Cusp*, done only just larger than the *Third Son*.

But from the position of that cruiser, it could fire in either direction. It could fire at the black bear ship, yes, but also at the smaller gryphon.

And the *Horizon Cusp* and *Third Son*, they weren't quite out of danger either. If the cruiser fired on that smaller gryphon, it might open up on the *Third Son* or *Horizon Cusp* or...

No. This all needed to end now. Before people started dying.

Too late.

Donal could see those great balls of green fire slam into the side of that double-headed eagle.

Its wards were crumbling already.

No.

Donal soared that direction.

Fionn's teeth clamped a warning Donal didn't need. He knew that the alchemical fire might prove dangerous even to his own astral essence. Spells worked into the alchemical ingredients made them more damaging to the pure magic of wards, which was a form of astral essence entirely too similar to the sublime substance that carried Donal's consciousness even now.

It might be too subtle a substance for those shots to harm him. But then again, it might not.

He had to risk it.

Closer Donal flew, and now he could see that those wards were down. Shattered entirely.

Donal pulled the astral form of his tuning fork, and rang it out.

Discordant notes from the double-headed eagle. The wards weren't the only things down. Those shots had begun unraveling the spells that held the ceramics together. If the navy didn't stop shooting...

Three more fireballs, incoming.

Donal reached for all the power he could grab in an instant. Even six month ago, it would have been nothing. Or at least, nowhere near what he needed now. But six months of training in program as intensive as Donal's — especially as Donal and his Esmeralda pushed each other to get better and better — and now Donal could accomplish things he'd never dreamed of while studying for his Bachelor's.

Now he could get between those great balls of green fire. He could hear the ringing tones of the spells that guided them.

And with his tuning fork in hand, Donal rang out a counterpoint.

He sang the Call of the Thirtieth Aethyr, the lowest initiation of the Enochian system, and invoked that Aethyr's governor.

And he channeled that power in the form of space aspected space of space. And he did it purely with the intention of disrupting every aspect of the spells on those fireballs.

He could do nothing about their alchemy. Nothing immediate to diminish their heat.

But he could batter at their coherency and at their aim. And every little bit might help.

The familiar tonic chords of Donal's own magic rang out, clashing with the tones of the spells on those three great green balls of fire.

And the fire gave first.

The aim was spoiled. Not entirely, but enough.

Their coherency shattered. Green flame erupted outwards seconds before those shots glanced off their target. The damage they'd done reduced by a factor of five, or perhaps more.

But alas, with no wards protecting that ship, even that much damage was too much.

The ceramics of the double-headed eagle's hull began to fray and break apart.

No.

Donal soared closer to that ship. He hunted down the life support systems. Found a single magician — a Journeyman — working herself half to death to try to hold those systems together.

Donal slid into the circle with her. Her spacer jumpsuit with all its pockets was as black as her pale, sweaty skin was chalky white right now. Her long black hair matted with more sweat.

Donal did not know this woman's name, but he could feel her signature. Could feel the notes vibrating through everything she did.

And Donal settled in with her, tuning himself to harmonize.

The woman shook her head in sudden surprise, but recovered quickly enough to take advantage of her sudden aid.

In that moment, they began working in tandem. Donal feeding her power, while she — who knew the systems better than Donal could learn them without a week's study — worked double-time to knit those life support spells in place.

They would hold. Donal could feel it. Not forever, but for a while.

But only if those gunships stopped their barrage.

***

"Damn it, Yamato," Jacobs yelled at his counterpart. "Stop this shooting! Even *we're* picking up their surrender notice!"

Captain Yamato just gazed back at Jacobs with a look of quiet distaste.

"Tell me, Captain Jacobs," Yamato said, his voice smooth as ceramics. "If you were still a navy captain, would you take orders from a civilian?"

"No, but I would sure as hell accept a surrender and immediately offer humanitarian aid."

"I have my orders, Captain Jacobs."

"Well, nothing about those orders controls *me,* Yamato."

The Japanese man's face lost all expression at a speed that almost gave Jacobs pause. "Do you threaten me, Captain Jacobs?"

"Not at all," Jacobs said with a nasty smile. "But you understand that recording all scanner data is a mandated part of space travel under General Space Regulation Three."

"That regulation is intended only to ensure that all ships aid in contributing to current charts."

"But in this case, we have scanner evidence of a civilian ship offering surrender to the Terran Navy, and the Terran Navy failing to accept the surrender. I'm sure the news agencies would love that."

"Captain Jacobs, this mission is classified—"

"Especially since feeling back home isn't entirely in favor of the Navy right now. What with that incident on Ganymede giving you guys a black eye. And I know there's some question about how Earth is handling the 'Mars Crisis.' I know you guys are in the middle of that, since there's a shooting war."

"Captain Jacobs, all data from this mission must—"

"Plus, you already accepted a surrender offer from the *Tsar Nikolai*. True, they surrendered without firing a shot, but under the circumstances—"

"All right!" Yamato roared, and finally Jacobs saw the fire that he knew had to be there. No man nor woman rose to the rank of captain without having some fire in the belly.

Jacobs could hear Yamato giving the orders for the gunboats to stand down and to offer humanitarian aid.

When Yamato turned back to face Jacobs the look on the man's face was decidedly unfriendly. But Jacobs didn't care if the man hated him. So long as he stopped the slaughter.

"I have given the orders, and you have heard me. So long as the *Boyar* does not fire another shot—"

"How could they?" Jacobs said. "They lost fire control more than a minute ago."

"*Captain*," Yamato snapped. "You will cease interrupting me or I will arrest you for interfering with a Terran Naval officer in the performance of his duty."

"Try it," Jacobs growled.

Yamato cut the link.

Jacobs continued fuming as he ordered Goldberg to grab Cromartie and take the shuttle out to aid evacuating the ship. An order that had to be belayed even before the shuttle left the landing bay.

"Captain," Mr. Hernandez called out from the communications station. "We have orders from the *MacArthur* to stand down. The Terran Navy will handle all humanitarian aid here."

"Figures," Jacobs muttered.

"Further," Mr. Hernandez continued, "we are to shuttle our VIPs over to the *MacArthur* for a meeting."

Jacobs snorted, but there was nothing he could do to countermand it.

Of course, such a meeting would give Jacobs an excellent chance to give Yamato a piece of his mind. The Terran Navy firing first? The

Terran Navy continuing to batter a ship that could not defend itself? A ship that begged for surrender?

Jacobs started down the stairway from his station to the bridge deck proper.

Tunold was waiting for him.

"No, John," Tunold said, arms crossed.

"You're out of line, mister," Jacobs said. "Stand aside."

"*No*, John," Tunold said. "You are not going to the *MacArthur*."

"I am the captain here—" Jacobs started, but Tunold actually cut him off.

"I'll go to Ramirez right now," Tunold said, stepping right up into Jacobs' face. It felt aggressive, but for a man who moved like a bear, he was visibly trying not to be aggressive.

He even lowered his voice.

"John," Tunold said, "Ramirez told me about the lack of sleep."

"That—"

"He was right to do it, and you know it. Now look. This is going to be tense, and you're already fraying a little thin."

"How dare you—"

"John, you had Yamato surrendering to you, and you kept battering at him anyway. And if I let you go to the *MacArthur*, I'm not convinced you won't say or do something that *does* give Yamato an excuse to arrest you."

Jacobs burned to deny that. His lips wouldn't open though. His heart pounded, and his nose flared in angry breaths, but his lips stayed pressed together in a tight line.

Because he knew his Ex Oh was right.

"John," Tunold said, "they're going to have to start sending over route data. Or they're going to ignore us during the meeting. The first means you'll have a chance to set alternate courses, in case of trickery. The second means you may be able to chat with the other captains without naval interference. Isn't that worth not spitting fire into Yamato's face?"

Jacobs had to move his lips around a little, then finally rub his weary forehead before he could get out another word. And when he did, the word was "No."

But he chuckled as he said it.

"You're right, Ex Oh," Jacobs said through a sigh.

"I know it, Captain," Tunold said, and he didn't dare crack the smile Jacobs could hear in his voice. "But I wish I wasn't. Believe me, nothing would make me happier than to watch you tear Yamato a second special hole."

Now they were both chuckling.

Jacobs sighed again. "Can you believe it? *You* telling *me* to keep control of myself?"

"Honestly, John," Tunold said, his face clearing quickly. "That's how I know for sure that you aren't sleeping right. Let Ramirez give you the potion, for Christ's sake."

"I'll think about it, Ex Oh," Jacobs said. "And since I'm not going, you get the special hell of playing nursemaid to our VIPs for this little flight. Bring security too. Not Mash. We need him here. Cromartie if you think it'll help."

"I'll handle it, Captain."

"I know you will, Ex Oh," Jacobs said, clapping the younger man on the shoulder.

And then Jacobs turned and went back up the stairs.

Someone had to mind the store while the diplomats played their games.

5

Donal wasn't thrilled with this whole idea. Rowan seemed to take it in stride, of course. As though it were the most natural thing in the world to be leaving their official escort ship for an unexpected meeting aboard a Terran Navy cruiser.

With a security team along, no less. As if in confirmation from the *Horizon Cusp* that things weren't quite right.

And yet, all Donal could do right now was sit here.

He and Rowan sat in the two center seats of the first row of the hippogriff shuttle's passenger compartment. Fionn was resting inside the silver faun pendant around Donal's neck.

The seats were cushioned well. Gold fabric, with red and silver trim. Silver carpets, and off-silver walls and ceiling.

The Starchaser Spacelines logo seemed to be everywhere. The backs of the seats, the tray tables, the dishware, along the walls...

At least the seats offered plenty of room. Donal would never forget riding on this one shuttle all the way to Kennedy from San Francisco. Tight little thing, smaller than most airships.

That had been one cramped seat. The miserable threshold by which all other seats were judged. When they set down in Kennedy, Donal practically had to unfold himself from the chair. And he definitely heard a litany of joints cracking from behind held in place too long.

Nothing like that here. The seat Donal sat in now could recline all the way, if he wanted. There was a pop-up table, currently holding a snack of mixed fresh vegetables and a steaming cup of black cherry tea.

Rowan opted for more of her blackberry tea, and her snack wasn't vegetables. It was some kind of honeyed pastry, and she'd seemed to take special pleasure in eating it. Right down to closing her eyes and making little sounds that frankly made Donal a little uncomfortable, sitting next to her.

Those sounds were just a little too private.

In fact, while she ate the pastry, Donal felt for the security team sitting a few rows behind them. If it was uncomfortable for Donal, how much more uncomfortable must it have been for them?

Fortunately, she finished, and Donal no longer felt as though he'd be interrupting a personal moment by speaking.

"What could they possibly need a meeting for?" Donal asked.

That got Rowan to blink at him, and frown. "You really are new to diplomacy, aren't you?"

Donal sipped his tea, but gave her a droll look by way of reply.

"Obviously," Rowan said slowly, "the Terran Navy is concerned about the unexpected ships. However, Earth isn't the only party invited to this meeting by the Fae Courts. Earth may or may not have known that..."

"What?" Donal said loud enough that Rowan immediately made shushing movements.

Donal had to shake himself before he could continue, softly.

"What do you mean, Earth wasn't told about other invitations?"

"Earth..." Rowan said, "has tried for too long to control the Fae Courts. Well, not control the Courts, of course, but try to control who knows about them. And information is power."

"So the Fae Courts..." Donal started, but he let Rowan finish.

"With the discovery of not only the Rhian people, but the Du Mak, the Fae Courts have decided that they will no longer allow

Earth to control access to them. That arrangement served the Courts as they learned more about how the world has changed since the rise of magic. But it is time for them to come forth in their full glory, and they wish to remind Earth that they speak for themselves."

"They don't expect Earth to support them about the Rhian and Du Mak peoples."

"Very good," Rowan said. "It's uncertain, of course, since nothing is resolved within the Fae Courts on the matter. But they do have a way of looking at what's to come."

Donal frowned. "You don't mean prophecy."

"No," Rowan said with a smile. "Not per se. Just planning."

"So," Donal said, trying to sound casual. He even added a sip of tea to play that up. "Is there anything else the Courts have told you about this upcoming meeting that you haven't shared with me?"

That got him a wounded look.

"Donal," she said, and even her neutral tone seemed to shame him. "I didn't know this was coming any more than you did. I didn't know the Courts had invited more parties to the table either."

"But—"

"I've been dealing with them all my life. You've only been dealing with them for a few months. Of course I can spot their angles before you can. But that doesn't mean they're giving me advance warning."

"We're supposed to be representing them," Donal said. "Why would they leave us both in the dark?"

"The Courts are not the most experienced when it comes to working together." Rowan gave Donal a lopsided smile he'd never seen on her before. It seemed more simple and honest — uncalculated even — than any other expression he'd ever seen on her face.

It was her single most attractive moment, to Donal. Not that he'd tell her that.

Following the quick smile, she continued, "They don't trust each other, and they don't always trust themselves." She shrugged one shoulder, and Donal almost swore that a mask was sliding back into place as she did. "So of course they don't trust us."

Donal lowered his voice to a whisper. "Just how long have you been working with them?"

"My whole life, Donal," she said, taking the reduced volume as an excuse to lean a little closer. Close enough for Donal to smell her fresh heather and clean air scent. "I was raised by humans, but I have always had a fae friend or guardian or watcher. Always."

Donal blinked at those bright, emerald eyes. Eyes almost exactly the same color as Fionn. Disturbingly close, actually.

Her whole life, dealing with the fae? With people so mercurial that most refused to call them anything but the good neighbors just on the *chance* of offending them?

Donal couldn't quite suppress a shudder at that thought.

EDIK EASED THE *THIRD SON* CLOSER AND CLOSER TO A FEELING OF impending doom.

All right, he was only flying in to the *MacArthur's* dock. He wasn't even flying in first, but following that hippogriff shuttle from the *Horizon Cusp*. And he wasn't last either. He was being followed by the *Spear's Tip* and the *Tsar Nikolai*.

But it still felt like flying to his doom.

Dola looked up from his cat bed, under the helm.

"They won't trap us. They can't risk it," Dola said, words tuned only for Edik's ears. Which they had to be, since Anna, Mason, and North were still on the bridge.

At least Mason wasn't meditating anymore. Or whatever he'd been...

"Just what did you do, if you don't mind my asking, Hierophant?" Edik said.

Anything to give the fluttering bats in Edik's gut a chance to focus on something other than the image of Edik getting arrested, his ship impounded, and spending the rest of his life on a penal colony or something.

Of course, that might have been a sign that Edik had been

watching too many shadow plays in his off hours. Carl swore up and down that Earth didn't have any penal colonies.

"Not much," Hierophant Mason said, and from his tone he wasn't happy about it. "I tried to get the ranking ship's mage of the *MacArthur* to overrule her captain. Magicians, strictly speaking, aren't supposed to participate in executions. And the continued shooting at the *Boyar* felt like an execution to me."

"Why didn't you go straight to those gunboats?" North grumbled.

"The ranking magician was the one on the *MacArthur*. She was the only one senior enough to challenge the captain's orders."

"Well," Anna said slowly, "obviously you were persuasive. They did stop short of murder."

"But that's just it," Mason said. "I wasn't. The ship's mage refuted my every argument." A quick sigh erupted out of him. "Never before have I wanted to *challenge* someone to the *Comórtas Draíocht*. But I wanted to challenge her."

"Why didn't you?" Edik asked. The *Third Son* was getting closer and closer to that landing bay. And the itch between Edik's shoulders kept getting stronger. Worse, he had a light sweat going under his shirt, and his heart was beating hard enough that everyone on the bridge could probably hear it. "You used to duel professionally. She wouldn't have stood a chance."

"She was a Journeyman. She wouldn't have stood a chance anyway. But I wasn't there physically. Wouldn't have been a proper challenge." Mason snorted. "Can you imagine how mad things would get if magicians could issue the challenge from the astral? Nothing would ever get done."

"I've never done it at all," North said. "Not in person or any other way. Only every dueled with this."

North tapped the cutlass at his belt.

"You couldn't fight a magical duel if your life depended on it," Edik said, watching the hippogriff shuttle disappear inside that gaping mouth of a landing bay.

"Izzat so?" North challenged. "Well, maybe I ought to challenge you and—"

"I forbid it," Anna said, voice cold and accent just a little thicker than normal. "There will be no duels between you two on this mission. Not between any two of us. We must present a united front."

"Fine," Edik said. He had no intention of fighting a duel anyway. Truth was, even if he and North tried it, they probably couldn't do much to each other. They were only Initiates, and neither one of them had any dueling certifications.

Would have made for an even sadder duel to fight than to watch.

"Here we go," Edik muttered, and guided his ship inside the cruiser.

The damned thing looked like steel on the inside too. Had to all be ceramics and carterite, but for the life of Edik, this landing bay looked as though it were made from dull, gray steel.

A great steel field, large enough to dock a dozen ships the size of the *Third Son*. Four shuttles appeared to already be in place, and they continued the seafaring theme. Edik didn't know what kind of boats they were, but they were definitely designed for water, not space. They looked to have flat bottoms, and came to a point in front, and they had blocky cabins built above what must have been the waterline.

Silliness. Absolute silliness, and a waste of good opportunity. To Edik, at least.

Worse, those shuttles all looked to have at least one weapons chute each. Just in case.

Well, they were all on the deck already, so the chances were that none of them were offering any threat right now.

That was something, at least.

The hippogriff shuttle had already landed as well, in a painted off zone nearest the other shuttles.

Edik picked a spot facing the hippogriff to set down the *Third Son*. He just liked the symmetry of it.

"All right," he said, as his ship's talons touched down, and the ship settled into place. "We're going out armed, no matter what Earth says. And I should probably go out first, just in case there's trouble. Anna, you behind me. Mason, you behind her, and North, you last."

"What about me?"

Carl's voice sounded strained and weak. That made sense though. He *looked* strained and weak there, leaning against the doorframe.

"You," Anna said in that imperious tone of hers, "will remain aboard the ship. Recuperating."

Carl opened his mouth to argue, but she stepped right in close. She looked like a kitten trying to stare down a Bengal tiger. But she didn't give a millimeter.

"You are still healing," she said. "And if you're even thinking of picking up that sword again, you need to be at full strength when you do it. I won't have you dying to protect me."

"You can't stop that," Carl said.

"He's right about that much," Edik said, standing and joining them there in the now-very-crowded doorway. "Anna, you know full well that any of us would stand between you and danger. But..." Edik turned to Carl. "...she's right. You're not ready. Let's keep you in reserve. Chances are, the other parties will treat this like a show of force. Which means you can be our hole card."

Carl seemed to accept that argument, at least. Which was good. Even this much effort was making the poor man sweat and shake.

Mason guided Carl back to his chair, and helped him strap in. Mason then mumbled a few more spells, and gave Carl a potion that put him right out.

"Was that a sedative?" North asked, accusation plain in his tone.

"Of course not," Mason said, twinkle in his eye. "However, in the process of speeding his healing, that potion might encourage him to rest."

"Thank you," Anna said. "Now, the correct order for us here is this. Edik, you shall go down first. Then North. Reach the bottom and establish flanking positions. I shall follow then, with Nicholas here beside me."

North and Edik both opened their mouths to argue, but Anna said, "Trust me. This will portray our strength as unified and dignified at the same time. If we look as though we don't trust them, they'll assume we have something to hide."

Edik sighed, but agreed. North grumbled, but Edik heard assent in there somewhere.

But before Edik could open the hatch, a voice called from the bridge.

"Repeat, no one is to leave their ship until all ships have landed in the bay."

"What?" Edik said, moving back to his captain's station. "Why are we just hearing this now?"

"I was given my orders, not an explanation," Mr. Nakagawa's head said, floating above the slap pad. Sounded a little terse, to Edik.

So Edik cut the link on him.

Anna gave Edik a raised eyebrow of disapproval.

"He didn't have any more information," Edik said with a shrug. "Why listen to him being officious."

"Someone's pissed off the locals," North grumbled.

Edik agreed, but he had no intention of pointing it out. He could still remember how their last conversation with the *MacArthur* had gone.

"And here I thought Captain Yamato didn't like power plays," Anna said.

"Maybe it's different if he's on the giving end," Edik said.

"Let's not get paranoid," Hierophant Mason said. "These ships are more than a decade old. While they've no doubt been retrofitted and upgraded in many ways, they'll have artifacts of their age. I suspect that while the bay doors are open, the life support spells in the hangar don't work. It's likely as simple as that."

"He has a point," Dola said in English.

"In either case," Edik said, "we wait."

Shortly after finally getting to leave that hippogriff shuttle, Kristoff Tunold was certain of two things.

The first was that Jacobs would have loved this cruiser. It truly did look like all the old ships he used to talk about. And not just from the outside. Inside were narrow corridors, tight ceilings and doorframes. Every centimeter of space at a premium, and all of it made to look like dull steel.

Tunold remembered serving on ships like this one, back when he was still in the Terran Navy himself. But he had forgotten how much he hated them.

They were just so claustrophobic. All that fake steel seemed to press in on him in every direction. Made him hunch as he led his VIPs and security team.

When Tunold was in the service, he'd probably had a seminar or two about the ship design that would have explained why a ship with the bulk of a cruiser couldn't have more room allocated to crew sections.

Stretching his mind as he walked, he thought he could remember being told about how the naval designs were both "efficient" and "traditional."

He had to admit that the "efficient" part was probably true. These things were powered by two of the early HK engines, and those things required a lot of room. Plus, most ships could expect to be at space for months at a time. They needed to carry a lot of supplies. Not just for the crew, but for the spells and alchemy.

The "traditional" part Tunold hadn't really comprehended, not really. Not until he'd come to serve under Jacobs, and Jacobs had regaled Tunold at length about the old ships he'd sailed on the seas, back before technology fell.

This cruiser certainly looked the part. But what Tunold could tell now was that the resemblance went beyond appearances.

The hangar and corridors smelled like oil and metal. And what was more, the ceramics of the decks must have been enchanted. They didn't just look like steel. They rang out like steel under Tunold's boots.

Combined with the rest of the team from Tunold's shuttle, not to mention the *MacArthur* security team he followed to a meeting room said to be "not far" from the hangar, those boots raised a ruckus like a whole orchestra of steel drums.

Yes, Jacobs would have loved this ship.

But Tunold was equally sure Jacobs would have hated the personnel. Or at least, he would have hated Warrant Officer Reynolds.

Warrant Officer Reynolds stood about a half-meter shorter than Tunold, and the puissant little punk tried to make up the difference in attitude and smarm.

Hell, even Tunold wanted to take a few minutes and rearrange the bone structure of the man's face into something resembling a garbage heap. But Jacobs? On as little sleep as he'd had, if Dr. Ramirez was right?

Guaranteed interplanetary incident, and Jacobs thrown in the brig.

As it was, Tunold had to pay extra attention to the little details of the ship around him. Focus on the smell of the oil to try to guess what kind of oil it was. He didn't recognize it. Try to find the memory of an old cadence in the rhythm of his boots (he thought he remembered one about the admiral's cat, but not quite how it went).

Anything to keep from picturing the smarmy fucking smile on that too-tanned face. What kind of naval officer had a tan in this day and age? Might as well scream at every passerby, "I'm vain and pay for alchemical treatments!"

Fortunately, that warrant officer must have seen a look of warning in Tunold's eyes. He put his own security team — Pacifiers and all — between himself and Tunold as he led the procession to that meeting room.

But when they reached the meeting room — after a small eternity that was probably only a minute or two of walking down these cramped, cramped conditions — the bastard had the gall to turn and challenge Tunold. His security team fanned out beside him.

"You, no further," Reynolds said in a tone that just begged Tunold to throw a punch. "VIPs only."

"Forget it," Tunold said.

"I have my—"

"Fuck your orders," Tunold said. "Our contract says that we have to see our VIPs safely to the rendezvous. *This*" — Tunold waved his arms as much as he could without striking a surface or the idiot — "is not the rendezvous. And given that you ships have fired first on civilian vessels—"

"Civilian vessels who were in restricted space."

"—space not listed as restricted on the commonly available charts," Tunold finished for the little bastard. "Given that the Terran Navy fired first on a ship that might have been carrying VIPs for all we know, we are not, in fact, permitting you to take our VIPs anywhere we cannot protect them."

Tunold gestured with his head. The *Horizon Cusp* security team behind him, as one, pulled the collars of their ship's uniforms to one side.

Reynolds gasped, a look of fury entering his officious little eyes. No doubt he recognized some of the finest protective armor available to civilians. If controlled in distribution.

"Safety skinsuits! You had no right to—"

"*You fired on a civilian vessel,*" Tunold reminded him. "We're only taking the steps necessary to protect our passengers from *malfeasance.*"

Tunold wasn't sure that was the right word, but Jacobs had insisted he use it.

Tunold then found out why.

Reynolds' jaw dropped open wide. He cocked back a fist.

"Try it," Tunold growled. "See what happens."

"Excuse me," Donal Cuthbert called from somewhere back in the ranks. "I trust there isn't going to be any more fighting. The Fae Courts were assured that our safety would be guaranteed by Earth, and so far Earth has not been convincing in its ability to keep us safe."

Tunold made a show of crossing his arms and gave Reynolds the most evil smile he had.

"Who is speaking?" Reynolds called back.

"My name is Donal Cuthbert. And I assume your captain told you—"

"Yes," Reynolds growled. "All right, security teams too." Reynolds turned and sent one of his men to carry this news to the ex oh with all speed.

Literally. The man went running down the corridor, his boots tapping out a cadence that Tunold remembered.

Ain't gonna die
Not if I fly
Ain't gonna die
Not if I fly
Be a navy man
Best I can
Fly the worlds
Cause the girls
Love a navy man…

Tunold's smile widened.

"All right," Reynolds grumbled. He stepped aside and waved one arm. "In you go. And don't…" Reynolds shook his head. "No, never mind that. You go ahead and cause all the trouble you want. I'll be only too happy to give it to you."

It was all Tunold could do to step on past the man and into the meeting room.

Jacobs would have been proud of him.

DONAL HAD SEEN MORE THAN HIS SHARE OF MEETING ROOMS OVER THE years. It seemed sometimes that two-thirds of the deliveries he'd made as a courier had been picking up from one meeting room and delivering to another (albeit continents or worlds away).

At the universities and conferences, more meeting rooms. And whenever he got to spend time watching Donatello Mancuso work his own brand of business magic, that had involved a nonstop parade of board rooms, meeting rooms, and the like.

Well, and restaurants. But around Donatello, even restaurants and bars seemed like meeting rooms.

This meeting room? Aboard the *MacArthur*? Had to be the worst of all of them.

First of all, the ubiquity of this mock steel theme was starting to get to Donal. Mock marble, in his cabin aboard the *Horizon Cusp*, made its own kind of sense. The pretense of luxury in deep space.

But all this steel? It was as though Donal had walked into one of those tin cans he'd seen in a museum display in San Francisco. They'd had all kinds of sizes, but none of them much bigger than his two fists combined.

The sight of them had stuck with Donal. He couldn't believe they used to store food in those things.

Today, it seemed, they stored people in them. Or in the appearance of them, at least.

Low ceiling. Low enough that Donal felt like hunching his shoulders. He could only imagine how the tall guys — Edik, Hierophant Mason or that Mr. Tunold — could handle it. They must have felt as though they'd bang their heads any moment.

The room was wide enough. A good eight meters across, both directions. Two big tables butted against each other's sides. Cheap wooden folding chairs surrounded the tables.

Donal couldn't help sniffing at the sight of those chairs. His parents would have called them a waste of passable scrap. Donal knew that even he could have dismantled them and built better chairs out of the same parts.

Glass pitchers full of water were spaced around the tables, along with small tumbler glasses. Small plates held biscuits that smelled fresh baked.

"VIPs only at the tables," Warrant Officer Reynolds called into the room as the *Horizon Cusp* security team filed in behind Donal and Rowan.

Mr. Tunold growled audibly.

Donal muttered to him, "Don't let him get to you. He's a petty tyrant of a tiny kingdom. He resents your freedom. And your height."

Mr. Tunold blinked at Donal, but smiled and clapped him on the shoulder.

Donal took a seat in the center of the far, short side of the combined tables, with Rowan sitting to his right.

"Well done," Rowan murmured to him as they sat, simultaneously.

"Just guessing," Donal admitted. Still. One of his lessons from Donatello Mancuso had been quite clear — know the names of all the support people around you. You need to support them as much as they do you.

The *Horizon Cusp* security team fanned out behind Donal, and for a moment he felt as though it were all too much. There had to have been some sort of mistake.

But one deep breath and that feeling passed. Probably helped that he'd known it was coming. That feeling had hit him just about every six hours like clockwork, ever since he agreed to this voyage.

Donal eased out a more relaxed breath as people he knew filed into the room. Captain Edik Barshai, stylish as always. Red shirt that matched the stripe down the side of his black pants, which disappeared into his boots.

Anna Lukyanova, wearing a turquoise business suit that flattered her pale skin and brought out her blue eyes. Her long blonde hair was done up in a complicated series of braids.

"Don't stand," Rowan muttered as a warning against Donal's more genteel habits. "Not appropriate under the circumstances."

Donal only nodded a fraction.

Hierophant Nicholas Mason came next, with his brown hair tied back in a long ponytail, and wearing a black airsilk suit with the kind of cut that Donatello Mancuso always seemed to compliment.

Dontello was forever trying to get Donal to wear suits like that one. Donal had always counterargued that magicians didn't wear suits.

Now here was Nicholas Mason. Not just a Hierophant, but Donal's personal hero.

In a suit.

Donal had to fight down a sigh. He knew he looked pretty good right now. Not as good as Edik or Hierophant Mason, true, but

Donal's blue-green airsilk shirt and black airsilk slacks were tailored for him, and he'd shined his black loafers just this morning. Still, his look was more casual than formal. And this was a situation that probably merited a more formal look.

Then again, Rowan wasn't wearing anything formal either. Not that it mattered much. In that sundress the various shades of a sunset, she managed to look elegant and casual at the same time.

Probably wore it instead of something more formal because she'd known Donal hadn't brought a suit. She could be thoughtful at the least expected times.

Speaking of informal...

Another man came in with Edik's crew. Shorter and barrel-chested, with black hair that seemed to jut out at all angles from his head. On the top, of course, but also in a chaotic sort of beard that might even have been coming out of his ears. He was dressed like some kind of shadow play pirate, right down to the cutlass. Surprising he didn't have an earring.

Edik worked with this man. Donal was sure of it. Couldn't remember his name though. Donal had been introduced to him, briefly, but the man had only cared about yelling at Edik, so Donal didn't bother trying to remember his name.

Apparently he might need to.

Anna sat opposite Donal, with Hierophant Mason sitting opposite Rowan. Anna had smiled a greeting at Donal, but now she fixed Rowan with a puzzled frown.

Hierophant Mason was staring at Rowan too, but with a slightly absent gaze. No doubt looking past the physical to her other aspects. The Hierophant probably immediately detected that there was more to Rowan than met the eye.

Just another reminder of how much Donal had to learn. He'd met Rowan how many times before finding out she was more than human?

The short man with the chaotic black hair was staring at Rowan in the way Donal had often noticed strange men staring at her. Albeit a bit more blatantly.

Edik gave Donal a wave and a smile as he took up position behind Anna. The other man stood behind Hierophant Mason.

"It's good to see all of you," Donal said, honestly. "It's been too long."

"Yes," Anna said, "you really must come visit us on Luna more often."

"Studies have been taking up a great portion of my time."

"Ah, how they do that," Hierophant Mason said. "I remember all too well how the classes and homework seemed to expand to fill all available moments. And maybe just a little more."

Donal shared a chuckle with him.

"But who is your companion?" Anna asked.

Rowan drew breath to introduce herself, but Warrant Officer Reynolds called into the room, "Save the introductions until all are present."

Donal and Anna shared a frown at that. Who else was coming?

———

EDIK COULD FEEL HIS NERVES JUMPING WITH EVERY BREATH. TRUE, IT was great seeing Donal again. And even better, it was good to see Donal traveling with so very beautiful a woman. That red hair, that clear skin, and the way she filled out that sundress. With a woman like her around, Donal was less likely to develop an interest in Anna.

Anna was beautiful, but this woman was practically Vasilisa the Beautiful, come straight out of a folktale.

Anna might have thought so as well. From the tone in her voice when she asked about the redhaired beauty, Anna might have had designs on Donal.

Surprising, given that Edik had thought Anna was interested in Edmund, back on Luna. Clever, compassionate Edmund, who still thought his two bosses — Edik and North — might one day find enough common ground to become friends.

Quite the dreamer, Edmund.

More likely Anna was just keeping her options open. Edik had to remember that she was still a member of one of Luna's great families, and likely didn't look at relationships the way normal people did.

But right now Edik's nerves were still jumping. As though he might actually have to fight. Every time someone's boots rang out on these ridiculously loud decks, Edik thought he had to go for his saber.

It was all he could do to keep his hands away from it.

He wasn't the only one who felt this way either. North had one hand on the hilt of his cutlass, and he kept twitching at the echo of boots approaching.

Might be better if they could get this over with.

"Who else is coming?" Edik muttered, hoping someone would answer him.

Instead the answer came as more people filed into the room.

First came what looked like the delegation from the *MacArthur* itself. Captain Yamato was taller than Edik expected. Thinner too. Looked long and lean and maybe a little mean, if that puckered scar under his right ear was any indication.

He took the center seat of the side of Edik's left.

Captain Yamato had no advisers with him. Just eight security personnel. A number that, if Edik's quick math was right, would just happen to be one more than Donal had brought with him.

Was that petty? Or was it smart?

Edik had to stop himself from shrugging. If this came to a fight, everyone was going to lose anyway. No way anyone would come out of it intact and looking good.

Donal looked ready to ask questions, but Captain Yamato held up a hand and said, "I see before me either some or all of the invited guests to the coming gathering."

He gestured to his left. "Donal Cuthbert and Rowan MacPherson, representing the Fae Courts of Earth."

"The Fae Courts," Donal corrected him. "The Courts recognize no restraints on their domain, and will not be identified as the Fae Courts of only Earth."

"Very well," Captain Yamato said with a bow of his head. "Donal Cuthbert and Rowan MacPherson, representing the Fae Courts."

"Thank you," Donal said with a nod.

Captain Yamato gestured to his right.

"Here we have Anna Lukyanova, representing the Rhian people of... The Rhian people. Advising her is Hierophant Nicholas Mason."

Anna nodded graciously.

"I do *not* see a representative for the Du Mak," Captain Yamato said, "which brings us to a portion of the day's difficulties."

Edik cleared his throat.

"There is one outside this room—"

Edik cleared his throat more audibly.

"—who claims the authority to speak for the Du Mak."

Edik stopped clearing his throat. Instead, he noisily scraped back a chair and took a seat next to Anna.

That got all eyes on him in a hurry.

"Only the VIPs at the table, please," Captain Yamato said.

"Well," Edik said, trying to ignore the way his heart had sped up. When had it gotten so hot in here? "That's why I'm sitting down, you see. You asked about the representative for the Du Mak."

Edik raised one hand no higher than his chin. "That's me."

"What?" Anna asked.

"I don't know about—" Captain Yamato started.

Donal Cuthbert spoke then, and just like on Ganymede, he seemed to grab everyone's attention without raising his voice, or using even an iota of magic.

"The Fae Courts acknowledge the representatives of the Rhian and Du Mak peoples, and welcome them to these proceedings."

That got the redhead staring at Donal, her lips parted just a little in surprise.

Anna's mouth, in contrast, closed. And she frowned in thought.

"I see," Captain Yamato said. "While I appreciate the position of the Fae Courts in this matter, Earth requires—"

"Earth is in no position to *require* anything until we reach the meeting place," Donal said, leaning forward just a little. "We have all been quite gracious to play along with this uncalled for and arguably unnecessary meeting. That we have done so does not mean that the Fae Courts are ceding any authority to Earth, nor permitting Earth to judge the fitness of any ambassador, liaison, or other representative designated by the Fae Courts, the Rhian, or the Du Mak."

Captain Yamato sat back in his chair, blinking at Donal.

Edik could understand it. Donal didn't seem like the type to throw his weight around in meetings. But then, Edik could remember the way he was in those meetings on Ganymede, and this wasn't surprising Edik at all.

Anna seemed to be watching Donal more closely now though.

"You must understand," Captain Yamato said. "We have someone outside this room who claims to have been given the authority to speak for the Du Mak people. And Earth had not been given the identity of their representative. This leaves Earth in a position of some uncertainty."

"Earth," Rowan MacPherson said, "has tried to flex muscles it does not have. Now, this man..."

Donal whispered something to her.

"This Captain Edik Barshai," she continued smoothly, "he has identified himself as the missing representative, and an ambassador of the Fae Courts has confirmed it. This should be all Earth requires."

"But proof would—"

"Ah, proof," Edik said, trying to emulate Donal's style and falling short, he knew it. "I could prove it, but the Du Mak people would not be happy about it. I'm not supposed to call them here until the meeting itself. And I don't think Earth wants me to—"

"Very well." Captain Yamato frowned as he continued. "Bring in the claimant."

Two security women, both holding white Pacifiers, led a man into the room.

A man Edik immediately recognized. Everyone on Luna would have recognized Rasputin Pajari. Short, but heavily muscled. His black hair cut into a widow's peak that Edik suspected was not natural. And his skin didn't seem to have the nearly translucent pallor that the Lukyanov and Romanov families had.

Still, Edik had to admit that even standing there under guard, he looked more noble that Edik probably ever would.

Anna snorted a laugh. Edik didn't dare.

"This man is Rasputin Pajari," Anna said. Then she spat out rapid-fire Russian Edik couldn't quite follow, followed by more English. "I presume the *Boyar* is his ship?"

"He has two other ships as well," Captain Yamato said, "hanging back at the edge of scanner range."

"The Rhian people did not invite the Pajari family to this gathering."

"Neither did the Du Mak," Edik said, hoping he was right. All he'd been told was to bring that stone to the meeting. The stone that Cinnamon — the only member of the Du Mak that Edik had met — had given him, back at Ganymede. Edik was to bring it to the meeting, and when he arrived, use it to call Cinnamon.

Technically, this made Edik their liaison.

"Nor the Fae Courts," Donal said. "The Fae Courts do not acknowledge the Pajari family's right to attend."

"More than that," Hierophant Mason added. "The log of the *Third Son* will show that Pajari ships fired on us as we tried to leave Luna."

"Thank you," Captain Yamato said with a small smile. "But without anyone else to vouch for him, Earth still requires me to give this man a chance to prove himself. Mr. Pajari, if you truly represent the Du Mak people, call them here."

"I could," Pajari said, sounding insulted at the whole notion, "but much like Captain Barshai there, I would be calling the Du Mak people early, which they do not wish."

Edik drew a deep breath, and took a risk. "I swear on my power that I am, in fact, a liaison of the Du Mak people, sent on this mission that I might summon a specific ambassador when we reach the meeting place."

"I confirm," Donal and Hierophant Mason said at the same time. Donal then deferred to Hierophant Mason to finish. "I affirm and attest myself witness that Initiate Edik Barshai just took a formal magical oath on his power. Captain Yamato, you know what that means."

"Thank you," Captain Yamato said with a nod. Then, to Pajari, he continued, "Can you provide similarly convincing evidence?"

"I cannot," Pajari said, not sounding at all cowed. "But if I might have the use of my hands, I can provide evidence that all of the other ambassadors and liaisons should accept."

Captain Yamato nodded at Pajari's guards. They released his arms.

What Pajari did next was a small thing, but it demonstrated an aspect of the great families that Edik always found frustrating.

Edik, in Pajari's shoes, would have looked nervous. Been sweating. Exaggerated his movements so that there could be no question of his doing anything he wasn't supposed to be doing.

Pajari, though, moved just as slowly. His movements, though, were precise, not exaggerated. He managed to look as though he had all the time in the world. As though this were the sort of simple, unhurried thing every nobleman might be doing at this time of day.

But he pulled out a small stone. A perfect oval of greenish brown shale. The twin of the one in Edik's vest pocket.

Edik had been carrying his for months now. He'd gotten so he could sense it wherever he left it on his ship. Even sometimes let Dola hide it, as a game.

"It's real," Edik said, hardly believing the words, but unable to deny them. He could sense the magic of the Du Mak in the stone Pajari held. It felt different from his own, and yet the same in many ways. "But why—"

"Not all members of the Du Mak people agree with the leadership of the one you call Cinnamon," Pajari said.

Edik felt himself blanch. This man could not have known that name. Not unless...

Edik sighed.

"The Du Mak people acknowledge and welcome this second, true liaison."

"He's right," Donal confirmed. He'd been there when Cinnamon had given Edik the stone, and his thaumaturgic senses dwarfed Edik's, the way Mason's probably dwarfed his. "I can sense the Du Mak in that stone. The Fae Courts also acknowledge and welcome this liaison of the Du Mak people."

"As do the Rhian people." Anna made the words sound as though they tasted bad, though her expression gave away nothing. "Though they hope the Du Mak people will work together at the meeting. And cease having their representatives attack other liaisons."

"That remains to be seen," Pajari said, giving his guards an imperious look.

Captain Yamato dismissed the guards with a nod, then gestured for Pajari to take a seat beside Edik.

Pajari, instead, took a seat on the unoccupied side of the tables.

A bad sign.

Captain Yamato turned a penetrating gaze on Edik.

"Captain Barshai? Can you produce..."

Captain Yamato let the sentence trail off, because Edik pulled out his own stone and held it up. Pajari nodded a stiff acknowledgment.

Captain Yamato then turned to Anna, but she had already produced her own stone from somewhere on her person. Edik suspected she kept it up one sleeve. Hers was the grayish green of lunar rock outside Kennedy's Barrier, but with the yellow-green glow Edik had seen about Oolaut, the only member of the Rhian people he'd properly met.

"I have not met the Rhian people before," Donal said, "but the echo of power within that stone resonates with that of the other two stones in a way I would expect to be consistent with Rhian magic. The Du Mak people described the Rhian as kin, but not in a way we know the word."

"I can confirm that the stone carries the power of the Rhian people," Hierophant Mason said. "I'll swear on my power if it's necessary, but as Anna here has been in the courts and the news representing the interests of the Rhian, I assume I need not."

"You assume correctly," Captain Yamato said. "But thank you Ms.

Lukyanova for producing the stone, and thank both you esteemed magicians for your confirmations. Earth appreciates the gestures."

He then glanced at each delegate in turn, apparently making sure no one else had anything to add right now. No one did.

Captain Yamato raised his voice to carry out into the corridor. "Bring in the other two."

The "other two" were exactly whom Anna expected them to be. They even entered the meeting room aboard the so-very-steel *MacArthur* in the order she expected.

Natalia Romanova came in first. After all, even if Romanov were not the more prominent family on Luna — which is was — she was a woman, and therefore would have been given the opportunity to enter before a gentleman.

And Father, Alexei Lukyanov, was nothing, if not a gentleman. To exactly the same extent that Natalia Romanova was a lady.

In public.

In the boardroom, it was an entirely other matter.

But that was how things were on Luna. Pretense in public, but a very different set of manners in private.

Though the great families defined "private" and "public" in ways that might not have been what most people expected. That much, at least, Anna had learned in her time around Edik, Nicholas, Roger, and especially Edmund.

Natalia, of course, entered looking very much the head of a lunar great family. Enough so that Anna felt a small twist of envy. Natalia wore an airsilk gown of silver, cut conservatively for business, but in a way that still complimented her lean figure.

And of course Natalia wore her golden hair in the same series of braids that Anna had chosen. She would say she did so to support her "sweet Anya," but Anna couldn't help but feel she did it to remind Anna which of them was the more beautiful.

As though any could doubt it. Even entering under guard, Natalia took command of the room as soon as she entered. She needed only a single sweep of her pale, pale blue eyes. She had that kind of undeniable charisma.

Once more, "dear Aunt Natya" made Anna feel awkward and inadequate by her mere presence. Even being ready for the feeling did nothing to diminish it.

Even that Rowan MacPherson probably envied Natalia. A true *noble* beauty, rather than MacPherson's peasant prettiness. But if so, Anna could not tell. The woman gave nothing away with her face, nor her posture.

Following Natalia, and also under guard, came Father. His own charisma outweighing even his heavy physique. Not that most would have guessed Father's weight. Not with the skill of his tailors.

Father wore a dark airsilk suit for the occasion, of course, but with a bold red and gold striped tie that no doubt kept any from noticing the way his own pale blonde hair had thinned on top.

On her own Natalia might have owned the room. But now she had no choice but to share it with Father. The two heads of Luna's two greatest families.

But what were they doing here?

"I presume," Captain Yamato said, "that neither of you intends to claim that you represent the Rhian or Du Mak peoples?"

"Certainly not," Natalia said.

"*Nyet,*" Father said, not deigning to look at Captain Yamato yet.

"And I likewise presume," Captain Yamato continued, "that you do not claim to speak for the Fae Courts."

Neither Father nor Natalia bothered with words for that one. Instead they gave a single shake of the head. Almost entirely in synchronicity.

"And obviously," Captain Yamato continued, "you cannot represent Earth in the coming proceedings, as neither of you are from Earth. Not to mention that *I* have that honor."

Natalia gave the captain a bored look. Father continued to look over the assemblage, as though making a series of decisions about the individuals.

"So," Captain Yamato said, "as there is no lawful reason for you to be here..."

Father and Natalia, again, began to speak at almost the same moment. Father, ever the gentleman, bowed his head and allowed Natalia to respond first.

"I daresay," Natalia said, sounding bored, "that if you had allowed us to speak in the first place, you would not have had to waste so many words. Nor, for that matter, would you have to do us both the indignity of having us guarded like criminals. I can tell you with certainty that neither of us are accustomed to such treatment. Would you not agree, Lyosha?"

"You are correct," Father said, "as you often are, Natya."

"However," Natalia continued, "as you have finally done us the dignity of allowing us to speak, I can assure you that I have every legal right to be here. As, I imagine, does Lyosha here, though I confess I do not know his reasons and am quite interested in hearing them."

"Oh," Father said with a smile, "you will be even more interested in my reasons than your own, I do suspect."

"And will we be getting to those reasons anytime today?" Captain Yamato asked.

Father tutted.

Natalia gave a small, scoffing sound.

"No sense of order or priority," Father said.

"Truly," Natalia agreed, "there are no standards anymore. Outside of our own, dear Luna, of course."

Captain Yamato opened his mouth to say something, and from his expression, it would have been scathing, but Natalia spoke first.

"I, of course, am Natalia Romanova. However, I am not here today promoting the interests of the Romanov Group. Rather, instead, my friends on Mars tell me that Earth has tried to deny them a seat at the table?"

"Mars is under Earth jurisdiction," Captain Yamato said. "They have no place at this table, for they are bound by any agreements Earth makes."

"Ah," Natalia said, "but that is a matter under some dispute, yes? Thus the shooting war happening even now out on Mars between the Terran Navy and the newly formed Martian Navy?"

"A fancy name for rebels," Captain Yamato said, irritation as plain on his face as in his voice. "But they can call themselves independent all they want. That doesn't make it fact."

"Perhaps," Natalia said, holding to a look of slightly haughty amusement while keeping her voice neutral. "Perhaps not. In terms of government, who can say until the last shot has been fired and some sort of truce agreed to?"

"*I* can say," Captain Yamato said, "because I speak for *Earth*."

"Ah," Natalia said, her smile managing to grow only the tiniest bit. Just the right touch of humor and arrogance entered her voice as she continued.

The woman had truly mastered the art of speech. Anna could only pray to become as good someday.

"However, there are more considerations on Mars than governmental, yes? You would surely not deny that, Captain Yamato. And when the shooting is done, Earth will have to deal with those considerations. No?"

"You mean the corporations?" Captain Yamato's turn to scoff. "They have less right to a seat at this table than the so-called Mars Confederacy."

"Perhaps," Natalia said with the perfect shrug. Fractions of a centimeter. Bare suggestion, and yet there was no way anyone missed it. "If that is Earth's final ruling, then of course I will be happy to take my leave. And when I do, Earth will have to figure out how it can build more ships without carterite."

She let the word hang in the air with the patience of a true master. As though the word itself had to have time to slowly expand to fill the room, until it managed just a slight echo against the apparently steel walls, floor and ceiling.

Carterite. The reason a flight from Luna to Mars took days instead of weeks. And Anna suspected as alchemists continued to study the substance, they might unlock yet more mysteries.

Oh, what she would have given to be part of such a study.

But those were thoughts for another time. She set them aside for now.

"The Mars corps—" Captain Yamato began, but Natalia cut over him with a tone that brooked no debate.

"Are united with their multi-planetary brethren in this. Earth will receive no more shipments of carterite if the Mars corporations are denied a seat at the table through their representative. They are *very* interested in opening up a dialog with the Fae Courts and the Rhian and Du Mak peoples."

Anna couldn't help a small smile at that. A brilliant move on the part of those corporations. Not so much as a single executive could be held prisoner by Earth, if Earth tried to fight them on this. Not with Natalia here as their representative. And if they took her, they would have a problem on the Luna front that might make Mars look like a Sunday picnic.

"And I have only your word on this?" Captain Yamato said.

"But of course not," Natalia said. "At least, not once I am given permission to move by your silly guards." She gave the captain a droll look. "Honestly. As though I need to be under guard."

The captain nodded at his guards and they stepped back.

Natalia reached into her belt sash and pulled out an actual piece of paper. It was a yellowish kind of white, folded into thirds.

Anna had to smile at that as well. No memoboard record of the transactions. The corporations could have full deniability if this did not go the way they wanted, and Earth could have had no warning through transferred copies of the document.

She passed it across the table.

Captain Yamato unfolded it. Scanned it. Turned to one of his guards. "I need an authenticator."

The guard left.

"Very well," Captain Yamato said. "If our authenticator can confirm those signatures, then I will accept your place at this table. Though Earth will note that such acceptance is under duress, and not an indication of Mars' right to participate. Further, the record will show that only the corporations are represented here, and not the so-called Mars Confederacy."

"As you would have it, Captain," Natalia said. "Though I would point out that you are missing an opportunity to gain recognition on Mars."

"Recognition I do not need," Captain Yamato said. He turned to Father.

"And you, Mr. Lukyanov. Are you here representing Mars corporate interests as well? I know the Lunar corporations all have too many ties on Earth to risk a play like this. And Luna doesn't have anything as valuable as carterite to use as a bargaining chip. So is Venus so arrogant that they're already trying to declare independence and doing it through you?"

"Nothing of the kind, I assure you," Father said. "My representation is of a sort much closer to my heart." He raised one hand in denial. "*Nyet*, I do not represent the Lukyanov Group in this matter. Of course. Most inappropriate, that would be. Especially with my own dear daughter already a party to the proceedings. One could hardly call that fair."

"So," Captain Yamato said. "Why *are* you here?"

"Why, to represent Luna, of course."

Donal couldn't help chuckling. He should have seen that coming. That Luna would have sent a representative to this meeting.

The Rhian were discovered on Luna. Lunar universities were leading the research to the extent that they were allowed. The local Lunar government was trying to establish precedents and pass laws surrounding their new population and what to do about them.

And that included the efforts by Anna and Hierophant Mason to get them declared Lunar citizens.

But when Donal chuckled, everyone in the meeting room turned to look at him. Including Mr. Lukyanov, who did not have a friendly look on his face.

Donal wasn't sure how to read that. He'd never met Mr. Lukyanov before. Ms. Romanova, of course, he knew. She'd tried to have him killed in Kennedy once. Then Donal had saved her life on a flight to Venus, and she'd quitclaimed all vengeance that she felt she'd been entitled to under Luna's code of moral law.

Donal still wasn't quite sure how any of that worked. How delivering a package could have been interpreted as a moral crime than merited a death squad from a private individual? Or a corporation, for that matter?

And Mars was the one considered more like an untamed frontier. Luna was supposed to be civilized. Or as civilized as Earth, at least.

He had met her again on Ganymede, where he had outmaneuvered her. No doubt she was here for a rematch of some sort. She seemed the type to keep score.

Which meant that Mr. Lukyanov likely was as well. And Donal had already slighted him. Albeit unintentionally.

"Excuse me," Donal said. "I mean no offense. It was just, well, of course he's here to represent Luna. I mean, he's the head of a lunar great family. He has business ties from Kennedy to Markowitz and beyond, I'm sure. It only makes sense."

Donal shrugged. "The unexpected obvious sometimes makes me chuckle."

"You can stop talking now," Rowan whispered, managing to do it without even moving her lips.

Donal had to fight down a blush. Fortunately, much training as he'd had with meditation and controlling his body's systems, that took little effort anymore.

Still, it was embarrassing to have started rambling again. Donatello would have rolled his eyes and lectured him for it. Once they were alone, anyway.

Never in front of others.

"Well," Ms. Romanova said, "while I have no doubt that Lyosha here means well, I do have some trouble believing that Luna would ask a Lukyanov to represent Lunar interests ahead of a Romanov."

"Well, dear Natya," Mr. Lukyanov said, "perhaps it is not intended as a slight against the Romanovs. Perhaps it is merely that you have been so busy away from Luna of late, while I myself have been bringing Lukyanov off-world interests to Luna to make deals, that—"

"Enough," Captain Yamato said, and Donal flashed on Captain Jacobs barking out that word in much the same tone. Had to have been a navy thing.

"I am less interested in your petty squabbles than I am in your current status," Captain Yamato said. "Mr. Lukyanov, if you have some evidence to back up your claim, present it now. Then and only then will I decide if your claim has merit."

"The Rhian people acknowledge the merit of the Lunar claim," Anna said. "The fact or absence of his evidence does not change the Rhian opinion. If he is here as their representative, fine. If not, Luna still deserves representation. If not by a member of one of the great families, then by a Lunar government official."

"That is not the Rhian people's decision to make," Captain Yamato said. "There has been no declaration of Lunar independence—"

"Hasn't there, Captain?" Mr. Lukyanov said, and produced his own folded pieces of paper.

This was the most *actual paper* Donal had seen in months. And, excluding specific thaumaturgic uses for paper, perhaps the most he'd seen in one place, ever.

Well, outside of books and refillables, of course.

Certainly, only magicians could properly work zephyrpads, but surely these people owned a memopad or two.

Mr. Lukyanov passed his papers across the table.

Captain Yamato's face grew still as he read them both.

"I see," he said at last. "You understand that a declaration of Lunar independence, presented only to me—"

"Would be most foolish," Mr. Lukyanov said. "I do agree, of course, as do my friends in the newly formed Lunar Council. Which would be why they have sent out their formal announcement today through every proper news network and official channel. This paper I give you, it is only a courtesy."

Mr. Lukyanov's words seemed to fill the room with their implications. No way Earth would allow Luna to declare independence. Not without a military challenge.

But then again...

Earth was already fighting one war out around Mars. And enforcing its control of Ganymede. And maintaining the no-fly zone here near Venus, where it kept another strong presence.

The truth was, Earth might not have the ships to force Luna to comply right now. Not if Luna had been building its own military.

Had it?

Ms. Romanova was giving Mr. Lukyanov a calculating look now.

"So," she said so softly Donal might not have heard if the rest of the room hadn't been so quiet. "You *have* been busy, Lyoshka."

"I have done nothing you would not do in my shoes, Natya."

"Perhaps. We shall see."

Meanwhile, Captain Yamato continued to look over the sheets of paper in front of him.

He drew in a deep breath. "Well, in this case my duty is clear."

Captain Yamato stood. Pointed at Mr. Lukyanov.

"Security. Place this man under arrest for treason against Earth."

When Captain Yamato made that declaration, a dozen things or more all seemed to happen at once. So many that Edik had trouble keeping them straight, especially with all the damned echoes off those fake steel surfaces.

First, of course, was Anna. She leapt to her feet, objecting with every iota of body and spirit she possessed, which, especially in the latter case, was considerable.

Lukyanov, of course, objected as well, in a voice that rang out so loud and clear he ought to have been an opera singer.

More surprising was that Romanova objected. Edik had expected her to sit back and enjoy while Lukyanov got taken away in chains, or something. Binders, anyway. But she objected just as strenuously.

Pajari, he jumped to his feet too, objecting every bit as loud as Romanova. Albeit a bit more shrilly.

All of this, while guards began to move in. And worst of all, North drew his cutlass.

Oh, he didn't leap to defend Lukyanov or anything stupid like that. But what he did was almost as bad. He squared off as though he thought the order to arrest Lukyanov applied to Anna as well, and he was *not* going to let that happen.

Loyal, North appeared to be. If stupid.

But then Donal and Hierophant Mason locked eyes, and reached their hands toward one another, chanting. Edik could feel the power build between the two of them. And it was a considerable amount of power. Enough that the hairs on his arms and the back of his neck all stood up.

Edik couldn't imagine what they could be doing. No way either one of them was going to take a direct magical action against the Terran Navy. That was a death sentence. Not even a trial, necessarily, at high space. Magicians were deemed too dangerous to await trial, after the MacIntosh Incident last year.

But whatever it was they meant to do — whatever it was they *were* doing — it went away all at once. Just fizzled out, when the mist rose.

And that was the only way Edik could think of it.

It was definitely mist. Grayish white, cool, and faintly moist.

And it definitely rose. It seemed to seep up through the deck and fill the room.

All the shouting that was going on? It was all eaten by the mist. Even those damned echoes.

There *was* magic of some kind to the mist. Edik could feel it, not that he doubted it. After all, wasn't as though mist just regularly arose on ships at high space. Edik was pretty sure he'd have heard about something like that.

And yet...

And yet this didn't feel like magic, not the way Edik knew it. He wasn't the most knowledgeable or experienced magician, that was true. In fact, if it didn't concern the thaumaturgy involved in travel, odds were pretty good that Edik wouldn't know it.

Unless the topic was something really basic, like rudimentary wards or something along those lines.

But this, this mist, it was definitely magic. Edik could feel it the way he felt magic. Like a tugging just beyond his sense of touch. A sensation he could refine if he focused on it.

And this mist, it tugged at him.

But the force *behind* the mist. It didn't tug the way anything else did. Not like elements, or planetary magic. Nor even like the pure and simple energy that seemed to flow pretty much everywhere in the universe.

This mist, this was something different. Different the way the Du Mak and Rhian peoples were different. But not like them either. Edik knew how they felt.

This mist wasn't their work. Which meant...

What did it mean?

Anna grabbed Edik's hand. He shifted his grip quickly, and gave her hand as comforting a squeeze as he could...

...then felt embarrassed. Of course she wasn't seeking comfort. She was making sure they didn't get separated.

Edik grabbed the nearest table leg with his other hand.

"Can anyone hear me?" he said.

He couldn't hear his own words. He felt his lips and tongue move, felt the vibration in his throat. But he heard no sound at all, except the mist itself. A soft, gentle susurrus. Barely loud enough to register.

But he could smell the mist now too, and what he smelled made his stomach clench.

When Edik had been a boy, back on Earth, his father had taken him camping from time to time. And this one time, they'd hiked deep within a Russian forest near St. Petersburg. On their third day out, they'd found this lake. It wasn't on any maps. It might not even have been a proper lake. Edik's father had insisted it was only a pond.

But Edik, he couldn't have been more than eight years old. And to him, the "pond" seemed so vast and huge it had to be a lake. The only reason it wasn't an ocean or sea was that Edik could see the other side of it.

He pretended he didn't though. He dubbed it "Lake Barshai" which made his father laugh. It became their secret then. Their own lake, out in the middle of the forest, where nobody else could bother them.

The lake smelled like clean water, pine and fresh fish. It was so full of salmon that there had to be some underground stream feeding it, as well as taking water away. No other reason Edik could think of, once he was old enough to think about this, that salmon could have been caught in something that wasn't more than a large pond or a very small lake.

But that smell, it stayed with Edik. It was a secret smell. Something he told no one about. Not even Dola, though that was only because it never occurred to Edik to say anything about Lake Barshai.

But Edik smelled Lake Barshai in the mist.

Sweat began to form at the back of Edik's collar, and under his arms. He found himself gripping Anna's hand tighter.

"CAN ANYONE HEAR ME?" he yelled.

But still, he could not hear his own words.

The table leg slipped from his grasp.

That shook him. Hard. The leg wasn't pulled away from him, nor he from it. His grip never faltered. It was just that one moment he held that cold metal leg tight in his right hand.

The next moment, his hand was an empty, clenched fist.

The table leg was gone. And so was the table when he groped for it.

His chair went next, but Edik didn't fall. The chair vanished beneath him, but Edik was simply standing. Standing on that steel deck. Assuming it still appeared to be a...

No. The feel under his boots was wrong now. He no longer felt the perfectly level deck beneath his boots. The surface was just a little irregular.

More like a natural surface, than fired ceramics...

The mist began to lift then.

No. Not lift. Not really. It wasn't that it rose up and went away. It just seemed that whereas a moment before, all Edik could see was that gray-white mist, now he could see Anna's arm. Then all of Anna. And on the other side of Anna, he could see Hierophant Mason, holding her other hand.

And North, alas, holding Mason's other hand.

But that "alas" felt hollow, even in the privacy of Edik's mind. While the thought of North getting lost in the mist was one that should have brought him visceral pleasure, Edik found that, deep down, he didn't actually want North to just vanish into the mist.

An odd thought, that one, and new.

But this was not the time to worry about it.

Edik could see more now, as the mist continued to thin. He could just make out the sight of Donal, standing a handful of meters in front of him. Holding hands with Rowan MacPherson.

Now he could see Captain Yamato, and Alexei Lukyanov, Natalia Romanova, and Rasputin Pajari.

None of them were holding hands. But they were all standing there, looking just as mystified as Edik felt.

And yet, he noticed that exactly one person present did *not* look mystified by what had happened.

Rowan MacPherson.

At least, Edik *thought* that was Rowan MacPherson.

6

GOING OVER REPORTS FOR THE THIRD TIME DID NOTHING TO EASE Jacobs' nerves. He didn't like deviations from procedure. Especially when they came unilaterally from the Terran Navy, at high space.

Bringing all the VIPs together aboard the *MacArthur* was never part of the plan. The plan, in fact, had been simple.

Ships meet at the rendezvous point, on the edge of the no-fly zone near Venus.

Terran Navy ships fly escort from that point, into the no-fly zone to the location that, apparently, had been agreed to by all parties as the site for this big, important meeting.

Ships that could dock there would dock. Ships that couldn't sent their VIPs over in shuttles.

Earth changed the rules.

Without warning.

Had to be orders from above.

Too big a risk for a career man like Yamato to take on his own. No, odds were that Earth knew about the other ships, but because they lacked a formal invitation, used their arrival as an excuse to seize control.

They had the ships here. They had the firepower. And now they had the VIPs.

The tension gripping muscles from his butt to his brains told Jacobs that this was as far as the *Horizon Cusp* was going to be allowed to go. Earth was going to find some pretext to ferry the VIPs the rest of the way.

Separate them from their support. Create a strong-arm position to advance whatever Earth outcome wanted out of this deal. Not much finesse, but Earth was stretched pretty thin right now.

Jacobs looked up from his phantasmal display and out of the transparent ceramic dome toward the *MacArthur*...

...and saw something impossible. Something Jacobs hadn't seen in all his years at space. Hell, something he hadn't seen since his days of sailing the seas.

Mist.

But that was ridiculous. Mist was air and water. And while Machado had nattered on once in a while about what space really was, Jacobs was pretty damned sure it didn't involve a whole lot in the way of air or water.

But that sure as hell looked like mist arising around the *MacArthur*.

"Mr. Hernandez," Jacobs said, "get me the *MacArthur*. And tell Mr. Machado I want him on the bridge *now*. Mr. Grabowski, what the hell is that mist?"

"Mist, sir?" Grabowski sounded more puzzled than Jacobs, which was not what he wanted from his scanners officer.

"Yes, mist. Around the *MacArthur*. Sure as hell doesn't look like a nebula. And there wasn't a nebula here five minutes ago, unless there's something you'd like to tell me."

Grabowski fumbled with the handles of his scanners, while making little confused sounds about not seeing any mist.

Jacobs marched down the short spiral staircase from his captain's station to the deck of the bridge.

"Captain," Mr. Hernandez said as Jacobs passed communications, "I can't raise the *MacArthur*."

"Keep trying. If you can't then get me the *Kansas* or the *Lexington*." Jacobs stopped right behind Grabowski, who had his face screwed up in concentration, while working his handles for all he was worth.

Jacobs tapped Grabowski on the shoulder.

The poor kid jumped so hard Jacobs almost felt bad.

Jacobs didn't say anything. Just fixed Grabowski with a commanding glare and point up, through the dome, and at the now-almost-invisible *MacArthur*.

Grabowski's jaw dropped. "What the hell is that?"

"That, Mr. Grabowski," Jacobs said in a dangerously quiet voice, "is what you have five seconds to tell me."

"But, sir, there's nothing. I mean, I can't." Grabowski grabbed the handles again and turned paler than Tunold.

"Sir," Grabowski said in a small voice. "It's gone."

"What do you mean, gone?" Jacobs said. "The *MacArthur*—"

"No, sir," Grabowski said, taking his life in his hands as he interrupted his captain. "I mean the space there. In that ... mist? Our lacuna says there's no space there."

"Then what is there?"

"That's just it." Grabowski turned a miserably scared and confused face to Jacobs. "There's *nothing* there. Not space. Not a planet. Not a ship. The lacuna is saying that there's nothing at all there. Not even space."

"That may be what it's saying," Jacobs said in a soothing tone, "but we both know that's not possible. Which means the lacuna is detecting something it's never detected before and doesn't understand. Maybe it doesn't even want to look there. But you make it look, Mr. Grabowski. You keep making it look until it sees something you can understand. Just focus on your job. Leave the rest to me."

"But, sir, Mr. Tunold... And we have security people..."

"And I'm going to bring them home, along with our passengers." Steel in Jacobs' voice now. And the steel of it did more to settle his nerves than anything else could have.

Jacobs didn't know what game Earth was playing, but it was fucking with the wrong captain.

"I will bring them back," Jacobs said. "But right now I need to know everything you can tell me about that mist."

"Aye, sir."

"Hernandez," Jacobs said, turning and heading back toward his station, "any luck raising the *MacArthur*?"

"No, sir. It's like they're out of range. But I've never run across that before."

"And you're not likely to again," Jacobs said, continuing his way back to his station. "Our links can reach from here to Mars and maybe beyond. And they'll get upgraded if Starchaser Spacelines starts going to Ganymede."

Normal things. Jacobs knew he had to give his crew some sense of normalcy, or the stress would eat them alive.

Much like it was eating his guts right now. And his muscles. Jacobs shook his head as he ascended the stairs to his station. He'd need a potion from Ramirez. No doubts about it. But he couldn't risk one that took away his edge right now.

"Sir, I have the *Lexington*."

"Good man," Jacobs said as he eased down into his chair and pretended not to sigh as he did. "Put him through."

"Her, sir," Hernandez said as a warning.

The head that appeared above Jacobs' slap pad was younger than he expected. Again. So many kids these days running ships. This one barely had any good command lines going in her yellow-brown complexion. Hardly any gray in her short, straight black hair.

But she had a pretty good command glare. Jacobs had to give her that. Wasn't as good as his own, of course, but still, it was a good one. Time would make it even better.

"Captain Paulson here," she said, her voice a little too nasal for proper command weight. "Can we make this quick, Jacobs? We have something of a situation here."

"What you have is my VIPs and my crew aboard a ship that has vanished from our scanners behind some kind of mist. So I'd like to know just what the hell is going on?"

"So would we."

"You're saying this wasn't planned?"

"Let's not get paranoid, Jacobs," Paulson said with a raised eyebrow. "We've been playing this above board. We're as in the dark as you are. You figure something out, contact me. Otherwise, I'll link you when I hear something. *Lexington* out."

She cut the link before Jacobs could object. Punching his palm made him feel a little better. And the sting was good. Real. Not just stress.

"Captain?"

Machado. Standing at the base of the Jacobs' stairs. Jacobs hadn't even heard him come onto the bridge. How could Jacobs have missed that? The big man wasn't exactly known for his stealth.

"That mist, Mash," Jacobs said, looking down, but pointing up. "What is it?"

"What mist, sir?" Machado asked, puzzled. But he was looking in the right direction.

At the same moment, Mr. Grabowski yelled from his station.

"Captain! The *MacArthur* just vanished!"

THE MIST CLEARED, AND JUST AS DONAL HAD EXPECTED BY NOW, HE NO longer stood within the meeting room aboard the *MacArthur*. Rather, instead, he stood within a wide ring of toadstools atop a green, grassy hill.

In the distance, he could see a shimmering white castle to the north, and an light-devouring ebon castle to the south. To the east, a vast forest of primarily evergreens. To the west, a crystal sea.

The sky above was the royal blue of deep summer, with fluffy clouds gently floating by in a breeze that barely kissed Donal's cheeks down on the hilltop. And the sun in that sky looked like molten gold.

The air was so fresh and clean, it smelled like nothing Donal had smelled before. Not even Santa Cruz on a spring morning smelled as fresh and clean as this. The grass lent a slight spice to the air, like a touch of pepper in a glass of spring water.

After the mist — which had smelled like fresh-mown grass and his mother's soda bread — Donal had expected a more familiar scent here. Something that would make him feel relaxed. At home.

Because Donal was sure he stood in Faerie.

Everyone was here. Well, everyone Donal expected to be here, at least. Rowan, of course, and himself. Still holding hands to ensure they weren't separated during the passage.

Edik, Anna, Hierophant Mason, and that scruffy, barrel-chested man who came in with them. They were all here, and all holding hands.

Ms. Romanova was here, as was Mr. Lukyanov, and even Mr. Pajari. None of them held hands. No real surprise though.

And from the *MacArthur*, only Captain Yamato was brought through. Not one of his ship's security forces seemed to have followed him through the mist.

Donal looked behind himself. Sure enough, Mr. Tunold and the security team from the *Horizon Cusp* were absent as well.

Rowan released Donal's hand. Held up both of hers in a gesture of welcoming.

For the first time since the mist cleared, he got a good look at the woman standing beside him.

Everyone *else* had come through the mist looking exactly as they had in that meeting room aboard the *MacArthur*. Down to their clothing and weapons.

But not Rowan.

Oh, she still wore that sundress in various shades of the sunset, and her hair was still red. But otherwise…

Her skin glowed. A gentle yellow-white light seemed to emanate from her pores. She stood taller now. Perhaps as many as ten centimeters. Easily taller than Donal now.

Her once-crimson hair fell that had fallen just past her shoulders fell all the way to her waist now, in waves the deep red shades of late sunset.

And her face. No one could look at her now and call her beauty anything but otherworldly. She shone now with such radiance that even the *leannan sidhe* at her finest would have been put to shame, had Morna been standing beside her now.

How could Donal ever have mistaken this woman for having only a little fae blood? For being nothing more than a human-fae hybrid child?

She was exactly what she'd claimed to be. Rowan MacPherson, or whatever her true name was, had been born one of the *Daoine sidhe* herself. Even if she had been raised by humans, as she'd said.

Donal closed his jaw. He wasn't sure exactly when it had fallen open, but at least he wasn't alone. Pretty much everyone was staring at her right now, and only Hierophant Mason's jaw wasn't slack.

"Ladies and gentlemen," she said, and her voice came out higher and clearer than Donal was used to. Indisputably a voice made for singing. "Welcome to the true rendezvous point."

"Captain," Mr. Hernandez called up from communications, "the *Lexington* says they don't know either. They'll update us when they know something."

"Well you tell them," Jacobs said, his voice seething with the need to punch something, "that's *not fucking good enough*. I have crew and passengers on that ship."

"Captain," Machado said, carefully, from the foot of the stairs below the captain's station.

Jacobs looked back down at his ship's mage, who had a thoughtful expression on his face as he stared up through the transparent ceramic dome and into nearby space.

"You said there was a mist. Is that right?"

"Yes."

"An actual mist. Not a slip of nebula. Not—"

"I said a mist and I meant a fucking mist. Are you going to tell an old sailor what mist looks like?"

"No, sir," Machado said, maddeningly calm. "I just want to make sure that the word was precisely chosen, under the circumstances."

Jacobs didn't give that any response but a raised eyebrow. But from Jacobs, a raised eyebrow could speak volumes.

"I've been studying up on the Celtic fae," Machado said. "The stories tell of people getting lost in the mist and ending up in Faerie."

Jacobs blinked at that. "You mean…"

"I mean that no magician has ever reported on real interactions with the fae. At least not since the rise of magic, which means that the old sources are hard to trust. We don't know which are reportage and which are fictive. But it seems to me that, especially with the Courts involved, that they might be able to control when and where that mist appears."

"You're suggesting that the goddamn faeries just pulled an entire Terran Navy cruiser into Faerieland?"

"That's my working hypothesis," Machado said with a shrug. "I didn't get to observe it. Perhaps if I coordinate with the naval magicians, I can figure out more."

"Do it," Jacobs said. "And if they refuse, you let me know."

Machado hustled down the stairs and into a cross-legged sitting position against the transparent outer bulkhead of the bridge.

Jacobs turned to the rest of his bridge crew. "Mr. Hernandez, try getting me the *Kansas*. Maybe they'll be more helpful. Mr. Burke, you get ready to take us into that no-fly zone. Just in case. Mr. Grabowski, scan just as far into the no-fly zone as you can. The Terran Navy knows more about this than they're letting on. I can feel it."

That wasn't all he could feel, unfortunately. The stress of this was getting to Jacobs. Too little sleep, and now too much sudden pressure. And he just wasn't a young man anymore.

He found himself sitting in his chair without meaning to. Feeling lightheaded, which didn't jibe with all the muscles in his system being so tense.

Well, he had to admit that his breaths were a little short and quick…

Jacobs stabbed one finger into the right spot in the middle of the tiny illusory facsimile of his gryphon ship. Twisted.

The owlish features of Dr. Ramirez appeared above Jacobs' slap pad.

"John," Dr. Ramirez said immediately. "You're sweating like you've been boxing. Any numbness? Pain?"

"No," Jacobs said, shaking against some dizziness. "Nothing like that, just…"

"I'm on my way," Dr. Ramirez said. "As senior medical officer of the *Horizon Cusp*, I order you not to leave that seat. Don't even try to stand."

Jacobs nodded and cut the link. Gritted his teeth at the way the bridge seemed to swim around him.

"Communications," he said, and it didn't come out as loud or sharp as he wanted. "Get me…"

Jacobs dropped back in his seat. Panting. Ramirez was right. He was sweating like a pig. Jacobs took off his cap. Wiped his forehead with one sleeve.

Damn it, he thought. *Not now.*

Jacobs forced his breaths slow and deep. Focused through the spin of his surroundings. Made his voice louder.

"Hernandez, I want someone official on that link and I want it now. Grabowski… Grabowski … get me…"

"I don't have anything yet, sir. I'll keep at it."

"No good," Machado said, from the place he'd been sitting. Then called up, "John!"

Machado was standing over Jacobs now. Surely the big mage didn't move *that* fast. Goldberg would never have believed it. But Jacobs would have sworn that Machado was…

"John," Machado said, hands checking his captain's wrists, as he stared into his eyes. "John. What day is it?"

"It's … the day you die … if you don't…"

"Belay that shit, Captain," Machado said. And just *hearing* a naval term escape Machado's lips was jarring enough to get another deep breath down Jacobs.

It wasn't enough. Captain Jacobs passed out.

<hr>

THIS WAS ALL A LITTLE TOO MUCH, TOO FAST FOR EDIK.

One moment they were all sitting in that fake-steel meeting room. Someplace Edik really didn't want to be. True. But it was someplace that made sense.

Then the mist.

Then Rowan MacPherson looked like something straight out of a fairy tale. And not a proper Russian tale either. Maybe one of those Irish ones. Scottish maybe. Something like that.

Still, he had to admit that where she'd been beautiful before, she was something else now. Something too much, the way all of this was too much.

Looking at her almost caused physical pain.

Unless he was mistaken, Edik was not the only one who felt that way. He certainly thought he heard Anna mutter, "Oh, come *on*."

So instead of looking at the dangerously beautiful woman, Edik tried to figure out where he was.

A hilltop? Surrounded by mushrooms? Under a sky that looked for all the world like Earth?

Green grass on the hill, with none of the oddities of the lunar attempts at replicating Earth terrain. None of those in the air, either. The air here smelled better than anywhere Edik had ever been before.

Well, maybe except for Lake Barshai. But this place just smelled fresh and clean. Not like anyplace Edik had been before.

Then there were those castles in the distance. They looked like a choice between good and evil if ever Edik had seen one.

Forest and sea to round things out.

Sea. Not Russia then. Where? The UNAS? Somewhere in Europe?

Maybe Ireland? Seemed like it would suit ... whatever that MacPherson woman was. But surely Ireland didn't have forests that vast, or castles that ... clean. Both directions, they both seemed unreal.

The same way Rowan looked unreal...

Hells. This was Faerie.

Then Rowan offered up a formal greeting. Like she was the hostess. Cemented that idea in Edik's mind.

She was going to be a problem, like she was. Even her voice was such that Edik had trouble paying attention to her words, because just the sound of her voice was entrancing.

Edik called Dola out of his house.

"Why are we in Faerie?" Dola asked immediately. The shaggy gray cat looked solid here. Not translucent at all.

Edik started to say something about the MacPherson woman, but Dola acted before he could. Dola just hoisted himself up on his back paws, put his forepaws on Edik's shoulders.

Edik looked right into his familiar's cerulean eyes without being told.

He felt a burst of magic pass between them.

A sensation washed down Edik. Like stepping quickly through an icy waterfall.

Edik shook himself.

But now, the MacPherson woman looked ... tolerable. Still so beautiful she was fucking *glowing*, but now her sheer presence didn't seem to dig right down into Edik's essence and command his attention.

She was still more beautiful than any human had the right to be — if she was, in fact, human, which Edik was coming to doubt — but that beauty no longer called to part of Edik in a way he couldn't explain.

Dola glanced at Edik a moment longer, then dropped his forepaws down to the ground and took his place at Edik's right hand.

"A moment please," Hierophant Mason said. "It seems to me that only you are currently in any condition for a reasonable meeting right now, Ms. MacPherson."

Hierophant Mason raised an eyebrow. "Well, perhaps you and Donal."

"Where we stand now," the MacPherson woman said, "I cannot

appear other than as I am without using glamour. But if I use glamour…"

"I understand," Hierophant Mason said with a nod of his head. "May I level the playing field?"

"Of course," she said with a smile that, even now, seemed to warm Edik more than a little. "I was hoping you would."

Hierophant Mason mumbled a spell…

And felt a second waterfall sensation that made him need to shake himself as though he had as much fur as Dola.

Sighs, all around the group. But relaxed sighs. Not as though anyone was about to start spouting poetry.

Instead, people gushed out different words all at once.

"What do you—" Anna started.

"Where are—" That one came from both Romanova and Pajari.

"How did we—" Lukyanov started.

All of those questions crashed together, flooded quickly with more questions. A few accusations. And more than a few threats, implied and expressed.

That was as near as Edik could piece it all together. It was too much for him to really follow.

Rowan MacPherson held up her hands again. And this time she had to say something to get everyone's attention.

A tiny, silvery note of power sang through her words, but nothing she tried to hide.

"If I might have your attention, I'll attend to all your questions. After all, I wish you all to feel at ease here."

"Here?" North said, and there was nothing restrained about the way he openly drooled over MacPherson. "On a fucking hillside?"

"Very well," she said, "I'll address that one first. You might notice the ring of toadstools around us? Far easier to effect the transfer to a spot such as this one."

"But there was no ring of toadstools where we were," Hierophant Mason said.

"If I may," Romanova said. "While I'm sure we're all *very* interested in the technical aspects of this teleportation, I find more immediately compelling the need to know exactly where we are. How long we will be here. Where we are to hold this meeting. And how and when we should expect to be returned safely to our ships."

Romanova fluttered her eyelashes and somehow made the move look as though it promised violence.

MacPherson smiled. "I hear an underlying question to the ones you asked. If I might answer it first?"

"So long as the answer doesn't take too long. My explicit questions are more pressing."

"Very well." MacPherson took a step forward, into the circle they'd all unconsciously formed. "It is the opinion of the Fae Courts that Earth intended to try to seize control of this meeting. So we beat them to it."

"I see," Captain Yamato said. "So you admit to kidnapping all of us for purposes of—"

"Captain Yamato," Donal said. "We're never going to get anywhere if she isn't allowed to answer even a single question."

"I have no intention of playing a kidnapper's games."

"You were going to arrest Mr. Lukyanov," MacPherson said. "Luna was invited to participate in these proceedings, as was Mars."

"Earth was not informed of this, and denies that they have any right to participate."

"Which is why Earth wasn't informed," MacPherson said with a smile. "Ties it all together neatly, don't you think? And with you about to arrest Mr. Lukyanov, the Courts had to act in the immediate, rather than waiting until all invitees were someplace more ... amenable to the transportation."

"More amenable," Lukyanov said with a vulpine smile. "So there is such a place inside Earth's vaunted no-fly zone."

Captain Yamato's expression went completely blank.

Had to be one hell of a poker player.

Jacobs. Passed out.

Machado never thought for a moment that he'd see that tough old bastard unconscious anywhere except his own bunk. Unless it was because he'd tried to fight a dozen men singlehandedly. It was the sort of thing he'd do.

Machado called *Saravá* out of his house and started to give his familiar orders that would send the translucent *onça* into the captain's etheric fields. Machado's primer on medical magic had been ages ago, but he'd do what he—

"One side if you would, Mr. Machado," Dr. Ramirez said, dropping his medical bag beside the captain's seat.

Ramirez actually had his familiar with him. A spotted eagle owl, a half-meter tall and just as translucent as Machado's own big cat, of course.

It was just that Machado had never seen Dr. Ramirez's familiar outside of the med bay when the ship was at space. Even when the doctor himself was elsewhere, he kept his familiar in the med bay, running tests, or just ready. In case he was needed.

But Machado was glad to be able to step aside and let the professional do his job. Machado would match his own knowledge of the magic of transportation and space against anyone. But he'd afford Dr. Ramirez every bit as much respect in the medical field as he himself expected in his own field.

Machado stepped back while the doctor did his work. It also gave Machado the chance to glance over the captain's phantasmal workstation. Make sure it was operating as intended.

At least, that was what he planned to do, until he saw the bridge crew looking up at him. Looking lost.

Machado had to check the urge to glance around for someone in command. The captain was down. Tunold was off-ship. And right now, Machado was as close an authority figure these people had standing on the bridge....

"Back to it," Machado said in the same tones he used to censure Journeymen who were slacking in their training. "Our captain will be back on his feet any minute, and woe betide you if you haven't been doing your jobs."

"Um, sir?" Hernandez said from communications. Green as an Initiate that boy. Probably needed his hand held.

"Yes?" Machado said, adding a touch of impatience in an attempt to make the situation feel normal.

"I've got the *Lexington* on the line."

"Good," Machado said. *This* was something he knew how to handle. "Link them through."

She looked like a captain. Machado had to give this woman that. She had the right kind of determined jaw and glare to her dark eyes. Details that made her more attractive than her features alone would.

"Where is Captain Jacobs?" the woman said.

Not even properly identifying herself. Honestly. One little thing went awry and everyone lost their manners.

"Captain Jacobs asked me to take this link so I could find out why your magicians won't work with me."

She narrowed those dark eyes. "You must be Machado."

"That's *Magister* Machado," he said. "And you are?"

"*Captain* Paulson," she said. "And I need to speak to your captain. Right. Now."

"Well, you're going to speak to me. So tell me. Are you guys hiding important information from us? Is that why your magicians won't take my assistance working on a shared problem? Is this your way of saying it isn't a problem?"

She let out an irritated burst of sigh.

"Tell me, *Magister* Machado. Are you a licensed Terran Naval warrant officer?"

"No, but—"

"Can you provide the security clearances necessary for a civilian to work directly with Terran Naval magicians?"

"No, but I have more—"

"Then I don't care what certifications you have, or how many people want to kiss your ass. This is a tight situation, and we're playing it by the book. So classified information stays classified, and—"

"*Ora meu deus,*" Machado said. "Just how stupid are you?"

"I. Beg. Your. Pardon."

Yes, the look in her eyes was probably enough to kill an insect at ten paces. Most likely cowed everyone on her ship, when it was directed at them.

But Machado just matched her glare for glare.

"I asked, just how stupid are you? The answer could make the difference between whether we get these people back alive or don't see any of them again for a hundred years."

"Fairy tales," Paulson said. "Now get me—"

"*In case it has escaped your attention, Captain, we're dealing with faeries.*" Machado took a quick breath. "Fairy tales might hold the answers we need."

"Step aside, Mr. Machado."

That sounded like Captain Jacobs. Only weaker.

Machado turned and was amazed to see the captain conscious. Weak and sweaty as he got after hard workouts — and quite frankly, this sweat smelled even worse — but conscious.

Ramirez hovered over one of the captain's shoulders, and his owl over the other.

A hovering owl. Not something Machado ever expected to see.

"Captain Paulson," Jacobs said, sitting forward in his chair and sounding a little stronger now. "You will stop berating my ship's mage for attempting to bring all resources to bear on this shared problem. My log will reflect this conversation."

"Then I trust," Paulson said — a little too much sarcasm in her voice for Machado's taste — "it will reflect my reason."

"It will reflect the reasons we were told," Jacobs said, sounding stronger still. Machado shot Dr. Ramirez an impressed look as the captain continued. "Far be it for me to speculate on your true reasons."

"I don't like what you're suggesting, Captain Jacobs."

"I don't like suggesting it. I also don't like being kept in the dark."

"Captain," Mr. Grabowski called up. Jacobs waved his scanners officer off of reporting, and gave his hand the triple twirl that would tell Grabowski to send whatever information he had to Jacobs' station.

Jacobs called it up while Paulson dared try to lecture Jacobs about Terran Naval procedures.

The *MacArthur*. Grabowski had found it on a scan.

Deep inside the no-fly zone.

"Paulson," Jacobs interrupted her would-be diatribe. "You don't share with us, I have no reason to share with you."

That got her to blink and frown in surprise, both eyebrows coming down before she narrowed her eyes.

"You don't have anything," she said. "You're bluffing."

"Am I," Jacobs said, making it a flat statement, not a question. "Well, I'm going to pursue my lead. And I'm going to go *wherever it takes us*," — Jacobs shot a significant glance at the helm, where Mr. Burke acknowledged with a nod — "and as this mission was explicitly supposed to carry my ship into the no-fly zone—"

"With an escort. You have no right to enter alone."

"I have every right to pursue any avenue to save my crew and passengers. But," Jacobs said with an evil smile, "I acknowledge that you and the *Kansas* have the right to escort me, should you so choose."

Jacobs cut the link.

"Punch it," he said to Mr. Burke.

DONAL HAD KNOWN SINCE CHILDHOOD THAT THE FAE WERE SAID TO LIVE under mounds and hills. But he hadn't expected this to be so literal, even here in Faerie itself.

Faerie.

Donal was in Faerie.

Yeah, his mother wasn't going to let this one go anytime soon.

But, at least they were done with that over-the-top Q and A session. Rowan had handled them all well. More aplomb than Donal could have managed, even after all his lessons from Donatello Mancuso.

She seemed eternal in her patience, even when the lunar great families seemed to gang up on her, asking the same questions in different ways. Trying to trap her in a lie.

Donal didn't doubt that all three of them knew Russian folklore better than he ever would. But would it have killed them to have learned a little about the Celtic fae before coming to meet with them?

If they knew even the basics, they should have known that trapping a true fae in a lie is just about impossible.

Just about…

Donal had to think about that one. It might have been literally impossible, in the case of at least some of the fae. Certainly there were rumors that the *Daoine sidhe* couldn't lie. And Fionn acted as though that were true.

Still, Donal wouldn't count on that himself. Maybe that was all the lunar Russians were doing. Trying to verify information.

Certainly, thinking of it in that way made them seem better prepared.

Of course, for people who were always said to be at each other's throats, they worked together alarmingly well. Donal would have to remember that.

For now, he had a few minutes to himself to rest. And he knew what he needed to do.

Well, he knew he needed to do two things before he even met with Rowan to discuss the coming meeting.

He needed to meditate.

He needed to talk to Fionn.

But before he even did those things, Donal needed to check out these quarters he'd been given.

They were amazing. And not just because every millimeter of the place glistened and chimed with the magic of Faerie. Like spun sugar and distant bird song.

The whole network of suites appeared to have been dug into the hill itself, and Donal's was no exception.

The ceilings were high, though, or at least high enough that Donal didn't feel the need to crouch. And after huddling aboard the *MacArthur*, even ceilings he could touch by standing on his toes and stretching his arms up felt just *obscenely* roomy.

Everything was done in earth tones. From the brick shapes of the hard-packed dirt of the floors and walls and ceiling, to the wooden cabinets and dresser and bedframe.

The bed was big enough that Donal could stretch out on it any direction without his head or feet dangling. He knew. He'd checked as soon as he saw it. Just a little tradition of his.

And that bed was so very comfortable. Donal had never lain on anything so comfortable without earth magic being involved. But in this case, it seemed that whatever had been used to stuff the mattress had been just about the perfect choice for mattress stuffing.

Stressful as the day had been, Donal had almost closed his eyes and taken a nap. But that would have cost him precious time enjoying his surroundings.

There was a small shelf of books above the bed, all with leather bindings, and what felt like old parchment paper when Donal thumbed through a volume.

The pages were blank as he thumbed through it.

Donal frowned. Looked at the cover. "Title Me," it read.

Donal said, "Once on a Thursday." It was the first book he could think of. A gripping tale of a magician, hunting down the fiends who'd managed to steal his familiar.

Not possible, of course. But a great story nonetheless.

The title shifted to the title he'd named, and as soon as Donal opened the cover, he saw the right title page, and the first paragraph he knew well enough he could have quoted.

Amazing. Even refillables couldn't do that.

Donal shook himself. Hopped up to check out the rest of the place. There was an armoire that matched the bedframe and other furniture. Inside were elegant clothes that Donal suspected would all fit him perfectly.

And in the next room, a modern-looking bathroom, complete

with alchemical toilet, and a faucet that generated hot and cold water without the usual elemental feel to the magic of such fixtures.

More spun sugar and bird song magic.

Donal had to admit as he walked back out of the bathroom. It was all quite impressive. Everything he could ask for except…

The moment he thought of food, he saw a finely carved wooden platter on a shelf by the entry door, covered in meats, cheeses, fruits and cookies.

Donal started laughing. Couldn't help it.

"Contract or no contract, I'm not eating anything," Donal said out loud. "Surely you must all know that. No food. No drink. And I hope you all had the good taste to tell your other guests…"

Donal didn't bother finishing the sentence. Of course the others would get no warning about eating the food and drink of Faerie. He could only hope they'd done the research that the lunar great families all looked to have done.

With that thought in mind, Donal called out Fionn.

The emerald deerhound didn't look the least bit translucent here. Here, in Faerie, he looked every bit as solid and substantial as Donal himself.

"Well," Fionn said, looking around. "I was wondering just how long it would take you to actually come here. Do I have time to show you around a bit?"

"Alas, no," Donal said, patting his familiar on the head as he caught him up on everything that had happened since Donal had boarded the shuttle for the *MacArthur*. Seemed like an eternity ago.

When he finished that, Donal said, "I need a favor while I meditate. I need you to go around and warn the others not to touch any food or drink while they're here."

"Good thought," Fionn said. "Hope it's not too late."

"I just hope they listen. Go. And when you get back, bring me out of meditation. We need to chat before we meet with Rowan and prep for the meeting."

"You won't see Rowan before the meeting," Fionn said.

"Ridiculous. How can we coordinate if we—"

"You won't be coordinating," Fionn said, shaking his head hard enough to flap his ears around.

Donal frowned and waited for the explanation.

"She presented herself as hostess. That means she has declared herself neutral for these talks." Fionn's ears folded backward. "Or as neutral as possible, given her nature."

"So I'm on my own for this?"

"Naturally." Fionn sat and tilted his head, as though surprised Donal didn't already know this. "The Courts are not known for getting along. That they managed to agree to *you* as a representative is only possible because you, yourself, are human."

Fionn tilted his head back and forth. "Well, and you have the kind of ancestry they prefer in a representative. Both sides of your family go back to the Isles."

"But Rowan—"

"Rowan is a changeling. I told you. She is too human to be considered fae, but she is too fae to be considered human. She has a foot in each of two worlds, and does not truly belong in either."

"So," Donal said slowly, "in their eyes she has no clear allegiances, which means—"

"Which means the Courts will use her, but not trust her."

"Fine," Donal said with a sigh. "Bring Morna back when you return then." Donal shook his head. "I need at least *some* information before it all comes together."

And Fionn went out through a door that opened for him, instead of simply flowing through the closed door the way he would have, back in Donal's own world.

Interesting.

And with entirely too much on his mind, Donal sat down to meditate.

IF ANYONE HAD EVER TOLD JACOBS THAT HE'D BE FLYING STRAIGHT INTO a Terran Naval no-fly zone, pursued by two gunboats, well, he couldn't say he'd've been shocked to hear it.

That was the problem with no-fly zones. They existed for someone to violate them.

If Earth had really wanted everyone to ignore this space, they should have found some way that wasn't tempting enough to pull an old man out of retirement and risk his health on a journey he should have known better than to take.

For crying out loud. Things had gotten bad enough that Jacobs had needed medical attention on the bridge.

In front of his crew.

That was violating an unspoken code that said the captain is indestructible. Unquestionable.

True, no one really believed those things, but the fiction of them helped keep order.

It was true back on the seas when a storm could hurl waves five times the size of a ship and half that captain's job was to stand tall and firm, as though he could throw those damned waves back himself.

And these days, it was especially true on dangerous flights into parts of space where sane people shouldn't want to fly in the first place. Hazardous space, and no help from the navy. Enough to jolt fear even through Jacobs' own seasoned crew.

And after that little *incident*, Jacobs had to work twice as hard to look as though he were in peak health and ready for action.

Wasn't going to be easy with Dr. Ramirez hovering over his shoulder. And that big owl familiar of his, sitting on the rail on the other side of Jacobs' workstation, watching with unblinking eyes.

Ramirez had laid it all on the line, though. He stayed on the bridge, or Jacobs didn't.

That would have left either ... Burke or Mash at the conn. Running *Jacobs'* ship. With crew and passengers missing.

Not. Gonna. Happen.

So Jacobs commanded this violation of Earth space from a standing position, hollering out his orders.

Oh, and letting every link get patched through to his station, so he could have the singular pleasure of cutting that link the moment the gunboat captains started threatening him again.

What was it with today's young officers? Did no one ever teach them to listen? Maybe when he got back, Jacobs should let his old business partner Zoltan book him on those lecture tours, like Zoltan wanted. Maybe kick a little sense into the younger generation.

"Mr. Grabowski," Jacobs asked for the third time. "Anything yet?"

"No, sir. Far as I can tell, space between us and the *MacArthur* is..."

"Something, Mr. Grabowski?" Jacobs savored the humorous impatience in his own voice. Something regular for the crew to hook into.

"Aye, sir. Space around the *MacArthur*, sir. It's not reading right."

"How is it reading, Mr. Grabowski?"

"Like it's there and not there," Mash said from over Jacobs' other shoulder.

Honestly, with Ramirez over one shoulder and Mash over the other, they might as well have been wearing angel and devil getups. Would have suited them.

They were even positioned right for it. Ramirez over the right shoulder, and Mash over the left.

Jacobs spared his ship's mage a glance, then looked at his scanners officer for confirmation.

"That's ... that's right, sir," Grabowski said, slowly. "It's like ... it's kind of like space in that area is all like that mist was."

"Makes sense," Machado said softly, with a nod. He was rubbing his many chins, but his expression was speculative. "If the mist pulled them into Faerie, then it stands to reason there was some region of semi-permanent mist out here. A weak spot in space, if you will, where the barrier between our world and theirs was thinner than in most of space."

"Tell me you're kidding," Jacobs said.

"Not at all," Machado said, and his tone warmed as though he were gearing up to lecture. "There are places all over Earth where the veil between our world and another is thin. In the Celtic Isles, they called the other side Faerie ... or at least, that was one of their names for it ... but such places certainly exist in other cultures. In fact—"

"Mr. Machado," Jacobs said with all the patience he could muster. He was feeling his shoulder muscles locking up again, and Ramirez had warned him to avoid that. So Jacobs rolled his shoulders as he continued, "is this relevant to our immediate situation?"

"Obviously," Machado said with a shrug. "In fact—"

"Allow me to revise that question," Jacobs said, forcing a smile. "Do you have any information right now that is applicable and practical? Or is it all theoretical?"

Machado frowned, as he always did when he was interrupted while gearing up for a good lecture. "Only that we could possibly fly through into Faerie, and we need to be careful about that. Getting back might not be so easy."

Jacobs blinked. "Mr. Burke, slow to one-quarter. Do not, I repeat, do not approach any areas of space that Mr. Grabowski indicates as questionable. Mr. Grabowski—"

"On it, sir."

"Good man."

The link opened again, and this time it was a different face. A white man, with the kind of blonde arrogance that came from making rank too quickly, and probably getting promoted through family connections.

Jacobs hated this man the moment he laid eyes on him. He'd met the type too many times, going all the way back to that first seafaring ship, serving under Captain Nemeth.

Jacobs was looking at a man who came out of the academy and got all the plum assignments, handling them just well enough to justify more. When seen in the right light. And he had the connections to make sure they were always seen in the right light.

"Captain Jacobs," the man said, and even his voice was irritating. "I'm Commander McRae. You're not supposed to be here."

"What have you done with my crew and passengers, Mr. McRae?"

"*Commander* McRae," the irritating youth insisted, before smiling a grim smile and saying, "and the Terran Navy has the situation entirely in hand. If you would please allow our gunboats to escort your ship back to the—"

"We're not going anywhere without our people."

"Well," *Commander* McRae said. "I have a number of fireball chutes that want to remind you that you are traveling through restricted space without permission or an escort."

"We have permission, in writing, and my mandated escort is right behind us."

"Nevertheless," the smarmy kid said, "you will—"

"That's it," Jacobs said. "I'm done. You have thirty seconds to either find an adult or learn how to talk like one."

Jacobs cut the link.

"I'm not sure that was advisable," Dr. Ramirez started, but Jacobs stopped him with a raised finger.

"Doctor," Jacobs said. "You know I respect you. But if you interfere with my command without a solid medical reason, I will physically throw you off my bridge."

"He will," Machado said. "I saw him do it to a reporter once."

Ramirez shut up.

Jacobs nodded. Turned back just in time to see the link reconnect.

"Now listen here," McRae started, but Jacobs cut him off with the full weight of his decades of command.

"No. You listen." Jacobs pointed at him. Started to say something else, but then the pieces fell into place. "You don't have my people. Maybe you lost some of yours too. So either you cop to it, or I'm going to go looking for them myself."

"I was hoping it wouldn't come to that," McRae said, shaking his head. "Your crew members are fine, Captain Jacobs."

McRae gestured to someone Jacobs couldn't see.

A second head appeared next to McRae. A head Jacobs would recognize anywhere.

"Kris," Jacobs said with a smile at the familiarity of the sheer fury in his ex oh's eyes. "Good to see you in one piece."

"Glad to be in one piece, Captain. But, John, we've got VIPs missing all around, including the *MacArthur's* captain."

"I knew it," Jacobs said, shaking his head. "Now. *Commander.* Maybe it's time you stopped pretending to know what the hell is going on here and try *working* with us. Maybe, just maybe, we'll manage to get our people back safe and sound if we pool our resources."

Finally, a crack in that façade. For a moment the arrogant commander looked like the lost little boy he was.

"I have to do this by the book," he started, but Jacobs wasn't having it.

"Nothing about this is by the book, you damned fool. Now gather up all the magicians from your ships, and get them over to the *Horizon Cusp* pronto."

"But—"

"*You have my shuttle.* My magician can't come to you. And besides, I need my ex oh back, as well as my security team. Now give the orders and get your butts over here."

"Aye, sir." Commander McRae flushed a bright red as he squeaked those words out. As though Jacobs were the first man ever to censure him. Maybe his parents never spanked him, either.

Well, if the good commander didn't get his priorities straight, Jacobs might just do that job himself too.

WELL, THE PLACE WAS COMFORTABLE. EDIK HAD TO GIVE IT THAT.

Weird. Definitely weird. But comfortable.

Floor, walls and ceiling made of bricks, made from dirt? Without any dust?

Weird.

Almost as weird as the oversized bed. For a guy who was used to kipping in his hammock, a bed that big seemed ridiculous. More than big enough for Edik to share with Dola without either of them getting in each other's way.

Well. Maybe. Familiar or not, Dola *was* still a cat. He was just as good at spreading out to fill available space as any natural cat Edik had ever seen. And standing a meter at the shoulders, Dola could fill a lot of space.

The warm, earthy wood tones of the furniture were all right. The warm, yellowish light too. Not that Edik could tell where it came from.

The whole place reeked of magic, and none of it felt like anything Edik was used to.

Weird. That was just the only word Edik had for it.

"Is all of Faerie like this?" Edik asked, picking up a slice of yellowish cheese from the wooden plate near the door to his suite.

"Wait!" Dola said, leaping up to knock the slice of cheese out of Edik's hand, just before it reached his open mouth.

Edik started to ask a sharp question, but Dola's cerulean eyes were too full of worry for him to get the rebuke out.

"What?" Edik said instead.

"Don't touch the food here. Not the drinks, either. Not even water. If you didn't bring it, you don't consume it. Do you understand me?"

"Well, yeah, but we're going to be here a while, and—"

"Edik." Dola reached up and put his paws on Edik's shoulders again.

Twice in one day. That was a lot, even for Dola.

"Please," Dola said. "Listen to me here. The food and drinks can ... tie you to this place. Sometimes even make time run funny. We might not get back for a century, or we might get back before we left."

"How is that possible?"

"A lot of things are possible here," Dola said, looking around. The cat seemed oddly at home, yet as though he felt unwelcome. As though...

"Were you kicked out of Faerie?" Edik asked softly.

"What?" Dola turned a droll look at Edik. "I'm a *Russian* spirit, Edik. Not Celtic. We don't play their games. My own world is similar to this, but different enough that even I have to be extra careful here."

"Oh," Edik said. "We've never really talked about where I summoned you from."

"Nor should we," Dola said, but his voice was casual and he continued peering around, as though he expected to see tiny fae around every nook and cranny. "It's not really something we're supposed to discuss, once we take gigs as familiars. Something about not letting the wizards know too much."

"Magicians," Edik corrected. Edik had a hard enough time considering himself a magician. Wizard was just too much to ask.

"Them either," Dola said, then trotted back over to Edik. He looked about to sit, but there was a tapping at the door.

Dola spun in place in the kind of nimble move that Edik always admired in his familiar.

The door opened.

Donal's familiar, Fionn, stepped in, looking just as solid as Dola. Huh.

"Donal asked me to warn all of you about the food and drinks."

"I've already covered it with Edik," Dola said.

"Good," Fionn said, and Edik heard approval in the fae deerhound's voice. "I came to you last because I expected as much. All have been told now."

"Thank you," Dola said.

Fionn bowed himself out of the room. The door closed behind him.

"How long do we have in here?" Edik asked.

"The MacPherson woman implied that the meeting would begin before too long. I'd suggest meditating, but—"

"But we both know I won't."

"You really do need more meditation in your schedule, Edik. Especially if we're going to go on jaunts like this one. You need your head as clear as it can be."

"Trust me," Edik said with a lopsided smile. "No one has ever accused me of having too full a head."

Dola uttered a small yowl of disapproval at that, and his tail swished annoyance.

"Come on," Edik said. "Let's check on the others."

Edik stepped out of his front door and into the common area. So far as he'd been able to tell when he'd been escorted down.

Well, not down. Rowan MacPherson had simply gestured and they all sank into the hillside, to end up in some kind of central hall. Then Donal had been escorted one direction by a tiny man in a long, green cap, while all the others — Edik included — had been escorted another direction by a tiny man alike enough that, had they been standing side-by-side, Edik might not have been able to tell them apart.

Edik and the others had been taken to a common room that had a series of suites adjoining.

Edik had objected at the time. Said that Donal should be here with them. That all of the ambassadors and liaisons should be housed together.

But the little man with the long green cap had simply smiled and vanished. And everyone had gone off to their respective rooms to acclimate.

The common room had large, overstuffed couches the color of spring moss. More than enough seating for everyone to gather without anyone feeling crowded.

The room had no ceiling at all, though, as far as Edik could tell. The walls extended up and up and up. Easily a hundred meters that Edik could see. And yet, above was only darkness, that lent a faint echo to any noises in the common room.

Three large banquet tables had been set up to one side, with a feast. And between the couches, pale wooden coffee tables. Currently empty.

And though Edik's room had smelled like oiled wood and clean dirt, the common room smelled like a warm summer day in a field of wild grass.

Edik was the first one out into the common room, but only by a step or so.

Alexei Lukyanov was storming out there even now. Looking around as though he needed a servant to berate.

His eyes settled on Edik.

"What's this? What's this? We've all been brought here with assurances of safety, and yet I am told we dare not risk the food or drink?"

"Do your homework, Lyoshka," Natalia Romanova said, entering the common area herself. "The food of the good neighbors is not safe for human consumption."

"I have done my homework, Natka. But we are *invited* guests. Have these people no proper guest rights? And they call themselves good—"

"*Tishina,*" she hushed Lukyanov. "Not a game you want to play. Not here, especially."

"She's right," Hierophant Mason said, stepping into the common room. He had changed into a dark chocolate brown shirt and black pants combination, along with a pair of matching loafers that looked exquisitely comfortable.

How had he managed to bring along a change of clothes?

"Here," Mason continued, "you may call them fae, as well as good neighbors. But avoid calling any of them Seelie or Unseelie, unless you are absolutely positive that you are right. In fact, you would do better to avoid those words, and any value judgments at all."

"Fah," Lukyanov said, and stomped back into his room.

"Lyoshka is right about one thing," Romanova said, raising an eyebrow at both Mason and Edik in a single gesture. "We would be best to return to our rooms and rest. We may be called on at any time."

She didn't wait to see if anyone followed her advice. Or maybe, as a Romanova, she just assumed everyone would.

Either way, she returned to her own room and closed the door.

"She's up to something," Edik said casually. "You know that, don't you? No matter what it is she says, she had at least two other gambits going."

Mason tilted his head. "Is your hatred for her special? Or do you feel the same way about all the great families?"

"With one particular exception," Edik said with a nod.

As if on cue, Anna came in from her own room.

"Honestly," she said through a sigh. "I wasn't particularly hungry or thirsty. But now that I know the food and drinks aren't safe, I can think of nothing else."

"Yeah," Edik said, ignoring the way his own stomach had started to rumble.

"I keep flashing back to those grilled gruyere and tomato sandwiches you made us just before we landed aboard the *MacArthur*. And even those rolls in the meeting room."

"Well," Mason said, "then the best thing to do is take your mind off it. I myself am going to return to my meditations. Edik, I suggest you do the same. Anna, I know you are not a magician, but meditation might still be advisable. Or if not that, perhaps a nap."

"I believe I can determine my own course of action, thank you very much," Anna said, arching her eyebrow in a way that looked all too much like Natalia Romanova.

Mason opened his mouth to say something, but Edik beat a hasty retreat back to his room. Shut the door behind him.

He knew that Anna had some things in common with Romanova. No way she couldn't. All the great families, they shared a culture of their own, over and above both the modern lunar culture and the traditional Russian culture.

The great families, they were apart from Luna, as much as they were a part *of* Luna.

But that didn't mean Edik liked seeing reminders.

Dola sat beside the most comfortable chair in Edik's room. A huge thing that looked as though it had been carved out of a mossy rock, but as though Edik could just sink right down into it.

The look in Dola's eyes was pure hope.

"All right," Edik grumbled. "I'll meditate."

Took too goddamn long to get all those magicians over to the *Horizon Cusp.*

Yes, long enough that Jacobs had been able to wolf down a couple of ham-and-swiss sandwiches and a doctor-mandated liter of water.

Still. This was taking too long. But Jacobs suspected that was because the different captains were venting all over Commander McRae. Maybe even trying to demand their own ships as the proper meeting place.

McRae, however, was apparently smart enough to know when he was beaten. He never tried to link back and change what Jacobs had "proposed."

So Jacobs had stood down on the gangplank, between the rows of seats, and taken his updates from the bridge about shuttles flying from the *Kansas* to the *MacArthur*, and then from the *Lexington* to the *MacArthur*.

Until, finally, one shuttle had left the *MacArthur*, bound for the *Horizon Cusp*.

"About bloody time," Jacobs grumbled at Mash, who was standing next to him. His assistant ship's mage, Cromartie, stood behind Mash, lean and towering over both Mash and Jacobs.

"It's necessary," Machado said, a little too soothingly for Jacobs' nerves. "After all, we can only really handle two shuttles at most, or one of their large shuttles. So they had to get everyone together before they could come here anyway.

"In fact," Machado said, raising an eyebrow at Jacobs as he continued, "one might even suggest it would have been more efficient for them to send a shuttle for me."

"One might," Jacobs said, "but we're not getting both the captain and the ex oh off this ship at the same time. And if you think I'm missing this gathering, Mash, then you're not as smart as I think you are."

Machado chuckled and turned back to watch the shuttle approach.

The shuttle was a beauty. To Jacobs' eyes, at least. He knew Machado and Cromartie regarded it with distaste, but Jacobs found the archaic design like a refreshing glass of water after a long, intense workout.

It really did look like an old harbor patrol boat. A little too much steel for accuracy, but Jacobs wasn't going to quibble.

The shuttle zoomed in and docked with admirable efficiency.

And yet, no one seemed to be emerging.

"Mash," Jacobs said, and Machado sent his familiar straight into the shuttle to enquire about the delay.

The translucent gray pantherish familiar returned in short order.

As was custom, Machado allowed his familiar to report directly to Jacobs.

"Captain John Jacobs," *Saravá* began, "I regret to inform you that there is something of a disagreement transpiring between Executive Officer Kristoff Tunold and Terran Navy Commander Halford McRae."

Jacobs didn't stay for the rest of the report. He marched straight across the deck, his boots ringing off the ceramics, and pounded on the hatch of that shuttle almost as though he were trying to batter it down.

Almost.

He wasn't.

Not yet.

Machado and Cromartie caught up a step behind.

"Captain," Machado said, "I doubt this will help."

"Open this damned hatch," Jacobs said at command volume, "or you'll find out firsthand just exactly how good my ship's mages are."

Jacobs heart tapped out a rapid rate that made a few seconds feel like an hour. He was ready to pound again when the hatch hissed open.

Tunold stood there, looking fit to be tied. His pale complexion all blotchy and red with anger.

"Idiot's changing the rules on us, Captain."

Commander McRae, a step behind Tunold, looked composed again. And he had that light in his eye. That little light that promised payback for the abuse he'd taken from Jacobs earlier.

"Captain," Commander McRae said. "I have decided that it is in the interests of the Terran Navy to mount a rescue mission across the mists into Otherspace."

"Otherspace?" Jacobs asked, as incredulous about the man's terminology as his decisions.

"You are referring to Faerie," Machado said, sounding just as irritated as his captain. "If you can't even use the right terminology—"

"I know how these creatures present themselves," McRae said, in as condescending a tone as he could manage. "But has it ever occurred to you that they may be giving us a false front? They pretend to be fairies—"

"Tell me you didn't call them that to their faces," Machado said.

"—but we don't really know. Do we? I mean, the Seelie and Unseelie Courts are supposed to get along about as well as Heaven and Hell. And you expect me to believe they're sponsoring something jointly?"

McRae shook his head. "I don't buy it. I think we've been suckered. I think all our people are in danger. And I'm going to go rescue them."

"You're a fool," Jacobs said. "You don't have the assurances of safety given to the ambassadors and liaisons. If you go in there, you and your people, you're meat."

"I understand if you're afraid to accompany my expedition."

"*Mister,*" Jacobs said, snapping out the word with everything he had. "You are the executive officer of a Terran Navy ship. Your captain is already off-ship. *Where are you supposed to be?*"

There was only one right answer to that. At the conn.

"Not answering to you," McRae said instead. And the little bastard had the guts to get right in Jacobs' face. "You may have been hot shit once. *Captain.* But your time is past. You're not my superior officer, you're a *civilian.* And I don't have to listen to a word you say."

"You're going to get your people killed."

"So you say. Which is why yours aren't coming. I'd've taken volunteers from your ship, but clearly there aren't any"

"This is ridiculous," Tunold roared. "If there's a rescue mission, we first need to—"

"There should not be a rescue mission," Jacobs said flatly. "I don't know why the timetable got moved up, but one thing should be clear to all of us."

That actually got McRae to shut up for a moment and listen.

"Look. These are the goddamn Fae Courts of goddamn Celtic mythology. Do you understand me? Us humans have been studying magic for sixty-odd years. Compared to them, we're not even *toddlers.*"

"Well," Machado muttered, "much of what we've learned has been recovered from previous—"

"*Mr. Machado.*"

"Sorry, sir."

"Listen," Jacobs tried again, because he saw nothing but stop signs in McRae's eyes. "You've got to listen to me. If they took all the ambassadors and liaisons across, they did it to control the time frame and location of the meeting. Yes," — Jacobs held up a forestalling hand — "it was an end move. A trick, if you like. But they're calling the shots right now. You go in there with ... what? Pacifiers and slingers?"

"And safety skinsuits," McRae added, as though those things might swing the fight.

Safety skinsuits were great in physical combat. They were enchanted to reflect the force of an incoming blow with varying strength. Made them both defensive and offensive at the same time.

But they'd be useless against faerie magic. Even Jacobs knew that.

He shook his head. "You go in there like that, trying to mount a *rescue* mission, you'll all be dead by twenty-four hundred hours."

"Your objection is noted," McRae said.

Jacobs shook his head.

"You're still going to go through with this."

"I suggest you recall your people, Mr. Tunold," McRae said, turning away from Jacobs now.

Jacobs' fists itched to pound this man to so many component parts.

"Listen to me," Tunold growled. "And listen good. This man here" — Tunold pointed at Jacobs — "knows more about commanding through unknown space and space phenomena than anyone, anywhere. And *this* man" — he pointed at Machado — "knows more about the magic of space than all your magicians combined. If they both say this is a bad idea..."

Tunold turned to Jacobs and Machado who both shook their heads in slow unison.

"...then this is a mission that is going to get you *killed*. And maybe your people too."

"Killed if you're lucky," Machado said. "No maybes about it. You run into the wrong fae? One of the nobles? You'll be *wishing* you were dead before the first year's over."

"Your. Objections. Are. Noted," McRae said. "Now recall your people, or they're coming with me. Oh, and take this other one, would you?"

"Other one?" Jacobs asked.

"They found him on the *Third Son*," Tunold said. "Clearly wounded and recovering. I figured Dr. Ramirez should have a look at him."

"Bring him aboard," Jacobs said. Then raised his voice. "And if any of you want to object to your suicidally stupid mission, you're welcome aboard too. I'll give you sanctuary."

"You have no right..." McRae started.

"Actually," Jacobs said with a smile, "General Space Ordinance Seven says that—"

"Don't you quote space ordinances at me! I will—"

But McRae stopped talking when someone behind him stood up. McRae whirled on a young, mousy-looking woman, so hunched in on herself that it was hard to tell much about her except that she was a lieutenant, and she was pale with brown peach fuzz hair. "Back to your seat."

"No, sir," she said. "My objections have already been noted in the record, and with Magister Ronaldo Machado confirming my suspicions, I consider these orders in violation of Naval Code Section Three, subsection six-six—"

"Are you quoting regulations to a superior officer?"

Jacobs had to admit. The idiot had a decent intimidating growl.

"No, sir," she said. "Only qualifying my objection for the record, and accepting Captain Jacobs' offer of sanctuary."

"Why you—"

"Commander," Jacobs barked. "Considering the circumstances, perhaps this lieutenant could be assigned to my ship, to coordinate this end of the rescue efforts, alongside my ship's mage."

McRae whirled on Jacobs, almost apoplectic. But he stopped himself. The little part of him that knew how to navigate political issues must have been whispering to him that forcing this lieutenant to accompany him over her lawful objections would be a black mark on his record, even if he managed to survive this damned fool mission.

"All right, Medici," McRae said, turning back to the lieutenant. "You're tasked to the *Horizon Cusp*, to coordinate this end of the rescue effort." He turned to the rest of his people. "Anyone else too cowardly to stand between harm and the captain who needs your help?"

Medici winced as she stepped off the shuttle. But she did step off. And she was alone from McRae's crew in having the courage to stand up to him.

"Journeyman Carmen Medici at your service, Magister," she said, reporting to Machado instead of Jacobs.

Magicians.

Jacobs turned his attention to getting his own people off that shuttle as quickly as possible. Plus whoever it was who needed medical attention.

Who knew? Perhaps Jacobs could even get one or two more of McRae's to see the folly of this mission. The man had a score of spacers on that shuttle.

Every life Jacobs could save was worth the effort.

IF EDIK WERE TO COMPILE A LIST OF THE BIGGEST WASTES OF HIS TIME, meditation would come in ... third.

Yes. Third.

Spaceport bureaucracy would come in first.

Waiting for late clients would come in second.

Meditation, though, was hot on its heels.

Yes, Edik knew he *should* do more of it. Dola told him so. Carl told him so. Every teacher Edik had studied thaumaturgy under since high school had told him so.

Hell, even Donal had made a case study of it on their long flight out to Ganymede and back.

But the fact was, Edik was just not built to sit still and think about nothing.

All right. To think about *his breathing*. That was what they all told him to focus on. Or at least, it was what they all told him to focus on after he'd given them *the look* when they'd suggested things like a meditative mantra, or a symbol to gaze on, or something along those lines.

It was all the same as thinking about nothing, in Edik's book.

So though it felt as though Edik had been meditating for about an hour, when he finally opened his eyes he figured it had *actually* been more like ten minutes or so.

Dola sat there. Right in the center of Edik's room here under the hill, less than a meter from where Edik sat in that surprisingly comfy chair. The one that looked — and kind of felt — like a moss-covered stone.

"How long?" Edik said, fighting a yawn.

"Ninety-six seconds," Dola said, and a displeased ripple went up his gray fur.

"You've got to be—"

"I timed you."

Edik shook his head.

"Come on," he implored his familiar. "How can I be expected to meditate here? I mean, on the *Third Son*, sure. I know I'm safe. I have the place to just the two of us. Makes sense for me to meditate there — assuming I have to do it at all."

"Do I even need to answer that part?" Dola said through a sigh. "Again?"

"No," Edik said, sighing right back at him. "I suppose not. But out here? In freaking Faerie of all places? How am I supposed to relax when even the food is…"

Edik frowned.

"We went over the food," Dola said.

"No," Edik said, as thoughts came together in his head. In the common room, he'd seen Anna and Hierophant Mason. He'd seen Lukyanov and Romanova….

"Captain Yamato," Edik said, standing so quickly that the wave of cold passing over him felt like a burst of icy rainfall.

He started across the dirt bricks of his room and toward the door.

"What about Captain Yamato?" Dola asked, trotted right beside Edik.

"We didn't see him in the common room," Edik said.

"We didn't see Rasputin Pajari either," Dola said. "Or Roger North."

Edik threw open the door of his suite, shaking his head and continuing to talk as he strode past the huge, comfortable couches and coffee tables toward Captain Yamato's door.

"I don't care about Pajari. That jerk deserves whatever he gets. North too."

"Edik," Dola admonished.

"Captain Yamato, though. He's just doing his job." Edik shook his head. Pounded on Yamato's door. "Captain?"

He had to pound once more before the door finally opened.

Captain Yamato stood there, smiling a beatific smile. His eyes fairly sparkled.

He held a half-eaten cookie in his hand.

"Oh," Dola muttered. "No."

"Captain," Edik said. "Can you hear me?"

"Of course I can hear you, Captain Barshai," Captain Yamato said, his smile widening as he made a gesture of welcoming. "Come right in. Have a cookie. They're delightful."

"No," Edik said, stepping on in to the suite and closing the door behind him. "And you shouldn't have any more either."

"Won't matter," Dola muttered in syllables only Edik could understand. "One bite or a thousand, the effect is the same."

"Why on Earth not?" Captain Yamato asked, shaking his head slightly and taking another bite. "They're like... They're like spun childhood, and happy dreams. Don't you think?"

"I haven't tried one. And really, you should put that down."

Captain Yamato shook his head, smiling now like a little boy who's getting away with something naughty.

It was an odd look to see on a man with a lined face, as well as gray hair and beard.

"I'm not sure we're up to this," Dola muttered, sticking to tones only for Edik's ears.

"We have to be," Edik replied in similar fashion. "I'm not sure it's safe to tell anyone else about his condition."

Edik stepped in close to Yamato before he could return to the full plate of cookies.

"Captain, I need you to listen to me. You must not eat any more of those cookies."

"That's what the dog said. That huge green hound." A slight frown creased the spot between Yamato's eyebrows. "Do you know, I've never seen a hound like that one before. I do believe he is a hound, too, of some variety. He looks built for hunting something. But that color. I think he must be a familiar. Except that he couldn't be. Familiars are all spectral."

"Not here," Edik said, then shook his head to get the topic out. "Captain, had you already eaten when the dog spoke to you?"

"No," Yamato said, then smiled. "A dog spoke to me today. Do you know, I think this is the first time in my life that I can say that? I've lived quite some time, too. I was born only a few years into the rise of magic. I've seen a great many wonders in my day."

"Captain..."

"I've spoken with Oni. And Tengu. Would you believe that? My parents would never have believed it. But I have."

"Captain Yamato!" Edik snapped, trying to make himself sound … official. It didn't come naturally to him.

It did get Yamato's attention though.

"Yes, Captain Barshai?" But just as fast, Captain Yamato seemed to notice Dola for the first time. "Well, and aren't you just an amazing specimen of a feline? Are you Captain Barshai's?"

"My name is Dola," Dola said, in plain English. "And I am proud to be Edik's familiar."

"Edik?" Yamato turned back to Edik. "Is that your name?"

"Yes, I—"

"Mine is Haru. I think I would prefer you call me that. You seem like a good man."

"Thank you, I—"

"You can always judge a man by how his inferiors speak of him. And that your familiar would say he is *proud* to be your familiar. Well, that says good things about you, Edik. May I call you Edik?"

"Certainly," Edik said, exasperation as plain in his voice now as on his face. "But will you listen to me a moment?"

"Of course, Edik. Can I offer you a cookie? Or perhaps some coffee? It's delicious."

Edik's mouth watered at the thought of coffee, and at the same moment, he could smell it, coming from the tray next to the cookies. Strong and rich and just the way he liked it.

"No," Edik said quickly. "Thank you, though, Haru."

"What are friends for?"

"Oh, this is bad," Dola muttered, but only for Edik's ears. "Sure you don't want me to fetch Hierophant Mason?"

Edik made a line of his lips as he thought about that, while Yamato hummed a little song to himself.

"No," Edik said. "Get Donal."

"Donal's here representing the Fae Courts," Dola said. "He might not be allowed to help here."

"How are you doing that?" Haru said. "Your mouths move. Both of you. As though you are holding conversation. But the sounds you make are not words."

"All magicians can speak directly with their familiars," Edik said, then sighed. "Fine. Get Mason."

"Mason?" Yamato asked, and Edik realized he forgot to switch modes of speech. "That Hierophant? Oh, I'd rather not see him. I'm not sure I trust him at all. He is the sort who always seems to know more than he will admit. The type who would think nothing of using others to accomplish his own goals."

Yamato tilted his head and gazed thoughtfully at Dola. "And I've never gotten to hear from his inferiors."

"Nevertheless, I'd like him to have a look at you," Edik said, trying hard not to start talking louder and slower as though Yamato were senile. "You're under an enchantment."

"Oh, I don't think I am," Yamato said, frowning. "And if I were, I'd much rather you handle it. I like you. That Mason though."

Yamato frowned deeper and said something in Japanese.

Edik glanced at Dola, who shook his head. He didn't understand it either.

"I'm afraid," Edik said slowly, "I didn't catch that."

"An old Japanese saying," Yamato said with a smile, but got more serious as he continued. "Mason is a man who pulls water to his own rice paddy. You should not trust him. He ... focuses on his own benefits. You understand?"

"I understand," Edik said with a sigh.

He was going to have to do this. Just him and Dola. Against faerie magic.

What could go wrong?

THE PEACE OF DEEP MEDITATION. THERE WAS NOTHING ELSE LIKE IT. And with all the time Donal spent meditating these days, he could reach deeper states, faster, than he had ever known before.

Thus, Donal wasn't entirely sure how long he spent meditating before Fionn returned.

Donal did know this much. By the time he felt the small, inquisitive touch to his mind that was Fionn's way of telling him it was time to return, Donal had gone a long way toward both relaxing and refreshing himself.

He fluttered his eyes open. Let them acclimate quickly to the yellowish light in his room here under the faerie hill. His nostrils flared deep to take in the woodsy smells of his room.

But Donal smelled something else then. Something deep and primal. Sexual. Not quite a musk, but something along those lines. Something he could not so much find words for, as feel, all the way down his spine.

Even before he saw her, Donal knew that Fionn had found Morna for him.

Donal had wondered if the *leannan sidhe* would look different here in Faerie, but no. She looked much the same as when Donal had first seen her. Slender and beautiful, with silver hair that trailed down to her calves, and a gossamer gown that looked as though she'd been wrapped in moonlight. Her eyes like the setting sun.

Right now she stood two respectful steps in front of where he sat on the dirt brick floor, cross-legged. Fionn stood beside her.

"Morna," Donal said, greeting her with a smile as he rose straight to his feet. He reached to dust himself off, but not a mote of dust stuck to his pants "Thank you for coming."

"Thank you for calling me, master."

Her voice tinkled like silver bells once more, each sending a gentle chill down Donal's spine.

One problem at a time.

"Donal, please. For so long as you are in my service" — Donal quickly held up a hand to stop the objection — "let me say it that way, even if your service can only end in one of our deaths."

She nodded.

Donal continued.

"For so long as you are in my service, I would prefer that you call me Donal."

"If I must, Donal."

A simple sentence, but she made it sound surprisingly intimate.

As though those words had been a promise whispered in darkness, in the early hours before dawn.

Donal shook his head.

"I have not called you here for sex."

"You can't blame a girl for trying," she said, and just like that, her voice changed. It still tinkled like crystal bells, but no longer did her words send shivers down Donal's spine.

"Perhaps not," Donal said. "But I'm more interested in knowing what's been going on at the Courts."

"You've been the talk of everyone. The Winter Court is impressed that the Duke of Shadows has managed to help you without aid from the Duchess of Mirrors countering him. You have given him quite a coup."

"Have I avoided anything from the Duchess of Mirrors?" Donal asked Fionn.

"Difficult to say," Fionn said. "I am accustomed to shunting many small distractions away from you. If an attempt to contact you was made along the wrong lines, I would have intercepted it instead of allowing it to reach you."

Donal frowned. "Such attempts are common?"

"More so than you likely wish to know," Fionn said, not meeting Donal's eyes just then. "Ever since you took up your current post, there have been small attempts at spying and influence."

"And you didn't tell me that because…"

"He is your familiar, Master Donal," Morna said. "It is his role to protect you from the minor distractions as part of aiding in your study and focus."

"She is right," Fionn said with an ear-twitch-nod.

"Just as it is my own small role to aid you to greatness. You need only let me please you, and—"

"As I said," Donal said firmly, one interposing hand raised against her natural reach out for him. "I wish to hear your report. Nothing else."

"Nothing else *at this time*," Morna said, her voice almost pleading. "Allow me that much?"

Fionn gave Donal a nod.

Donal sighed, but said, "Nothing else at this time."

"Thank you, Master Donal."

"But drop the 'master.' I prefer Donal."

"If I must. Donal. The Duchess of Mirrors was beside herself for a day and a night, but then she returned to court composed and smiling as though she had some hidden trick to reveal, when the time was right."

"Any sense of what that could be, or when?"

"Mas... Donal, had I the wit to puzzle through the machinations of Her Grace, the Duchess of Mirrors, I'd be named queen by the fall."

"Fair enough," Donal said. "Do you have any way of providing me with warning about it? Is there anyone who would know that you can—"

"Please don't finish that sentence," Fionn said quickly. "Master, you do not want to give her that order. It would bring her into conflicts that could violate portions of your contract in ways that will make you vulnerable."

"Why does he get to call you master, but I cannot?"

The *leannan sidhe* actually sounded put out about that.

"He is my familiar." Donal shrugged. "I confess, I don't care for it. Not really. But it's tradition. I was warned not to violate it."

"Well," Morna said with a small smile on her raspberry lips, "it is also tradition for a defeated *leannan sidhe* to refer to her master by his proper title. Just as, were you my servant instead of my being yours, you can believe that you would call me mistress as you knelt before me."

"You aren't..." Donal started to point out, but Morna quickly knelt.

Donal looked helplessly at Fionn.

"She is right," Fionn conceded. "It is tradition. And there is magic in tradition. It may also be a fact of her nature. The truth is that you might be taking risks by having her call you Donal. I cannot be certain."

"Oh, all *right*," Donal said, frowning even as he said the words that made the *leannan sidhe* beam with delight.

"Thank you, *master*," she said, and shivered when she did.

Donal refused to think about why the word made her shiver.

"All right." Donal sighed and shook his head. "What about the Summer Court? What are they saying?"

"In the alcoves, of course, they discuss Her Grace. But in the court itself, they speak of the Queen's promise."

Donal felt his stomach try to sink through the ground beneath him. "Promise?"

"It seems the Queen of Summer has promised—"

"*Stop reporting,*" Fionn said quickly.

Morna stopped mid-sentence, and lowered her head. After all, Donal had commanded her to obey Fionn as she would Donal.

Donal looked the question at Fionn. Fionn answered in tones only Donal could understand.

"Remember that you are, technically, in the employ of both Courts," Fionn said. "If one queen makes a promise about the outcome, and you know about the promise..."

"I would be expected to fulfill it," Donal said, the same way. "Giving one Court an edge over the other."

Suddenly his face felt clammy, and there was a chill down his spine that had nothing to do with Morna.

"They're already using her against me, aren't they?"

"It is *their* nature," Fionn agreed.

"I can't send her back, can I?"

"You shouldn't."

Donal looked over at Morna. And though she could not have understood his conversation with Fionn — it was literally impossible to eavesdrop on isolated conversations between a magician and his familiar — Donal would have sworn that the look in Morna's eyes was knowing.

Took Edik three tries to draw a halfway decent chalk circle on the floor around Captain Yamato. Too used to only working on the smooth ceramics of his own decks. Had trouble adjusting to the little grooves separating the flawless dirt bricks that formed the floor of Yamato's suite here in the middle of a faerie hill.

A hill. Edik was in the middle of a freaking *hill*, in the Celtic Faerieland.

Edik couldn't think about that too much though. Not right now. Right now he needed to focus on what he was doing. He needed to not let his thoughts run to where he was doing it. Or why.

Focus on the spell.

That had always been Edik's mantra when he was working on his ship. But working on his ship, that had come naturally. Piloting was what Edik loved the most, and so anything to do with his ship was just an extension of that.

But this? This wasn't magic intended for Initiates. Low-grade practitioners of a single type of thaumaturgy. Two types, at the most, if they had enough certifications.

Nobody got a certification in faerie magic. Wasn't possible. Not even an option in Ireland, so far as Edik knew.

Edik stopped. Shook himself.

Brought his mind back to what he was doing. Drawing a nice, regular chalk circle around Captain Yamato.

The first step.

"This is why meditation matters," Dola muttered as Edik erased yet another attempt. "Helps your focus."

"You know what doesn't help my focus?" Edik asked, in tones pitched just for Dola. "Criticism."

Dola ducked his head, then brought his tail down to the dirt floor and traced a circle. Edik had only to follow it with the chalk, and just like that, he had a more perfect circle than any he'd drawn outside of his own beloved *Third Son*.

At least Yamato seemed patient about the whole process.

No. Not patient. Amused.

Yamato didn't believe he was enchanted, but he was flattered that

Edik would go to so much trouble for him, so he seemed willing to play along. Standing there in the circle, his hands folded behind his back. His sparkling eyes watching every movement Edik made, but his lips held closed as though to hold back a torrent of questions.

"Do the words have to be Gaelic?" Edik asked Dola. "I know for the ship stuff they don't, but for this—"

"Your Gaelic is pretty good," Dola said, "but if you're uncomfortable, you can stick to English. Or Russian."

"English, if you'd please," Yamato said. "I don't speak either Gaelic or Russian, and I would very much like to understand what you say. I do speak Spanish, German, and French, though, if you'd prefer one of those."

"Trust me," Dola said, "you don't want to hear Edik attempt German or French."

"Hey," Edik said, but then made himself chuckle. Trust Dola to find just the right words to distract Edik from his stress but not his goal.

"Right," Edik said, standing tall in front of Yamato. Easy to do here, even under the hill, because the fae had at least provided ceilings of a decent height.

"Start with earth?" Edik asked Dola, who nodded, but said, "Soon as you're done with the circle."

Right. But the circle was drawn and closed. So, on to earth.

Edik drew three deep breaths, then focused on the earth center within himself. Deep within his guts. Within his core. Here was where he most felt the cool, dryness that was earth, the element, not Earth, the planet.

Earth the element was stability. Solidity. An anchor against the hurricane or the tsunami.

Earth, the stable core at the center of all things physical.

Earth, as Edik continued to contemplate it, the foundation of his body. Earth, his flesh and bones...

"Edik," Dola muttered in plain English. "Spark the circle first."

"Oh!" Edik stopped his contemplations and slapped himself in the forehead. He'd been getting ahead of himself. Too nervous.

Edik drew a simple spark of power from within himself and projected it into the circle.

"Circle round," Edik muttered as his touch of energy flowed into place, activating the circle, "become a barrier. Separation. World within, world without."

At that very moment, someone knocked on the door. A simple three-beat knock, but it felt insistent to Edik.

Edik said to Dola, "See about that, please."

Dola trotted off as Edik returned to his contemplation of earth, the element. Reaching down into his own natural connection to that element. The connection he had deepened through his training and practice.

And as he touched that connection to the element of earth, he felt its stability remind Edik of his own accomplishments. His own power.

Edik might only have been an Initiate, but he was still a magician.

He could do this.

"Edik," Dola said, "we have a visitor you cannot ignore."

"Oh," Yamato said, turning, "do come in. The more the merrier. Edik here was about to show me some magic, but you're more than welcome to stay and watch the show."

"About that," a voice said. A voice with a thick Celtic accent. Thicker even than Fionn's.

Edik looked up.

A tall man stood in the doorway. His skin was the pale of early sunrise, and his hair the black of midnight. His eyes, disturbingly, were the same cerulean blue as Dola's.

He wore rich, simple clothing in summery colors.

"I'm afraid," the fae man said in a velvety baritone, "that I must ask you to cease and desist your current casting, Captain Barshai."

The interruption felt like a gut punch, but with so much recent connection into earth, Edik took it well.

He smiled at the interloper.

"My friend here was just having a little trouble with the food. I thought I would help him ... digest it."

"Oh, it's sitting quite pleasantly in my stomach," Yamato said. "Honestly. Can't remember when I've had such good cookies."

"Sounds to me as though your friend needs no help."

"You know exactly why he needs help," Edik said, stepping over toward the fae man. "He's eaten the food of Faerie. I know what that means."

"I see." Those cerulean eyes danced with mirth. "And you think to negate the effects? You?"

"He's not just some hapless farmhand, wandering off into the mists to find himself at a party," Edik said. "This man is an *ambassador* from Earth. You know. The planet where all your people come through when they come into our universe?"

"Now that's hardly true, is it?" the man's voice held as much amusement as his eyes now. "After all, you didn't get here from Earth, did you?"

"Stop playing games and listen," Edik said.

The fae man folded his hands and turned a mock attentive expression on Edik.

"He is an ambassador here to negotiate. But after eating your food, he is hardly in any condition to negotiate, wouldn't you say?"

"On the contrary," the fae man said. "I think he seems in excellent spirits."

"I'm fine, Edik," Yamato said, then turned an apologetic expression on the fae man. "Honestly. He's such a worrier. Have you met his cat?"

"I have not," the fae man said. "You must be the one known as Dola. I am called the Doorman."

"Under the circumstances," Dola said slowly, his fur standing up, "I'm not certain I can say I'm pleased to make your acquaintance."

"This man has been enchanted," Edik said. "As liaison for the Du Mak people, I…"

An idea sparked in Edik's head. He found himself smiling.

"You what?" the Doorman asked, suspicion plain on his face now.

But Edik stepped past him into the common area.

"Everyone!" Edik yelled. "Come out here please. I need you all for this!"

"Really," the Doorman said, "I'm sure you and I can come to an—"

But Edik didn't let the Doorman finish. He kept yelling and yelling until all the others came out to see what was the matter.

Edik kept at it until they were all out here. Anna, Mason, Romanova, Lukyanov, and Pajari. Even North.

No Donal, but Donal might have been too much to ask.

And besides. Dola was right. As ambassador for the Fae Courts, Donal might not have been able to take a stand here.

The Doorman and Captain Yamato came out as well, which meant that the latter had broken Edik's circle. But if this worked, the circle wouldn't matter.

"Captain Yamato tried the cookies and coffee," Edik said.

"Marvelous," Yamato said, drawing out the word. "Truly, if you haven't, you must."

Edik watched as every face around him showed understanding of the situation.

The heads of the great families, of course, got calculating. But at least Anna, Mason, and North immediately got indignant.

"Now the Doorman here," Edik said, "he seems to see nothing wrong with this. But it seems to me that Captain Yamato—"

"I *have* asked you to call me Haru, Edik."

"—that Haru here is not in fit mental shape to represent the interests of Earth in any kind of serious capacity."

"Oh, I don't know that that's true," Yamato said, but Mason spoke over him. "You're right, Edik. He wouldn't be."

Mason turned to the Doorman. "I request permission to attempt to free him from the enchantment he did not mean to seek."

"Honestly," Yamato said, "I *do not* feel enchanted. Why..."

Yamato kept talking, but everyone else continued the conversation without him.

"Denied," the Doorman said, with a pretense of sadness. "I'm afraid I can't have you casting spells on the ambassador from Earth."

"As a designated representative of the Du Mak people," Edik said, doing his best to talk over Mason's inevitable rejoinder and North's bluster, "I demand that the ambassador from Earth be freed from the unsought enchantment, and that all food and drink made available to us for this visit be free of any enchantments or personal consequences."

"We are what we are," the Doorman said simply. "It is the *nature* of our food that you dispute, not any deliberate acts of malice or glamour. Would you have us be such bad hosts as to not offer refreshment?"

"Free him," Edik said, heart pounding as he went for his hole card, "or I will not call the Du Mak. They will be absent from the coming meeting."

"As liaison for the Rhian people," Anna said immediately, "I support the words of the liaison from the Du Mak. Free Captain Yamato from the effects and consequences he suffered by eating and drinking, or I will not call the Rhian to the coming meeting."

"Luna is already here," Lukyanov said, "but Luna objects to what it sees as trickery on the part of the Fae Courts."

He held up a hand to forestall any objections on the part of the Doorman.

"*Nyet*, waste not your breath on denials."

Lukyanov shook his head, showing as much sadness as the Doorman had a moment ago. And likely with every bit as much sincerity.

"Luna objects to our being provided food and drink that carries any kind of risk, regardless of its nature. As such, Luna supports the words of the Du Mak and Rhian liaisons. Free this man, or Luna will not join in the meeting either."

"And Mars," Romanova said, picking up as smoothly as though she and Lukyanov had rehearsed this, "concurs with the objections from Luna to the state of the provided refreshments, and joins in supporting the Du Mak and Rhian demands. If they are not granted, Mars will absent itself from the coming meeting."

Everyone turned to look at Rasputin Pajari.

"Well," he said with a slow smile. "It all comes down to me, does it?"

"Please," Edik said. "Consider—"

Edik stopped talking when Pajari waved him to silence.

"There are two liaisons for factions of the Du Mak," Pajari said. "If one faction is not called, the other benefits. In that respect, I should not support the words of Captain Barshai."

Anna drew breath to speak, but Pajari waved her to silence too.

"However," he said, obviously enjoying himself a great deal, "it does occur to me that if the Fae Courts gain an advantage over Earth, that advantage might turn against the faction of the Du Mak whose interests matter most to me."

He stepped right up to the Doorman. Pajari was short, and the Doorman tall, so he had to crane his neck back to meet the Doorman's eyes.

But Pajari must have been looking up at men all his life. He sounded completely sure of himself when he said, "Release Captain Yamato. Free him from all effects and consequences of what he has eaten and drunk. And bear no ill will against any of us for making you do this. Agree to these things, or the Du Mak people will be entirely absent from the coming meeting."

Edik chimed in. "Won't be much of a meeting without any of us, will it?"

The Doorman frowned, but acceded.

WHEN CARL LAST CLOSED HIS EYES, HE'D BEEN ABOARD THE *THIRD SON*, finally confident that, for a time at least, his opinion and his sword would not be needed.

Thus, he had allowed himself to sink once more in the healing meditation.

This was not a skill taught to most magicians, as far as Carl understood. But perhaps it should have been. Goodness knew that Carl had come to rely on it over the years.

Healing meditation was a method of sinking deep into silence, while shunting and filtering the right kinds of energies into the etheric body, where their effects would filter smoothly and directly into the physical...

Then again, perhaps it wasn't for everyone. As Hierophant Mason had pointed out, Carl's etheric body had been modified as part of his training. Changed in ways that would speed his healing under all circumstances. And when healing meditation was available?

His recovery time was nothing short of miraculous.

When Carl opened his eyes now, though, he was not on the *Third Son*. He was not in anything like one of Edik's leather seats.

No. He was lying in a hospital bed.

Check that. A medical bay bed.

The differences were small, but significant. Little details in the materials. The feel of them, under Carl's head. The thickness of the pillows. All the little corners that were always cut for space travel, but not worth cutting anywhere permanent. Not even on a military base, much less a civilian hospital.

Four beds total in this med bay. Carl's was the only one occupied. Charts on the way of the meridians and winds and channels of the bodies. The power centers. All, typical doctor's office kind of stuff.

The herbal smells were consistent with a ship's med bay. Coriander, golden seal, buckeye and the like. The treatments for more typical ailments.

Carl sat up. His muscles felt a little stiff, but otherwise good.

That was as it should be. The stiffness would be gone within a few minutes of moving at stretching.

At long last, Carl felt like himself again.

He was getting up — and irritated to realize he was in a hospital gown — when the door at the far end of the room opened.

An owlish man entered. Carl would have known him for a doctor, even without the caduceus on his ship's uniform, or his aura of power. He had that look.

And as for his aura of power, he felt like ... either an advanced Journeyman, or a Magister. Tough to tell. So many doctors went in for certifications instead of the usual channels of progression magicians favored.

Thinning brown hair, and smiling big brown eyes.

Carl knew at once that this man had top notch bedside manner. Especially compared to the last doctor he'd seen, on Luna.

"Up already?" the doctor said with a chuckle. "Seems none of my patients want to slow down today. I'm Doctor Ramirez. And you, I believe, are Carl Jones?"

"That's right," Carl said, and his throat rasped a little more than he expected. Used too much of his body's water-of-water in his healing.

Dr. Ramirez started getting Carl a glass of water from the tap at the side of the room as though it were the whole reason he entered in the first place.

"Well, Carl Jones," Dr. Ramirez said, still smiling as he handed over the glass of water. "You were unconscious when they brought you aboard. Didn't figure you for coming out of it that quickly."

"Wasn't unconscious." Carl paused for a swig of water, and ended up draining the glass.

First rule of healing that Carl had been taught. If anything tasted that good, he needed more of it.

Carl walked over to the tap and refilled the glass himself while Dr. Ramirez took notes on his zephyrpad.

"You *aren't* going to tell me you were meditating," Dr. Ramirez said, slight admonishment to his tone. "You're not licensed to practice magic — though your champion's license includes magical dueling, I noticed..."

Carl knew that pause. Dr. Ramirez was hoping Carl would explain the discrepancy. Carl only smiled, and drank his water.

"Have it your way," Dr. Ramirez continued. "But I have a pretty good feel for magic, and you don't feel like more than a Journeyman to me. I find it a little difficult to believe that a Journeyman could be so proficient at meditation as you would have to be to have been meditating this whole time. Including a shuttle ride from one ship to another, and plenty of manhandling."

"I understand," Carl said slowly, "that Journeymen, in training, often prank each other by moving their meditating friends. Is what I did so much more difficult?"

"Yes."

Those owlish eyes did bore into Carl. But Carl had been bored into by the best.

Carl only smiled back. "Let's hear it for private tutors, eh?"

"Honestly," Dr. Ramirez said, making a note in his zephyrpad. "As though a doctor can't figure these things out. Now, back to bed."

"Why? I'm fit enough to—"

"Until I've given you a complete examination, I refuse to certify you able to get up and move around."

"But if I certify myself—"

"You're at high space, Mr. Jones."

Carl grimaced.

"Oh," Dr. Ramirez said with the smile of a cat who's caught a mouse. "Know a thing or two about space law, do you?"

"Enough to know how it applies to me." Carl shook his head. "All right. Let's get this over with."

Carl popped back onto the edge of his bed while the doctor gathered his tools.

At least Dr. Ramirez liked to talk. By the time the examination was over, Carl would know more about what was going on. Most important, he'd know where his friends were.

From there, it would just be a matter of figuring out how to help them...

7

One good thing about having the *leannan sidhe* around. She had an excellent sense of fashion and color. Much better than Donal's.

Left to his own devices, Donal would have chosen something in a midnight blue to wear to the coming meeting. Morna had talked him out of it.

"The key," she'd said, "is looking casually powerful. Those dark colors project power for you, true, but they lack the ... relaxed nature that a representative of the Courts should bring."

"Do I have to worry about color affiliation and the Courts?"

"Of course not," Morna said, puzzlement all through her features. "The Summer Court wears dark colors betimes, and the Winter Court such light colors as they choose. It—"

"But what about those castles?" Donal said. "White and black. Can't get much more polar opposite than that."

"Castles?" Fionn asked, leaning forward and ears wary. "There are no castles allowed near this hill."

"They're glamour," Morna explained. "If humans came through the mists and didn't see gleaming castles, they wouldn't believe they were here."

Nerves fluttered through Donal at the casual intimation of the power of fae magic. A himself a handful of slow, deep breaths helped calm him. Deception magic was one of Donal's specialties, but he hadn't actually *looked* at the castles. They were background.

Made perfect sense. The best illusions were always the ones no one had reason to suspect.

"I'm sorry," Donal said. "That's not important right now. You were saying about the Courts and clothing selection."

"It is their natures that make them what they are," Morna said, as though Donal had never interrupted her, "not their trappings. Tis the same with you, of course, master."

"Then if my nature doesn't matter—"

"In terms of who and what you are," Morna said. "In terms of the image you project for the coming meeting, trust me. Please, master. I know a great deal about image."

Donal had nodded, and Morna had gone through the armoire and the choices that had been provided for him. She had pulled out a shirt that looked ... well, blousy. It poofed in the sleeves, and it didn't have anything like what Donal thought of as a masculine cut. And it wasn't entirely opaque.

But Donal held his tongue as she laid it across the bed and looked at it. It was a creamy, off-white color. Donal wasn't sure about it at all.

Back into the armoire Morna had gone, and returned with a kilt. The ... colors of the Black Watch, unless Donal was mistaken.

"That's casual?"

"Casual *power* is what matters," she said. "The meeting is still formal, and this will serve you better than a suit. The other men are likely to wear suits. You'll be the only one in a kilt."

"That's true enough. But I thought we weren't going with dark—"

"Please," Morna said. "Give me time, master."

Donal nodded. He looked over at Fionn, who sat very still. As though that could hide the amusement fairly vibrating out of him.

Morna returned with a sporran, belt, knee socks and shoes that looked almost wooden.

"You're sure about this, Morna," Donal said, but she only smiled.

Once she had the clothing laid out on the bed, she looked at it.

Then she looked at Donal. Frowned slightly. Tilted her head one way, then the other.

"May I brush out your hair, master?"

"I can comb it quick, if it needs it."

"Allow me to rephrase," she replied with a bow. "Please allow me to prepare your hair, master."

Donal looked at Fionn. "How is that different?"

"You'll see. Let her do it. At least this once."

Donal frowned, but nodded.

The *leannan sidhe* stepped behind Donal, but she was so tall he didn't need to lower himself as she...

Oh, but that felt marvelous. Was she just running her fingers through his hair? Donal could feel it all the way down to his toes. And it seemed as though she had dozens of fingers, moving different directions.

Then, just as swiftly, the wonderful sensation ceased.

Donal almost objected, but caught himself.

From the look in Morna's eye as she stepped in front of him, she knew the objection had been there.

"There, master," she said, and held up a small pocket mirror to show Donal his hair. "Much better."

Donal had to admit she was right. He looked as though he'd just sat in a stylist's chair for an hour, getting his ends evened, and his locks washed, dried, and brushed out just so.

"All right," Donal said, "you have a point."

"Then you'll love what I can do with clothes." Her smile gained another dimension as she said, "Please, master. Strip."

"I don't think—"

"Or allow me to disrobe you. Oh, do please allow me that, master."

"I can handle it myself, thank you, Morna," Donal said. "I'll just step into the bathroom then, shall I?"

"Must you?" she asked, fluttering her lashes and giving him a hopeful look. "I know you must be feeling the stress of the coming meeting. I could help with that—"

"No, no," Donal said quickly, stepping over and into the bath-room. "Stress is good for me. Keeps me focused."

"You'll have to do better than that one," Fionn said, in words only Donal could understand. "She's going to be around for a while, after all."

Donal shut the door.

Looked at himself in the mirror. He wasn't used to beautiful women falling all over themselves for him. Much less women whose beauty was downright otherworldly.

"How do I cope with this?" he asked his reflection.

"I can't help with that," his reflection said back, making Donal stand up straight while a wash of cold ran down through his system.

"What—"

Donal cut off his own words when he realized he knew the answer.

The Duchess of Mirrors.

"I believe you know," his reflection said, and bowed slightly. "But I have a gift for you."

From one pocket, Donal's reflection pulled out a small velvet box. His reflection reached out of the mirror and set the box down on the wooden counter.

"Her Grace bids you wear that to your coming meeting. She says you will find it quite useful."

And then Donal's reflection was just a reflection again. And Donal waved both hands and jumped around for a moment to make sure.

Then he frowned. Was there nowhere safe to take off his clothes?

A gentle knock on the bathroom door.

"Master." Morna's voice. "Your garments are ready for you. May I clothe you?"

"I can dress myself."

"Have you ever worn a full kilt before, master?"

"As a matter of fact, I have."

Cuthbert family reunions only happened every few years, but when they did, full kilts for the men were mandatory on day one.

After that, the filibegs were good enough for the rest of the reunion.

"As you wish then, master."

She sounded disappointed, but that was just fine with Donal. She'd have to get used to disappointment.

Donal opened the door only just enough to receive the clothing she handed him. He noted that her eyes tracked him anyway, and showed more disappointment that he was still dressed.

The shirt was the same material as it had been, but now it was the pale blue of late spring.

The kilt no longer felt like wool. It felt ... lighter. Almost ... nebulous. And it held a different tartan pattern. One Donal had never seen before. And the colors had changed to shades of blue with only touches of black.

The hose matched the shirt, and the shoes were now low boots of a soft leather. Deerskin, if Donal was any judge.

Donal noted that Morna intended for Donal to wear the kilt ... traditionally. Not that this surprised him. Still, he *was* accustomed to underwear.

Donal gritted his teeth and trusted her fashion sense.

Donal dressed in the bathroom, and when he regarded his own image, he had to admit he looked pretty good. The shirt, now on him, didn't look blousy at all. Or even at all translucent.

It all worked together, and...

...it almost made him look like one of the fae.

The outfit. He wore it as though he were wearing a piece of the sky, much the way Morna's gown fit her like spun moonlight.

"Whose tartan am I wearing?" Donal called out through the closed door.

"It's a new pattern, great one," Morna called back. "You'll need it one day when your children and grandchildren are called not Cuthbert, but O'Donal."

"Getting ahead of ourselves, aren't we?" Donal muttered to his reflection.

"It *is* a good look," his reflection said. "And the tartan suits you."

Donal frowned, but thanked his reflection, then picked up the velvet box and walked back into the main room of his quarters.

"Perfect," the *leannan sidhe* said, sounding almost like a teenager mooning over a shadow play star.

"What is that?" Fionn said, immediately focusing on the box.

"It's a gift from" — Donal closed the bathroom door and glanced around to make certain there were no more mirrors in the area — "Her Grace."

"You mustn't refuse it," Morna said immediately. "Master, please, trust me on this. If it is to be worn, wear it. If it is to be consumed, consume it. Refusing a gift from such as her would carry consequences you cannot soon grasp."

"She's right," Fionn said, "unfortunately. After the meeting you can put it away, but for now..."

Donal opened the box. Inside was a small golden pin, shaped like a harp.

Morna immediately picked it up and pinned it to Donal's kilt at his left shoulder.

"But—" Donal started, but Fionn hushed him.

That was surprising enough that Donal stopped talking.

"What did you sense?" Fionn asked Morna.

"As any harp, played well, moves the heart, so *words* of the heart are clear to the wearer of *this* harp."

"More poetic than I would have have said it," Fionn said, "but that's what I sensed as well."

"I'm supposed to go into a political meeting able to hear what people really mean? Kind of an unfair advantage."

"But one you cannot refuse," Morna said urgently. "Please."

"I need time to think this though," Donal said.

A knock on the door.

"I'd say you're out of time," Fionn said.

"No closer, Mr. Burke," Jacobs said, staring out the transparent dome of his bridge at the great floating area that looked for all the world like an Earth mist.

Not a nebula of any color or variety. But a mist.

And the *Horizon Cusp* was now as close to it as Jacobs was willing to get. Closer than any of the three Terran Naval ships out here would get, but Jacobs didn't blame them for that.

Their crews weren't likely as good as his.

"Be ready for full reverse," Jacobs said. "Just in case."

"Aye, sir," Burke said, his own eyes wide but his voice and hands steady.

"Anything, Mr. Grabowski?"

"Only that the lacuna doesn't like being this close to it, sir. It refuses to even try to look at the space there, no matter what I do."

"Sir," Hernandez called up from communications, "I have Chief Jang on the link for you."

Jacobs nodded and Jang's irritated face showed up at his station. Her hair was even untidier than usual.

"Just what the hell are you doing up there, Captain?"

Jacobs only raised one eyebrow.

"Sorry, sir." She didn't sound sorry *enough*, but she kept going. "The Deception Drive's lacuna is going nuts. And it's nothing going on down here."

"Mr. Grabowski," Jacobs said, "send the scanner information to Ms. Jang."

Grabowski nodded, and a moment later Jang frowned.

"That ... doesn't make sense. Lacunas can't help but sense *everything*. It's in their nature. As long as they aren't in range of a planet's sylphs, they..."

"Wait," Machado called up from where he'd been talking with Cromartie and Medici down along the outer ring of the bridge. "Say that again."

"I said." Jang raised her voice. "As long as they aren't in range of a planet's sylphs, lacunas can't help but sense everything. It's in their nature."

"Curse me for a novice," Machado said. Then louder. "Jang, I owe you dinner when we get into port."

"Damn right you do!" she called back. Then, quieter, to Jacobs she added, "Why does he owe me dinner?"

"I think you just helped him solve a problem he's been working on. I'll get back to you. In the meantime, if the lacuna is acting up, try the sylphs. Maybe you'll get somewhere with them. Bridge out."

Jacobs cut the link and looked down to see what his mages were up to. But the three of them were deep in conversation. So Jacobs turned back to his bridge crew.

Just then the door to the bridge opened, and a man walked onto the bridge. A man who looked like violence made flesh, right down to the steel-handled saber at his side.

This was the man who'd been brought aboard unconscious not that long ago?

"This is the bridge," Jacobs said, managing to sound both official and gentle at the same time. "If you're looking for the mess hall, you should try one of the restaurants down on the Main Deck."

"I was told the ship's mage is—"

The man turned away from Jacobs and to Machado.

"One. Second." Jacobs said, and the man understood rank well enough to stop mid-step and look back at Jacobs. "Who are you and why are you on my bridge?"

"My name is Carl Jones, Captain. I'm ... ex-Terran Navy. I'm also a magician, and I'm carrying links to Anna Lukyanova, Edik Barshai, Roger North, and Hierophant Nicholas Mason."

"You are?" Machado asked the question at the same time as Jacobs, but Machado sounded more impressed.

"They're friends. Well most of them. And I thought that I might be able to help find and bring them back."

"Then, Captain," Machado said, glancing up, "may I formally requisition this man's assistance in dealing with our extant problems?"

"You may, Mr. Machado, and thank you for following protocol. Keep me informed."

"Aye, Captain."

Jacobs turned back to his station, but a thought occurred to him.

"Lieutenant Medici," Captain Jacobs called down.

"Sir?" Medici responded, coming to attention.

"Does your ship have emergency links to its crew?"

"No, sir. I was just telling Magister Machado that the Terran Navy had to discontinue the practice last year. The Terran Assembly decided that it was a violation of the Basic Right to Privacy."

"Idiots," Jacobs grumbled. It probably was, he knew it, but still, privacy didn't mean much to the dead. Louder, he said, "Ah, well. Thank you anyway. Carry on."

She saluted, and Jacobs was impressed enough to return the salute.

"Sir," Grabowski called from scanners. "I heard what you suggested to Chief Jang about the Deception Drive."

"And?"

"And I'm getting something from the sylphs. Didn't think to check them, 'cause we're at space. But still—"

"Details, Mr. Grabowski. What do the sylphs tell you?"

"They tell me there's air in the mist, sir. And land on the other side of it. Land that feels to them a lot like Earth, sir, but not quite."

"That may be," Jacobs said, "but I don't want to trust that means it's safe."

"No, sir." Grabowski said quickly. "The sylphs seem more comfortable than the lacuna, but not by a whole lot. I just wanted to assert that information is coming in. I'll keep trying for more and better, sir."

"Good man." Jacobs turned to his helmsman. "Mr. Burke, have you tried the planetary engines?"

"No response, sir. Maybe that mist has air, but the sylphs in the engines can't find much where we are."

Interesting. Jacobs had never been entirely sure that there wasn't air in space. True, when he'd been a child, he'd been told that space was frozen vacuum. But since the rise of magic, no one seemed to agree exactly what space was and was not, anymore.

"Well, keep testing, all of you. We need as much information as we can get our mages here, while they figure out how we can get our people home."

"Sir," Tunold said from his own station. "May I remind you that you're due for a break?"

"You may not," Jacobs said. "This is an emergency, Mr. Tunold. I belong right where I am."

"Sir," Tunold said, "may I remind you that Mr. Ramirez was already called to the bridge once today to revive you?"

That seemed to stop all activity on the bridge, as the crew turned to look at their captain.

Well, all but the magicians, who were deep in discussion.

"Very well," Jacobs said. "The conn is yours for thirty minutes, Mr. Tunold. I'll be in my office. I expect to be alerted immediately of any developments."

"Aye, sir," Tunold said.

As Jacobs stiff knees carried him down the stairs from the station, he had to admit to himself that a break sounded like a good idea.

Not that he'd ever admit it aloud.

When Edik saw where the meeting was to take place, he felt rather foolish.

He'd been expecting a *meeting*. Office chairs. Big, vaguely rectangular table. Room with four walls and a ceiling. Maybe several shades of gray for the color scheme.

That was what Edik thought of, when he thought of meetings.

But when the tiny man in the green cap returned to escort everyone to the meeting, he didn't take them anywhere like Edik was expecting.

Instead, he led them down a tunnel out of the common area. A tunnel that hadn't been there a moment before.

Literally. One moment, it had been solid earth — or whatever the ground should be called here. Solid Faerie, maybe — and the next, it just melted into a nice, roomy, regular tunnel.

The little man led the way, and light seemed to precede him by maybe about two meters.

The heads of the great families insisted on going first. Romanova and Lukyanov side by side, with Pajari trying to stay in step but not quite allowed to.

Anna followed, with Mason beside her. Then Captain Yamato.

Finally, Edik and Dola. And North.

For some reason, North was back here, walking with Edik instead of walking up beside Anna and Mason, where Edik had figured North would be.

North didn't look quite like himself, either. He frowned deeper than normal, and he kept glancing back over his shoulder as they walked. One hand always hovering near his cutlass.

Edik almost wanted to ask what was bothering him. But the truth was, Edik wasn't sure he wanted to know.

Anyway, Edik had been more interested in keeping an eye on Captain Yamato, to make sure he truly had shaken off the effects of eating and drinking, earlier.

But Captain Yamato's step had been steady, his posture erect, and his expression neutral.

Good enough.

Still, instead of leading them all into the kind of meeting room Edik had been expecting, the tiny man in the green hat led them straight outside.

Here, beside the hill, it was twilight. That time when the sun was absent, but the sky was not yet truly dark. No shadows to be seen anywhere on the ground, or among the thick, green grass.

Just ahead, a fire pit, currently unlit, but full of neatly chopped logs. Surrounding the fire pit, a series of large stones, nine in all. Stones of a size that would be comfortable to sit on...

One each, for every ambassador, adviser and liaison. Even one for North.

Well, there was one additional stone, but it was already occupied by Rowan MacPherson.

There was something less ... staggering about her, as she sat there on the rock. She still looked too beautiful to be real, with her hair down and wild, but no longer did it seem so difficult to look away from her. To think about anything other than her.

Whatever it was that had changed, it certainly wasn't her tailor.

Rowan MacPherson wore what looked like a piece of the twilight sky itself, wrapped around her in ways that did conceal everything that modesty would expect, but the dress seemed to have a sense of movement about it. As though, even as she sat still, the dress fluttered in a breeze that Edik didn't feel.

And there was no breeze this evening. Edik could still smell fresh air and clean grass, but nothing more than that.

"Is there a preferred arrangement?" Romanova asked.

"Sit as you choose," MacPherson replied, gesturing to the stones. "As Hostess my concern is your presence, not the choice of seat."

Romanova sat at MacPherson's right hand, and Lukyanov at her left. Anna sat almost opposite MacPherson, with Mason on her right and North on her left.

Pajari sat beside Romanova, and Yamato beside Lukyanov.

That left one seat, between Pajari and North.

Not the place Edik would have chosen for himself, but he took it all the same. Perhaps it was better to have the two Du Mak liaisons side-by-side anyway.

At least the stone was comfortable. Felt like the thing was padded. Couldn't have been, but that didn't seem to matter here.

"What about Donal?" Anna asked, and Edik realized that all the stones were full, but Donal wasn't here yet.

"Donal will be here ... ah, there he is now."

With those last words, MacPherson smiled as much with her voice and posture as with her lips.

Edik turned and saw ... yes, that *was* Donal, wasn't it?

Edik almost didn't recognize the man. He was dressed like one of the fae, in clothes that didn't seem quite real. And that he was wearing a *full kilt* only seemed to enhance the effect. Especially with Fionn on Donal's right side, and just behind him...

Did this man just collect women or something?

Another fae beauty was following behind Donal, looking every bit as amazing as that MacPherson woman, only this one was more willowy, with silver hair that reached her calves, and a low-cut gown that shimmered and flowed as though it were made from water and moonlight.

"Guess it's me that's got to stand," North said, his shoulders still hunched. But before he could get up, MacPherson spoke again.

"No," she said, "as Hostess, I have no seat, once the meeting is begun. Donal shall sit here, and I shall stand and facilitate."

Donal did smile, when Edik met his eye, but he looked troubled.

Donal took his seat, Fionn sitting on the ground as his right hand the way Dola sat next to Edik. The silver-blonde woman stood behind Donal on his left, looking very pleased to be there.

Wait. Donal had Fionn with him. Edik, of course, had Dola. Why was Mason's familiar not here?

"Liaisons," MacPherson said, "if you would please call forth the people you represent, we can begin this meeting properly."

<hr>

Machado enjoyed attempting new forms of thaumaturgy. It was one of the reasons he subscribed to as many different trade magazines as he did, along different specializations.

Yes, his first love was the magic of space. But deeper than that ran his love of magic itself. And there was no way he wanted to risk missing out entirely on any new developments in the art.

But this. This was beyond anything that anyone had ever attempted. At least, so far as Machado knew.

What he needed to do could never have been accomplished from the bridge. He stood down on the Observation Deck now.

The Observation Deck was easily one of the most popular attractions among tourists who flew on the *Horizon Cusp*. All the way down at the bottom of the gryphon's belly, it was a deck all but entirely transparent.

Almost, because standing seemingly unprotected in space proved to be too much for some passengers possessing more delicate constitutions.

Thus, there was a gray walkway, that led from the bubble, one path out to the port bulkhead, back, and over to an enclosed, gray-walled lounge. A haven, for those who were fine ... until they weren't.

A couple of years back, Machado had inscribed two large magic circles in the floor of this deck. As a matter of fact, he'd done it after Cuthbert had — unintentionally, at least — drawn two zuglodons to attack the ship.

Not one, but two of those gigantic space spirits. Either one of them could have ripped through the wards and torn the ship apart.

Machado had had some time getting rid of those things. Might not have been able to do it, without Cromartie working himself into unconsciousness.

Yes, and some help from Cuthbert.

After that flight, Machado had inscribed the two circles. Just in case he ever had to do something like that again.

What he was up to right now was nothing like that.

And yet, this deck was still the best place to do it.

Sure, he would have preferred working in the marvelous, fine-tuned circles in his lab. But he needed everyone involved to have their physical eyes on that great mist in space.

Links were all well and good, but there was nothing like having one's eyes literally looking at the target.

Or in this case, as close as they could come.

Machado stood at the arbitrary northern point of the circle. Yes, it was arbitrary. There was no north in space. No poles, after all. And yet, for ritual purposes, it worked well enough to simply assign a direction and go from there.

North, of course, was to the fore, and south to the aft.

With that in mind, Machado had positioned Cromartie in the

relative east (starboard), Medici in the relative west (port) , and Jones in the relative south.

Jones. An unusual man, this Jones. No certifications at all. No record of training that Machado could find.

And yet.

And yet.

And yet this man was a Journeyman. Machado was quite sure of it. He had no license, but his aura of power was decidedly that of a Journeyman.

Though his aura of power felt ... off. As though he'd achieved this status not through the sort of generalized thaumaturgic training one would expect, but rather through a series of Initiate-level intensives.

Yes. That was as close as Machado could come to it. If Machado talked theory with this man, Machado was certain Jones would display a Journeyman's understanding of a good many topics, but some ... interesting gaps.

Machado could only hope that Jones could hold up his end of this. Bad enough that Cromartie was only an Initiate. This effort really did require at least a Journeyman in all four quarters.

Machado could only hope he himself was good enough to make the difference.

In the center of the circle, the links Jones had provided. Tiny snippets of arm hair, taken recently enough to still be potent, from Anna Lukyanova, Hierophant Nicholas Mason, Initiate Edik Barshai and Initiate Roger North.

Arm hair. An interesting choice. Most would take hair from the head for this, but Jones had taken hair from the arm. Machado almost had to wonder if the four in question knew Jones had taken those hairs.

Curiouser and curiouser, this man's training.

Beside the links in the circle, Machado's small copper brazier. Its coals burning hot, and kicking out incense heavy on the dragon's blood. Dragon's blood added a power on its own, but more than that, it would activate the alchemical formula anointing each magician present at the wrists, the heart and the forehead.

Saravá passed along the edge of the circle, touching each celebrant with his nose. Creating a connection among the four of them, over and above the connection of their positions in the circle.

Links. Everything always came down to links. The more the better. The tighter the better.

When *Saravá* returned to Machado, touching nose to forehead once more, the ghostly *onça* took his position behind his master.

Machado activated the circle with a small flare of power. With his consciousness already flowing along the right lines, he could see the white circle now shimmer electric blue.

Machado reached into the depths of his own power, and stretched to relative east for Cromartie, who added his own as he stretched toward relative south to Jones.

Test one. Jones passed. He added his power and passed along to Medici.

Medici finalized the connection to Machado.

The four of them began flowing power through that connection. Swirling and building. A circle within a circle. Power within power.

Machado reached deeper inside himself to his personal connection with the element of earth. Dug down deep into its cool, stable power. Raised it up, and sent it along that cord between himself and Cromartie, who pulled the element of air from within, and added it to the mixture.

Jones came next, and he pulled fire from within himself as smoothly and naturally as though he did this every day. He sent it along, blended with the others, to Medici, who added water.

The heady combination reached Machado again, and he led the chant.

The chant, properly speaking, was derived from ancient Greek papers, and involved names of gods that were long gone when even the Greek empire rose.

But those words, their meaning forgotten now, yet served to build power and focus it.

The chant built, and the power built with it. Doubled. Tripled. Now five-fold. Ten-fold.

Cromartie's voice got thick with effort. But Machado had to push. Twelve-fold. Fifteen-fold.

Machado could hear the strain in Jones and Medici now. Cromartie was almost overcome. His voice not much more than a rasp.

But if this was to work, they needed all they could get.

Machado spread his hands wide, ready to act when the moment came.

Eighteen-fold. More power than Machado needed even to run the shields at their highest levels.

Twenty-fold.

Peak.

Cromartie, sweating, collapsed, and Medici followed right behind him.

Jones staggered but kept his feet. Flung his hands toward the links in the center of the circle. Might even have been drawing further on his own personal connection with those Machado was trying to reach.

The more links, the better.

Machado flung all that massed power into the links, channeled through one simple command.

Come.

It was a summoning. It used the format Machado knew best for other forms of summoning, but it was unlike any previous effort, because he was not summoning some elemental or distant spirit.

He was trying to summon human beings.

It sounded impossible. It might have been impossible. Certainly anywhere else, under any other circumstances, it had to be impossible.

But right now it was the best shot they had.

And so Machado stretched through those links with all the power he and the others had gathered. He reached through those links and straight through the misty barrier between this world and Faerie.

If he were summoning fae, it would have worked like a charm. But to summon humans?

Machado could only try. And hope.

And focus as he had never focused before.

———

Anna withdrew the stone from where she hid it up her left sleeve.

Oolaut had never really told her *how* to use it to call him. But Anna *had* been given instructions in the basics of thaumaturgy as part of her education — never more than that, Father would never have allowed it — so she hoped she had the principles correct.

Anna reached into the stone. Not with her fingers, but with her thoughts. Her attention. She tried to extend a part of her own mind into the stone, so cool and smooth in her hand. Even here, it glowed with a faint yellow echo of Kennedy's Barrier.

Anna then thought of Oolaut. His stony shape, his three thick legs, the little spots at the end of the sloping neck-head that she thought of as his eyes.

And Anna thought as hard as she could.

Oolaut. It is Anna Lukyanova who calls you. The meeting is ready to commence, and your presence is requested.

The stone vanished from her hand. Her fingers closed on the gap it left behind.

And before her stood a living god.

That was the only way Anna could think of this ... individual.

It was masculine — undeniably so — but far too perfect to disparage with any term so mundane as "man."

He stood a full two meters tall. Maybe more. Every centimeter of his skin that Anna could see — which was considerable, as he was clad in nothing more than a short toga, the white of starlight — was golden, and muscled just the right amount to be enticing.

Not over-muscled, like those men who spent all their time with their weights. But everywhere she could see, he was toned to perfection.

Anna was a Lukyanova. She would not allow her jaw to drop, nor saliva to drip from her lips. She would not even allow her eyes to open as wide as they wished, that they might take in even more of this magnificent sight.

But the temptation to do all these things was every bit as strong as the temptation to reach out and run her hands over that perfect, golden skin. To look up into those eyes like mid-day suns. To run her fingers through that russet hair, so curly, all the way to those perfect shoulders.

"Anna," the living god said to her, in a voice like a Beethoven symphony. "I thank you for calling me. But I fear I must ask more of you than that."

"Oolaut?" Anna asked, blinking in shock and folding her hands in her lap to keep them to herself.

"Of course." Oh, but his smile was like a ray of sunlight in the middle of the worst winter storm. A ray that shone out only for her.

"And I thank you," Oolaut continued, adding a slight bow that finally made her blush. "You have done myself and the Rhian people immeasurable service."

"It was nothing, really," she said, then bit the inside of her mouth. "I am pleased to have been of service, and honored to aid you in recovering your proper place, whether it is with these Fae Courts, or elsewhere."

Then she realized she'd missed part of what that wonderful voice had told her.

"What further service could I be?"

"I should probably answer that," said that annoying MacPherson woman. Honestly, putting on a faerie face to pretend to beauty she did not possess.

Anna turned away from the glory of Oolaut all the same.

"Much as the Fae Courts themselves take no place at this table but through their ambassador, Donal Cuthbert, it would not be proper for either the Rhian or Du Mak peoples to claim their places, save through their own representatives."

Anna turned to look the question at Oolaut, but he nodded.

"She is right, of course. Some of us have not seen the others since your race was still quite young. And others of us, I believe, have not yet met at all."

Anna turned to see about these others.

Standing in front of Edik now was a lizardlike man, slightly more than two meters tall. He had four arms, and, on closer inspection, no actual scales. His smooth skin appeared to have scales, but Anna believed they were only a pattern in the browns and grays of his skin.

At least, Anna assumed it was a him. She could see no evidence of male or female features on this person in front of Edik. But then, she would not likely have known the gender of a lizard or snake on first sight, and those were all she could compare this being to.

Another such being stood in front of Pajari. The same coloring, but in different patterns. This one had diamond shapes here and there among its colors, while the one standing in front of Edik had more elliptical shapes in his coat.

And the one in front of Pajari had seen battle. He — if it was also a he — appeared to have three black scars running across his torso, and his lower left arm had been burnt off at the elbow.

If elbow was the right word. Anna wasn't sure.

Both these individuals had crests flaring behind their heads as they regarded one another.

"I would remind you," MacPherson said, "that you will only be allowed to represent your people here if you set your enmity for each other aside for now. If you cannot stand together without blood, you will accomplish nothing this day."

Both of them nodded. Slowly, and without looking away from each other.

"Should I still call you Cinnamon?" Edik asked. "I mean, you still smell like cinnamon, but—"

The Du Mak individual standing in front of Edik smelled nothing like cinnamon. He did have a pastry smell to him though. More like honey cakes.

Now Oolaut, he had a sort of masculine scent Anna had never smelled before. She did know she liked it.

"Cinnamon will do for this meeting," the one in front of Edik said, in hissing kind of high-pitched voice. "But I thank you for asking."

"I prefer to be called Hrissapkuss," the Du Mak in front of Pajari said. His voice a little deeper than Cinnamon's, and it seemed to carry a growl underneath it.

"How is this to work then?" Oolaut asked. "We are here. The Du Mak are here. But where are the Fae?"

No sooner did those words escape those perfect lips than two birds fluttered down to land on Donal's shoulders. A large raven on his left shoulder, and a tawny owl on his right.

The birds looked at each other across Donal's head.

"We represent..." the raven started.

"...the Fae Courts," the owl finished.

"I from Winter," the raven croaked.

"I from Summer," the owl hooted.

The birds leaned down and began whispering in Donal's ears. Anna marveled for a moment that Donal actually seemed to be listening to both, albeit with a frown, but she felt Oolaut tense up behind her.

"Whatever is the matter?" she asked as she turned.

Oolaut was staring at the birds, with thunder in his eyes.

"An old memory. From the time before. It is as I thought." Oolaut spoke louder. "We do know each other, do we not?"

"Please," MacPherson said quickly a touch of pleading in her voice. "Speak to each other through your representatives only from this point on."

"The Fae Courts wish it known," Donal said slowly, "that they have never before met the Rhian people. However." Donal drew a deep breath. "They do remember their old foes the *Fomhóraigh*, driven so long ago from the Emerald Isle. And in particular, they recognize the person of—"

"The representative of the Rhian people," Anna said quickly, "wishes to remind all present that he is to be referred to as Oolaut." After a momentary prompting from Oolaut, she finished, "And he also recognizes the children of Danu."

"The Du Mak," Edik said, "do not know either of you, and hope that old enmities can be put aside as easily as new ones."

"Only a fool would believe that," Father said.

DONAL FELT ONLY TRUTH FROM LUKYANOV'S WORDS. AND WORSE THAN that, he felt the truth of those words hanging in the air like violence, waiting to happen.

Not just from the unmasked "Rhian people." He felt it from Morna. From the fae masquerading as birds on his shoulders.

Even Fionn felt only one step away from action. And his eyes stayed glued to the one who insisted on being called Oolaut.

"The representative of Luna is right," Romanova said. "And Mars must ask if the Fae Courts and ... well, let us continue to call you the Rhian people ... can set aside their old differences for purposes of determining what we can determine here today?"

"Earth echoes the question," Captain Yamato said, smoothly. "We have all traveled far and risked a great deal to be here. If, perhaps, this new information sheds light in ways that must be dealt with before talks can proceed, then perhaps we should all return to our quarters for now and resume later."

Half -truth there. Yamato wanted to find a way to leave. Donal couldn't blame him for that.

"Question," Hierophant Mason said, his eyes darting back and forth between the Rhian and the fae. "If we *do* adjourn for the time being, will we be provided with food and drink from our own worlds?"

"There will be no adjournment," Rowan said, which surprised Donal as much as the desperation she hid under the surface. "You must all understand that if we step away from this table, it may occur to some to claim that negotiations, and thus any temporary truces, are concluded."

"Ah," Lukyanov said. "You fear all will return to the business of killing one another."

"The Fae Courts," Donal said, "are not interested in adjournment, either temporary or permanent. They are ... surprised to learn the truth of the Rhian people, but—"

Donal muttered to the birds, "you sure you want me to say this part?"

They nodded.

"—but they are pleased to know what became of their old enemies after the battle."

"We drifted at sea for quite some time," Anna said, and the words were not hers, nor were the tone.

"Silence!" Rowan said, and a wave of magic swept over all.

She turned an admonishing finger on Oolaut.

"You will not turn your representative into a puppet."

"What else is a representative, really?" Pajari asked, but it sounded like his own voice. "What difference does it make if they whisper words into our ears or our heads?"

Rowan ignored him.

"You will release Anna Lukyanova's mind at once, or be banished from this meeting."

Anna suddenly sat forward, her face in her hands.

The golden man stood tall and terrible in his rage.

"The *Fomhóraigh* cast aside the name Rhian and reclaim our name of old. Just as I now cast aside the name Oolaut and reclaim the name you wished to call me. Nalacha."

The name rang in the twilight air. And in the distance Donal thought he felt something stir. A good many somethings. Especially in the direction of that crystal sea.

It was a name Donal knew from the old stories, but he could not remember what role Nalacha once played.

"Further," Nalacha continued, "we do not recognize the right of the Fae Courts to banish us from this meeting. Nor from this land *they* call Faerie."

Nalacha gnashed his gleaming teeth.

"It is ours as surely as the isle we fought over so long ago. Our swords have slept for thousands of years."

He leaned forward just a little. Raised hands as though he would strangle Donal from across the fire pit.

"But they are awake now," Nalacha continued. "And we are coming for you."

Nalacha leapt at Donal.

The birds on his shoulders flew to meet their ancient foe.

Morna grabbed Donal's left shoulder and Fionn his right. The *cú sidhe's* jaw clamped down, but it must have been some fae quality that kept Fionn from biting through Donal's skin and drawing blood.

Both yanked him back and began dragging him across the grass.

"Wait!" he cried out.

"No, master," Morna said. "You must flee."

Even as she said that, Donal saw Cinnamon turn and grapple with Hrissapkuss. But not like they were trying to hurt each other. More like Cinnamon was keeping Hrissapkuss from interfering.

At just that moment, Edik, Dola, Anna, North, even Hierophant Mason all just vanished.

"Stop!" Rowan yelled in a voice like a thunderclap at ground zero.

The birds were thrown back from Nalacha.

Cinnamon and Hrissapkuss were thrown apart.

Romanova, Lukyanov and Captain Yamato were all flung to the ground.

"I am the Hostess," she said in something like her normal voice, only more menacing. "Accepted in my role by all of you."

The birds looked up at her from the ground, as did Nalacha, Cinnamon and Hrissapkuss.

"You will not fight here," she said, and Donal felt power in those words.

"How dare you use that—" the raven started, but Rowan finished, "—you forced my hand."

She ran a glare across them all, and Donal could hear the words of her heart. She would pay a price for wielding this power. The Courts would never forget it.

Rowan might not survive this.

"Several humans are gone from us. Which of you took them?"

Those last five words echoed like thunder, and Donal even heard himself saying, "I did not."

But everyone at the table said the same three words. Even the captain and the heads of the lunar great families.

Lukyanov followed his own denial with rants and accusations until Rowan used more of her Hostess magic to silence him.

"Notwithstanding all honest denials, they are gone from us," Rowan said. "This meeting was stipulated to with the understanding you would be addressing each other through representatives. That is no longer possible for those invited here as the Rhian."

Donal could hear Rowan try to avoid more violence by drawing on the name of the ancient enemy.

"As Hostess, I claim that role, and the right to cut short negotiations to simple questions."

Rowan turned to Cinnamon and Hrissapkuss.

"One of your representatives is gone. Will you agree to work through the same representative?"

To Donal's surprise, they nodded.

"Earth," Rowan said, turning to Captain Yamato. "Will you welcome among your lands those commonly known as the Rhian?"

"Earth cannot," Captain Yamato said. "We have an existing agreement with the Fae Courts that precludes us from coming to similar agreements with their known enemies."

Nalacha started to respond, but Rowan spoke over him.

"Mr. Pajari," she said, "what do the Du Mak ask of Earth?"

"A moment," Donal said, pulling himself free from *leannan sidhe* and familiar to resume his seat.

"First," Donal continued while dusting himself off, "the Fae Courts wish to thank the Hostess for appropriate use of the rights and powers of her role, without descending into abuse. It is the opinion of the Courts that she should be commended."

The raven and owl immediately flew back to Donal's shoulders. Donal could feel their objections. He kept talking before they could voice them.

"Second. Earth cannot agree to anything regarding the Du Mak until the Fae Courts establish ground first."

That stalled the raven and owl.

"I should hardly think—" Captain Yamato started.

"And if the Fae Courts declare the Du Mak as enemies?"

Captain Yamato frowned, but nodded.

Donal drew a deep, focusing breath. He'd need to conclude this as quickly as he could. He desperately needed to find out what happened to Edik, Dola, Anna, Mason and North.

But first came the politics. And those always seemed to take forever.

MACHADO REDOUBLED HIS EFFORTS. FELL TO HIS KNEES BODILY WHILE his mind did nothing but focus on the call. On shunting power through those links. On demanding that those he called cut through that mist and appear here before him.

Cromartie was down, all but unconscious on the deck. Likewise Medici. Even Jones was flat on the deck now, drenched in sweat and lips unmoving, though his hands yet stretched and Machado could feel wisps of power still flowing from him.

Machado forced his own efforts to even greater heights.

And something burst, flinging him backwards to the deck. Slamming his head on the transparent ceramics.

Dazed, Machado rolled over to see what answered his call...

Into the circle they tumbled. Four, so it had to be all of them. Anna Lukyanova, Initiate Edik Barshai — and a large, gray translucent cat that had to be his familiar — Initiate Roger North, even Hierophant Nicholas Mason himself.

Machado sighed and smiled. Wiped sweat from his forehead and tried to stand. Took a moment, but he got a hand and his feet under him.

"What have you done?"

Leave it to a Hierophant to criticize even an effort of a sort that had never been accomplished before in modern thaumaturgy.

"Saved you," Machado said, "from fae kidnappers."

"That was the meeting," said the beautiful blonde woman who had to be Anna Lukyanova, looking every bit as angry as the Hierophant. "The entire reason we were out here."

There was just no justice in this life.

"Donal." Initiate Barshai. Had to be, based on Jones' description from their earlier conversation. He had the blonde Van Dyke and the familiar. "He's still back there. They'll kill him."

"So," Machado said with a small smile. "You *were* in trouble. No need to thank us."

"*Thank* you!" Machado didn't recognize that one, but by process of elimination the little pirate had to be Initiate North. "Send us back, you damned fool!"

Machado started laughing.

"Wait," Hierophant Mason said. "How did you get us here in the first place?"

Machado started laughing even harder.

"Excuse my master, Hierophant Nicholas Mason," *Saravá* said, taking up position between Machado and the Hierophant. "He has expended a great deal of time and effort into recovering you after your unexpected disappearance from the *MacArthur*. Employing the links provided by magician Carl Jones, my master fashioned a derivation of a summoning spell and led the ritual that succeeded in calling you back from across the mists."

"Send. Us. Back."

Initiate North had a lot to learn about gratitude, but Machado was too busy laughing. Though he was, he had to admit, a little surprised at being so giddy.

"Can't happen." That was Jones' voice?

Yep. The man was back on his feet, and looking steady, despite all the sweat.

Unfair. Jones was on his feet, and Machado was still half sitting on the deck.

Then again, Machado had done the bulk of the work. Plus, Jones looked to be fighting trim. Possibly from actual fighting.

Maybe there *was* something to this modern workout trend among magicians. Still, Machado would be damned before he gave up his *feijoada* or *cachaça*.

Machado shook himself and forced himself to his feet while Jones was explaining to the Initiates and Anna Lukyanova why the same links couldn't send them back.

Machado took that opportunity to send *Saravá* to the bridge with word of their success.

"We have to go back," Hierophant Mason said, once *Saravá* was away. "Donal—"

"Please," Machado said. "If there's anyone who can wriggle his way out of a tight spot, it's Donal Cuthbert."

"You don't understand," Hierophant Mason said, notably not denying what Machado had just said. "Romanova, Lukyanov, Pajari, and Captain Yamato of the *MacArthur*. They're all still there too. We can't just abandon them all."

"They can't have the meeting without us anyway," Initiate Barshai said, frowning and tugging on his blonde Van Dyke. "Can they?"

"Assuming they stop trying to kill each other long enough," Initiate North grumbled. "And don't forget Rowan MacPherson."

"She might not need our help," Anna Lukyanova put in. "She looked fae to me, and she did declare herself Hostess."

"Regardless, I don't see what we can do about it," Machado said with a frustrated shrug. "I don't have links for Donal or MacPherson."

"We both know Donal's signature though," Hierophant Mason said slowly.

"My master is spent," *Saravá* said, drifting down through the ceiling of the deck, apparently having delivered his report. "He will not be up to such a venture for some time. And forgive me for saying so, Hierophant Nicholas Mason, but if you intend to attempt to bridge the gap between here and Faerie on the basis of a magical signature, even you will need the help of at least a Magister. A *rested and ready* Magister."

"All right," Hierophant Mason said. "Machado, you rest. Your people too. You too, Carl. We'll likely need you for this."

Jones nodded.

Machado wanted to object, but *Saravá* stopped him by nuzzling his face.

"He does not intend to challenge your demesne, master. And you *must rest*."

Machado hated admitting it, but his familiar had a point. He was drenched in sweat, and all his muscles felt as though he'd tried to swim through space from Earth to Mars.

Machado started walking over to one of the viewing benches. Stretched out. He tried to keep listening, but already he could feel a nap creeping up on him.

"Anna," Hierophant Mason continued, "talk to the ship's alchemist. Maybe the two of you can work together to assemble some concoctions that would help."

"What about us?" Initiate Barshai said, clearly including Initiate North in his question.

"You know Donal's signature too, don't you, Edik?"

Initiate Barshai nodded.

"Good," Hierophant Mason said with a smile. "I have an ace up my sleeve. You two can help me plan how to best use it."

Machado wanted to know what that ace was, but the nap won.

8

When the meeting finally ended, the owl and raven flew straight off into the sky. The two Du Mak representatives phased away, as though they melted into the night air.

Nalacha approached Donal. Fionn immediately lowered his head and began growling, while Morna hissed and raised hands that looked more like talons now.

"I come in peace," Nalacha said in that deep voice of his.

Donal nodded. He hoped the move looked calm and smooth, but the truth was he didn't want to speak because he worried his voice would crack.

This was Nalacha of the *Fomhóraigh*. Straight out of the old myths.

At Donal's nod, Fionn stopped growling, but held his defensive pose. Morna held hers as well.

"I smell the Isles on you," Nalacha said, ignoring the fae hound and *leannan sidhe*.

"My mother's family goes back to Ireland, and my father's to Scotland."

Nalacha nodded. "The fae hold on you feels ... temporary."

"I negotiated a short-term contract. With lawyers."

"Really?" Nalacha said, russet eyebrows high. "Impressive accomplishment."

"Thank you," Donal ventured, worried even more now about where this was going.

"While your contract holds, you are my enemy," Nalacha said with a frown. "But I hold no personal grudge against you. My people were once gods to yours, even as the scions of Danu are now. When your contract ends, perhaps we could talk."

"I ... cannot commit to anything right now." Donatello Mancuso's words, coming out of Donal's mouth. A default answer for a proposal one could not simply refuse outright.

"Of course," Nalacha said with a small smile. "*Slán.*"

And with that Gaelic goodbye, Nalacha became an albatross flew off toward the crystal sea.

While Donal and Nalacha were talking, a tiny man in a long green hat led Romanova, Lukyanov and Captain Yamato away. Donal could hear Lukyanov pepper the tiny man with questions about his daughter and what had happened to her, but the tiny man seemed to pay him no mind.

Donal was escorted back to his room not by a tiny man in a green hat, but by Rowan, with Fionn beside him and Morna trailing, apparently watching Donal's back.

Donal tried to speak as they walked, but Rowan stalled him with a raised hand.

"Not yet," she whispered.

Once they reached his room, Rowan asked, "May I come in?"

"I don't think so," Donal said, frowning with uncertainty. "We need to talk, but I need time alone first. And a chance to talk to Fionn."

"I understand." She raised both hands. "As Hostess, I declare this private space."

Donal felt a bubble of fae magic pass though him. It tickled, like feathers across his skin. Made him twitch all over.

"I cannot take long this way," she said, and raised her hand to forestall any objections. "And I do not intend to engage you in the conversation you wished to delay."

She hesitated until Donal nodded.

"Thank you," she said, sounding as though she were thanking him for more than just permission for a moment's conversation.

Those two words came out of her with such urgency that Donal felt them slip down his spine and twirl in his guts.

"Really," Donal started, but Rowan wasn't finished.

"No, Donal. Don't downplay this. You saved my life back there. Maybe more than my life."

"I think that's—"

"It's not an exaggeration," Fionn said. "She's right. You forced the Fae Courts to both formally commend her for her actions."

"When those two in particular," Morna added, "would have been as happy to torment her slowly over the course of a decade for interfering with their excuse to battle Nalacha. Especially because he initiated the attack."

"And they might have taken turns tormenting me," Rowan said, and shivered.

"Who were..." Donal stopped himself with a grimace. "Not the queens or kings. Let me guess. The—"

"Use no names or titles," Rowan said quickly. "Even a Hostess' silence cannot keep them from hearing themselves spoken of. Not here."

"The ... two peers who have taken an interest in me?"

"The very same," Rowan said. "And you have stayed their hands, and done so without shaming them or embarrassing them. I owe you my life."

"You don't," Donal said quickly. "I didn't do anything they shouldn't have done themselves. And the last thing I want coming out of this is more fae debts."

Donal's turn to hold up a hand. "Changeling. *Sidhe.* Whatever you are, Rowan, you're fae enough that debt where you're concerned might be just as bad as debt to one of the peers."

"Tell me you don't believe that, Donal," Rowan said, looking crestfallen. "I'm not like them. I am of their blood. I have had to learn to play their games. But I am not them."

"I'm not sure what to believe anymore." Donal shook his head. "Too many surprises. Too much. I ... I'm not sure I can keep it all straight."

"All right," Rowan said, her eyes shining but no tears escaping. "I can understand that. But know this, Donal, that in matters of love and friendship or of business and debt, I am far more like you than I am at all like them."

"That's true, master," Fionn said.

Rowan looked at the *leannan sidhe* and raised an artful eyebrow.

"It's true," Morna said through a sigh. "She is more human than you currently believe, master. Though she may also be more fae than you know. But," she added quickly before Rowan could object, "she is human enough in matters of love and debt."

"All right," Donal said. "I'm not sure what that means right now, but all right."

"Then allow me this much." Rowan leaned in, and Donal held himself still.

Rowan kissed him on the cheek. A gentle press of lips that lingered, and as she pulled back Donal found himself smelling spring heather, and a touch of honey.

"The kilt really suits you, by the way," Rowan said, her eyes roving over Donal. She smiled at him. "Until we may speak again."

And she left.

Donal felt the magic of her bubble leave with her. He shook himself quickly. Glanced at Fionn and Morna.

Fionn watched Donal with a neutral expression.

Morna, for her part, looked jealous.

"Come on, then," Donal said. "We have much to discuss."

Donal opened the door to his room.

And a giant spider was waiting for him.

DONAL'S ROOM HAD REMAINED LARGELY UNCHANGED SINCE THE LAST time he'd been in it. Hard-packed bricks of clean dirt for the walls, floor and ceiling. Warm woods for the furniture, from the armoire to the writing desk, bookshelf, table and even the frame of the so-comfortable bed.

However, the last time Donal had been in it, there had been no insects or pests of any kind.

Now, right in the center of the room, sat a huge freaking spider.

It was black and chitinous. Easily a meter tall, and probably a meter across, not including the legs, which would have made it perhaps three meters across.

Just the sight of it was enough to make Donal's heart lurch to speeds it hadn't hit since Nalacha had tried to kill him earlier.

No one's heart should have to go that fast twice in one day.

But Fionn did not leap to attack, nor did Morna.

"Please, Journeyman Donal Cuthbert," the spider said in a high, clicking voice, "close the door that we may speak with privacy."

Fionn cocked his head to one side. Spoke quickly in that vaguely Gaelic-sounding language that all familiars seemed to speak, but Donal could never understand.

The spider responded in kind.

"It's safe, master," Fionn said. "He is from a friend."

Donal entered his room, trying not to think about that time, when he was six, and he had woken up to find a big, ugly black spider crawling up his arm.

Oh, how Donal had howled and shook his arm. Leapt out of his bed, intending to find something to give the spider a quick, certain end.

Bran, of course, wouldn't hear of it. Bran had scooped the spider up in his two hands and taken it outside. He left it on a tree, near a trail of ants.

But Donal had never quite been comfortable around spiders ever since.

And this one, well, it was too big for him to pretend to anything other than discomfort. His hands shook as he closed the harp pin in its velvet case.

"Perhaps," Fionn said, "if you shrank yourself a bit."

The spider shrank to half its size.

"Does this suit you better, Journeyman Donal Cuthbert?"

"I guess," Donal said, feeling not all that much better. His heart was still pounding, and he couldn't deny the trickle of sweat working its way down from his temple.

Nevertheless, the spider bowed, using its forelegs.

"I have the honor of being the familiar of Hierophant Nicholas Mason," the spider said. "I am called Clixic."

"A pleasure to meet you, Clixic," Donal said, even though he wasn't being entirely honest. Not even as grateful as he was to be hearing from Hierophant Mason.

"The Hierophant sends you his greetings. He has had me patrol out during your meeting, and bid me bring you the results before returning to report them to him."

"He's no longer anywhere near here," Donal said. "He vanished during the meeting."

"He did," Clixic confirmed. "He is no longer in Faerie at all. I don't know where he is, and that troubles me."

"Why have you not pursued him?" Fionn said, and Donal was pretty sure that tone was meant as admonishment.

"My master gave me a task," Clixic said, in the same tone. "I will fulfill it before I seek him out."

"Of course," Fionn said.

"I have learned of other humans in this area, Journeyman Donal Cuthbert. I do not know them, but believe they carry a similar quality to Captain Haru Yamato."

"From the *MacArthur*?" Donal asked, forgetting his discomfort and stepping closer to the great arachnid. "What are they doing here?"

"They were kitted out for battle. I suspect they were intended as a rescue team. They were taken by a party of fae knights from the Summer Court. That queen holds them even now."

"That must be the secret behind her smile," Morna said. "She somehow knew in advance of their coming."

"Where are they?" Donal asked urgently. "Where does she hold them?"

"I know not."

"You can't save them," Fionn said.

"The hell I can't," Donal said. "I'm the ambassador here, and this is a diplomatic incident."

"If *she* holds them," Morna said, "you must not interfere."

Donal turned to Clixic.

"I'd say…" Donal cut himself off from telling the spider its report was complete. He didn't want it leaving just yet.

"I have information for your master," Donal said instead. "Mars and Luna acknowledge each other's independence. The Rhian, under their proper name the *Fomhóraigh*, will find no home on Earth right now. But Luna and Mars will welcome them."

Donal shook his head, trying to keep it all straight. "The same is true of the Du Mak people, but that's not the Courts' fault. The Du Mak made agreements with Luna and Mars first, and Earth refuses to acknowledge the independence of those places. They won't work with the Du Mak until the Du Mak abrogate those agreements."

"They will not," Clixic said, with more certainty than Donal expected.

"They're not happy with Earth in the first place, after what happened out at Ganymede. The Du Mak will not choose sides between the Courts and the *Fomhóraigh*, expressing a desire to work with both. So that leaves things in kind of a tight situation. And now, if one of the Courts is holding Earth citizens…"

Wait. *One* of the Courts was holding Earth citizens.

"I need to see the queens," Donal said quickly, to Fionn. "Both of them."

"I advise against this, master. The fae monarchs are not noted for—"

"You don't want to finish that sentence," Morna said in a singsong voice. "Not here."

"True," Fionn said, giving the *leannan sidhe* an appraising look.

"I am his now," Morna said with a shrug. "I know where my loyalties lie."

Fionn nodded. "My sentiment stands, master. Don't do this."

"I have to," Donal said, then grimaced and sighed. "Like it or not, this is what I signed on for."

THERE WAS A TIME WHEN EDIK COULD EASILY NAME THE THREE strangest days of his life. Back in those halcyon days, they'd been 1) his first failed attempt at conjuring a familiar — odd little magical effects had kept happening that whole day — 2) the day he'd first realized he could speak to spirits — his first conversation with an earth elemental named Ruum would stay with him forever — and 3) the first time he set foot on the moon.

That one felt like cheating. Growing up on Earth, and then one day being able to look up at a green sky, and smell air scented with licorice. It was something that seemed out of a dream.

None of those three days were even in Edik's top ten anymore. The top spots kept shifting on him.

And this day, it was turning out to be the strangest of all.

When Edik had found himself back in his own universe — just that concept alone was enough to kick today to the top spot — after the strangeness that was his little jaunt in the freaking Celtic Faerieland, he'd figured the weirdness for the day was over.

Nope. He found himself floating in space.

No. Not floating in space. He was standing on transparent hull, surrounded by more transparent hull, with the only visible part of the ship being above him.

That was weird.

Not quite as weird as realizing he'd been summoned out of Faerie like some kind of spirit. *That* was weird.

But still. It was enough that Edik had needed Dola's help to orient himself. And meanwhile, Hierophant Mason had just stepped up and taken charge, as seemed to come so naturally to him.

For crying out loud, the man had just been summoned out of Faerie, same as Edik, and yet he was acting as though this sort of thing happened to him every day.

And now Mason was talking about using Donal's signature and the fact that his own familiar remained in Faerie as links to try to bring Donal across too. Or maybe it was to open a gateway, so he could go back through.

Edik wasn't too clear on that point.

Right now, Edik and North were sitting just outside a great magic circle, inscribed in the transparent deck. A handy bit of magical preparation, Edik had to admit. Wouldn't have minded a circle on the *Third Son* done right on a viewport.

Mason was in the middle of the circle, doing ... something. Edik wasn't quite sure what. The man was casting spells at a rate that Edik had never witnessed before. He was tuning the circle, Edik was sure of that much, but there were other things he was doing that were beyond anything Edik could begin to understand.

Even Donal, working fast as he could, couldn't have kept up with this man.

Must have been why Mason was a Hierophant.

Anyway, Magister Ronaldo Machado — a man Edik desperately wanted to talk magic with over drinks, when all this was over — was sacked out fast asleep there on a viewing bench that must have been near the port bulkhead. Hard to say, as the deck and bulkheads were completely transparent.

Magister Machado's gray, pantherish familiar stood guard over him.

Edik wasn't sure what kind of cat that familiar was, but the pose looked very much like the way Dola would have done the same thing, if Edik needed.

Two other magicians were sacked out on the deck near Magister Machado. A tall, dark man, and a short, pale woman. Edik had no idea who they were. The woman wore a Terran Navy uniform, with a lieutenant's bars. The man wore spacer's clothes, as opposed to a proper ship's uniform. Much like Machado did. Maybe Machado's assistant.

Carl was conscious, though from the slight waver in the way he sat, Edik wasn't sure he should have been. He looked like he was paying closer attention to what Mason was doing than Edik was. Maybe he could follow more of it.

Anna was gone. Off talking to the ship's alchemist, wherever he or she was.

And standing off to one side, what looked to Edik like an officer of the ship's watch. Either keeping an eye on all these magicians, or handy in case they needed any—

Just then something appeared next to Mason. A great, ghostly spider.

Edik jumped. Couldn't help it. His only consolation was that North jumped too. And North swore.

Mason looked surprised, but not so much as Edik expected. At least, not until Mason started having a quick conversation in that vaguely Russian-sounding language that all magicians shared with their familiars.

"Don't suppose you can pick any of that up," Edik muttered to Dola, who shook his head.

"Spider," North said, rubbing his beard. "Odd choice for a familiar, wouldn't you say?"

"Back when he conjured it," Edik said with a shrug, "he'd been planning on spending his career as a professional duelist. Maybe he felt a spider-formed familiar would be a help there."

"All right," Mason called out in a ringing tone. "I have word from Donal. And apart from the meeting results, he also tells me that the Queen of Summer has hostages from the *MacArthur*."

"Why?" Edik asked, at the same time that North asked, "How?"

"Same answer to both," Mason said with a frown. "Sounds like they sent a rescue party through, and they were captured by fae knights, since they weren't part of the ambassadorial team."

"So what do we do?"

"We have to find a way to get back there and help Donal," Mason said. "Summoning him isn't even an option now."

"As though it were ever possible," North grumbled.

"We need," Mason continued, "to get back there and assist him before he ends up in even bigger trouble."

"I don't know," Edik said, tugging on his Van Dyke. "Donal's pretty good at getting out of trouble. We might get in his way."

"He's good at getting out of trouble," Mason said, "but he's even better at getting into it. I've had to save his bacon twice before. I'm not above doing it again."

"Still," Edik said, "he's been handling—"

"Edik," Mason said with a flat look, "Donal knows about about this 'rescue team' and their predicament. What's he going to do?"

Edik sighed. "Try to save them himself."

"Fine," North said, standing and drawing his cutlass. "I need to work off some o' these nerves anyways."

"We can't fight them. Not that way." Mason shook his head while North swore. "Oh, one on one a couple of us might have a chance."

Edik was pretty sure Hierophant Mason meant himself and Carl. As Mason continued, Edik tried to figure out whether or not he should feel slighted.

"But it won't be one-on-one fighting. It would be a skirmish. And they've had millennia of warfare. If we fight them with weapons, we'll lose. But their nature gives them mental blind spots. If we're careful, we can out think them."

With an opening like that, Edik had to check himself from reflexively insulting North.

It wasn't easy.

THE ENTIRE TIME FIONN WAS OFF SEEKING A PAGE, DONAL SPENT PACING back and forth in his room. The *leannan sidhe* watched him from her seat on his bed, moving only her eyes to track his path back and forth.

Donal was tired, but he did not feel safe to rest. He was hungry, but there was nothing here safe to eat. He was so tense that half his muscles seemed to be threatening to break in half, but there was nothing he could do about it.

It did keep occurring to him that Morna probably gave a massage worthy of an entire series of ballads. But much as Donal would have loved a massage, right now that seemed like a bad precedent to set.

And besides, if he relaxed, his fear might catch up to him.

Fionn finally did return with a page. No more than perhaps ten minutes had elapsed, but to Donal those ten minutes felt like ten days.

The page was male, maybe a meter tall, and looked as though he were made entirely of sharp, pointy angles, from his feet and knees to his elbows, shoulders, chin and ears.

The page bowed in the doorway of Donal's room.

"How might I serve the ambassador?" the page asked, in a tone that sounded as though he wasn't at all sure he was at the ambassador's service.

"I must meet with both queens at the same time."

"Impossible," the page scoffed.

"All right," Donal said with a smile. "I will meet with first one and then the other. Your task is to bring me to the more important queen first."

Morna hissed in a breath.

The page paled until every centimeter of him was whiter than snow.

"Ambassador, it is not for this lowly page to make such a distinction."

"I tell you I must meet with both at the same time," Donal said. "What I must say is urgently important to both courts. And yet you tell me that I cannot. In that case, I must speak with the most important queen first. As you are of Faerie and I am only a lowly human, it is not my place to determine which is which."

"Lord Ambassador," the page said, and Donal was pleased to hear more and more respect — and maybe a little fear — in the page's voice, "if I were to choose one above the other—"

"Then do not," Donal said. "Arrange for me to speak with both, as I ask. Otherwise, I leave the choice to you."

"I ... shall do what can be done, Lord Ambassador. Will you do me the service of awaiting their pleasure outside by the fire pit?"

"I will wait there," Donal said, "but I will not wait long. If an hour passes and only one queen arrives, then I shall assume she is the more important queen, and she will be the only queen who shall hear my words. If neither queen shows up, then I shall take from that a statement that my critical information does not matter to either court, and as dismissal from their service."

The page vanished in a puff of smoke.

Fionn looked up at Donal. "You really have been paying attention to what Donatello Mancuso's been trying to teach you."

"Surprising how often his lessons come in handy," Donal said, allowing himself a tremor of nerves before Morna began leading him back outside and to the fire pit.

Thirty minutes.

Jacobs had agreed to take a rest for thirty minutes. He'd let Tunold talk him into taking a break for *thirty freaking minutes.*

And now, this.

Jacobs sat behind the large oak desk in his office. And damn it, if he was the captain who had to deal with this mess, he was going to think of it as *his* office. However temporary the situation might be.

Benny Sugg, alas, was nowhere to be seen. Jacobs would have loved to have the big old tomcat curled up on his lap right now. But Benny was smarter than he was. Benny had taken off as soon as the knock on Jacobs' office door came.

So Jacobs was alone on his side of the desk.

On the other side of the desk, a crowd Jacobs would *never* have allowed to see the inside of his office all at once. When he was the regular captain of the *Horizon Cusp*, Mr. Kelly would have known better than to admit a group this size.

Tunold's doing, no doubt. Even now, the ex oh stood at the back of the group, arms crossed, giving Jacobs a *see what you've been missing?* look.

Or maybe it was a *sure you still want command?* look. Hard to say with Tunold these days.

Between Jacobs and Tunold, the mob.

Just to Jacobs' right, the "guests:" Hierophant Nicholas Mason, Anna Lukyanova, the previously unconscious Carl Jones, that too-young captain Edik Barshai — with his huge gray cat familiar right beside him — and some short, would-be pirate whose name Jacobs didn't know.

Just to Jacobs' left, the crew: Chief Goldberg, Machado, and his assistant Cromartie.

That visiting Lieutenant Medici stood with the crew. Or she stood with the magicians, which was more likely.

Ten people, not including Jacobs himself. In his office.

That alone was enough to get his blood going.

But to have them all come in talking at once? That was just too much to be borne.

"Silence," Jacobs roared. And Jacobs had a voice that used to carry across the deck of old seafaring ships, even through heavy storms and huge waves.

In a room the size of Jacobs' office, his roar made more than one of them wince in pain.

"While I'm quite certain that more than one of you are accustomed to cowed silence while you speak, I would remind you all that this is a helioship at high space, and *I* am the captain. I trust you all realize what that means."

"Captain Jacobs, you must understand—"

Of course it was the young woman from the lunar great family who interrupted him. Jacobs didn't let her finish her sentence. He just spoke louder.

"What I understand," Jacobs continued, "is that I am the legal

authority aboard this ship. And so long as I am, all matters relating to this ship, its crew, its passengers and its cargo will be dealt with in an organized fashion. *Not* through the ranting of a mob."

The young Lukyanova gave Jacobs her best glare. Not bad, for someone her age, but not even enough to register on Jacobs' scale.

"Now," Jacobs said. "Mr. Tunold, would you care to explain why these people are on my ship, let alone in my office?"

Tunold's response contained information, but not much of an explanation. He didn't seem to understand how they got here either, but it sounded as though Mash had done the impossible again. This time, yanking people bodily out of another world.

"Mr. Machado," Jacobs said, "so long as you were summoning back people from Faerie, why exactly didn't you summon our *passengers?*"

That explanation made a little more sense. But to Jacobs it sounded an awful lot like Mash had used up his quotient of impossible tasks for the day.

"Captain Jacobs, if I may." This from the Hierophant Mason, who had done a better job of gathering himself than the others. He was the only one in front of Jacobs who didn't look either flushed with anger or frustration, or thoroughly spent from effort.

Jacobs gave the Hierophant a nod.

Mason got as far as mentioning the rescue attempt when Jacobs cut him off with a raised hand.

"We know about that. Did you not explain Commander McRae's idiocy, Mr. Machado?"

"I did, sir." Mash sounded winded even now. "But matters are complicated by Donal Cuthbert."

"Well of course they are," Jacobs said with a heavy sigh. Jacobs liked Cuthbert, despite himself. The boy had heart. Not much wisdom, but a lot of heart. "What's he ... oh. Of course. He's trying to rescue them, isn't he?"

"We think so, sir," Mash said, and Jacobs was pleased to note that the Hierophant was following rank and procedure here. Perhaps he wasn't a total idiot.

"Well, good luck to him," Jacobs said. "Is there any way you can help him from here?"

"We want to try to rescue him," Captain Barshai said.

"Well, Mr. Machado, you pulled four people out of Faerie today—"

"Forgive me, Captain Jacobs," Mason said, "but that won't work. We don't have the links. While my familiar was there, we might have been able to—"

"If you are trying to suggest mounting a rescue party," Jacobs said archly, "I would remind you what happened to the previous effort."

"Forgive the immodesty, Captain Jacobs," Hierophant Mason said, "but I was not with them."

"We help him from here or we don't help him," Jacobs said.

Several of them tried to talk at once, including a great deal of swearing from the would-be pirate.

"Enough!" Jacobs slapped his desk hard enough to ring out.

"I am not spending lives and resources on a fool's errand. I—"

"Coward!" the would-be pirate bellowed.

Jacobs stood. Glared at the upstart with such intensity that the untidy man found his mouth closing.

"Let us be clear about something," Jacobs said, his voice quiet and menacing. "Whatever meeting happened, that's over. That you served as ambassadors and liaisons may not afford you any protections. And forgive me for saying so, Hierophant Mason, but if you match your spells against a fae noble, you're likely to lose."

"Not necessarily," Mason said.

"Inevitably," Jacobs said. "Because even if you manage to save yourself, you'll lose whoever comes in with you. You are one Hierophant. How many equivalents and better do they have, Mr. Machado?"

"Unknown, sir," Mash said, sounding subdued. Or exhausted.

"Exactly. One Hierophant against all of Faerie is trying to extinguish a forest fire with a single pail of water."

"I wouldn't have to take on all of Faerie," Mason said, calm once more. Calmer than Jacobs, whose heart was pounding pretty hard right now. "Slow, careful infiltration, and with a small team, I could extract all our people safely."

"Interesting proposal," Jacobs said, "though I have no reason to consider it likely." Jacobs stopped Mason's rejoinder with a gesture. "Tell me, Hierophant Mason, do you have a ship?"

Mason frowned. "I do not."

"Mr. Machado," Jacobs said, his eyes still locked with Mason's. "In your honest assessment, is this proposal anything more than a fool's errand?"

"I'm sorry, Hierophant," Mash said, shaking his head, "but I cannot certify this as anything more than a fool's errand."

Mason's nostrils flared in a long, slow breath.

"So, Captain Jacobs," Lukyanova said. "You wish to abandon these people to their fates?"

"Not at all," Jacobs said. "But I will not consign others to those fates." Jacobs made a point of looking from Mason to Machado and back. "You are two of the brightest thaumaturgic minds humanity has to offer. Find a way to help from here, or wait with the rest of us."

"But—" Lukyanova started.

"Dismissed," Jacobs said. "Ex Oh, clear my office."

Jacobs sat perfectly still while Tunold and Goldberg escorted everyone out of his office in a crisp, orderly fashion.

The moment they were gone, Jacobs walked over to his own, impressively large portholes and looked out at the mist in space.

Jacobs sighed.

"Donal," he muttered, "I hope you haven't used up *your* miracle for the day."

EDIK FELT MORE THAN A LITTLE DEJECTED, GETTING USHERED OUT INTO the hallway after that clusterfuck of a meeting.

Edik didn't know why. Captain John Jacobs had a reputation as the best helioship captain alive. The man had more accolades and mentions in the history books than any other non-magician since the rise of magic.

But this. This didn't require a helioship, or its captain.

This, trying to figure out how to help Donal and that good-hearted, idiot rescue party, that was a job for a magician. Not a helioship captain.

And right now, the two most qualified to do something about it — Hierophant Mason and Magister Machado — were too busy arguing about approaches and ideas to just buckle down and try something.

"Well?" North muttered to Edik. When had he matched his step to Edik's? "What do you think?"

"I think any effort to reach through to Faerie from here is too much even for Hierophant Mason. But Magister Machado looks half-dead even after his nap. Carl probably shouldn't be off his back either. That Journeyman lieutenant isn't in much better shape, neither is that big Initiate. The assistant ship's mage."

"So you're saying it's down to us?"

"No," Edik said with a frustrated sigh. "I'm saying Donal better have one hell of a trick up his sleeve."

***

THE FIRE PIT. NOW THAT HE COULD TAKE A PROPER LOOK AT IT IN THE growing twilight, the fire pit looked to Donal as though it had seen a fire every night for centuries. And yet it was not lit right now.

Donal stared at that dead fire pit, and the wood waiting for a spark, for perhaps five minutes before turning to Fionn to ask his opinion.

That was the moment two women arrived who could only have been the Queens of Winter and Summer. Each perhaps two meters from the other, and three meters in front of Donal.

They were both so surpassingly beautiful that Donal could barely keep himself from falling to his knees in worship.

One was truly all things summer. Her hair like wheat stalks and sunshine, her eyes all the greens of grass and leaf and tree, her skin the warmth of woods, and her skin the shades of flowers in bloom, shimmering from one to the next with each movement.

Her smile gleamed out and warmed Donal to the core.

The other's smile drove that warmth out with a chill that felt no less unwelcome. Like a cool drink on a blazingly hot day.

Nor was it able to settle in place of the warmth. It was more that the two smiles seemed to strike a confusing balance deep inside Donal.

The Queen of Winter had skin all the shades of winter skies and snow. Her eyes shone out in the variances of the aurora, and her hair shimmered with all the colors that ice can take on.

Neither woman seemed to be clothed, but Donal's eyes saw only what the queens wished him to see, and so even his peripheral vision could take in no more than the vagueness of their forms below the neck.

Despite their smiles, neither queen seemed overly pleased to be here.

"We are unaccustomed to being summoned," the Queen of Summer said, and the heat under her words scorched.

"Nor do we appreciate being summoned now," the Queen of Winter said, and the freeze of her words burnt just as surely.

Donal's heart pounded a slow, terrified beat. His throat refused to work. Sweat poured out of him, only to vanish in steam or freeze and fall away.

Donal needed to kneel. That much was certain. He needed to kneel as Morna did. He could not see Fionn, but Fionn was surely kneeling too. These were the Queens of Faerie. Donal had to kneel before them.

He *had* to.

But he refused.

The power of the queens washed over Donal. But all of his training had not been for naught. The core deep inside Donal had been strengthened through consistent, intensive training for some time now.

And that core knew who it was. Donal Cuthbert. Human. Free

citizen of the United North American States. An ambassador by agreement, and not a subject of the courts.

Donal gritted his teeth.

"It will go easier for you if you kneel," the Summer Queen suggested.

"Far easier, in the long run," the Winter Queen added.

"I ... am not ... here ... to ... *kneel.*"

With that last word, Donal pushed back with all the will he could muster...

...and the urge to kneel passed.

He found himself panting for breath as though he'd run all the way here from Earth. He had to lean forward, one hand on each knee.

"Not much of a bow," the Winter Queen said.

"Still," the Summer Queen said, "I suppose it will do. For now."

"I..." Donal had to swallow and pant a few more breaths before he could continue in anything like a normal tone. And his empty belly rumbled loud enough that the queens had to have heard it, but that couldn't be helped.

"I had not intended anything that could be construed as a summons," Donal said, wiping his forehead. "That was never my intention. I only wished to address you both at once, for fear of being seen playing favorites with information that could be critical to you both."

"He speaks well," the Summer Queen said to the Winter Queen.

"All right," the Winter Queen said with a small nod, "I admit you did well to choose him."

"Although," the Summer Queen added, sounding slightly more cross, "I am not convinced he did right in backing the Hostess in our names."

"I had the selfsame thought," the Winter Queen said with a smile that made Donal see her as a stalking cat and himself a wounded mouse. "I trust what you have to say will put you back in our good graces?"

"That is not for me to judge, but for your Royal Selves." Donal bowed from the neck. "However, as I have contracted to represent you both in negotiations with Earth among others, I must inform you your agreements with Earth have been placed in terrible jeopardy. And with the return of the ancient enemy, the loss of such an ally could prove dangerous."

"How have they been placed in jeopardy?" the Winter Queen said. "Is it something done by the Hostess?"

The Summer Queen only narrowed her eyes at Donal.

"No," Donal said quickly. "The Hostess has acted well at all times in this. No, the error lies with a handful of knights who thought they had encountered some of the old sport. Humans who had strayed through the mists, to find themselves in fae hands."

"That is tradition," both queens said in a disturbing unison, the memory of which would sometimes make Donal awaken in a cold sweat in the years to come.

"It is," Donal said, "but now the Fae Courts hold a formal arrangement with Earth. Earth will interpret the arrangement as providing protection from the human follies of old."

"We have no agreements," the Summer Queen said, "that guarantee safe passage through our lands."

"Nevertheless, if Earth learns that knights of a Fae Court have taken stray humans and kept them against their will, the government of Earth will take exception. They will demand not only their safe return, but reparations."

"Reparations?" the Winter Queen asked. "They would dare?"

"They might not have before, but with the Du Mak around now, and the return of your own ancient foe, Earth may decide they cannot trust an ally who would capture their people for sport."

"Who are these knights?" the Summer Queen asked. "And how do you come to know this?"

"No stray humans have entered Winter," the Winter Queen said with a certainty that could not be denied. And she looked at the Summer Queen with icy curiosity.

"I am a magician," Donal said with a modest bow. "I presumed my extensive resources were one of the reasons I was asked to serve as ambassador."

"And the identity of the knights?" the Summer Queen pressed.

"I would withhold their names," Donal said, muscles tense, because he knew how fine a line he walked, "as I would see them spared any repercussions for their actions. After all, they saw themselves only as continuing the old tradition. They had no reason to believe they were violating a treaty with Earth. I wish only to see those humans released and returned promptly, unharmed. Or at least, any harm healed."

"I do not know that I would agree with sparing the perpetrators their proper retribution," the Winter Queen said, still watching her counterpart. "After all, if an example is not made, others may not learn."

"It was a small error," Donal insisted, "and understandable. Far more important to return the humans, unharmed, than to worry over punishing those who did not know they had erred."

"I agree," the Summer Queen said. "Where is the fun in punishing the guilty when they did not intend to commit a crime?"

"I find that the punishment is its own reward," the Winter Queen said.

"Ah," the Summer Queen said with a smile that radiated light as well as warmth. "But you have admitted the humans have not entered Winter's domain. And thus, ultimately, the decision is not yours to make."

The Summer Queen turned to Donal. "You have shown wisdom beyond your years, to withhold the names of those poor, foolish knights. I would grant you a boon, but your contract prohibits it."

Donal would have sworn she was asking him to lift a portion of the contract. As though he'd risk that annulling the whole thing.

"The sentiment is appreciated, but no boon is needed." Donal bowed from the neck again. "I shall accompany their return, along with the other ambassadors and liaisons, and ensure that Earth bears no ill will over this mischance."

"Ah," the Winter Queen said, "the other ambassadors and liaisons. We are missing rather a few of those, are we not?"

"I am given to understand," Donal stretched truth quickly, "that they were called away on an important matter."

"Truly?" the Winter Queen asked, and Donal could feel the freeze of her stare penetrate deep into him. "And how did you come by *that* knowledge?"

Donal forced his rigid body to bow once more.

"As ... I ... said." Donal swallowed, and drove his next words out with all his will. "I am a magician. I have my sources."

Donal was taking a chance. He knew that. But he also knew that Hierophant Mason had been pulled out of Faerie, which meant that the others likely had as well.

He could only hope they were all right.

"Come, dear cousin," the Summer Queen said to her counterpart. "He has done all we could have asked of him. And perhaps even a little more."

"Shall we return him then? For now?"

"You need not trouble yourself. I must see to those wayward humans, after all. I shall return him and the others."

And just like that, they were gone.

Donal fell to his knees, panting for breath and sweating so badly his mouth grew dry.

"Well," Morna said, shaking her head. "I never stood a chance against you. Did I?"

"Help him up," Fionn said. "We must gather his things." Then, as the *leannan sidhe* helped Donal to his feet, Fionn's voice gained a touch of humor.

"And no, you never did."

DONAL HAD BARELY HAD TIME TO GATHER HIS POSSESSIONS — WHICH included the harp pin on Morna's insistence — and none at all to change his clothes, before the mists arose and took him once more.

A moment outside time.

The world around him, only cool, moist mist. On the dark side of gray at first, but slowly lightening.

Fionn was with him. Donal felt certain of that. He could not see the *cú sidhe* any more that he could see his own hands — or even his nose — but Donal could feel his familiar's presence. Part of himself, and yet not part of himself.

Beyond that, only the mist.

Mist that slowly grew lighter. From the dark side of gray, though a gray that felt almost like seeing nothing at all. But then, smoothly, yet so slowly that Donal could not spot a single change of shade, that gray lightened further and further.

The mist itself thinned as well as lightened in color. Soon Donal could make out his nose, and then his own arms and hands.

Then, the mist was gone altogether.

And just like that, Donal found himself once more in that oh-so-steel meeting room aboard the *MacArthur*. Standing beside the chair he'd been sitting in. Fionn to his right, and Morna just behind him, on his left.

Captain Yamato stood once more by his seat, and the heads of the lunar great families by theirs.

And not just them. The room was flooded with at least a score of heavily armed security personnel, all in Terran Navy uniforms. And every one of them looked as though they'd stared straight at the most terrifying aspect of the Morrigan herself.

The Summer Queen had come through, and released them. That alone was worth a sigh that came all the way from the soles of Donal's feet. A sigh that didn't happen, because of one other little detail.

Rowan MacPherson was nowhere to be seen.

"What about Rowan?" Donal asked, but his words were lost in the explosion of speech from the other recent arrivals.

Fionn must have felt the question, because he could never have heard it. He responded mind-to-mind with Donal, a mode of speech they used infrequently these days, because speaking to one's own familiar in words no one else could understand was simply part of life at grad school.

"You specified the ambassadors and liaisons," Fionn said. "She was neither once she officially took on the role of Hostess."

The fear for her that washed over Donal was as cold as it was unexpected. For so long he had accounted Rowan an enemy. Even now, he was not positive she was a friend.

But still ... to think of her left behind, when the Fae Courts were clearly displeased with her...

"Is there any way I can help her now?" Donal asked the question directly to Fionn's mind, rather than compete with Mr. Lukyanov's shouting match with Captain Yamato.

"Not at this time."

"She will be safe for now," Morna said, leaning in to speak directly into Donal's ear. He was pleased to note she'd added no touch of thrill to her voice, beyond its own bell-like tones.

"How did you—"

"I guessed," she teased. "But you forced the Courts' hands to commend her for what she did, and that will prevent even the peers from seeking retribution."

"Her points are fair," Fionn added, continuing mind-speech with Donal. "But also consider that the Courts will find her more useful working for them in this realm than dead or tortured. She acquitted herself well. Given time, they will admit it."

Captain Yamato had finally managed to impose silence on the great families, through the threat of guards with Pacifiers.

It was a good threat. Pacifiers wouldn't cause harm. All they did was drain all aggression from a person, even on a near miss.

But the heads of those great families were unwilling to surrender their aggressive nature, even for a few minutes.

Of course, it probably helped that Captain Yamato appeared to have given up thoughts of arresting Mr. Lukyanov.

Donal spoke out in a calm clear voice, before Captain Yamato could gather himself enough to speak without yelling.

"Mr. Lukyanov, your daughter is back in this realm, somewhere. *I know"* — Donal held up both hands and spoke louder, but only a little — "because I ran across Hierophant Mason's familiar, and was told that the Hierophant is no longer in Faerie. Ergo, none of the others who vanished at the same time are in Faerie."

"They're aboard the *Horizon Cusp*," Captain Yamato said, consulting a memopad handed to him by a crewman. "All of them. Safe and sound, and worried about us."

All three Russian oligarchs started to speak again, but Captain Yamato silenced them through sheer volume.

"Before we cope with any of that." He glared from Ms. Romanova to Mr. Lukyanov to Mr. Pajari, then threw a glare at Donal for good measure before turning to one of his security officers. "Lieutenant, bring them food and get them to their ships."

Donal found himself chuckling. He was back from Faerie. Safe and sound.

For the time being, anyway.

9

"All right, stop." Jacobs drew a deep breath. Let it out nice and slow.

He sat at his station above the bridge on the *Horizon Cusp*. At the foot of his station, Mash was trying to persuade Jacobs to bring the *Third Son* and her passengers aboard for most of the flight home.

Jacobs was pretty sure Mash just wanted a couple of days to talk theory with a Hierophant. But was that worth the hassle of taking on more passengers?

On the link, Captain Yamato was trying to convince Jacobs to send the *Third Son's* crew and passengers back to the *MacArthur* for an "after action meeting."

Jacobs only wanted to focus on the important questions.

"You have Cuthbert there with you, right?"

"Yes," Captain Yamato said, eagerly, "along with the heads of those three lunar great houses, which is why we need only—"

"*All stop*," Jacobs said. "What about MacPherson. Is she there?"

"No, and Cuthbert says she isn't coming back with us. So all we need is—"

"All *I* need is my one remaining passenger returned to me immediately, so I can get him back to Earth while he's still in one piece."

"Captain Jacobs, this is a golden opportunity."

"No," Jacobs said, "this is a risk none of us need to take. Get all these people in one place again and the fairies might decide to yank them back."

"Please don't call them that," Machado said, sounding pained.

"Well," Captain Yamato hesitated, and Jacobs filled the gap.

"You know I'm right, Haru. You need to get back and report in. So do all the others. Another meeting right now is all risk, no reward."

"Damn you, John," Captain Yamato said, though not as though he meant it. "You're tough as your rep, aren't you? You old salt."

"Old salt?" Jacobs chuckled. That wasn't a term he'd heard since his own youth. "How fucking old are you?"

"Younger than you, but who isn't?" Captain Yamato teased, then got serious. "If there's no meeting *here*, then their royal graces from Luna all formally request permission to come aboard your ship."

"Denied, one and all. They came here in their own ships, they can go back in their own ships."

"That's how I feel about it, but I had to ask. Someone coming back for the *Third Son*?"

"If it were your ship, would you abandon it?"

"Hell no."

"I'll send my shuttle over with your lieutenant and its people."

"Sir," Machado called up. "What I asked you about?"

Jacobs almost said no, but then remembered he had a full crew all the way down to the restaurants and shops, but only one passenger for the flight back.

"All right, Mash," Jacobs said with a sigh. Then to Captain Yamato he said, "Correction. Their captain will pick up his ship, but apparently the *Third Son* is coming back here. Looks like I've got more passengers for the flight back after all."

"You're not leaving Earth out of an important meeting," Captain Yamato said, one eyebrow high.

"I'll pretend you didn't insult me with that question, Haru. Far as I'm concerned the diplomacy for this trip is *done*. *Horison Cusp* out."

Jacobs cut the link.

It would be fine this way. Get them underway sooner. Maybe make all the passengers more happy in the process. Happy passengers made for easy flights.

And right now, Jacobs could use an easy flight. Hadn't been sure what he'd been thinking, taking the captain's chair one more time. For a voyage like this one.

Once he got back, he'd be more than happy to live the rest of his life as the captain of nothing larger than his own *Sweet Dream*.

<hr>

WITH A BELLY FULL OF FOOD, EDIK STRETCHED OUT ON A BED THAT WAS sinfully comfortable. And large enough that Dola could sprawl right next to him, without feeling intrusive.

True, this was not so big a bed as he'd been offered in Faerie. But this one had two tremendous advantages.

One, it had earth magic running through it that did more to relax and soothe the muscles than anything this side of a deep tissue massage.

Two, and this was the important one, *it wasn't in Faerie*. Here, Edik could actually relax.

The suite of rooms Edik had been provided had more livable space than the entirety of his own dear *Third Son*.

The bedroom alone had a chest of drawers bigger than anything Edik had ever owned. Might have been able to fit his entire wardrobe in it, with two drawers to spare.

The bathroom had a counter big enough that Dola could stretch out on it, while Edik enjoyed a long, lingering shower with positively wasteful amounts of hot water.

The suite even *smelled* high end. If he tried, Edik could pick up a kind of subtle, floral scent. But only if he tried. It was subtle as a classy kind of perfume.

The whole suite was like the kind of high-end, fancy hotel that Edik had seen in shadow plays, but never expected to enjoy in real life.

So he was going to enjoy it thoroughly for as long as he could.

Edik stretched again on the bed. He burped and Dola chuckled.

"Nice eating someone else's cooking for a change?" Dola asked.

"Nice enough to make me consider going to restaurants once in a while. That salmon was amazing. And those asparagus. Oh. I didn't know they could taste that good. And that chocolate cake. Donal was *so right* about that chocolate cake."

"Terran food," Dola said. "You won't get as good on Luna, not without spending a lot more money than that menu would have charged you here."

"And the setting," Edik said, voice full of wonder. "If I hadn't known better, I really would have believed we were eating on a hillside in ancient Greece, on a balmy summer evening."

"Whoever cast those illusions really knows their stuff," Dola agreed.

"Best of all it was all *free*," Edik said. "Still don't know how that works."

"Trip's sponsored," Dola said. "Gotta be."

"Preserved Terran food? Still just-caught fresh a week out of port? Who's got that kind of money to throw around?"

Dola rolled over. Opened those cerulean eyes and gave Edik a droll look.

"Throw around? Whoever fronted for this is getting something out of it. You know that."

"I suppose," Edik said, stretching out and yawning. "Wish Anna had stayed for the flight. Would've been nice to hear how this luxury compares to what she's used to."

"Well," Dola said, "I, for one, am pleased that she's flying back to Luna with her father. Those two have a lot to talk about."

Edik thought about the look of abject relief on Alexei Lukyanov's face when Anna had stepped off the *Horizon Cusp's* hippogriff shuttle and into the landing bay of the *MacArthur*.

The way he'd charged over and seized her up in a hug, saying nothing but her name over and over.

It was the single most human moment Edik had ever seen from

the head of any of Luna's great families. Made him miss his own father.

"You may be right," Edik said, settling back into his pillows.

"*May* be?" Dola clucked his tongue. "When am I ever wrong, Edik?"

"Still," Edik said, stretching for the sheer pleasure of it, "I'm glad Carl went with her. Just in case Lukyanov gets ... too fatherly. Tries to make her come home or something."

"I don't think he'd try it. Anna's been doing a good job of asserting her own independence. And you're evading the question."

"Independence. Luna's declared independence." Edik shook his head. "That'll never stick. Mars might pull it off. They're distant enough. But Luna? We're too close, and we import too much from Earth."

"Edik..."

"And the Du Mak. Didn't look at all like they did on Ganymede, did they?" Edik shook his head. "Same with the Rhian. What was that other name for them?"

"*Fomhóraigh.*"

"Man, that's a mouthful." Edik snorted softly. "Didn't look at all like they did on Luna either. Why so very different, I wonder."

"Faerie is a more hospitable environment for them," Dola said. "Though there might be more to it than that."

"I wonder if Cinnamon will still talk to me," Edik said. "I hope he does." Edik frowned. "And I hope he gives me a better name. I felt silly calling a huge, four-armed lizardman kind of person 'Cinnamon.'"

"Edik..."

"Hrissapkuss. Hriss-ap-kuss. I wonder if Cinnamon's real name is like that, or as different as, say, mine and Haru's."

"Edik..."

Edik yawned. "I hope Haru's okay. That fae food hit him pretty hard."

"You're evading the question." Dola made a song of the statement.

Edik frowned at the shaggy gray cat. "What question?"

"When am I ever wrong?"

"Right now," Edik said through a yawn.

Dola gave Edik an expectant look.

Edik smiled. "You're talking when we should both be sleeping."

Dola chuckled.

And with that, they settled down to sleep.

His own clothes. A much-needed massage. An even more-needed dinner of rare rib eye steak, asparagus, and garlic-roasted mashed potatoes. Plus the best conversation of theoretical thaumaturgy Donal had been part of outside of school.

And none of it was setting Donal's mind at ease.

He paced now on the faux-marble of the sitting room of his suite. Eight long steps toward the space outside the viewing wall. Turn. Eight long steps back toward the entry door of the suite.

Then back again. Hands behind his back. Mind whirling in ways that weren't productive.

Fionn sat, prim and proper, his emerald eyes tracking his master's movement.

If Fionn spoke, he would no doubt suggest meditation. And he would be right to suggest it.

But Donal wasn't ready for that level of deep contemplation. He felt too unsettled, in ways that he was unaccustomed to feeling unsettled. He wanted to understand that feeling first, and for that he had to embrace it.

Morna sat draped across the overlarge couch. Also watching Donal with her eyes. Also saying nothing.

She didn't have to. Donal knew what she would suggest, just as she knew he'd refuse her. So she sat there, in a pose that might have been tempting, had Donal been of a mind to be tempted.

Finally, Donal spun on Fionn.

"All right," he said, but the tension in his brow was anything but.

"Question. That really was one of the *Fomhóraigh*? As in the invasions of Ireland?"

"It was," Fionn said with a nod. "Nalacha."

"And he recognized his ancient foes. The children of Danu."

"...Yes. Technically speaking."

"But the gods I worship. My family worships. The Dagda, Lugh, the Morrigan, all of them. The *Tuatha Dé Danann*. They're—"

"*Not* the fae," Fionn finished, and Morna nodded agreement.

"Explain," Donal said. "And this better not be one of those things you can't discuss."

"The *Fomhóraigh* have returned," Fionn said. "That opens up a number of things I can say. But the one that matters now is this. The *Tuatha Dé Danann* are children of Danu. But they are not the only children of Danu."

"Wars are not fought," Morna chimed in, "only by the generals and great heroes."

Fionn flicked his ears, irritated at the interruption, but his tail began a slight wag, as though this were a subject he'd wanted to address for some time now. He tilted his head as he spoke.

"You are familiar with the concept of apotheosis, I believe?"

"Essentially ascension to godhood," Donal said, starting to see where this was going.

"Just so. The gods you worship, the *Tuatha Dé Danann*, they are the children of Danu who became gods. But all of Danu's children held a great deal of magic. Those who did not become gods, became what you know of the fae."

"And it's the same for the *Fomhóraigh* then," Donal said, tapping his chin now with his tuning fork. Not that he remembered taking out his tuning fork. "Balor. Bres. Ethniu and the others whose names we know. They became gods. And the rest ... became like the fae?"

"I wouldn't have thought they had enough magic," Fionn said, "but all evidence says that's just what they did."

Donal frowned. There was another people he remembered from the invasions. "Does this mean the *Fir Bolg* are running around someplace?"

Fionn's ears twitched in a canine shrug. "Until today, I didn't know any remained of the *Fomhóraigh*. I cannot discount the *Fir Bolg*."

"If they are," Morna chimed in, "I've heard nothing of them."

"Had you heard about the *Fomhóraigh?*" Fionn asked.

"Rumors only."

"That's more than nothing," Donal said, then slumped to the floor.

"I can't ... I can't put it all together. The Du Mak. The Fae Courts. The *Fomhóraigh*. All these declarations of independence and mutual support. I don't know what it all means."

"It's too big to put together at once," Fionn said. "Mars and Luna themselves don't know what independence means yet. And Earth, it will have to decide if a two-front war is really worth what it would gain."

"Three, if Venus gets involved," Donal said, then shook his head. "I don't know. The Du Mak and the *Fomhóraigh*. Allies like those might make Mars and Luna pushier. Or they might make the Fae Courts push Earth toward war."

"Maybe," Fionn said.

"It wouldn't surprise me," Morna said. "Winter and Summer have not gotten to war against a common enemy since the invasions of Ireland. They'll jump at the chance."

"We can't let that happen," Donal said. "The scale of death would be beyond anything we've ever seen before."

"I don't see how we can stop it," Morna said, but Fionn said nothing. The *cú sidhe* only stared right back into Donal's eyes.

"There has to be a way," Donal said. He jumped to his feet and started pacing again.

"That doesn't mean *you* have to find it," Fionn said.

"Time does not press," Morna said. "Neither the Fae Courts nor the *Fomhóraigh* would begin a war until Samhain. They'll observe the traditions there, and want the ... qualities of the time."

Samhain. Not only the Celtic new year, but also one of the two times during the year when the veil between worlds was thinnest. Yes. Donal would believe they would wait for that.

That meant he had just under ten months to stop the war.

Donal was quiet for a few minutes as he considered his options.

"So you agree?" Fionn asked, his voice urgent. "You'll return home and see your family? Then return to your studies?"

"Yes," Donal said, smiling with sudden realization. "Yes, I will. And while I'm at school, I'll begin a research project."

Fionn cocked his head expectantly, but Morna couldn't resist asking, "What?"

"Fintan mac Bóchra," Donal said. "The only man to survive the invasions. He's not of the *Tuatha*, and he's not of the *Fomhóraigh*, and I don't think he became a god. But even back then, his wisdom and magic were legendary. That means he's probably out there somewhere."

Donal smiled at Fionn. "I just have to figure out where to look."

SIGN UP FOR STEFON'S NEWSLETTER

Stefon loves to keep in touch with his readers, and loves to keep you reading. The best way for him to do both is for you to sign up for his newsletter.

Sign up at http://www.stefonmears.com/join

If you sign up for Stefon's newsletter, you get...

- Monthly updates about his publishing and travel schedules
- His latest news, in brief, and answers to reader questions
- A free short story for signing up
- List-only offers and occasional specials
- Plus a free short story every month!

ABOUT THE AUTHOR

Stefon Mears knows not to eat the food in Faerie. Stefon has more than thirty books to his credit, and he never stops writing. He earned his M.F.A. in Creative Writing from N.I.L.A., and his B.A. in Religious Studies (double emphasis in Ritual and Mythology) from U.C. Berkeley. He's a lifelong gamer and fantasy fan. Stefon lives in Portland, Oregon, with his wife and three cats.

Look for Stefon online:
www.stefonmears.com
himself@stefonmears.com

9 781948 490061